"An enjoyable madcap caper."—*The Guardian*

"Hackwith's writing, her characters and her scenes are each a delight. This book is as rich as chocolate and as refreshing as sherbet."—*Morning Star*

"Hackwith builds her world and characters with loving detail, creating a delightful addition to the corpus of library-based and heaven vs. hell fantasies. This novel and its promised sequels will find a wide audience."—*Publishers Weekly*

"Elaborate worldbuilding, poignant and smart characters, and a layered plot... An ode to books, writing, and found families."—*Library Journal* (**starred review**)

"Hackwith writes a fast-paced, suspenseful story set in an intriguing world where storytellers can duel with words and souls are not what they seem."—**Booklist**

"Wow! A.J. Hackwith puts a whole new spin on libraries and librarians in *The Library of the Unwritten*! The imaginative plotline coupled with lots of phenomenal action and a solid dose of humor keep the reader engaged even as we wonder what twisted turn of events will happen next."—**Fresh Fiction**

"Prepare to laugh and to cry, to have your mind bent and your grip on reality loosened as you embark on the wild ride that is *The Library of the Unwritten*. This is the ultimate novel about the power of storytelling. Librarian Claire, who must deal with the denizens of assorted Afterworld realms, is a stand-out creation, complex and memorable. A novel brimful with imagination, with emotional undertones that run deep. I loved it!"—**Juliet Marillier, author of the Blackthorn & Grim series**

"Clever, charming, full of intricate worldbuilding and delightful characters, *The Library of the Unwritten* is the first book in your new favorite series."—**Christina Henry, author of *The Girl in Red***

"It's like *The Good Place* meets *Law & Order: Bibliophile Crime Unit*. Highly recommended. This book is so much fun, and you should be reading it. Trust me. Stories about story are some of my favorite kinds. This book definitely makes the list. I am so glad I read this."—**Seanan McGuire, author of *In an Absent Dream***

"The most intriguing story I've read in a long time. I shall never again turn my back on an unfinished book."—**Jodi Taylor, author of *Just One Damned Thing After Another***

"*The Library of the Unwritten* is a tiered dark chocolate cake of a book. The read is rich and robust, the prose has layers upon layers, and the characters melt like ganache upon the tongue. A saturated, decadent treat. An unforgettable, crave-worthy experience. A book lovers' book; a supreme and masterful concoction that makes fresh fiction out of dusty Dante and boring Bible bits."—**Meg Elison, Philip K. Dick Award Winner**

"Like *Good Omens* meets Jim Hines's Ex Libris series, a must-read for any book lover. Hackwith has penned a tale filled with unforgettable characters fighting with the power of creativity against a stunning array of foes from across the multiverse."—**Michael R. Underwood, author of the Stabby Award finalist Genrenauts series**

"A muse, an undead librarian, a demon, and a ghost walk into Valhalla... what follows is a delightful and poignant fantasy adventure that delivers a metric ton of found family feels, and reminds us that the hardest stories to face can be the ones we tell about ourselves." —*New York Times* **bestselling author Kit Rocha**

"Hackwith has artfully penned a love letter to books and readers alike and filled it with lush, gorgeous prose, delightfully real characters, a nonstop, twisty, and heart-wrenching plot, and an explosive ending that gave me chills."— **K. A. Doore, author of** *The Perfect Assassin*

"A delightful romp through heaven, hell, and everything in between which reveals itself in layers: an exploration of the nuances of belief, a demonstration of the power of the bonds that connect us, and a love letter to everybody who has ever heard the call of their own story."—**Caitlin Starling, author of** *The Luminous Dead*

"A wry, high-flying, heartfelt fantasy, told with sublime prose and sheer joy even at its darkest moments (and there are many). I want this entire series on my shelf yesterday."—**Tyler Hayes, author of** *The Imaginary Corpse*

"The only book I've ever read that made the writing process look like fun. A delight for readers and writers alike!"—**Hugo Award Finalist Elsa Sjunneson-Henry**

"It's fun, creative, some great humour and a solid mystery at its core."—**Books, Tea & Me Review**

Also by A.J. Hackwith and available from Titan Books

The Library of the Unwritten
The Archive of the Forgotten

THE GOD OF LOST WORDS

A. J. HACKWITH

TITAN BOOKS

The God of Lost Words
Print edition ISBN: 9781789093216
E-book edition ISBN: 9781789093223

Published By
Titan Books
A division of Titan Publishing Group Ltd.
144 Southwark Street, London, SE1 0UP.
www.titanbooks.com

First Titan edition: February 2022
10 9 8 7 6 5 4 3 2 1

A CIP catalogue record for this title is available from the British Library.

Printed and bound by CPI Group (UK) Ltd, Croydon CR0 4YY.

To Becky

Wherefore do you so ill translate yourself
Out of the speech of peace, that bears such grace,
Into the harsh and boist'rous tongue of war,
Turning your books to graves, your ink to blood,
Your pens to lances, and your tongue divine
To a trumpet and a point of war?

William Shakespeare, Henry IV, *Part 2*

I

HERO

Maybe a library isn't defined by what it holds. Maybe it is
defined by what it does.

Librarian Bjorn the Bard, 1433 CE

WHEN A BOOK RUNS, a librarian follows. It was the law, part
threat, part promise, of the Unwritten Wing. Hero knew this; all
the books knew this. It was thoroughly *known*.

What was unknown was what a book was supposed to do
when the librarian ran.

The Arcane Wing had become a carefully layered thicket. No,
not a thicket—a fort. Hero danced between half-crumpled crates
of artifacts, malice and wonder dribbling out from between the
cracks. A stack of folded gold cloth tilted precariously, and Hero
sidestepped the silk avalanche.

It was worse than Rami had described when, in the low,
gentle tones of a worried sheepdog, he'd asked Hero for help.
"She hasn't conducted an inventory in a month. Not since…" He
trailed off, finding it either impossible or unnecessary to indicate

the epicenter of Claire's distress. Of everyone's, really. A mysterious ink that stained and threatened to possess Claire, a muse angling for revolution, Hero's book… gone. No one emerged from that nonsense with the unwritten ink okay. Under different circumstances, Hero would still be sunk into a dark corner of Hell and an even darker corner of whatever passed for a bottle of ale in these parts—he suspected Walter could point him the way. But those were different circumstances, and this… well, this was Claire.

The Arcane Wing had been ruled by Claire's discipline, iron will pitted against magical chaos. But now order had been discarded, however temporarily, in a search for answers that weren't there. Hero cleared the last wall of defense—a particularly cluttered table where ornate jewelry lay in a tangled nest—and found the center of Claire's warren.

"Go. Away."

Ah, this was why Rami had asked Hero to help. Ramiel was a steady assistant, could lend infinite wise guidance and support. That patently wasn't what Claire needed right now. People only ever brought Hero in when there was monstrous prodding to be done.

The Arcanist was slouched in the chair behind her desk. She had an absurdly large book held up like a shield. Hero cleared his throat. Predictably, Claire ignored him.

"Sulking doesn't suit you, warden," Hero said.

The book lowered a fraction. Claire's face did an enjoyable contortion before settling into an arch frown as she saw him. Bodies didn't change much in Hell, but Hero thought he could detect new, exhausted lines around her eyes that had not been there before. She rose and brushed past him with precisely the brusque, offended air he'd been hoping to elicit. "I don't have time to sulk—or for you."

"But I'm a delight." Hero shadowed Claire's steps as she stopped to straighten a particularly teetering stack of crates. Even when cultivating chaos, Claire was tidy. "And you must have time. You've wasted nearly a month on self-pity."

"Not self-pity. Research."

"Ever your vice. Personally I would prefer if you were a drunkard. It would be infinitely more entertaining for the rest of us."

"I apologize for boring you."

"Never that, no." Hero smiled as Claire finally halted at the head of a row of shelves to look at him. "You are never that."

Claire sighed, but Hero could see her shoulders relax by inches. "What do you want, Hero?"

"The same as you—answers. But we already know we won't find them here." Hero stepped closer, still feeling a thrill of wonder when he reached out to touch her chin and she allowed it. "We've already faced the worst, Claire. What are you hiding from?"

There was a moment when Claire drew a breath and her lips parted and Hero thought he'd reached her. But then the answer came out of the darkness behind him. "The consequences of her own actions, if I was asked to wager a guess."

The voice crashed against them like ice water. Hero stepped back out of reflex. Claire's mouth snapped closed and she turned with a poise she reserved for only the worst things. "Why, Malphas. To what do we owe the pleasure of a visit, Grandmother of Ghosts?"

Malphas was seated at a worktable near the front doors, enthroned in a brown-red cloak. She was a lean older woman, although demons could appear any age they wished. Age sharpened her edges rather than softened them. The soft light from the lamps deepened her wizened features and made the fabric appear to puddle into dried blood in the folds. At least, Hero reverently hoped it was a trick of the light. A smile pinched her wrinkled features and she raised her voice to carry. "Never cared much for that name. 'Grandmother' insinuates I'd claim anyone as kin."

"A shame; she'd make a delightful evil stepmother," Hero mused under his breath.

No one should have been able to hear him at this distance, but Malphas pinned him with a glance. It was precisely like a pinning, so much steel and malice in her regard that a cold smear of terror streaked up Hero's spine. He felt a small bit of relief when Malphas turned to Claire with a trip-wire smile. "If only it were bloodshed. No, nothing so pleasant. Worse: *accounting.*"

Malphas said the word with the precise feeling with which Hero might say "polyester," or Claire would say "coffee." Claire's lip twitched. "Poor thing. Don't you have a lesser devil of details to see to that for you?"

Malphas appeared to miss the wordplay. "They're the ones who brought it to my attention. I need an inventory."

The amusement faded off Claire's face. Hero was fairly certain only he could notice the muscles in her jaw as they twitched. "An inventory? Surely you don't mean my wing."

Leather stained the color of dried blood creaked as Malphas folded her arms and tapped a sharp claw against her elbow. "For a start. Don't get your knickers in a bunch, child. I'll be asking the Unwritten too."

Claire smiled, and it was a very particular smile. One she reserved for disasters and imminent death. Really, it was alarming how familiar Hero was with that smile. "I'd be happy to comply; unfortunately, Hell doesn't have authority over the Library to make such a request. We're sovereign, remember."

"A right shame—we do so love cooperating with Hell," Hero added.

"You aren't sovereign, not when it disturbs the power balance of the realms. There was a sudden drop in the ambient power of the realm a short while ago—coincidentally centered on the spaces where we generously host the Library wings. Almost as if something was removed."

"Well"—Claire gestured with a theatrically loose shrug— "your measurements are inaccurate. As you can see, here we are."

"It isn't your whereabouts that concern me—for once," Malphas said. "In our realm, the inventory of souls might as well be our borders and defense. We have a right to protect our assets." The trap in Malphas's smile sprang, and she stepped forward. "I find it strange that a soul loss would register here of all places, given your attendance. Don't you?"

Claire had her right hand clutched behind her skirts. Only Hero saw the flinch and reflexive clench of her fingers, hard enough to turn the knuckles pale. It was the same hand that had been stained black with the ink of destroyed unwritten books mere weeks ago. A stain that had subsequently spread, had haunted and nearly destroyed her. Hero might have—they might have—lost her had it not been for a fateful confrontation in the Dust Wing. In a struggle with Probity, a muse set against the Unwritten Wing, Claire had unleashed the ink. Rami had recognized the tattered souls in the ink, like had called to like, Claire had been saved, and the fragmented souls had joined their brethren in the Dust Wing.

At least, that was the current theory. Hero wasn't sure any of the Library's little family knew precisely what the hell had happened to any of them.

Claire had been haunted and then purged. Brevity had been

tattooed, then scarred. Hero... well, Hero had been a character from a book. With that book destroyed, he wasn't sure what that made him now.

Ramiel, their angelic resident soul expert, insisted it all came down to the revelation of the secret the Library had been hiding: books are made from fragments of soul. Or, at the very least, human souls and stories were made of the same stuff.

Souls were one thing in Hell: power. When they'd released the ink, Hell had taken notice.

Hero's mind spun up a dozen ways to divert Malphas from this line of inquiry and discarded all of them as doomed to fail. His spiraling dread was only interrupted by an irritated *tch* sound as Claire clicked her tongue. "Well," Claire said after a moment, sounding irritated. "No need to make it out so dramatic, General. I don't have time to meddle with your little power plays and schemes. I'm positive you'll find all our inventories in order, but if you insist—"

"I do," Malphas said.

"—then I suppose we can produce yesterday's inventory. Will that suffice?"

"With proper authenticity, perhaps," Malphas allowed. Claire turned on a prim heel and strode toward the far aisle of shelves, waggling a hand over her shoulder as an invitation to follow. Malphas did so, shouldering past Hero with more weight than her fragile old grandmother appearance warranted.

There was no inventory, at least not one completed yesterday, or last week. Only years of professional villainy kept the blasé smile on Hero's lips. Years, and the firm belief that Claire was not so foolish as to let slip what the Library had discovered to the blood-soaked grand general of Hell. He wiped a palm over his face before hurrying to follow Malphas.

HE CAUGHT UP TO them back at the oubliette of paperwork that Claire liked to call her office. It was more of an alcove, really, inset off the back corner of the Arcane Wing, conveniently located adjacent to Claire's twin priorities of tea and secrets. Even Malphas didn't care to follow the curator all the way into the bookkeeping stacks. Claire resurfaced after a moment with a box not quite succeeding to contain its pile of vellum sheets.

"Here, the most recent inventory, signed and countersigned by Walter, as a matter of fact. I assume that's sufficient?"

Malphas frowned, but even Hell's general wasn't going to question the good name of Death. The terrifying yet oddly charming gatekeeper of Hell was a rather clumsy giant and, secretly, one of Claire's greatest allies. Malphas eyed the box with significant prejudice. "This is your idea of filing?"

"Oh, I defer to my predecessor. All Andras's files were kept in just such a manner. Who am I to change the system?" Claire's smile was delightfully malicious, and Hero was glad he had a moment to admire it as Malphas reluctantly took possession of the box.

"You're hiding something," she said.

"It's Hell. Of course I'm hiding something." Claire made a vague shrug of her shoulders. "The only question is, Is it the same thing you're looking for?"

Malphas's expression grew warmer, if no less suspicious. "Careful, little librarian. Get too good at this game and Hell may decide to keep you for themselves."

"Hell could not afford to keep me in the damnation to which I am accustomed." Claire gestured vaguely to the collection of problems around her, with a finger flick for Hero. A warm feeling beneath his breastbone immediately decided it was a compliment. It nearly distracted him from noticing how Claire's eyes slid past

Malphas's shoulder, and she abruptly cleared her throat.

"If that's all, General Malphas, I do have an Arcane Wing to run."

Not being a fool herself, Malphas turned her attention behind her. In the shadow of the Arcane Wing's wide double doors, Ramiel waited. His trench coat was even more rumpled than usual, feathers escaping the epaulets to stick up around his collar like some disgruntled owl. It was an atrocious look, absolutely horrid, and it never ceased to fill Hero with an inexplicable fondness. So much so, in fact, that he nearly missed the other visitor.

Pallas, smooth and perfect as a statue, was hard to miss normally. The—what was he, an attendant?—attendant of Elysium was no more than a blond sliver clutching Rami's sleeve. There was no official title in the Library for Pallas. His mother was the librarian of the Unsaid Wing and wore his body like a puppet when the mood suited her, a feat Hero hoped to never have to witness again. One trip to Elysium's library had been enough for him. Pallas should not be here, and his presence could only indicate a new problem.

More important, Hero noted with irritation, Pallas should not have been so forward as to clutch Rami like that.

These calculations occurred in the split second it took to glance back and catch the particular level of superiority in Claire's frown that she reserved only for deep alarm. If Pallas was here, then that likely meant other members of Elysium were here—for some ungodly reason—and Hell would not take kindly to visitors of a paradise realm encroaching on their doorstep. Hell barely tolerated the Library, which held a distinct policy of moral neutrality when it came to the afterlife. The Library could hardly afford more suspicious attention from Malphas.

Claire's lips parted but closed again as Hero made an irritated sound. He wasn't quite foolhardy enough to nudge Malphas aside, but he put extra dramatics into his sigh as he stepped around her. Attention was an easy thing to manipulate, once you knew the trick. "Ramiel, you scoundrel! You terrible cad."

The way Rami's brows inched together, like two anxious caterpillars in the middle of his forehead, never ceased to delight. He was excessively attractive when confused. Hero continued forward, slipping an arm through Pallas's elbow and stealing him away with a graceful turn. "Bringing a damsel down here, really! And while I was away visiting your senior, to boot." Hero squeezed Pallas's elbow, and the youth had the good sense to stay quiet. "I know you Arcane Wing types flaunt the rules, but leave our poor charges out of it."

Rami's broad olive features did a complicated twitch before regaining control. Bless his heart, the angel was just not wired for impromptu subterfuge. Hero said a silent thanks when Pallas cleared his throat.

"No, it was my fault. I swear it, Sir Hero. I begged Sir Ramiel until he agreed to take me along. I wanted to see the"—Pallas's eyes darted around the dim wing for a flicker of a heartbeat—"the tables... so awfully much."

"The tables are impressive. Connived your way into it, did you?" No damsel, indeed no self-respecting book of the Unwritten Wing, would call Hero "sir," but Pallas's wide blue eyes and cherubic cheeks, which flushed with performative guilt, would have sold a lie to the devil himself. "Not that an angel should lose out to a mere book."

Perhaps it was his time in Hell. Perhaps it was Hero's bad influence, but Rami managed to recover in the time Pallas had bought him. "One would think. But I appear to have a weakness."

Rami's constructed poker face almost hid the amusement in his eyes. Any flush of color in Hero's cheeks could be dismissed as annoyance, surely. He made a scoffing sound in his throat.

He'd nearly forgotten about Malphas until she spoke. "Behaving like children, as usual. I expected a better level of control from you, Claire."

"The misbehavior of unwritten characters is not my concern, alas," Claire said, hands primly clasped in front of her. She was the picture of buttoned-up propriety, which just made Hero want to pluck at her buttons. "As the general keeps reminding me, I am no longer the librarian."

Malphas offered Claire a smile that didn't pretend to reach her eyes. "That would mark the first time you listened to me, child." She hiked the sizable box against her hip with one hand, a relaxed reminder of her superior strength. "We will speak again. Pray you listen to me then."

"Quite," Claire said in that particularly British way that simultaneously said both *Sure* and *I'd rather eat dirt*. She held her placid mask in place until Malphas disappeared down the hall and the air colored with a sharp burst of anise and cinders, which signaled her true departure. All pretense dropped when Claire whirled on Rami and Pallas in alarm. "What for hell's sake are you doing here?"

"Language, ma'am," Rami muttered. He swallowed a particularly worried sound but was beat to the answer.

"Mother wants to see you," Pallas said simply.

2

CLAIRE

There's not much time. The Library is—no, me, I am failing. The songs are failing. Darkness grows in the stacks. Malphas will find her way in soon.

I will keep writing until the pen is taken from my hands. I owe the books that much. I can't save it, at least not in the way that I'd planned, but I can preserve it. The Library has to grow to become a force for good. I will change the Library, or I will perish in the attempt.

Librarian Poppaea Julia, 48 BCE

"MOTHER" WAS A COMPLICATED term to humans, even at the best of times. Memory of her own mother was another bit of Claire that Hell had snipped and nibbled at the edges. She was left with a vague sense of a sufficient childhood and an excess of books and candies slipped to a small, persistent child. That would have been practically indulgent child-rearing by the standards of Claire's day.

Pallas's mother was trouble by any standard. Claire had never had the occasion to meet the woman who held the Unsaid Wing as librarian, but Rami's report and the way the color drained from Hero's face was reputation enough.

"I don't believe I'll have liberty to travel to Elysium anytime soon," Claire pointed out.

"Oh, no." Pallas broke into a shy smile. "Mother is here. Waiting in the Unwritten Wing."

"Oh shit," Hero muttered.

Claire didn't run through the hallways, but perhaps only because she could use Hero's long strides as a reason to sprint.

"INVENTORY?" HERO KEPT HIS voice pitched only for her as he drew up alongside. The hallways of Hell flashed by in a distracted blur.

Claire had been expecting the question. "It was *an* inventory. Malphas will find everything in order."

"Signed by Walter yesterday? He'll attest to that?"

Claire shrugged. "Death has as subjective a sense of time as one would expect."

"You're playing fast and loose, warden."

"Your influence, no doubt." She hesitated as she rounded the stairs. "Any idea why Elysium has sent people?"

She caught motion in the corner of her vision as Hero's mouth twitched down. "No. None."

Alcoves and staircases flashed by the corners of her eyes, unimportant and ignored, as she reassessed the situation. Pallas's presence in the Unwritten Wing was bad—Malphas would have had every right to be suspicious—but the librarian of one wing abandoning their own realm to interfere with another? That was a disaster.

Claire should know; she'd been that disaster. She'd had a clear and thorough rationale, of course. Strange, it felt different on this side of the experience.

The doors of the Unwritten Wing were open, and distant voices leaked out of the stacks as they entered the lobby. The librarian's desk—Brevity's desk—sat empty. Claire paused, fingertips resting on the desk for a moment, but the air was still. The books stacked on the nearby cart lay quietly, and the lamp on the desk remained a cheery soft white. Nothing wrong, not yet. Claire took a slow breath and exchanged a glance with Hero and Rami.

Hero shrugged eloquently. Rami gestured down one of the far aisles that wound deeper into the thicket of stacks. "I left them near the damsel suite."

"Your books are funny," Pallas mused, fingertips drifting over the returns cart. "They talk."

"So do yours," Hero pointed out.

"No," Pallas said with a touch of regret. He began to drift down in the direction Rami had indicated. "They only echo."

"Why are the pretty ones always so creepy down here?" Hero complained as they followed after him.

"You would be one to talk," Claire said.

"I'm too well-bred to be creepy." Hero placed a hand on his chest in mock offense. It didn't keep him from knocking shoulders with Claire. "Hey. You called me pretty. Warden, I'm touched."

Once, Claire might have assumed Hero was being annoying for annoyance's sake, instead of trying to ease her with a distraction. Once, she would have risen to the bait—well, she would still rise to the bait, but it would be accompanied with a comfortable easing in her chest. "I said nothing of the sort—"

"I will accept this confession of admiration with grace—"

"Oh, bugger off, you—"

"You are both well-proportioned beings of many attractive values." Rami's voice rumbled behind them, making Hero startle.

"A fact that I fear will not benefit us with the librarian of the Unsaid Wing."

"Unless she wants to wear one of us," Hero said with a shiver. Claire noted the paleness in his cheeks. The banter had drained out of him.

The damsel suite's door stood open, cutting a cheery light across the shadows of the Library stacks. Just inside, Brevity stood with her back to the door, shoulders up around her ears with obvious uncertainty. The damsels clustered around her like a shield. The characters of the Unwritten Wing were protective of Brevity in a way they'd never been of Claire. That was not unusual.

What was unusual was the pond that appeared to flow out of the fireplace and pool in an indentation in the floor. Against the diffuse lights of the damsel suite, the water reflected a dark, murky surface. *Not ink*, Claire told the sudden incendiary in her chest. She concentrated her gaze on the waterlogged doily that was just visible through the edge of the water near her toes. *Water, not ink.*

Feathers brushed her cheek as Rami stepped forward, offering his grounded presence. On his other side, she could see Hero's hand gripped tightly. Brevity made an effort to disentangle herself from the wary crowd of damsels before joining them.

"I brought them, Mother." If Pallas noticed the combined distress of the Unwritten Wing, he made no sign of it. He stepped lightly over a tilting ottoman to kneel on the waterlogged carpet. "Will you speak with them now?"

"*Now*," the pond echoed. Without the benefit of high canyons, Echo's voice was quieter, limited to a flutter of sounds rebounding against the pond surface.

"Is that really necessary—" Hero made a nauseated sound as

Pallas reached toward the surface of the water and his reflection reached back.

"Steady, Hero," Claire said quietly. She had never met the Unsaid Wing's librarian before. Hero and Rami had eventually described their foray into Elysium, but she was keenly interested in observing Echo for herself. Each wing of the Library chose unpredictable librarians, all especially suited for the nature of their wing.

The Unsaid Wing, it appeared, preferred the heart of a mimic. Claire watched with a clinical eye as Pallas tipped to the water's edge and his reflection rose to meet him. The exchange, when it occurred, was eerily seamless, though nothing outward appeared to happen. It was as if the dynamic of life switched places. The reflection stepping out of the pool was now the living image, and the boy slumped against soggy carpet was just a reflection.

People stepped out of books in the Unwritten Wing. There seemed something not quite right about stepping into people.

"Greetings, Librarian," Claire said as Echo straightened. She unfolded her hands behind her back enough to nudge Brevity forward. To her credit, Brevity fumbled only a moment before clearing her throat.

"Welcome to the Unwritten Wing." Brevity appeared to wipe the palm of her hand off on her pants before offering it. "Brevity, the current librarian. You've already met Hero and Rami. And Claire is the curator of the Arcane Wing, as you might know." Claire felt a flash of pride for how smoothly Brev rattled that off. No flinch, no pause.

Echo-as-Pallas took her hand after a weighty moment. Echo stopped, appearing to search Brevity's eyes before her expression drifted into sorrow. "*No*," she repeated softly.

Hero had described how Echo, true to her myth, could only repeat what others said, in whole or in part. The Greek librarian lifted a hand and gestured to her daughter. A flicker of annoyance crossed Iambe's fine features before she stepped forward with a sigh. "Mother has a request. I suppose she brought me to save us time."

"*Time*," Echo repeated, though Pallas's lips never moved.

"I'm getting to it, Mother." Iambe straightened, appearing to choose her next words with uncharacteristic seriousness. "The Unsaid Wing is in danger. We require the assistance of fellow librarians."

Hero made a disbelieving click of his lips. "From what? You lot are in paradise, for gods' sakes."

"That would, it appears, be the problem." Iambe was able to match Hero down to his precise lip curl. "Elysium took note of your visit. The resident heroes started asking questions."

"I imagine your mother was as helpful as she always is."

"That's precisely the problem; she was." Iambe rubbed her temple. "They followed the trail that you neatly left, and then did something you weren't clever enough to do: ask Mother a question."

"It's not as if one ever gets a straight answer," Rami grumbled.

"Straight enough, when the questioner is as clever as Herodotus. And the question is, 'The made and the maker are the same. Why is the Library concerned about books so old?'"

"*Books so-ol*," Echo repeated, voice watery as she elided the original phrase enough to transform it. Books soul.

"Oh, *bugger*," Claire breathed.

"Cheating!" Hero almost stamped his foot. "That's cheating. Why wasn't she so helpful when we needed information?"

Iambe exchanged a look with her brother-mother, then lifted her shoulders in a blunt shrug. "You didn't ask the right question."

"Elysium knows, then. About us." Rosia spoke up from the front of the cluster of damsels. Claire had quite forgotten she was still in the room. The girl was still moonlight and shadow, but more solid now. Her gaze no longer wandered but appeared to look straight through you. She considered Echo for a long moment, and even the eerie librarian appeared caught off guard. "They know we have souls."

"Are souls," Brevity corrected, looking pained. "Not just partially made up of souls, like inspiration, but are as soulful as any human."

"They will try to use that," Rami said quietly, and Brevity's worry took on a nauseated hint.

"They have already tried." And at that, Iambe looked ill. "The Unsaid Wing is in… I suppose you would call it lockdown."

"Elysium has moved against its own library?" Claire's voice was low with a streak of horror.

"They have tried. They believe souls are better off in their custody." If Iambe understood the danger of the situation, she did an admirable job of not showing it. She studied her nails. "Heroes, they're like that. What paradise realm has never met a soul it didn't want to save?"

"We don't," Rosia said with a peak of color in her cheeks, "need saving."

"I agree. Your people are so much luckier here in a damnation realm."

"Yes, here they just want to consume you," Hero grumbled. "And only if you're lucky."

"*Key*," Echo said.

"I was getting to that, Mother." Iambe sighed. "We were forced to… relocate." She made an impatient gesture toward the pool of water.

Brevity glanced back and forth between the pond and Iambe. A bewildered look sprouted on her face. "Your entire Library wing is in there?"

"Temporarily. It is not a long-term solution, of course."

"How—what—all of it—wow, really?" Brevity's brain appeared to short out and take a moment to recalibrate. "Can you show me how to do that?"

"I doubt it. Not every library is as… inflexible as the Unwritten." Iambe looked impossibly smug.

Claire jumped straight to the point. "Then what can you possibly want from us?"

For the first time, an uncertain shadow crossed Iambe's face. She glanced askance at her mother, who nodded. When Iambe turned back, she had straightened her expression into a military kind of dignity. "We request sanctuary."

3

BREVITY

Churches gave sanctuary, in my time. To the unwanted, the unloved, and also the criminals, whether they repented or not. I don't see why a library in Hell shouldn't be a kind of church—lord knows that we have enough altars to longing, to regret, to mistakes, here in the stacks. Few souls find their way down here, but if they do, what shelter we can provide, the Library should. Libraries have always been a kind of church, a kind of sanctuary.

Librarian Fleur Michel, 1784 CE

THERE WERE TIMES—MOMENTS, REALLY, no longer than a swig of tea—when Brevity longed for the simplicity of the Muses Corps. Take this, go here; love this, break your own heart. It was hard work, but there was a certainty to it. Certainty was good; it kept quiet the beehive of anxiety that she held in her chest.

As Echo and her daughter turned their expectant gazes on her, Brevity swore she could hear buzzing.

"Sanctuary?" Rami repeated, breaking the silence and earning

Brevity's eternal gratitude. His brow tucked in on itself in disapproval. "You intend to stay here?"

"Them and their entire wing," Claire said.

"On a temporary basis." Iambe had maintained her icy composure. Echo, wearing Pallas's face, continued a placid kind of eye contact with Brevity. As if completely confident in her fellow librarian to navigate this bombshell.

Sanctuary. Brevity wracked her brain but couldn't remember any relevant protocol. She risked a glance at Claire. "Is that possible?"

She expected a clear signal from Claire. As former librarian, Claire always had an opinion on the goings-on in the Unwritten Wing. Brevity had leaned on it, up until recently when they'd disagreed over the ink of unwritten books. Brevity had tried to restore them, Claire had tried to isolate the threat, and the result had been a disaster. The ink had nearly killed Claire and Hero. Brevity had traded her beloved inspiration tattoo for scars. Perhaps both of them had been wrong, but Brevity wasn't sure they could survive being at odds again.

Which is why the distracted glaze in Claire's eyes was so alarming. "Claire?" Brevity prompted again.

"Hmm? Oh." Claire shook herself, razor-edge focus returning. "Gregor referenced an agreement of mutual support and allegiance between the wings of the Library." She pursed her lips. Claire had always avoided mentioning her predecessor by name. "But I don't recall anywhere in the log where it's actually been done. We're a standoffish lot in the Library."

If Claire had an opinion on the matter, she hid it well. Brevity didn't have the time to panic over what that might mean. A glance said Hero and Rami were just as lost.

Only Rosia looked at her with clear understanding. "You

are the librarian," she said simply.

The librarian. Brevity sucked in a breath. It was a title, but it was a duty too. Spending so much time with the log and books, one couldn't help but draw some conclusions. Librarians protected the books with ferocity like Ibukun's. They cared for the books with skill like Ji Han's. They considered the power of books and humanity with the wisdom of Gregor. They bucked tradition and expectations for the sake of the books with the abandon of Fleur.

But they also, whether in Hell or on Earth, didn't turn away anyone in need.

She'd learned that one from Claire. For all Claire's harsh manner and harsher words, she'd never turned away anyone who really, truly needed what the Library could offer.

Brevity was the librarian. There was no question what a librarian's answer was.

"Okay, then," Brevity said.

Hero blinked. "What? Are you sure that's wise? You may want to—"

"I... On behalf of the Unwritten Wing, I grant you sanctuary." The words swept past Brevity's lips, as if stolen on a snatch of wind. A susurrous sound rippled through the damsel suite like a tide as millions of pages ruffled. It was a prelude to a sonorous creak, which turned into a rumble that shook the floorboards beneath her feet. The world tilted. And the Library rearranged itself.

"May want to open that door," Iambe suggested, a second before a gust of wind tossed the entrance to the suite open hard enough to crack the inset glass. Outside, a feral thunder rumbled through the wing.

Brevity grabbed the corner of the couch, squinting against a shiver of dust that fell from the suite's rafters overhead. Light splintered on the shoals of dust particles, forcing her to squint. The air, when it cleared, was accompanied by a bite of green.

The damsel suite, in itself, seemed unchanged. Echo's pool had dried up, leaving Pallas's sleeping body inert by a merely damp carpet. But Brevity could hear the raised voices of damsels outside. She hurried out the door, with Hero close on her heels.

At the threshold, Hero let out a low whistle into the dim aftermath. Dim, that was, because the globes of Brevity's faerie lights filtered through new obstacles. Spider-thread vines and silky drifts of heather hooked carelessly up the sides of bookcases and across strings of lights, painting everything in a mossy kind of watercolor. Wood-slat crates punctuated the formerly tidy shelves, overflowing with haphazardly rolled paper and clapboard notebooks. On the book cart nearest them, an old unwritten epic appeared in a struggle for territory with an elaborately folded envelope. Its jaws were still sealed with red wax, but it nipped and stabbed creases into the larger book.

The Unwritten Wing remained; it hadn't been harmed. But it had been... subject to revision. Brevity bolted down the stacks, overcome with the sudden desire to check the front desk, to anchor herself with some sense of solidity. She had to pick her way over fast-growing vines and sandstone vessels popping up like mushrooms over the top of impeccably polished wood floors. She slipped, once, when a fresh patch of moss decided to sprout under her heel. It was Claire who caught her elbow and kept their forward momentum. They sprinted between dappled foliage and familiar shadowed shelves to slide to a stop at the edge of the lobby.

"I just inventoried that section," Hero complained.

"Unacceptable," Claire muttered under her breath, more than a little scandalized. Brevity was prone to agree. There appeared to be a turf war brewing between the stack of books she'd been in the middle of repairing on her desk and a clatter of rickety papyrus that was emerging from a drawer that hadn't previously existed. The unmistakable sound of tearing paper prodded her to action.

"Excuse—wait, y'all, listen, just—SETTLE DOWN!" To Brevity's ears, she always sounded more like a frazzled babysitter than an authoritative librarian, but she was used to that by now. She drummed her hands on the desk until the sound of textual warfare eased.

"How nice," Iambe said with a tone devoid of said quality, which Echo repeated with a more sincere "*Nice.*" They trailed out of the stacks with the others, accompanied by a handful of damsels, whose expressions ranged from wide-eyed wonder to deep judgment. Iambe carried her brother's sleeping form as if he weighed nothing.

Brevity had been trying to pry a scroll out of the maw of an angry gothic horror, but she paused. "Is… is your mom okay?" The floor had gone concave underneath Echo-as-Pallas's feet, and water—water! in a library! again!—was seeping in from the floorboards beneath her toes. She beckoned with a waft of one slender arm.

Iambe grunted a prolonged complaint under her breath as she hefted Pallas's limp form over one shoulder and deposited him without reverence into the growing puddle. "Oh, she's happy as a sea hag." She made a small adjustment so Pallas was merely slumped over and not at risk of drowning as the small flood of water grew. "Good luck getting rid of her now."

"Surely this is just a temporary—" Claire made an arch noise as Echo-as-Pallas ignored her. The spirit laid a gentle hand on top of her sleeping son's head and began to sink.

The shallow water swallowed her up, and inch by inch Pallas's reflection returned to him. Hero shook his head and turned to Iambe. "Your mother is kind of an asshole."

Iambe smiled. "You just noticed?"

A crack, like a popping log, thundered from the doorway, drawing Brevity's attention. The greenery had spread a trail of tiny white flowers out the door, but Brevity couldn't see how such tiny plants could make such a ruckus.

Claire's brow furrowed, then smoothed with a dawning kind of horror. She broke into a run. "Oh, bugger."

By the time Brevity caught up, Claire had frozen to a stop at the edge of the hallway, just before the gargoyle alcove.

The gargoyle's empty alcove.

The flowers swarmed over the wide hallway, blanketing the alcove in blooms. Dark red-purple leaves and wide lilies the color of turmeric had joined the foliage now, and evidently driven out the stone inhabitant.

Claire was forced to shield her eyes to protect her sanity. Brevity stopped beside her and barely managed to drag them both out of the way to avoid a stone wingtip. The gargoyle flailed across the expanse of the hallway, churning up freshly formed moss under his stone claws. The greenery climbed up the creature's sides, moss clinging to stone flanks even where the flowers couldn't find purchase. The gargoyle's frantic movement, coupled with his non-euclidean nature, made it hard to discern the details, but Brevity was almost positive it was yellow daisies encircling the shifting, fractal blur of his head.

The gargoyle let loose another growl that sounded like an aggrieved rockslide. It ripped at the offending greenery, but new moss just sprang up in its place. Brevity hesitated, then had a thought. "Rami?"

"Yes, ma'am." Ramiel stepped forward, shrugging his sword out of the folds of his coat. It ignited into a controlled blue flame.

Claire spun. "This doesn't call for violence—" She cut off when Brevity squeezed her elbow. It didn't take words to convey *trust me, watch* between them, and Claire folded her arms with a huff. Rami stepped past them, dodging around the gargoyle's frantic movements with a grace that Brevity was always surprised to see he possessed.

Rami ducked and spun, waiting until he had an opening in the gargoyle's guard. Then he tapped the burning tip of his sword to a mass of flowers clinging to the creature's chest.

The foliage ignited, far easier than green moss should have. Violet, yellow, and white shifted into flames racing over the gargoyle's stone body, stripping it of the offending flowers. When the embers tried to jump from the ankle to the floor, Rami stamped them out neatly.

The gargoyle was left with one singed daisy clinging above the fractalized cliff of his face. His panicked movements stilled, until the giant creature hunkered to a stop in the middle of the hallway, huffing great, gritty breaths.

"Aren't you clever." Claire cupped the side of Rami's face with her palm before stepping past him as he sheathed his sword. She tutted at the gargoyle, "There, now. No need for all this fuss." She began brushing ash off his shoulders. The creature let out a pitiful low croon.

"When do I get a flaming sword?" Hero complained as he joined them. He cast a loaded look toward Rami. "What do I need to do to get you to show me that trick?"

Rami's stoic expression barely twitched but appeared to melt into something warm and shy. "You could train with me if you like."

"You minx."

Brevity cleared her throat, which made Rami step back, but Hero only made a wretched face at her. She left them to it and joined Claire beside the gargoyle. "At least now we don't gotta bother the dryads for flowers." She tilted her head. "Hey, do you suppose the Unsaid Wing grows their own tea leaves? That could be handy."

"It overflowed the Library," Claire said as if she hadn't heard her. Her face was grim and slightly speckled with ash. "Hellfire. We'll need to move fast."

The relief Brevity had felt drained away quickly. She glanced up and down the hall but couldn't see any discernible threat. Claire's shoulders were clenched as if an attack was imminent. "What do you mean?" A flutter of doubt grew. That swooping sensation Brevity got at the fear of having done the wrong thing bottomed out her stomach. "I had to help them. It's what the Library does."

Doesn't it? Tell me I was right. Please tell me it's what you would have done, a terrified small voice said in Brevity's head.

Claire waved that away like an irritating fly. "Of course you did, but the timing is terrible. I didn't have time to tell you before. Just before the Unsaid Wing arrived, Malphas was poking around the Arcane Wing. She's suspicious."

"Malphas is always suspicious." Hero appeared to have put aside his flirting enough to join in the conversation. He shook a spot of moss from the tip of his polished boots.

"This is different." A graphite streak of certainty in Claire's voice managed to draw everyone's attention. "The Library provides some obfuscation, but they noticed something changed when we freed the ink." Claire's left hand grasped her right wrist, as if attempting to stem the memory. She straightened. "The spillover of the Unsaid Wing into the Unwritten will have created a signal flare of power that even the weakest demon won't have missed. There's no way an inventory will satisfy her suspicion now. Malphas will demand answers. If Hell discovers that the Library they host is actually stuffed full of fragments of souls, they'll be on us like carrion birds."

"Perhaps this is a conversation best held inside." Rami cast a wary eye down the hall. The gargoyle had calmed under Claire's attention and shook the rest of the ash from its shoulders to dust the lot of them. Brevity wrinkled her nose and stepped back so the giant could lurch back to his alcove.

"You're right." Claire dusted her hands. "Besides, we have guests."

THE GUESTS, IAMBE AND Pallas, had not followed the noise into the hallway and instead appeared to have made themselves at home. They found Iambe lounging on a couch across from the front desk, idly flipping through a book with one of Brevity's pens in her mouth. "I'll grant you that it's more exciting reading, but however do you work with books with writing that trips all over the page like this?"

"Carefully." Brevity rescued the book from Iambe's hands and returned it to the desk.

Iambe's pink lips made a displeased moue, and she continued to chew on the pen thoughtfully. "As you say. You'll be pleased to hear that Mother has asked the Unsaid to play nicely with the Unwritten for the duration of our stay."

It was true. The alarming sound of paper warfare had trailed off. A cursory glance at the nearest shelves showed that books and letters were cooperating, if quite overstuffed in their cubbies. "Thank you," Brevity said, and meant it.

"Where's your brother?" Hero asked.

Iambe fluttered a vague hand over her shoulder. "He allowed himself to be swept off by those books you have walking around—"

"Damsels," Hero and Brevity corrected at the same time.

"Damsels, whatever." Iambe examined her nails. "They couldn't wait to coo over him and coddle him off. Pallas has that effect on people."

"The suite might be the most comfortable for both of—" Brevity cut off at yet another crack of sound coming from the hallway. Her pulse spiked as she wheeled around. Rami and Hero both had their swords out. What had the greenery of the Unsaid wrought now? Or was it demons, demons already champing at the bit to—

A large, elderly raven came careening through the great doors, cackling up a ruckus. It was the old mortal bird Claire kept as a—well, "pet" was too strong a word, as she still only referred to it as Bird, but she'd allowed it to stay in the Arcane Wing. She complained, but Brevity had caught her feeding it crackers.

The giant black bird was hampered in its flight. It had a large oversized envelope in its claws. It reeled once over their heads before dropping its package into Claire's open hands. It cursed loudly at all of them before landing inelegantly on the desk. Probably to wait for its reward.

Claire made no move toward her pockets for crackers. She pinched the large envelope at the edges and ripped. She read the short note inside, then continued staring at it with stony resolve.

"What is it?" Brevity drew closer and realized the envelope was singed. Sulfur and anise filled the air.

"A summons," Claire said. Her voice was nearly as low as the gargoyle's had been. "Malphas moves fast. We're being summoned to the high court of Hell."

"When?" Hero asked, and Claire's grimace spoke volumes.

"Now."

4

HERO

Malphas tried to warn me off this foolish quest, in her way. Don't tell anyone, old book, but I think she's always had a fascination with, if not a fondness for, the Library. Or maybe just with souls—she doesn't know the secret, that they're one and the same. If she did, I wouldn't have lasted even this long.

She'll come for me, but she won't dare destroy the books. She won't dare to touch the Librarian's Log; even she doesn't have that much power. So listen close, Book. This is not mere indulgence; this is strategy. Hide these words from the others if you must, but listen to that which I failed to learn.

To win a war against Hell, you have to know what you are willing to lose.

Librarian Poppaea Julia, 48 BCE

Hell is a natural bureaucracy—that would figure. But don't underestimate the threat process and paperwork can present. Good men have been felled by less. The demons have been at

this game far longer than you or I, apprentice. If you walk into
Hell's courts, tread very lightly indeed.

Librarian Gregor Henry, 1988 CE

HELL ONLY EVER OPERATED on a now time frame. The time in
the afterlife was always either now or never, whichever was most
painful. Hero didn't know why he'd hoped for otherwise. Claire
was already conferring with Brevity, concocting some kind of plan
that would surely lead them to skimming along the edge of chaos.
"... they'll want to see both of us, at a minimum."

"I'm going," Hero said. It was a fact. He was. He lifted his chin
and dared Claire to deny it. Not so long ago, she would have denied
the sky was blue if it fit her preferences.

Miraculously, a resigned look flickered across her face instead.
Claire screwed up her nose and frowned at him for a long moment
before nodding. "Fine, then, we'll all go together."

Together. A sliver of his unease settled at the word. He was an
exceptionally skilled man—humble, too—but as capable as they
all were, the story seemed to go right only when they were together.
It made a fierce, protective streak bloom in his chest, as strong as
any ambition he'd ever had. Together; all of this would be all right
if he could just keep them together, the story in arm's reach.

It felt like the kind of irritating, honorable rot that Rami
excelled in. Hero cast a glance over his shoulder, expecting to see
their angel pleased at the pronouncement. Instead, Rami's eyes
were trained straight ahead as if facing a firing squad. Hero hadn't
thought it possible for color to leach out of the angel's craggy stern
face, but Rami's warm olive cheeks were pale and gray as his trench
coat. Tension sang across his cheek.

"However," Claire said slowly. She was studying Rami too. She threw a significant glance Hero's way. He was ashamed at how long it took him to put it together—Ramiel had been cast out of Heaven. Even though he had not joined with Lucifer, he had also fallen. The Watcher took pains to differentiate himself from the demons, but he had been colleagues with infernal creatures like Malphas. He'd strived to regain his place in Heaven, only to end up here, once again. Even angels could falter when faced with past mistakes and old betrayals. Claire cleared her throat. "It would be irresponsible to leave the books unguarded, wouldn't it, Librarian?"

Brevity had been preoccupied with her preparations but read the emotional charge of the room in a single glance. She slapped the Librarian's Log shut. "Right. Good point. Rami, could I ask you to stay? I know the damsels trust you."

If it was difficult to be a villain among these heroic misfits, it had to be even harder to be an angelic being in Hell. Ramiel shook his head as if waking himself. "I— Of course I can, but, ma'am, you shouldn't go into the vipers' den unprepared—"

"I'm quite capable of handling a few bureaucratic demons myself," Claire reminded him. She made sure that fact was given time to be understood and acknowledged before relenting. "In any case, Brevity and Hero will be there."

Hero knocked his shoulder into Rami's before he could work up a proper bluster. "I can follow orders as well as you." That was a bald-faced lie, which he softened when he lowered his voice. Their cheeks touched. "You don't have to face them. Not today. Let me do this."

No one was as skilled at damning himself as well as a Heavenly being. As close as they were, Hero could feel the telegraph of relief and agonizing doubt flicker across Rami's face before his shoulders sagged. "Be careful. These demons—"

"You're not the only one with relevant experience," Claire said gently. She straightened as Brevity came around the desk to join her. "Besides, Hero's sword may not set things on fire, but he's capable enough with it."

"Such praise! Listen, if we're going to start comparing my sword to Rami's, it's only fair—"

"Hero." He was rewarded with the way Claire's voice was the perfect frisson of reproach and scandal. Hero grinned despite himself as they departed for a meeting with Hell.

THE WAY TO HELL'S inner court wasn't nearly as long as Hero had thought it would be. Claire and Brevity both appeared familiar with the route, down a flight of stairs, across a burnt-out cathedral that opened into a field of swords, and up another flight. They came to a stop at a door in an empty courtyard just as unremarkable as its kin.

"This is Hell's court of demons?" Hero had thought demons had higher standards than the rotting moss that dotted the cobblestones at their feet.

"Everywhere has the potential to be a part of Hell." Claire hesitated at the door, frowning at the distressingly modern brass knob. Hadn't it been oak and knockers a moment before? Hero mistrusted changing architecture. Which is why he listened when Claire began speaking low and urgent.

"Hell's court is a traveling one. It never convenes in the same place. Any place that has seen the worst that humanity has to offer can host Hell's court. They simply snip a pocket of time from it—the moment an orphanage burned, war was waged, or a boardroom voted some people not worth saving. They have a demon in their employ that can snip that moment out of the world and use it for their own for a time. I don't know what Malphas will have chosen for this affair, but I suspect she will choose something upsetting. It may be useless to say it, but I need you to be on your best behavior in there. Brevity—I know you've been to court before, but that was a social call. This will be different. You're librarian now. They will test you."

"I'm ready," Brevity said, with only a minor pallor to her cheeks. Hero could nearly see her counting her breaths in her head, *four in, four out*. Practiced and in control. Hero admired that in the little muse.

"Then, let's go." Claire took a steeling breath for herself and opened the door.

A FAMILIAR, MUSKY SCENT assaulted Hero's nose the moment he crossed the threshold. His childhood had been one of rural poverty, so his first thought had been *barn*. An ill-kept barn at that. The smell of nervous animal was familiar: urine and sweat and the vague tang of exhaustion. But it lacked any of the fresh smells of the barn. No must from old feed, no sharp cut of green hay in the mow. It was the smell of beastly treatment, lives made sour.

The ground beneath his toes was gritty concrete, however. And the lights overhead were modern and apathetic, buzzing with a canned kind of light that didn't reach the far walls. No windows broke the gloom, and the concrete walls only radiated a chill into the air. There were no animals to be seen, but metal chain-link fencing rose in the center of the room, dividing the large space into square pens.

Concrete would be terrible for living creatures, Hero's distant childhood reminded him analytically. Too cold, hard on the feet.

Perhaps the vague shadows he could just make out on the floor were intended to be padding. When he approached the pens, the smell of urine increased. Security cameras lurched like vultures at the top of the fencing. "What is this place, a cattle pen? This is some spot of great evil?" Hero used his best sneer and made sure his voice carried.

"Yes, it is." Claire's voice was subdued. Hero followed the line of her gaze through the chain link. There were indeed some kind of cheap foam pads scattered amid piles of tissue-thin silver fabric that reflected and scattered the cold light in fractured shadows. Nestled forgotten under the nearest pile was one small sandal.

Child-sized.

A squelched noise escaped Brevity. She stepped back, edging closer to Claire. "What is this place?"

"I don't know," Claire said quietly. "It's too modern to be anything from the Great War."

"'The War,' as if there's ever just one." An old soft voice, gently creased with malice, reached them from the other side of the cages. Malphas stepped out of the gloom. The general of Hell's forces was deceptively matronly. Gray-haired and wide-hipped in rust red leather, but the crow's-feet at her eyes bracketed a sharp, cutting gaze. "But you've been dead awhile, Claire. I suppose this was after your time, and you've been too busy with your books. Pity you can't appreciate it."

"You and I have different values of appreciation, Grandmother of Ghosts."

"Still with that nickname. You'll call me General here." Malphas clicked her tongue, and in an instant the title was true. She wore a dress uniform, though Hero had no hope of identifying the army. He recognized the primary-color flag patched on her shoulder. Other shapes moved in the darkness, indistinct and black-clad.

His eyes were adjusting to the gloom. A pair of children's underthings, soiled, was caught on the chain fence closest to him. The air was tangy with sweat and sick. Hero had distinct experience with the possible evils conducted in the trappings of uniforms and authority. He'd led armies, worn crowns, once upon a story. But this place took even his breath away.

"No need for drastic action from your paper tiger," Malphas said sharply. Hero hadn't even realized his hand had been creeping toward the hilt of his sword until the cold metal was between his fingers. The gates on three of the pens swung open on sour hinges.

One for each of them.

"Oh, hell no," Hero whispered with emotion.

"Is this really necessary, Malphas?" Claire did an admirable job of sounding bored.

"General." Malphas's smile was as chill as the cages. "Afraid it is, girl."

"The last demon that called me 'girl' is now an ornament in the Arcane Wing." Claire let the fact hang before stepping forward into the leftmost pen like an idiot. Brevity followed her lead, cautiously inching into the middle pen. Hero resisted the urge to scream at them for being foolish heroes, and stepped into his own.

5

BREVITY

The Librarian's Log keeps its secrets. I've observed myself how I can read a page five times and discover new entries every time I return to the page. So I'm asking you a favor, book of mysteries. Hide these words. I'll not index this; I won't even assign it a code word. I'm attempting a thing no librarian should, and I am doing it alone. Alone except for you. I need somewhere to write these thoughts. Indulge me in this, old book, and don't bother my future heirs with the nattering of an old woman.

I'm off to interrogate a demon.

Librarian Poppaea Julia, 48 BCE

BREVITY KNEW COLOR, BREATHED color, saw colors, wherever she went. But now she stepped into a place colors fled. The cotton toe of a child's sock, gray from filth from the floor. Vomit, hours or days old in the corner. The shred of a foil blanket crinkled under her shoes. If this had been the worst of it, Brevity might have been calmer. But the colors of the place were all wrong. The places of children were some of her personal favorites. Kids were like little books in that way. Stretching and reaching in all directions with colors they had not yet been told were impossible. Imagination, budding and feral, radiating off their little minds. Kids were the closest humans ever came to the world of muses, of color and possibility. Brevity liked kids. There was a kinship there.

The colors that lingered in this cold room were the furthest thing from the colors of freedom. The whole place was washed with a light the color of bile, and the gray concrete spotted with so many dark stains that Brevity couldn't tell what was physical and what was manifested by the horrors it had seen.

It was a room where innocence went to rot.

Malphas was still speaking in cool undertones she couldn't decipher, to which Claire was responding in kind. Claire stood ramrod straight in the middle of her pen, and the debris at her feet might have been a stack of books rather than bits of inhumanity. Only Brevity could see the way her knuckles whitened into a fist behind her back.

A wrongness screamed in Brevity's head. The one time she'd accompanied Claire to Hell's court, it'd been a posh affair. Some Italian manse snipped out of time a moment before a massacre. Tables upturned but still gilded and pristine. She'd been there to be introduced as the Unwritten Wing's newest assistant librarian. The demons had embellished themselves in kind, as courtiers and nobles of an indeterminate era. Well, courtiers with horns. Her relationship with Claire had been so strained, she'd been worried she'd use the wrong fork and shame the Library.

This room was the furthest from a noble court. The evils here weren't gilded; they were as blatant and bare as exposed iron.

"Eyes forward, spirit." A figure separated itself from the gloom and approached the fencing. The demon was dressed as some kind of authority figure, designed to intimidate. Clad head to toe in modern riot armor—Brevity could discern nothing more than that. A flicker of white on their shoulder caught her eye, an armband with three letters stenciled in bone white paint. They slapped a baton against the chain link before Brevity could decipher it.

Brevity was too tense to flinch. She was mildly proud of that. She unclenched her jaw enough to swallow and find her nerve. "Librarian. My title is librarian."

"This isn't the Library," the figure barked.

"No," Brevity said quietly, "it is not."

"Answer truthfully. Date and time of your most recent inventory." The demon guard barked it like an order, not a question. Brevity felt ill as she answered. Thank god she'd had just enough time to review the log before they came.

"The results?" the demon asked next.

"All books accounted for." She'd been able to answer truthfully so far, and Brevity was of a naturally hopeful nature. Perhaps they could talk their way out of this yet.

All that hope shattered on the rocks of the next question. "Irrelevant." The helmet tilted as the demon paused a moment, studying her. "Define 'books.'"

"What?"

Her interrogator took a step closer to the fencing that separated them. "Define 'books.' What, precisely, Librarian, are the books in your care? Surely you can tell me."

Ice crept into Brevity's gut, and a hollow kind of ring echoed in her ears. *They know. They know.* The sour air of the pen suddenly seemed too thin, chain fencing too close. She couldn't breathe.

They know. Her thoughts hammered and the panic set in.

6

HERO

Know what you're willing to lose, and what you are not. Because the demons certainly do.

Librarian Yoon Ji Han, 1800 CE

THE THIN DEMON THAT approached Hero's pen wore a disappointingly pedestrian pinstripe suit. Really, he was insulted. Brevity had gotten an armor-clad ruffian, Claire had gotten the demon general herself, and Hero rated no more than a bean-counting imp? Rude. Incredibly rude.

He crossed his arms, not even bothering to reach for his sword. "Who are you supposed to be, Hell's accountant?"

"A friend." The demon did a good approximation of human, with a bald head that was just a little too pale and spectacles obscuring eyes that were a little too fiery to be brown. The creature adjusted his glasses, briefly blinding Hero with a flash of the overhead lights before continuing. "They are going to leave you here, you know. We didn't do this; they did."

"Is that something you cooked up just for me, or is that what you tell every poor soul who passes through here?" Hero affected a dismissive glance around the pen. He had to swallow his revulsion to look bored, but that was practically his profession at this point. "I'm not a helpless child."

"No. You're not a human at all. Everyone agrees on it. There was a motion and executive order. We released an official statement on the matter. I have the paperwork right here." The demon leaned closer. "How does it feel to be a mere book?"

Hero paused, letting the question linger. They were suspicious, had inklings even, but they didn't know. They didn't know his book had been destroyed. And if they didn't know that, then perhaps they didn't know the real details of the rest. Not yet, at least. This whole act was to tease more information out of them by pretending they did know.

Hero glanced to his left. Brevity looked a particularly pale cornflower shade of blue, and beyond her, Claire and Malphas faced each other in evident isolation. Claire could stonewall the gods themselves; that just left two.

The demon clerk waited patiently for an answer. They certainly knew how to get under his skin; Hero hated feeling analyzed and itemized, like a mere oddity. "How does it feel to be a transdimensional leech?" he asked instead.

The demon smiled, nodded, and made a note on his clipboard. Demons always did have a flair for prop work.

"Does resisting make you feel as if you have a modicum of control over your life?"

Even knowing what he was doing, the question twisted a knife somewhere in Hero's guts. He translated the pain into a smile that could skin a bear. "I can trade pointed questions with you all day, demon. But then, I am just a book." He drew out the word and added an extra barb on the end of the *k*.

"Strange that the librarians would allow a book to accompany them outside the wing."

"Strange that you would care."

The demon didn't blink. Hadn't blinked for the last several minutes. Hero felt his skin crawl. The demon paused before asking his next question. "What have you done to earn your place?"

Claire called him vain; Hero didn't argue. It was less shameful than the truth, that Hero had no idea what he was doing—or who he was. He preferred to keep that, and anything else real enough to hurt, private.

But these were demons; demons fed on secrets. The more they tried to obscure and evade, the deeper the demons would dig in.

Fine, then. Hero would starve them of secrets.

"I seduced them, of course," Hero said. "And then, annoyingly, they seduced me."

The painstakingly slow blink and pause were as good as a trophy for Hero. Right, then. Time to do this right.

"Do you know how difficult it is to court an angel? How absurd it is to try to seduce a being of literal divine goodness? I mean, I am perfect, but even I have my limits. We all know I don't work miracles. And that doesn't even get me started on Claire." Hero mustered a brazen smile he did not feel and forced his shoulders to relax. He sauntered toward the front of the cage, hips first. He let a lazy hand fall to his chin in thought. "You know what it's like to want to do bad things all the time, don't you?"

The demon's clinical expression didn't change, but Hero caught when his infernal pupils widened with surprise.

Or perhaps interest.

"Well, then." Hero cracked his knuckles and grinned. "Let me elucidate."

7

CLAIRE

It was my mistake. I thought I had nothing to lose, but there was so much I wasn't willing to give up. The idea of redemption. The passage of time. Dear, sweet, stony Revka. I couldn't lose her.

Malphas knew that from the start. I was doomed to failure, then. Doomed not because of what I lacked but for what I already had and would not relinquish.

I wish I could say I was sorry.

Librarian Poppaea Julia, 48 BCE

"SURELY MY PAPERWORK WAS in order," Claire said. Sound was restricted to inside her pen, but worry for the others distracted her. Out of the corner of her eye, Claire could see Brevity fidgeting, and beyond her Hero making some vague gestures. Probably telling the demons where to stick it, knowing him. It was difficult to focus, but fear was a great clarifier when Malphas smiled.

"Perfectly in order. I would expect nothing less from our dear Arcanist." Malphas tipped her head. "Which is why you are here."

The hair on the back of Claire's neck prickled with warning. "I don't understand."

"We requested an inventory from the Unwritten Wing as well, of course. Standard practice." She paused, and her fingers tapped the cuff of one perfectly tailored sleeve. Malphas in a pantsuit was almost more terrifying than when she was enrobed in the leather of her enemies. "What do you think we found?"

"Really, General, the intimidation of hypothetical questions is a little below you, isn't it?"

"Not in this case." Malphas looked pleased. "I'm honestly interested in your answer. What does the Library contain, Claire? Don't tell me books. Because the discrepancies I've been finding are tantalizing."

"I have no idea what you're going on about." Claire studied her nails and flicked an imaginary speck of dust away from her skirts. "What possible discrepancies? If the inventory is too complex for a demon to understand I'll simply have to walk you—"

"No need to explain the entire Library, girl. Just one book. His." Malphas pointed a finger, maintaining a steady, smug gaze all the while.

Claire's heart bottomed out. She followed the line of Malphas's finger, though she already knew where it pointed. Hero was in the midst of explaining something to his demon with broad, possibly fruit-related gestures. The demon looked uncomfortable. Hero looked delighted. Completely clueless of the danger he was in, as usual. Claire swallowed her fear before returning her gaze to Malphas. "Hero is no longer in my care. As you should well know, I am no longer librarian—"

"Indeed you are not. And I am not as young and quick as I used to be. So perhaps you can explain something for me." At no time, in no reality, could Malphas be described as dull-witted. Her tight-lipped smile widened into what felt like the jaws of a trap. "The Unwritten Wing's inventory indicated all books accounted for—except for his. An oddity, since I understand there are limits placed on your so-called Special Collections. But I was reassured when Librarian Brevity annotated that the book was in the care of the Arcane Wing for the time being."

The air was already cold, but the frost in the realization made Claire finally shiver.

"Strange, then, how your inventory states everything is in its place. And makes no mention of a book on loan from the Unwritten Wing."

They'd accounted for this. In the days of hollow clarity after the ink had disappeared into the Dust Wing and it became evident that Hero's book was not coming back, Brevity and Claire had devised a simple plan. Falsify the inventory to cover up the loss of the ink, and should anyone inquire about Hero's missing book, it would be on loan. They hadn't accounted for Malphas actually understanding the workings of the interworld loan system, and Brevity had been forced to make up an excuse on the spot.

And they'd never thought Malphas would compare inventories. Stupid. *Stupid.* The only bureaucracy Hell loved was its own; there should have never been a demon with a mind for the details of paperwork.

Except, it seemed, Malphas.

"The Arcane Wing is not a lending kind of library." Claire prayed her voice was not as unmoored as it sounded to her own ears. She built up her reasoning as fast as she talked. "As well you know—otherwise we would have every upstart demon at our door seeking items of power. Our inventory doesn't have a line item for items in the wing on temporary loan."

Rather than seem appeased, Malphas appeared to have been waiting for such an argument. "Then your curation process is flawed." She stepped closer to the fence, making the cheap metal screech with one gloved hand. "Whatever shall we do about that, Claire?"

Claire's nerves were screaming some very solid advice. To run, to take Hero and Brevity and run. But there was no escaping Hell; of that much she was certain. She'd already tried once before.

Instead, she heaved a loud sigh and forced herself to saunter closer to the fence herself, as if impatient to have this matter settled. She had to pick among the detritus on the floor. Her toe caught on one of the foil blankets and a soiled diaper tumbled out. Bile rose in her throat. "It's a perfectly fine system, General. There are merely exceptions—"

"Claire, dear Claire." Malphas interrupted her, lowering her voice to force Claire even closer. "There can't be exceptions. You have always run such a tight operation. Really, I've always admired you for it. You could have almost been one of us." She paused and then shook her head. "You've falsified inventory and lied to me. Either you have failed to meet your duty as Arcanist or you stand in treason to Hell. Which is it?"

"The Library does not owe allegiance to Hell," Claire said lowly.

She hadn't answered, but Malphas acted as if she had. She stepped back, nodding thoughtfully. "We host you, we grant you shelter, we exempt you from the fate of most mortals bound to this realm, and this is how you betray us. With secrets."

"Hell thrives on secrets," Claire snapped.

"Ah, but the Library isn't of Hell," Malphas echoed her softly. "So when power spikes and seeps out from around the edges of your little corner of the fiefdom, we notice. Power, Claire. The power that is only produced by new souls, unbound souls at that. What have you little bookworms stirred up? Failure or traitor, Claire. Which are you claiming to be?"

Words failed her. Claire remained silent.

Somewhere a fan had kicked on. As if the chilled and desolate concrete needed any cooling. It succeeded in taking away none of the stench of despair, but it dried out Claire's face. She was forced to blink first, and Malphas clapped her hands together.

"We can clear all this up easily." She made an imperious gesture and the other demons stepped back from the pens. There was a pop and sound returned to the world outside the pen.

"—and then I'd dribble honey on his…" Hero trailed off into the silence.

Malphas folded her arms. The tailored suit she wore was beginning to melt at the edges. A dark rust brown stain crept in at her cuffs, slowly muddling the pinstripe into bloody leather. "Show us his book. One stab is all it takes, correct? Send our little man here back into his book and that will verify what you say is true, that the book is functional and in the proper hands, and I can let go of more interesting questions."

Claire could hear Brevity's sharp intake of breath. A scuffling sound, as if Hero had stepped back. It wasn't fear that Claire felt, for just that moment. It was a churning heat, of thirty years of struggle and grief coming to a red-hot head in her chest. Malphas toyed with her the way demons toyed with all mortals. The agony was that Claire had *let* her. It had been so easy to back her into an unwinnable choice. It would be suicide to refuse Malphas in her own court, but it would be murder to harm Hero, who was now very much fragile without his book.

"I will not," Claire said softly.

The fans clicked twice more. The churning shadows of demons stirred. Malphas tilted her head back to smile at the ceiling. "Traitor, then."

"Brevity! Hero!" Claire raised her voice, feeling frozen in place even as Malphas raised a hand. "Cut a path."

"With pleasure." Hero spun, flicking his sword out and hacking at the locked gate behind him. Sparks flew, and one solid kick sent the cheap metal screaming.

"I told you once, little Claire. Do you remember?" Malphas was still speaking. Her transformation was complete, again swathed in blood and leather and smoke. Red seeped from her eyes. Grandmother of ghosts, crone of the battlefield, warrior of the damned, general of Hell. "You will know it, when Hell comes for you."

A clatter behind her, hopefully Hero freeing Brevity. Claire began to back up, stumbling over the soiled blankets but not daring to take her eyes off Malphas. Her back hit the pen fencing, and it was already vibrating as Hero hacked at the gate and smashed the lock.

"It's been an enjoyable game, girl." Malphas tilted her head. "Try to make it last."

Only when Hero's hand found her wrist did Claire dare to look away. Brevity was already at the door—curiously unchallenged by the guards—and held it open. Hero yanked Claire into a run.

Shadows turned to shards around them, threatening but distant. "Forget them," she could hear Malphas mutter behind her. The next pronouncement sent ice through her veins. "Burn it. Spare nothing."

8

HERO

The Unwritten Wing is not beholden to Hell. Hell is the wing's host, not its sovereign. But never mistake that for safety, young apprentice. Hell cannot command the Library, but it can do so much worse. The demons know the foundations of this realm far better than we ever will. They have their hands buried deep in the roots from which the Unwritten Wing has grown. It would take so very little effort for them to shake the ground out from underneath us. You asked me once what could possibly make me afraid. Little tremors; that's what I fear in Hell. Tremors of change.

Librarian Yoon Ji Han, 1799 CE

NO GUARDS OR ARMORED horrors waited for them on their flight from the court. The crumbling courtyard was just as they had left it. Hero didn't have time to pause and be suspicious. They cleared the pavers at a dead run and hurtled back down the labyrinthine hallways of Hell.

"Where are we going?" Hero asked.

"The Unwritten Wing." Claire stumbled to keep up with his long legs. She was wheezing but stubbornly refused to slow down. "We have to get there before they do."

"The books—we need to evacuate the wing!" Brevity shouted over the noise.

Beside him, Claire's lips tightened to a thin white line and she ran harder. Hero didn't need her to state the obvious. There was no way to move everything, even with all the time in the world. They couldn't just up and relocate through a pond like the Unsaid Wing had. The Unwritten Wing was not just books. It was art and rugs and—

Hero staggered. "Oh gods. The damsels."

"Almost there." Claire urged him down the hall. Their arrival roused the gargoyle, still grimy from the flower attack. It appeared the Unsaid's foliage had stayed in bounds since they'd left, but Hero nearly skidded on moss as they rounded through the archway.

Though he'd expected it, the chaos of green and vines still startled Hero to a standstill. His gaze picked through the noise, automatically landing on Rami, who was bent in conversation with Rosia. Both of them turned at the sound of their entrance. Rami's hand was on his sword pommel. Rosia simply looked skeptical.

"They're coming," Claire said. Neither she nor Brevity slowed down, continuing their sprint to the desk.

"Lock down the wing. Rami, Hero—the doors." Brevity's voice was surprisingly steady in the face of impending destruction.

Rami broke away from Rosia, already joining Hero at the entrance. "Who's coming?"

"The in-laws. Who else? The demons," Hero snapped, if only to burn off the terror running high in his veins. He gave an uncertain look at the doors. One was still swaying on a broken hinge, and vines had further wedged themselves up into the locking mechanism. "The doors may… be a problem."

"Then drag Echo out of the nearest teacup to clear up her mess." Claire was barely restraining herself from interfering while Brevity flipped frantically through the logbook. Her fingers flexed, and Hero could see the struggle in her dark eyes before she diverted herself to pacing, loading up the nearest book carts with whatever was at hand.

"No time," Brevity mumbled into a drawer before she surfaced with three delicate pieces of colored vellum. "There's the wards; they held up once—"

Rami was already shaking his head. "That was what Andras managed to cobble together with scraps. The wards will be a mere inconvenience to Malphas's forces, should she be so determined."

Claire sighed quietly. "Oh, she's determined."

Hero had begun to hack at the vines engulfing one of the door's giant latches, but it was a bit like wrestling a pig. He twisted the blade between the door and the bolt, a move that would have surely damaged a normal blade and made the swordsman in him cringe, but unwritten materials were made of stiffer stuff. "The doors are thoroughly bu—fucked." He'd nearly said "buggered." Claire was having a terrible influence on his thoroughly American cursing repertoire. "It's going to take an hour of work to shut them securely. Which means we're screwed."

"Then we barricade it. The gargoyle will help." Claire raised her voice. "Buddy!"

"Buddy?" It took Hero a moment to understand, but when he did, he snorted. "That's its actual name? You actually named the migraine-inducing stone monster 'Buddy'?"

"A man self-named 'Hero' has no place to judge."

"This makes the raven named 'Bird' make more sense," Rami mused, earning a rare glare from Claire. The sound of grit on marble heralded the gargoyle's approach, but when no giant wings shouldered the doors open, Hero frowned and stuck his head out into the hall.

The gargoyle was there, all right, filling up practically the entire width of the hallway. The floor was still mildly littered with ash and greenery, and Buddy had churned it all into a green-gray pulp under his claws.

"Claire… Brev," Hero called back without taking his eyes off the beast. "You may want to see this."

"They can't be here. Not yet." Brevity was breathless as she came up behind him. "I thought we'd have more time."

It was terribly difficult to gauge the mood and emotional state of a non-euclidean gargoyle. Buddy's edges kept on twisting and warping at impossible angles, threatening to twist Hero's stomach contents along with them. The gargoyle's head was nothing but a static cloud of reality that went *Nope*. But Hero knew the pacing of a cornered beast, and the howl Buddy made—on several unpleasant frequencies—was agitated and aggrieved.

Brevity skittered under Hero's arm into the hall. "Whoa there, it's been a bad day, yeah, but…" She paused, nearly getting clipped by a warped wing when she stopped with her nose in the air. "Wait, do you smell that?"

Hero thought it was the wrong time to complain about the stench of Hell, but he sniffed gamely. The hallway smelled much as Hell did, overwhelmingly of anise and embers, haunted by smoke. But there was a different feel that clung to the roof of his mouth as he breathed in. Smoke, yes, but it wasn't the faded, chemical memory of fire that most of Hell was. This was warm… present.

"A fire?" Hero barely echoed the word before he heard Claire make a startled noise behind him.

"No… it can't be." He had half turned when Claire collided into him, shoving him to the side as she pushed her way into the hallway. She paused, eyes wide, as if confirming something. Then she took off at a run down the hall.

"What…" Hero looked worriedly to Rami as the angel, sensing impending disaster, emerged from the stacks to join them.

Brevity made a small wounded noise. "Oh…" She turned, horrified and pale, to the others. "It wasn't the Unwritten Wing they wanted to burn."

Rami went still as stone. "The Arcane Wing." He cursed something in a language Hero didn't know, but it drew gooseflesh up his arms all the same, and then the angel, too, was running.

If there was one thing, Hero reflected, that Hell's Library did well together, it was to sprint headlong into disaster when any sensible creature would flee. Hero was still putting the pieces together even as he and Brevity ran after the others. He easily caught up to Rami—long legs, which he would have to make sure to be smug about later—but he barely caught sight of Claire throwing herself down the stairs that led, in a winding way, from the Unwritten Wing to its Arcane counterpart. The smoke hit him in the face as he descended. It was no longer a faint scent on the air but a corruption in the lungs. Coils of oily smoke, thick and searing, flooded the stairwell and landing. By the time Hero reached the landing that should have been the entry hall to the Arcane Wing, he could barely see the steps beneath his feet.

He made the mistake of looking up.

The flames that wreathed the doors of the Arcane Wing weren't red. They weren't oxygen-gobbling orange. They weren't any color of a fire that could exist on Earth. The fire burned green, pine and lime and every hellish shade in between. It roiled and licked around the doors, which hung broken on their hinges. Through the choking smoke, it coiled around everything in a way that bizarrely mimicked the green vines of the Unsaid.

Claire stood, a silhouette in the doorway, struck into stillness by the sight. Had to be, or she would have seen the movement to one side as a wraith-like imp peeled itself from the shadows. Hero crossed blades in time to divert the demon that had targeted Claire. The shuffle of metal on metal brought her back to her senses, and Claire whipped around. Hero dispatched the snarling creature with a twist of his wrist. It felt less satisfactory when enemies just collapsed into shadow. Bad sports.

She had hollow eyes and hunger-pang cheeks, already grieving. He had just enough time to see the way the fire lit up Claire's blank, determined misery before she ran through the Arcane Wing's double doors and disappeared among the flames.

Hero made a half step after her, but something deep inside him ground to a halt when the heat hit his face. Maybe some part of him still remembered being fragile paper and ink, the part of him that locked his knees and that swam his mind when he tried to force himself forward. The rabbit pulse in his chest nearly drowned out the distant voice in his head that told him Claire was in danger, Claire needed help. Hero needed to go, he needed to just go. Hero... He called himself Hero, what good was it for if not...

"Hero." Hero blinked and Rami's wide shadow fell over him, blocking the flames. "I'll go." The fire and shadows made it hard to read Rami's expression, but from the gravel in his tone it was obvious Rami had grasped Hero's fear in a glance. His fear, his failing. "Stay here—help Brevity."

Hero dimly became aware that everyone had caught up and there was now a small huddle of horrified damsels at the base of the stairs. At its center, Brevity stood, rigid and lifeless, her skin so pale it had almost lost its blue entirely. Her temples were glittering with sweat, and she was breathing with hard, forced breaths.

Hero wasn't the only one who held the memory of fire in the wounded parts of their soul.

He forced himself to nod, anchoring himself on the determined look in Rami's eyes. "Go. Be... be careful." His voice sounded weak to his own ears, hollow and frail. Like paper. Like all things that burned. He loathed himself in that moment, but a soft thing crept onto Rami's face. He nodded once, squeezed Hero's hand, and was gone.

His movements were mechanical as he put an arm around Brevity's shoulders. Her breathing hitched into a question he didn't hear. He said something reassuring, reassuring and meaningless and forgotten as soon as it left his empty lips. He gripped his sword tighter in his free hand, but no targets thoughtfully presented themselves. And Hero waited for the two parts of his heart to emerge from the flames.

9

RAMI

There's a cleansing element to fire. It's terrible—no one wants to see it lay waste to their lives—but it's a purifying ritual, walking through fire. You come out the other side burned and scoured. You come out the other side, knowing what is needed to grow anew.

Librarian Madiha al-Fihri, 608 CE

CONTRARY TO POPULAR IMAGINATION, angels were at home in fire. Indeed, Heaven was just as flame-filled as Hell, though Rami would grant it smelled better. Righteous fire burned clear and sharp, like good incense. It didn't clot the throat with thick, anise-oily smoke that seemed to wrap around your eyes like a blind.

But Rami had no fear of fire. So that could not be the reason he was terrified. Could not be the reason his pulse sped up and his muscles cramped with adrenaline as he crashed between two tables that had already tumbled to glowing matchsticks. It couldn't be what clenched around his throat like a fist, making it hard to yell over the crackling inferno for Claire.

"Here." The reply was muddled, made distant by the roar and crack of burning wood. Rami unsheathed his sword and used it to impatiently lever back the wreckage of a fallen shelf. Things were snapping under his feet. Bones and crowns, seeds and skin, pearls and flutes. The dormant relics of the Arcane Wing snapped and charred around him. And what could not burn began to scream. It was a miracle he could still see, that he and Claire weren't both immediately suffocated by the roil of smoke and heat. The Arcane Wing must have been venting the worst of it somehow. Trying to save itself and its charges even now.

It was losing the fight. But if a wing mirrored its caretaker, it would never stop trying.

He shoved and hacked his way down the far side of the wing and found Claire, wrestling with a hunk of burning shelving. The ripped skirts she used to protect her hands were already charred at the edges. Her hands were already seared and tender.

His impulse was to grab her by the arms, haul her away from the fragile realm turning to ash around them. But that was not the duty he had.

"Back!" Miraculously, Claire heard him and gave him enough room to cleave the wood with his blade. The smaller bits of the shelving crumbled, and Rami realized it had been blocking the opening to the cluttered little alcove Claire had claimed for her desk. She dashed forward before the debris had even settled. Rami lunged forward as part of the archway began to give. He shoved it up with his shoulder and winced as the heat began to eat through his feathered coat. "We have to leave!"

"Not yet." Claire's hands worked swiftly across the shelves crammed over the desk, deftly snatching the important books into a pile. Ash was in her braids and sweat cut hairline fractures through the soot on her face. She couldn't stop coughing. "Grab a box and start pack—"

A fantastic crack like thunder cut off her words. Rami glanced behind him just in time to see an arched beam sag down from the ceiling, descending like some slain beast as it crashed into the far shelves. He felt the vibration through the floorboards.

Rami placed a hand on her shoulder. "Claire." She didn't look at him. "We can't save them."

A shudder ran through her collarbone and then was ruthlessly suppressed. Smoke clotted the alcove by now, and even Rami was finding it difficult to breathe. He sensed, more than saw, her straighten and sweep the odds and ends of baubles on the desk—whatever happened to have been up for inspection that morning—into her arms. "We—" She wheezed. "We can try."

"Claire!" She was fighting with the bottom drawer of her desk. Her hair was in her face, one of the braids perilously close to the flames. Rami's patience broke. He manhandled an arm around her waist in a way that he hoped she would forgive later. She worked the drawer free just as he hauled her back, and came away with one more bundle in her hand.

Rami didn't wait to see what was worth burning over. The smoke was thick as night now, descending and stealing each breath they took. He dragged her back just as the framework of the alcove gave way. Claire's desk disappeared in a bloom of embers and falling debris.

Claire didn't fight him as he dragged her into the corridor. The world had turned to soot and rage around them. It was amazing how fire could turn from searing to impenetrable black at a critical point. Rami was forced to ignite his blade to keep them upright. Even the floorboards cracked and splintered beneath them now.

The Arcane Wing had lost the fight and was folding up around the corpses of its artifacts. What it couldn't protect it would entomb.

Just a little longer, please. Hold out just a minute more. Rami prayed, and he wasn't sure exactly to whom. They clawed blindly back to the front tables by memory. The air was a vacuum of smoke in his lungs. With the last of his senses, Rami heaved them through the flames where the doors should have been.

There was a confusing moment that muddled into a watercolor of sensations. The roar of a void at his back, and a gust of cold, mercifully cold, air slamming him in the face, followed by cool floorboards as Rami's legs gave out. Noise and touch whirled into an eddy before he was able to anchor himself on cool fingertips touching his cheek. He centered on stunning green eyes that were furious and a little wet and wobbly.

"I—" Rami gagged on the soot in his mouth. Hmm, he had never vomited before. Not in all his years. That would be a new experience—but he was able to swallow after a moment. "I was... careful."

Hero made a broken sound, half laughter and half relief, that ended with an angry shove. "You absolute idiot. Idiots," he corrected, looking over Rami's head. It took effort to turn over.

Claire lay like a broken toy sprawled across the floor, a sight that made Rami's throat clench worse than the smoke had. But her head was turning and she let out a violent cough that was strong enough to reassure him that the woman was too stubborn to die a second time. Around her, bits of rescued artifacts scattered the floor like stars, still smoking from their fall.

Clutched in her hand, nearly welded to her seared fingers, was a dagger. A dagger set with a tiger-stripe stone and a blade that seemed malicious. And awake.

BREVITY

Revka says I'm selfish, selfish in this quest to free the Unwritten Wing from its shackles. She's right, but it's so much worse than she knows. I'm not selfishly willing to sacrifice everything in pursuit of my goals. It's much worse than that. I'm selfish enough to want it all, and to lose nothing.

If there's a shred of humanity left in me, after so many years down here, it's that. I almost had it; I almost had it. Then Malphas threatened Revka, and I never even got so far as to speak to Lucifer.

It's true: I'm selfish.

Librarian Poppaea Julia, 48 BCE

"CLAIRE," RAMI'S VOICE SOUNDED rougher than normal, as if the anchor stone of his calm was beginning to fracture. Hero gripped him a little tighter as he struggled to sit up. "Ma'am. Please reassure me that we did not nearly burn ourselves to oblivion in order to save a traitor's soul from the flames."

Claire gripped the dagger in her hand tighter, and Brevity

knew when she finally released it there would be a burn imprinted in her palm. Really, Hero was the only one around here who was supposed to scar himself up. She got an elbow underneath herself and raised her chin in precisely the manner that told Brevity exactly how guilty she felt. Behind her the assembled damsels shifted uneasily. Some began filing out of the room, like smarter creatures smelling a storm on the horizon. "It was my duty as Arcanist to rescue whatever artifacts I could."

"Artifacts, not prisoners." Rami recovered his strength quickly. He stood, gently shaking off Hero's offered arm. The feathers under the epaulets of his trench coat were singed, some burnt back terribly. He began brushing himself off—which only managed to smear the soot around. He didn't seem to notice behind the thunderhead of judgment building in his eyes. "I saw you in there. You went right for that drawer. You risked everything to save that dagger."

Claire couldn't match Rami for pure supernatural stamina and recovery, so she settled her filthy skirts around her as if she were at a picnic rather than on the ash-covered floor of what had been the entrance to the Arcane Wing. "Your opinion is duly noted, apprentice."

"My opinion," Rami seethed, "is we should have left that thing to burn in Hell where it belongs and saved something more worthy. Are you aware we just lost the *entire* wing?"

Claire's shoulders twitched once. She studied the dagger and her folded hands in her lap. "I am aware."

The air in the room had simultaneously dropped several degrees and still managed to boil. Hero had a frozen look on his face—no help there. Brevity coughed and jumped forward, opening her mouth and praying something good fell out. "That's not anyone's fault, right? Why are we yelling at each other instead of Malphas?"

"Because some of us are too new here to have learned that this is Hell," Claire said calmly. "Justice is not in the cards. We don't get to choose who gets saved."

"Don't... Don't lecture me on Hell, Claire. I've known more demons than you ever will." Rami bit his lip, appearing to try to get his temper under control. Brevity would have been fascinated if she hadn't been so drained by terror; Rami was always the calm one, never angry, not since he'd joined them. He breathed once through his nose, then picked up and stowed his sword. "I will see all of them burn for this." He flicked a look down to Claire's lap and up again. "All of them." Rami strode back up the stairs the way they'd come.

Brevity half expected Hero to follow him. Instead, he crossed over to drop to one knee next to Claire. "Hands," he demanded flatly.

Claire startled and started to turn away with a sniff. "I don't know what you're—"

"Hands, Claire." Hero stopped her by her shoulders but declined to do more than that. "You can drive off Rami with your monstrous side, but not me."

"Because, as they say, it takes one to know one?"

Hero's mouth curved up at the side. "Just as you say. So from one monster to another, show me your hands, warden."

Claire relented with the grace of a sullen toddler. When she turned over her hands—one still gripping the dagger—Brevity let out a gasp. "Claire!"

"It's not as bad as all that," Claire tutted. "Don't make such a fu—" She let out a hiss as Hero gently peeled her fingers from the handle. "Peeled," here, being the correct term, as some skin appeared to remain behind, seared in painful bits and drabs to the heated metal. Claire's palms were red from the fire, but her right hand, which had held the dagger, was positively raw.

"I have never understood how, for a dead woman, you injure yourself so easily in the afterlife." His hands were gentler than his words, turning her palms and taking care not to touch the exposed burns.

"We can't all be fast-healing characters from books." It must have still hurt, because a sensible Claire would have noticed the way Hero winced at that. Claire's face was a paler shade of brown than normal. "And it's Hell: they can't let me off easy. I'll be fine in a few hours. It may not be a real physical body, but it's amazing what inconvenient physics your mind can convince you of."

"I'll go find some bandages," Brevity volunteered. She paused at the base of the stairs. "Hero, you'll…?"

"Any demons that come back to check on their handiwork will be a welcome excuse to work out my frustrations." Hero sighed and stood to readjust the sword at his hip. "We'll wait right here. Ma'am."

That last part was Hero's way of trying to soften his words. He did that more often lately. Had more soft bits, as if his time with Rami and Claire were wearing down the more barbed parts of his defenses. Brevity nodded and took the stairs two at a time.

SHE WASN'T ENTIRELY KEEN on the idea of running into Rami while he was still in a black mood, but the Unwritten Wing was the only reliable place for something as mundane as a first aid kit. She didn't see him when she bustled past the front desk and found the neatly folded linens and thread Claire had kept in the bottom drawer for the more mortal kinds of repairs. She turned, arms full, and nearly tripped.

"Oh! Rosia, what are you doing?"

"Reading." The small young damsel had no book in her hands.

"On the floor? Under my desk?" Brevity crouched down to pick up a linen she'd dropped. Rosia lay under the librarian's desk, knees neatly pulled up. It wasn't the oddest place that Brevity had found the girl, not since she had sunk into the unwritten ink and emerged again without her book. Brevity would have said it was impossible for a character to survive without their book if Hero hadn't just pulled the same miracle. Now both of them, Rosia and Hero, had a somewhat honored and entirely unique status in the Unwritten Wing. No longer books, but still a part of it. Hero wanted nothing to do with the damsel suite, so Rosia had inexplicably become their eccentric leader.

"I can read anywhere now," Rosia explained simply.

Brevity squinted but could see no writing anywhere on the underside of the desk. She suspected further inquiry along that line would not be helpful anyway. She straightened back up. "Well, there's been… an accident, at the Arcane Wing. I'm going to take these to Claire. I'll be right—"

"We should take the shadow way," Rosia interrupted.

"Oh, you're coming? I mean, you're welcome to come, I guess." Brevity tried not to grimace. She could shadowstep around the Library—little in-between blinks that *real* muses could do for long distances. She'd been restricted to the Library, though it had still come in handy when she'd been evading Andras's monsters during the standoff. Somehow, she'd been loath to use it much since then. There was no reason for Rosia to take such an interest.

"This way." Rosia rolled to her feet and took Brevity's hand—which required some swift juggling on Brevity's part. "Don't worry," Rosia added over her shoulder as she led them out. "I like this next part."

SHE HADN'T INTENDED TO eavesdrop. Not really. It was just that the gargoyle had been taking up space with its moping in the hallway, so Brevity had gotten impatient and—just as Rosia had suggested—used her shadowstep to get around him. Hell being Hell, it dumped her out in a side passage. It had taken her a moment to get her bearings, but it was easy enough to orient herself. She could return to Claire and Hero taking the roundabout, and she was nearly there when a raised voice made her pause.

"When do you plan to tell them, then?" Hero's voice practically cooed with accusation. Brevity slowed, creeping up to the end of the hallway with an instinctive quiet. She frowned, only half hiding—honest—as she peered around the corner.

"I don't know what you're talking about." Claire still sat on the floor, cradling both her hand and the soul dagger in the folds of her skirt.

"Oh, pish. Come on, warden." Hero lolled against the banister of the stairs, cleverly positioned where he had a strategic view of the room—all except the nook of the service hallway Brevity stood in. "No one here but us monsters now. You can stop pretending you saved that little demon trap by chance."

Claire's chin took a mulish jut. "I don't—"

"Why, Claire?" Hero interrupted softly.

The air deflated out of her. She said something too soft to hear, then appeared to repeat it. "We need him."

That caught Hero off guard. He nearly straightened from his lazy pose—to make a character break character was a feat. He eased back down again, eyes narrowed. "You mean Andras."

Claire nodded grimly. "Malphas went after the Arcane Wing first. And we're still breathing. Therefore, I'm assuming she's not at the Unwritten Wing's gates now. That means she's settling in for a long campaign, to control the books rather than destroy them. She took our arsenal, the closest thing the Unwritten Wing has to weaponry"—she made a placating gesture—"aside from you and Ramiel, of course."

"Charmed," Hero muttered.

"She's making her move for the Unwritten Wing. She's been patient and careful, but we've given her too good an opportunity, with you and the cover-up over the ink. I don't know if she knows books are soul stuff yet, but if not, she will soon. Then wards and brute force won't be enough to hold her back. We'll need to play like demons."

"We'll need to play like Andras," Hero supplied with a bitter tone. "You thought of all this in the mad dash from one wing to another?"

"I've thought of all this since the moment the wing shoved ten tons of demon antagonist into a six-inch blade."

"Oh really, I'd say five at most." Hero didn't appear to be in the mood to be generous.

"I don't know how we'll do it yet, and I certainly am not doing anything until I know we have a damned good way to leash him," Claire continued. "But we lost a great many weapons of power just now." She paused, taking a slow, staggered breath, the loss still smoking behind her. She pressed her lips into a thin line before continuing. "And of all the artifacts in the Arcane Wing, this little bauble may have been what Malphas had hoped to melt down to slag the most." Claire made a gesture and a distasteful face at the dagger cooling on the floor. "She's scared of it. That means we can use it."

"Or he can use us."

"As I said, I'll figure out a way to leash him."

"Oh, trust me, warden, I know how good you are at binding bad men to your cause."

Claire's face lost some of its doom. Her grim frown gave way to the slightest smile. "You're not a bad man, Hero."

"You're right—I am a terror." Hero crouched down next to the silver blade. It had cooled enough to be picked up, which Hero did as if it were a particularly stinky fish. "I'm your monster too. We can handle one pissant demon."

"And the army waiting in the wings?" Claire asked with amusement.

"Those I trust to you. You've handled worse before," Hero said with complete confidence. He dropped the dagger again and sniffed. "But say the word, and I'll serve you Andras's throat on a platter. I haven't forgiven him for the delightful makeover he gave me." He tilted his scarred cheek to the light with a frown.

Claire chuckled. "Vain as always."

"Clever as always," Hero returned.

It seemed as good as any point. Brevity exchanged a look with Rosia and stamped her feet in place loudly, mimicking a clatter of a run before emerging from her hiding place. Rosia followed. Brev hoisted the box of bandages in the air like a trophy. "Found them!"

"It took some time," Claire commented, worry knitting her brows together. "The Unwritten Wing?"

"Quiet," Brevity assured her quickly. "The doors fixed themselves, and no sign of demons. The gargoyle's on high alert and I did lock the way, just in case."

"Whatever do you keep me around for?" Hero said with a wink. He approached and, taking the box from Brevity, leaned close enough to whisper, "Couldn't have given me another minute, Librarian?"

Perhaps Brevity hadn't been as stealthy as she'd thought. However, Hero didn't seem bothered. He followed her over to Claire and efficiently selected the necessary materials to bandage Claire's raw palm. Of course, a character from a war-torn book would be well versed in basic first aid. And Claire'd been right. The burns were already healing, at a slower pace than either Brevity or Hero recovered, but Claire would be fine enough after a rest and, likely, a cup of tea.

"We shouldn't linger here," Hero announced once he was done.

"Quite right," Claire said. She stood and dusted off her skirts out of habit, though she was so soot caked it hardly had an effect. She grimaced at herself. "We should regroup and let our guests know what trouble they've caused already." She frowned. "Assuming Rami hasn't rethought his alliances and…"

"He's waiting for you both," Rosia said with confidence. Of course he was. As if any disagreement could dislodge him from his loyalties. It was obvious to Brevity how tightly enmeshed the Watcher had become with the Library. But she saw the relief flicker between Hero's and Claire's expressions like a firefly. For a moment Brevity thought she could almost see the thin shimmer of the magic that wound around all of them, binding them together like matching books. Humans sometimes called it many things: love, duty, family.

Brevity called it hope.

11

RAMI

A library is people. Just as much as it is books and archives. You want to know the heart of a library, don't look at its most famous books; look at the people it serves. Who it comforts, who it protects. The heart of a library may be its books, but its soul is its people. Humans and stories, impossible to separate the two.

Librarian Madiha al-Fihri, 603 CE

A CLATTER OF NOISE signaled the arrival of the rest of the Library crew in the front lobby. Ramiel gradually slowed his step. He'd been pacing a path in the Melodrama (Korean) section, close enough to keep an eye on the lobby without being found by pesky helpful ex-muses. Walking helped him think, though it was a distant replacement for flying.

And he was thinking he'd been, as Hero would say, an *ass*.

Ramiel had been dealing with humans for a long time. As a Watcher, then as a wannabe angel at the Gates. He'd never been invested in one, cared about one, as he cared about Claire, Hero, and Brevity. He was finding the pure, fragile madness of humans more of an issue when he cared about the particular outcome. He'd been afraid when he'd hurtled after Claire into the fire. When he'd realized she had risked her life for that damned knife, he'd been angry. But not at her. At a world that felt made to break vulnerable mortals at every turn. It was terrifying. He didn't know how Claire even functioned with it.

Probably not by losing one's temper with one's allies and storming off like a clod.

Ramiel rubbed the remaining soot off his face and peeked around the corner of the stacks. The sight and sound of Brevity clattering around the desk was comforting, at least. Hero had dropped himself over the armchair that gave him a view of the front doors while Claire hovered, obviously uncomfortable for more reasons than just smoke-singed clothing.

"Shouldn't we make this official?" Brevity said, her smile soft and hopeful. "Rejoin the Unwritten Wing again?"

A torrent of emotions flinched across Claire's face, stowed away by reflex. Rami cleared his throat and stepped out of hiding to join the conversation. "Of course. We'd be grateful to assist here with the Arcane Wing gone."

"Assist. Pssh." Brevity yanked open a lower drawer on her desk and began scrounging in its depths. "I can do better than—aha! Found it."

"Should we get cleaned up first?" Rami asked uncertainly. Claire was holding the burnt edges of her skirt with one hand. Brevity hauled a small box to her desktop and set it beside the Librarian's Log carefully.

"Nonsense! The books won't care." Brevity was already in the process of herding Claire toward the desk. She shuffled things around until Rami was squeezed into the oversized armchair with Claire. The previous disagreement was forgotten—at least by the muse. Claire tensed, obviously ready for Rami's withdrawal. It made shame stew in his stomach.

He squeezed his knees together in an awkward attempt to not take up more than his allotted share of space. Claire risked a glance to her side and Rami grimaced and bowed his head gently. An apology, of sorts, though he knew he would need to explain later.

"Okay. Just a little... and Claire... and... oh, Rami, you don't have a last name, do you?" Brevity held her pen poised over the Librarian's Log. Rami gingerly extracted himself from the chair to peer over the desk. Brevity had turned the book to a blank page, and scrawling in her looping, exuberant script, she'd improvised an attempt, in plain language, at a basic decree stating he and Claire were hereby inducted into the service of the Unwritten Wing.

"We can do that?" Hero muttered from Brevity's other side.

"Course we can. Just need some fine print annnnnd..." Brevity said with no trace of doubt. She tightened her script to a few minuscule lines at the bottom of the page. "... and done. Sign here."

"Fine print?" Rami echoed blankly.

Hero elbowed his way to squint at the book. "It says... did you just write 'peanut butter and jelly' over and over?"

"The details don't matter." Brevity shooed him off in order to spin the heavy book around on the scarred wood surface. "Sign there. Both of you."

"I don't—" Rami hesitated and glanced at Claire. Her lips were pressed in a pale line of discomfort. For a moment, it appeared she would object. Finally she released a terse breath through her teeth and snatched up the pen. "Give it here."

Claire's signature was swift and complete—*Claire Juniper*

Hadley—and then she pushed the pen into Rami's hands. "It's fine. Let's just… be done with it."

There was an undertone to Claire's voice that was wound tighter than a harp string. Rami quieted his concerns and adjusted his grip on the stylus. He'd… never signed something before, not in the sense of indicating his own agency, at least. Angels didn't have agency. Fallen angels, only shame. The first choice Rami had made was to lend assistance to rescue the soul of Leto, Claire's lost nephew.

The choices had come fast after that. To abandon Uriel's senseless thirst for blood, to protect Leto and help Claire and the others retain the Library. Decision after decision, with no moment to wait or breathe. Decisions cared nothing for his duty, or his sins, just action.

He wrote his name under Claire's and set down the pen swiftly. He expected a change. A thrill of magic, a chill, that susurrous wave of whispers that the Unwritten Wing had when something important happened. The air felt dry and stale without it. Everything was still. Rami coughed and stepped back. "What now?"

"Now…" Brevity bounced on her heels. She seemed eminently satisfied by whatever had—or had not—happened. She wafted a hand over the book long enough to allow the ink to dry before shutting it again. "Now we make tea."

It felt like the stacks of books released a held breath. Brevity enlisted Hero's help in making tea.

"Claire?"

"Hmm? Oh yes, thank you, Rami." Claire accepted the cloth and absently wiped at her face. The tension hadn't abated despite their supposed safety. She held still in the armchair, and eventually even her hands fell to her lap as she frowned into the distance.

Is something wrong? seemed like a particularly obtuse question, even for Rami. So instead he reached for an irrelevant question. "Do you think the Unwritten Wing has accepted us back in?"

Claire's laugh was short and bitter. "Who knows? I thought I knew everything about the Library, and this entire endeavor has been a constant string of disproving that." She caught Rami's alarmed look and waved him off before burying her head in her hands. "The books cast me out and I thought I was done with this place. But here I am, right back here. Here! And this time a refugee, filthy with failure, begging them for the mercy I never once showed them."

"It's not a mercy to welcome an old friend."

"The books and I were never friends," Claire said warily.

"You had to be once. You dreamed of writing, didn't you? Writers are readers first." Rami sat gingerly on the arm of the chair, not quite turned toward her. "I have learned a lot about books and stories since I came here. And the first thing I learned is that there's a love between a reader and a story that no one can harm or possess."

"I can't remember the last time I've simply enjoyed a book for pleasure."

"Now, I know that's not true," Rami murmured.

Claire chuckled to herself and slanted her eyes at Rami between her fingers. "I see what you're doing, Ramiel. This isn't about Hero."

"No, it isn't," Rami agreed gently. "It's about your attempts to isolate yourself again to punish yourself for your perceived failures—"

"I burned the Arcane Wing down, Rami."

"Hell burned the Arcane Wing. You did everything in your power to save it."

"Much to your disapproval."

"My disapproval doesn't matter." He paused, making sure Claire understood what he was saying. "The Unwritten Wing accepts you returning because you never really left here, Claire. You are a writer, you are a reader, you are human. You are a part of the continuum of untold stories and will always have a place here."

"Says who?"

"I do. You read books; I read souls."

"Same thing," Claire said into her lap.

"Same thing," Rami affirmed.

12

CLAIRE

History is told by the victors, isn't that how it goes? Fight for something and lose, you're insurrectionists, conspirators, terrorists. Fight for something and win, you're rebels, freedom fighters, founding fathers. History is a story told in past tense, the best kind of propaganda.

What everyone forgets is that, at one point in the story, every villain thinks they are the hero.

History happens in the edit.

Librarian Gregor Henry, 1986 CE

CLAIRE TOOK THE TIME to scrub the soot and ashes from her skin once they returned to the Unwritten Wing. Brevity had never moved into the restoration room that Claire'd used as an office, and there was still a small wardrobe of clothes—mostly castoffs and knitted monstrosities from the damsels—tucked in the back corner. She found a pair of loose trousers that didn't have nearly enough pockets for her taste, but Claire paired them with a cardigan with deep enough pockets to hide half an encyclopedia.

All pockets were best judged by book size, in Claire's opinion.

She left her streaked and singed clothes behind in a hamper. She'd been in the Library long enough to know that, given a few days, the next time she went seeking the wardrobe her garments would be whole again. Hell was a place for forgetting; even items wanted to forget their damage after enough time.

By the time she emerged from the back room, Brevity—bless the muse down to her toes—already had a pot on. It appeared to have just come off the hot plate, and Brevity was deeply engrossed in flipping through the logbook, the cup at her elbow still steaming but already forgotten. Claire poured herself a cup and took a sip, pleasantly surprised to find it was a strong Darjeeling rather than the fruity nonsense Brev preferred.

"Hero doesn't like Earl Grey, else I would already have your favorite," Brevity explained without looking up.

"Bergamot is a scent, not a flavor, thank you," Hero said.

"Only because you've never had good Earl Grey." Claire eased into a seat nearby. "Americans."

"We should discuss what our next course of action is," Rami said, perhaps because he knew how Claire and Hero enjoyed a good tiff.

Claire shrugged her shoulders with a defeated air. "What action? She'll cut us off. Malphas isn't stupid. She knows from watching Andras what a direct assault on the Library will bring."

"Damn straight," Hero muttered.

"But we can't wait her out, either," Rami cautioned. "Malphas will not be idle while she's got us cornered in here. And Malphas has had eternity to cultivate superior strategy."

Claire tilted her head thoughtfully. "How lucky we have our own immortal being as well."

Rami nearly dropped the fragile teacup in his big hands. "I beg your pardon?"

"Both you and Malphas are angels—were angels," Claire corrected when Rami opened his mouth to argue. She tapped her fingers on her knee contemplatively and her glance veered between Hero and Rami. "You know how she thinks, how she'll try to root us out. And you, Hero, you've already fought and won a war."

"A fictional one," Hero reminded her with a dry air.

Claire made a dismissive noise. "It makes it no less real. You have told me that often enough—will you deny it now?" When Hero merely pursed his lips, Claire nodded. She didn't have a plan, not yet, but she could see the pins on which they would hang it. "If I asked you two to put your heads together, can we hold the Library?"

"No," Rami said grimly.

"Definitely not," admitted Hero.

"Not forever, obviously. Can we buy ourselves time?" Claire said. "They'll loot and burn this place to the ground, as has been done to libraries countless times through history. Hell is not an option anymore. So what are our options?"

The silence was painful, needling all of them. No one wanted to say the obvious option, so Claire did it for them. "We could run, of course. Tell the damsels they're off the books, then every soul for themselves. Abandon ship; maybe those of us with souls can work our way to Mdina for sanctuary before Hell notices. The Library will have an interest in Hero, of course, and I'll be in another ghostlight situation, but Rami, Brevity, you two would have no trouble slipping off—"

"Shut uuuup." Brevity's outburst startled everyone. She made a dramatic show of flopping back in her chair. "Heck and Hades, boss, you know none of us are doing that. We can't do that; we can't just abandon the books like that." Brevity paused, pinning Claire with an uncharacteristically stern look. "You would never do that. And you know it."

Wouldn't she? Brevity sounded so certain. It was a kindness. Claire sifted through the burst of gratitude and doubt. There was some time, at some point in the past, when she would have. It was exactly the kind of abandonment and escape she'd planned with her own main character, Beatrice, wasn't it? And even after then... given a guilt-free excuse to walk away. To escape the Library. To choose freedom. She couldn't say for sure that she wouldn't have taken it.

But now... now.

"I suppose I wouldn't," Claire said. "But I am honest when I say I don't know what option that leaves us instead."

"Besides pointless heroism," Hero muttered.

"No. No more martyrs," Rami said with a heavy look at the rest of the room.

"Hell would not accept a single sacrifice anyway." Claire spared a glance for Brevity. She appeared distracted, dragging her thumb over the edge of the logbook pages with a rhythmic *thrrrrrp* sound. Claire considered leaving it there. Simple, agreeable, unsaid. Unfortunately she had lost that right, lost the assumption of good, humane intentions over her checkered history with the Library. She had to say it, for herself. Claire sighed. "But the books here have souls, in some way. They're... they're individuals. I brought them to this point, whether they were my books or not, whether I'm librarian or not." She felt the weight of Brevity's sudden attention on her. "Whether librarian or not. I can't walk away."

"People are not a cause," Hero said, almost to himself. "You admit that you're granting stories personhood?"

"I am not in a position to grant anything. We should not be in the business of arbitrating the worthiness of souls," Claire said harshly. They were all facing her with encouraging looks. She frowned. "Don't you dare try to give me a gold star and a pat on the head for finally wrapping my brain around the obvious and performing the bare minimum of humanity."

Hero shrugged. "Sure, but you won't be half as fun to mock now."

Claire's frown deepened, and Rami was the first to return to the point at hand. "Is moving the books an option? Does every Library have the ability to relocate as the Unsaid Wing did?"

Claire shook her head. "Libraries tend to take on the nature of their charges and their librarians. The Unsaid Wing is full of letters and secrets—those are never meant to stay in one place. The Unwritten Wing is more staid."

"A place meant for waiting, eternally," Hero said, and Claire nodded.

"Brevity can confer with Echo, of course…" Claire paused. It appeared Brev still wasn't listening. "But the Unwritten Wing was never made to move. Books only leave by means of their human authors via muses—normally." Claire was reasonably sure that Hero didn't even require eye contact for that remark.

"Humans…" A tenor in Brevity's voice made Claire turn. She still had that faraway look. Her gaze was simultaneously on the logbook and beyond it. Then her chin snapped up. "But that's what humans do. That's it."

"What?" Claire couldn't help her skepticism. The memory of Probity's accusations was still too fresh in her mind. "What do humans do, besides burn and destroy?"

"Rebel," Brevity breathed, more animated every moment. She drummed her palms on the book in front of her with emphasis.

"It's all right here. Create and rebel. What's more human than that?"

"Oh, I don't know: cruelty over superficial differences, sticking flags in things, frozen yogurt, performative gender roles, war…" Hero counted off on his fingers.

Claire was well practiced at ignoring Hero by now. She tilted her head at Brevity. "I don't understand."

"What is frozen yogurt?" Rami asked in a fascinated tone.

"Oh! Poppaea." The connections fired in Claire's brain all at once. She stared as Brevity's smile grew. A chill shot up Claire's neck as the idea took hold. She glanced down at the giant weight of the Librarian's Log in Brevity's hands. "You're talking about the story of Librarian Poppaea Julia."

Brevity nodded.

"That's… devious and suicidal." Hero tilted his head. "I love it."

"Um." Rami cleared his throat. "Not all of us have been thoroughly versed in the history of the librarians."

"Librarian Poppaea was the most interesting one of the lot. Present company excluded," Hero explained. "She was a delightful librarian's librarian during the—what? Early Roman? Or after? It's all Greek to me. She got the idea in her head to defy Lucifer himself and contest the Library's place in Hell. Her entries are incredibly cagey about it. A full-on rebellion. Against everyone." Hero practically clapped his hands. "She failed, of course. Set off the whole Dark Ages—"

"She did not set off anything. And really, Dark Ages, Hero? That's an outmoded view of history that lacks any nuance." Claire sniffed, despite the blatant fact that he'd learned the history from her.

"Point is, she was frightfully clever and makes even our own dear Claire look like a teacher's pet in comparison." Hero waved away any pesky details. "She appeared to believe the Library should be sovereign of its own realm."

"Maybe she was right," Brevity ventured slowly. "Would any of this have happened if the Library was free from Hell—and free from anywhere, really? Would this have happened if we—the Library, all of us—worked together?"

Hero was always eager for a bloody revolution, but Claire caught the way words like "freedom" and "cooperation" began to catch Rami's interest. She shook her head. "The point is, she failed. She failed, she disappeared, and the Unwritten Wing was rudderless for a century. We have no reason to think an attempt now would end any different."

"Unless we avoided her mistakes," Hero suggested.

"We don't even know what she *did*." Claire gestured to the desk. "The Librarian's Log doesn't say. As I recall from the official chronicle, she talks about challenging Hell and establishing a new realm and gets all very vague and ominous and then it just… ends. I've never found anything specific about how she did it. Unless the log has deigned to reveal something more to you, Brev?"

She could see by the way Brevity's smile fell that it hadn't.

"We could ask the books," Hero insisted. "Obviously they were here to witness it."

"Not necessarily." The hope seemed to be deflating out of Brevity as she spoke, and Claire felt a deep stab of guilt. "Something happened to the Library after Poppaea failed. I don't know if any books were lost, but I've never seen a book wake up that would have witnessed that time. Books that old either don't know anything or just… don't wake up."

"And it would be too dangerous to try to wake them," Claire said.

"As you would know," Hero said cheerily.

"Who else would know?" Rami asked, before Claire could entirely murder Hero with her eyes.

"No one that would talk to us," Brevity said after a long pause. She sank down in her seat behind the desk. Her fingers plucked listlessly at the scars on her forearms. Her blue skin was rough there, with a thin thread of black barely visible between puckered bits of skin. The aftermath of their encounter with the unresolved ink of lost stories. Claire thought of the Dust Wing again and shuddered. She could still almost taste the air clogged with regret and death.

… Death.

It was a particularly foolish idea that she had just then. Really, Hero-like in its ridiculous scale. But as she watched Brevity fold in on herself, the idea stuck like a sliver and started to grow. Claire let out a long sigh. "Actually, there may be someone who knows and who might talk to us."

Brevity looked up, hope so easily returning to her. Claire wished she had that skill. "Who? Who can we talk to?"

13

BREVITY

No one will read these words, will they? So I can admit it here. I considered Malphas a friend. She reminded me of my own grandmother, spinning me tales of Ariadne before bed. Grandmother carried a wicked blade too, and she never asked me when I was to be married. In any case, that's why I had my guard down. I told her about my idea, my dream. To build the Library a realm of its very own, a place for souls that don't belong anywhere else.

I only came to my senses when she asked, eyes like covetous gems, *why*. Why would human souls be drawn to such a thing as a library?

I forget the nonsense answer I gave her, but I knew those were not the eyes of my friend. I should make a contingency, just in case.

Librarian Poppaea Julia, 48 BCE

THE TRANSPORT OFFICE HAD always been located relatively near the Library. It made sense—muses came and went, and perhaps originally the idea had been to have Death keep a close eye on the independent part of Hell stuffed to the gills with tempting mortal souls. Brevity walked beside Claire with a tension rising in the silence. This had been her idea. They were going to talk to Death because of her idea.

She'd always liked Walter—Brevity generally found something to adore in everyone she met. But since muses didn't typically die, she understood Walter's role only as a vague construct. Sure, she understood that Walter was part of a universal constant called Death—there were many Walters in a way, in every realm and in every world. But in practice, Walter had just been their gatekeeper. The gentle giant with a dust rag and an ill-fitting suit who Brevity waved to on her way in and out of the realm.

But Brevity had become acquainted with death during her time in the Library. She'd become a scholar of it, a death anthropologist. She had held the hands of damsels—friends—as the story of their life had wilted away. She'd fumbled to help Claire over the grieving and loss of her own past. She'd seen how the wrong kind of death had haunted Leto. She'd feared for the lives of those she loved over and over again, and realized how fragile and fleeting and white-hot real mortal lives were. Even in Hell. Perhaps especially in Hell.

Brevity had begun to have an inkling of what Death threatened, and what it promised. And now they needed answers that only that unpredictable question mark could provide.

Claire's step didn't hesitate when they reached the archway with three interlocking wheels carved above it. She descended the steps lightly and seemed no more bothered than she'd be on any errand. It was a lie. Brevity could understand that much. If Brevity had become acquainted with Death, then Claire had befriended it.

Out of necessity, out of loneliness, out of spite.

If Claire could face this with calm, then so could Brevity. She straightened her shoulders and hurried down the stairs after Claire's retreating shadow.

Walter's office was a reassuring constant, at least. The stairs emptied out into a muddled curio of a room, stacked with glass jars of varying sizes and shapes containing even more varied worlds. There was a perpetual film of puttering and time that clung to every surface, a sepia-toned filter to the world. But Brevity's favorite part was, as always, the colors.

Bits of light escaped each jar, like steam rising off a fresh cup of tea. Never as plentiful and vivid as the colors that bubbled and burbled inside the jars, nor as questing and reaching as the tendrils from a book, but faint trail signs of worlds yet to be explored. Walter had left a single jar out on the counter, and a misty curlicue of saffron dribbled onto the counter. It took some doing to resist reaching out to touch it and to turn the jar to see what faraway realm was reaching back.

But that wasn't why they were here. Nothing so joyous. Claire stopped an appropriate distance from the counter and peered past it into the gloom. Brevity had to stand on her tiptoes. Claire cleared her throat. "Hey-ho, shop. Walter, are you about?"

A shadow moved farther back, and Brevity quickly knew it was Walter because it didn't grow any smaller as he approached the light. Walter shrugged between shelves, emerging shoulders first. He was surprisingly agile for an individual in possession of boulder-like shoulders and hands as big as Brevity's torso. It added a gentleness to his demeanor that Brevity always suspected was cultivated, which just made her even more fond of him.

"Miss Claire! Miss Brevity!" Walter always seemed pleased to see them, but his brows dipped in an uncharacteristic line of worry. His voice was always a bit like a nightmare that was fond of you, and concern was ill fitted to it.

"So you've heard the news," Claire surmised.

"The missin' hallways and the like were sure to spread gossip, ma'am," Walter said with an apologetic dip of his head. "I'm just glad to see you and Miss Brev in one piece."

"Whole, hale, souls relatively intact." Claire straightened. "We came to seek your advice on staying that way."

The floorboards couldn't help but groan as Walter fidgeted from foot to foot. Claire tilted her head, studying him a moment before precisely folding her hands on top of the counter. "Or did Malphas already get here before us? Perhaps to fume and fury and order you against helping us?"

"She is terribly terrifying when she gets in a state, ma'am." Walter studied the scar-studded knuckles of his big hands. "You ruffled her over quite good this time."

"I thought Death, above all, was sovereign from the petty squabbles of realms." Claire could be awfully terrifying herself when she wanted to be. Brevity hopped up to the counter to defuse the accusation.

"She's locking kids in cages," she said with her voice at a level for scandal and gossip. "It ain't right."

"If only it was just the demons to blame for that," Claire said. "But Hell can't borrow anything man didn't create."

"I'm in a bit of a predicament, ma'am," Walter said, apparently still wrestling with Claire's original question. "I don't answer to no one, y'see, but I'm not supposed to pick favorites either. Did that once. Didn't go well, no, sir. Did *not* go well…"

"Mortal lives are at stake—it's not as if you can recuse yourself!"

Claire would badger Death, if needs called for it. Brevity attempted to nudge Claire with her foot, to no effect.

"Malphas isn't an easy person to say no to," Brevity said. "Shoulda seen her face when Claire protected Hero from her."

"Not the pretty young gent!" Walter looked horrified. One had to wonder what criteria there were for Death to find you pretty, but Brevity supposed if anyone could manage it, Hero would.

"Hero's okay," Brevity reassured him. "But Malphas burned the Arcane Wing."

"The Unwritten Wing is next, to be certain," Claire said grimly, then lifted her brows. "We have run out of diplomatic options. I suspect you understand why."

"The souls kerfuffle, yeah." Walter appeared to look around the counter for papers to shuffle sheepishly, but there were none. He settled for fussing with the ragged cuffs of his suit. "I'm awful glad you got that ink off, but I told ye that you wouldn't like the answers none."

"You did." Claire inclined her chin. "But now I need more answers, whether I like them or not. You were here when Librarian Poppaea attempted to declare the Unwritten Wing sovereign."

Instead of surprise, a grimace roiled across Walter's face, as if he'd been expecting it. "Course I was, ma'am. But I can't—"

"You know, then." Claire leaned forward like a dog on the hunt. "How did she do it, Walter? What was Poppaea aiming to create?"

Walter's eyes were not much more than sunken black holes swirled with red, but he managed to make the voids look sorrowful. "Miss Poppaea lost, though."

"She said she'd claim a home for the books, to take the Library back from its host realm." Claire was not one to be diverted from an inquiry. "How? Can a new realm really be created? That's not possible, is it?"

"It's—" Walter caught himself and grimaced. "Ma'am, please."

"There has to be a way, or Poppaea wouldn't have attempted it," Claire said, more to herself than to either of them. By her side, Brevity could practically see the gears turning, bearings falling into place. She could feel the lockup and free fall when Claire's resolve kicked in. It was a terrifying kind of calm, like the stillness one felt before taking a plunge from a great height. "And if there is a way, you have to be the one to know it. Please, Walter. Tell me."

"Miss Claire—"

"Walter."

"I don't want to watch another war!" Walter jolted to his full height all at once. His head nearly reached the distant rafters. Even Claire startled. His fists were opening and closing at his sides. Could Death panic? The jars on the shelves nearest them began a low, tremorous rattle. "Rebellion near destroyed the Unwritten Wing once. Ma'am, please—"

"Submission will absolutely destroy the Unwritten Wing now." Claire's voice was low. Even if no less resolved, she knew when to be gentle with the facts. "Malphas will not rest until she knows the secret of the books. And once she does, every story dreamed of humankind will be forfeit."

"No one can survive without stories," Brevity whispered. Certainty came to her then. That was the fact. Though she'd suggested the idea of resisting Hell, exhaustion and fear hadn't let her believe it. She was a muse. She didn't want a war, a fight, a struggle, which would surely result in more destruction, not creation. But the depth of what was at stake drowned her doubts all at once. "If we don't do this, Hell will control the narrative."

"Sure it'll be bad for a while, but these things work themselves out eventually," Walter offered weakly. "Humans always manage to tell stories."

"Maybe." Claire refocused her gaze on him. "But not ours. Whatever Hell creates, the millions of souls living in the Unwritten Wing won't be part of it. You don't think that will change things?"

"We all reach a point we gotta choose, Walter." Brevity's voice was a whisper and she could not make it louder. It was too fragile a truth. "What stories are worth fighting for?"

Walter's gaze wobbled between the two of them. For a moment, Brevity thought Walter might grow again, might become something terrible and Death-like and scary. But in the end, his shoulders dropped and he heaved a great sigh. "I can't deny when you talk sense like that, Miss Brev."

"So you'll help us?"

"Yes," Walter said, then: "No." He held up his hands, which made a very effective shield as Claire threatened to object. "I can't get involved myself, ma'am! Even if I want to."

"So you can't tell us anything?" Claire crossed her arms.

"I can't," Walter said, then slanted his eyes to the side. "But I can't exactly be responsible for what I don't tell you."

Claire tilted her head. "Walter, are you about to be devious?"

"It's not cheatin' to say that Miss Poppaea was a lot like yerself, Miss Claire." Walter turned his head around the room slowly, looking anywhere but at the librarians. "Clever-like. Might be, she came to say good-bye before it all. Mighta asked if I could hold on to a little something for her."

Brevity's eyes riveted to the jar that had been sitting on the counter all this time, forgotten. It still whispered saffron, but she could now see threads of gold and umber swirling through it, like a very fine spice. "A jar? But we use jars to travel."

"Memory is just a different kind of travel," Walter said slowly. "Like stories. It takes you away when you gotta stay where you are."

"I don't need to point out that I don't have a ghostlight. I'm not approved for travel."

"This one stays in Hell, ma'am." Walter grimaced. "Trust me on that."

Claire eyed the jar, lips pursed into a skeptical thin line. She exchanged a glance with Brevity. "What do you think, Librarian?"

A soft thrill distantly warmed Brevity's cheeks, as happened whenever Claire could use her new title without grief or regret. Brevity nodded. "It can't hurt. I mean, we're already on the outs with Hell."

"Hell can always hurt," Claire said with a grim shrug. "But you're not wrong. Together?"

Walter cleared his throat. "I'll just be turnin' my back now, real innocuous-like—oh look, dust—"

He was a worse liar than even Rami. Brevity smiled and slotted her hand in Claire's. "Together."

The lid was stiff, and it was a bit of a feat to wrestle it loose one-handed, but Claire managed. She took a deep breath, squeezed Brevity's hand, and tilted the jar forward. Mist tumbled out in a thick fog and shifted course midair to swallow them whole.

I 4

CLAIRE

Memory is a fickle thing. Best not to trust it.
Librarian Ibukun of Ise, 818 CE

CLAIRE WAS A STEADY sort and dealt with all personal trauma in the time-tested way of her people: she folded it up very neatly and stored it away for never. Stiff upper lip and all that. Claire abhorred being a cliché, but some things were just efficient, thank you very much.

So the panic attack was a surprise.

There was simultaneously not enough air and far too much. Space pressed down on a small growing knot in her chest. A thorn quickly becoming a bramble becoming a fist.

Strange, Claire had always thought panic attacks, from the way Brevity described them, were thought focused. Some fear, gibberish repeated over and over. A problem the appropriately strong-willed could wrestle under control. But this was a panic that suffused the air, intoxicated her bloodstream. Panic wasn't a fearful thought; it just *was*. It was an undeniable storm front in her nerves. Anxiety was the atmosphere she breathed, and Claire thought nothing, saw nothing, felt nothing, for a molasses-thick moment.

Fingernails dug into her palm, but not her own. Small crescents of pain brought sharp focus. Brevity tugged on her hand. "Our thoughts are having anxiety," she said firmly, as if that would help.

"Seeing as I am my thoughts, that is a problem," Claire gritted through her teeth.

"But you're not. You're *Claire*, experiencing things. You're not your thoughts. Common mistake." Brevity tugged on her hand again. "Especially not here. Step back, boss. Step back."

The fist in her chest tried to yank on her throat, leading her like a tether. The imagery was so offensive Claire bit on her tongue. There. The panic was still there, gripped around Claire's windpipe, but she was not leashed. The panic wasn't her own. This was Poppaea's memory. But this wasn't any kind of flashback; there was formless space around them. Shapes formed only to crumble away into mist again.

Hell was an antithesis to memory. Hell was a place built for memories to wither, rot, and fade to dust. It was a place for forgetting, just as your life was forgotten in the living world. Claire had been here for thirty years, and it was really a miracle that she remembered her own name and homeland. No memory stored in Hell—even preserved in one of Walter's magical jars—could remain clear and whole. This was no tidy flashback to be played back for their benefit. Instead of following a map, they were going to have to dig through sand.

Trap-riddled sand.

"Poppaea," Claire said aloud. She had hoped that would stabilize something, and the saffron miasma around them did appear to shift and take the shape of a woman in the distance.

Brevity tugged her hand and they began walking toward it. Movement seemed to help the thorns of panic in her chest, even if it didn't lessen them.

"Librarian Poppaea!" Brevity called. The figure turned. At first Claire thought it was an echo, because the call came back to them.

"Poppaea." The voice was too familiar. Panic flash-froze into terror as Malphas stepped through the mist behind. Her robe bled at the edges, muddying the orange air with eddies of crimson. "My sweet friend, I wish you wouldn't do this."

Malphas certainly wouldn't refer to Claire as her sweet friend. Claire wasn't even sure Malphas was capable of having friends. The pieces fell together so rapidly that Claire nearly got whiplash. This was a fragment of memory. *She's not here*, Claire repeated firmly to herself, *she's not* here.

"You have the rest, I'll grant you," Malphas said with a nod that bordered on respect. "But you'll never have the Library. Not all of it."

I can talk to the other librarians. They'll listen to me. They have to, a voice surged up in Claire's mind. It wasn't her voice, or any she recognized. She didn't speak it, not quite, but Malphas nodded as if she'd heard it. More of her was bleeding away. Perhaps that's why she almost looked pitying.

"They won't. We have a great deal in common, your Library and Hell. We're not meant to unite. Demons and stories, we weren't designed that way. You will never be part of their story."

I write my own story, the not-Claire voice said in her head. A muddled, alien emotion cut through the fear. Resolve was sharp as steel and just as cold. Claire felt stabbed with it.

A strange expression seeped onto Malphas's face. It took Claire a long moment to recognize it as a smile—not the cruel, barbed thing she knew from the demon. A real, pleasant smile. Malphas cupped the air where a cheek should be and sighed. "I could never make you do anything, mortal. But I wish you wouldn't."

She lies, the voice whispered, but it was different this time. Sharper, purely directed inward. *She wants this. We have to try anyway.*

Malphas was growing taller—no. The mist was rising, taking the phantom with it but slowly sinking Claire and Brevity into its depths. A squeak escaped Brevity, which was her only warning. Claire had just a moment to tighten her grip on Brevity's hand before the bottom dropped out entirely.

She lost track of Brevity in the free fall. The voluminous fabric of Claire's trousers snapped back and forth, the only point of reference she had that she was tumbling. There was no horizon, nothing to pin her vision on but images that seemed to careen at her in all directions.

One of her favorite childhood books ridiculously presented itself in Claire's memory: *Down the rabbit hole with you, Alice.*

She breathed the space of an empty room, and her fall slowed. An infinite space spun around her, defined by her perception. *A wall there*, she wished, and it was. Like how the Library responded to a librarian. Oh, a home. Every family needed a place to call home. It felt ridiculous, calling a place home in the afterlife. But then, despite her best efforts to the contrary, she'd found a sort of family. Why not a home? But then, she hadn't *found* a family. Nothing was given in Hell. She'd built it, fought for it—fought against it, sometimes—with blood and tears.

A home would likely demand the same.

The floor of the space rushed up at her and she put her hands up out of reflex. She fell through the floor, but it still left her hands stinging. She tasted willing blood on her tongue, felt a hand in her palm. She couldn't see anything, but somehow she knew, *knew*, that the hand gripping hers knew the way. She let it tug her along. *A guide between gates*, the concept came to her like a punch. *We need a guide.*

The hand led her out of the darkness and let go, and Claire was falling again. She was distantly aware of shelves of books flying past her vision. Books, so many books. So many more than the Unwritten Wing could hold itself. *All of them*, Poppaea's voice said in a resigned tone. *We need all of them.*

She reached out, scrambled but couldn't find purchase. She was falling, falling into the Library. A room without a floor. A heart without a beat. Becoming the Library, as if it were swallowing her whole. It was terrifying and then it was calming. It was... divine. Claire felt more than god-touched; she felt *whole*. An infinite nothing—everything, *a god—no, a place—which is it, what was it, no*—the moment blinded her. *Hold it, hold it, step back and listen, this is important—*

It wasn't enough. The story was lost. Her heart broke.

Arms wrapped around her chest and squeezed tight. Claire stopped screaming. The floorboards of Walter's office were sharp slivers beneath her knees. Brevity was on the ground next to her, clinging to her shoulders.

Brevity was mumbling something soothing in her ear, but Claire couldn't hear it over the bile that screamed up her throat. She retched and coughed until puffs of saffron-colored smoke escaped and dissipated into the air. Her face was burning, eyes wet, all of Poppaea's bottled-up panic and resolve and despair still coursing through her veins. *A realm, a guide, a library, a god. A realm, a guide, a library, a god.*

"See, listen, touch, taste... step back," Brevity was whispering again, as if it were a mantra. "Pay attention to where you are now."

Claire forced herself to take a breath, release the simmering memory, and focus on the gritty reality of wood under her fingers. But she held on to the assault of senses she'd felt on the way down. An empty space, a sentinel's blood, a mind-rending taste of the divine.

Her mouth tasted sour as she raised her head. Brevity looked at her with wide, worried eyes but seemed otherwise unbothered. Muses were made for the madness of memory. She'd saved her. Claire had enough wits to hoarsely croak out, "Thank you."

The surprise that accompanied Brevity's smile never failed to sting. She still didn't expect Claire to express gratitude, kindness. Brevity always thought the best of her but never demanded it. Her grip on Claire's shoulders relaxed a little bit. "Malphas knew Poppaea."

Claire nodded, insides still hurting. "Malphas used Poppaea, and she'll use us now." Her voice was raw and ragged. She leaned on Brevity as they got to their feet. Walter was long gone, and the jar on the counter sat as empty as Claire felt. Brevity supported most of her weight. "I believe I know what we have to do."

A realm, a guide, a library, a god. The edict settled into repeating in her head like a heartbeat. *A realm, a guide, a library, a god.*

15

HERO

I know what I need from the hints Malphas dropped, the research I did: a realm, a god, a guide, a people. Common sense tells me that I, alone, cannot acquire a realm, let alone a god. My allies are few. I was not an easy woman to like in life, and I was not an easy woman to like in death. The ally I do have in Revka... no. No, I'm not willing to risk her. She'd help me, but Hell would make her pay for it.

I am surrounded elsewise by books and demons and all who want something from me. My hope lies in the other librarians.

Librarian Poppaea Julia, 48 BCE

"SHIT. MERDE. *FUCK*." HERO'S enunciation was excellent. His faux-royal air wasn't entirely put on just to annoy Claire after all. He'd had tutors in his time as a young tyrant-king. He'd ruthlessly beat out his common upbringing and now knew how to roll his tongue, gliding in a way that could draw out the sweet spots of words and phrases. He gloried in practicing the full extent of his skills as he ran through the filthiest vocabulary he could conjure.

He had learned some things from the damsels after all.

"Can't you do something about him?" Iambe asked, fingers pressed to her temple.

"No, and I don't try," Rami said with an unperturbed air, though Hero didn't miss how he flinched when Hero struck on something delightfully sacrilegious. Rami was particularly handsome from this angle. Sprawled with curated insolence across the desk, head hanging over the side, Hero had a particularly good view of Rami's jawline. It nearly distracted him from his amusement. Nearly.

"Come now, Librarian Echo, don't be rude. Cat got your tongue?" he said. And then, just as she was about to speak, with some terribly clever twist of "tongue," no doubt, Hero added a particularly crude insult in some language a book had told him was Klingon. And Echo closed her mouth again.

Books had become so much more fun since he had started actually reading them. Gave you all kinds of strange ideas. Hero could see why Claire was so fond of it now.

"Sometimes I wish Alecto really had mauled you on your last visit," Iambe said with a sniff. "Then again I doubt even a lion could have taught you when to back off."

"—ck off," Echo said primly.

"See?" Iambe looked smug. "Mother is much more practiced at this game than you."

Hero's hand flew to his chest. "Such language! I am shocked, Echo. Think of the children." Hero gestured vaguely in the direction of the children's books section of the collection. Though the Unwritten Wing had enough sense to secure any books at risk of expelling innocent characters far, far away from the front entrance.

"Must you be so rude?"

Hero shrugged. "It's not as if sentient ponds can complain."

"Don't antagonize the immortal reflection, if you please." Claire and Brevity entered at a brisk pace. Claire's pallor become evident as they drew nearer. Her warm brown cheeks had a tendency to take on a waxy, unhealthy quality under duress. There was a peculiar brightness to her eyes, too wet and too sharp.

"Walter was helpful," Hero guessed with a fair degree of certainty. In Hell, only *success* was that distressing. He rolled off the desk and onto the balls of his feet. He caught Brevity by the shoulder as she deposited her bag. "What happened?"

"We talked to Poppaea." Brevity's brow crinkled. She scrunched up her nose and rubbed a hand over her face. "Well, kinda. Kinda Malphas too—Hell is shit at this memory thing. We think—"

"Not here," Claire cautioned. Her shoulders were tight, arms crossed in front of her chest like a shield. Rami offered her a cup of tea and she took and sipped it absently. "Too close to the entrance. Perhaps the office—"

"We'll go to the damsel suite," Brevity said.

Claire shook her head. "Until we are decided on a course of action—"

"If we're deciding what to do, the damsels get a vote." A gritty resolution streaked Brevity's tone, and Hero cocked a brow at her. "This involves all of us. No more unilateral decisions."

Porcelain clinked against wood as Claire set her cup down and considered. She nodded, if slowly. "As you say, Librarian."

Out of habit, Hero scrutinized the tension in Claire's voice. He was surprised by what he found. Claire was able to defer to Brevity by her former title, without the throb of still-healing loss. The wound of "Librarian" had healed between them, or at the very least scabbed over. Both Claire and Brevity had the good sense not to pick at it.

With the Arcane Wing gone, Hero wondered if Claire and Rami had a title at all. Perhaps they were all simply patrons—or refugees—seeking shelter in the Library. That was part of what libraries were for, after all. Then again, perhaps they were as lost as Hero was. That was a disturbing thought.

"Librarian Echo," Brevity said after holding the silence a beat too long. She turned and cleared her throat. She straightened, a hand fluttering up to her face though she had no glasses to straighten. Hero by now recognized this as her "librarian" mode. "Will you and Iambe join us? I think this concerns all of us now." She paused. "I mean, Pallas is welcome too, but..."

She trailed off and made an awkward gesture at the puddle depression in the rug where Pallas's true form slumped at rest. Echo, in her not-Pallas image, shook her head.

"My brother can guard the doors," Iambe answered dryly. "He doesn't mind."

"Mind," Echo repeated with a reproachful tone. Mother and daughter had almost matching frowns when turned on each other. Brevity had the wisdom to simply nod and jerk her chin toward the widest aisle between the stacks. Claire and Rami followed, and Hero stretched before nudging past Echo.

"Come along then, Pond," Hero muttered.

"POPPAEA DIDN'T JUST REBEL against Hell," Claire announced once they were settled in the lounge. Brevity had commandeered the main sitting area, and the residents of the damsel suite were crowded to the walls. Their numbers had grown under her care.

Claire sat in an armchair near the center, hands twisted in her lap. "She tried to establish a sovereign realm of her own. For the Library."

"I..." Rami stopped, with a wrinkle of his brow so deep that Hero thought he'd hurt himself. "I didn't think that was a thing a mortal could do."

"It's not," Iambe said, a bit scandalized.

"But Poppaea tried anyway. I have a feeling she nearly got away with it."

"*A way with it...?*" Echo said.

Claire evidently had better practice decoding oblique questions than Hero did. She shook her head. "You would need a lot of things. Poppaea knew what those things were. A place to go, for one. And a realm is not an easy thing to secure."

"Not a lot of vacancy signs advertised in the local paper."

"But that wasn't the most important thing she lacked." Brevity counted on her fingers. "A realm, a god, some kind of guide, and—"

"Did you say a *god?*" Rami nearly dropped the delicate teacup that Rosia had offered him.

"There was one more thing." Claire ignored him and instead turned a steady gaze to Echo. "Poppaea was attempting to establish a realm for the Library—all the wings of the Library. For that, she would need the consensus and agreement of all the librarians of all the wings in the afterlife."

"The Library is already a single entity, though." Rami frowned. "The interworld loan signifies that."

"You haven't spent much time around libraries, have you, angel?" Iambe narrowed her eyes with amusement.

"By all means, enlighten us, then," Hero said.

"Libraries may be united in theory, but the job doesn't exactly attract the most conforming types, in case you hadn't noticed."

Iambe made a dismissive flick in the direction of her mother.

"We can be quite territorial and set in our ways," Claire said.

Hero conjured an appropriately theatrical gasp of shock.

"The IWL is more of an agreement," Brevity admitted. "We don't really, uh, talk."

"There hasn't been a universal concord among the wings of the Library since…" Claire stopped, frowning as she thought. "Since Poppaea's time, I suppose."

"And even she failed," Hero muttered. "So each wing is its own little fiefdom, in your practice? No wonder."

"Libraries are unique to the needs of their patrons," Claire insisted. Hero was kind enough to not mention that the Unwritten Wing didn't particularly have patrons, only benign demons at best. "The only thing we share in common is the artifacts in our care."

"The souls," Rami corrected gently.

Claire's brow twitched. "Yes. I mean the souls in our care."

Rami nodded. "So we gather them."

"Them," Hero muttered to himself, ruefully. "Yes, a reunion."

"We shouldn't just barge in… like last time." Brevity bit her lip. "It didn't go so well."

"I'll help you with whatever diplomatic niceties we need." Claire's voice curdled a little at the idea, but her gaze narrowed in Hero and Rami's direction. "But there's something else we can do in the meantime."

Hero leaned in toward Rami and pitched his voice at a false whisper that would carry. "Why is it, when a librarian says 'we,' I hear 'you lot,' and when she says 'something else,' I hear 'ludicrous peril'?"

16

HERO

What is a god? Bugger if I know, laddie. I've been here longer than most and I've yet to meet the supposed all-powerful beings that control the place.

The god of the Library isn't the librarian—or at least, isn't always the librarian. The patron god of the Library is the one who needs it, who claims the necessity of a place of stories and souls and is willing to build it. Sometimes that's the librarians and curators, sometimes that's the storytellers, but sometimes? Sometimes it's just you. You, the reader, who found your wild and winding way here to the pages. You have a library inside you, do you not? Stories, told and untold. That is the power of gods.

Librarian Bjorn the Bard, 1686 CE

"RAMIEL." HERO'S VOICE WAS low and dry. "You take me to the most romantic places."

"Only the best for you," Rami deadpanned, to Hero's delight. He really was having the worst effect on the angel; Rami was in danger of developing a sense of humor. It was a thoughtful gesture, giving something else for Hero to focus on besides the damp stone walls that swirled up around them like jaws closing. Hero's stomach did a lurch as Rami's transit—teleport, flight, whatever—landed them on solid ground.

Which quickly turned to wet ground.

"My boots!" Hero lifted one foot, then the other, to no avail. Water flooded the labyrinth hallway and sloshed around their ankles. A scent like aquatic death—brown and blue and dark as a cave—hit his nose, not dissipated at all by the open sky above them. It was the smell of wet clay and dead things, caught in the reeds. Hero caught an acrid edge that burned the inside of his nose.

First things first: we need a realm, Claire had announced, as calmly as one would order a glass of wine. Of course she'd had the worst, most run-down, godsforsaken one in mind. The abandoned labyrinth realm that had nearly killed Claire the first time around hadn't exactly improved with time. They were supposed to slip in, see if the god of the place was still in a cannibalistic mood or if it wouldn't mind a few million soulish neighbors. *Immortal squatters, that's what we're reduced to*, Hero thought grumpily. Of course Rami had volunteered immediately. And then Hero had to come, to make sure the labyrinth didn't acquire a taste for angels.

The feathered edge of Rami's coat dampened and darkened as he leaned down to inspect the flooding with a frown. "You never mentioned flooded sections."

"The labyrinth was too busy being flooded with ghosts and terror to bother with something as inane as water. Is this flooding from that damn river?" Hero took another step and winced. "More important, why was I not written with waterproofing? This is going to ruin the lining."

"You were a villainous king. You could afford new ones."

It didn't take much to encourage Hero to play along. He pulled out a brilliant smile. "Nonsense, I had servants to carry me everywhere."

Rami's snort was fond and he slid past him before Hero could hold out his arms. "I followed Claire's trace. We should be near the center of the maze."

"And near the minotaur."

"Claire defeated it," Rami reminded him.

"You haven't read enough fairy tales, dearest." Hero patted him softly on the cheek as he peered around the corner. "Defeated doesn't always mean dead and gone."

The flooding continued unabated, turning the open arena at the center of the maze into a lake. Hero had never been this way before, but he recognized the circle of pillars jutting up into the sky from Claire's description. This would have been the center of the labyrinth, the place she faced the monster at the middle of the maze and realized Death had been a companion all along.

The labyrinth had played its tricks on them both, before Hero had been magically yanked away by the IWL. He'd escaped, but not before facing a reminder of the story he'd left behind. Owen, the closest thing he'd had to family in a story in a book that no longer existed. If he picked too much at that open wound, it would bleed again. And Hero didn't have time to bleed.

Still, it was better that he be here rather than Claire. Rami hadn't wanted either of them to return to this realm, but someone had to go who had been inside the labyrinth. Someone who knew the tricks and taunts the place played on a mind and who had walked across the back of the cannibal crocodile god they'd come to seek out.

That logic didn't warm the chilly water sloshing in his boots now—Hero was beginning to lose the feeling in his toes. But at least it would win him sympathy when he got home.

Faint ripples in the water traced away from him as he stepped into the arena. Ripples that stretched out and rebounded against anything that broke the surface, sending a thousand crisscrossing tiny waves across his path. They didn't seem to abate. The water had a kinetic energy to it that Hero didn't trust.

"There." Rami had drawn his sword without Hero's notice, though he hadn't lit it yet. He gestured, and Hero followed the line of the blade to the shadow of the far wall. It had an uneven shape, and Hero had to squint until he could separate the long shadows from the outline of a tattered hulk, half-submerged, leaning against a pillar.

Hero exchanged a look with Rami, then edged forward before Rami could advise caution. "Walter?" To be fair, Hero didn't call out too loudly—who knew what else lurked in this place? But if Claire's story had been right, the minotaur that guarded the center of this realm was its gatekeeper, and the gatekeeper of every afterlife realm was Death. In Hell, Death happened to sport a ridiculous cockney brogue and the name of Walter. That would have been preferable.

Rami grunted a warning in his ear, the only indication he'd followed Hero's lead. How did an angel so broad and trudging move so damn quietly? Hero was supposed to be the elegant one. But he splashed along in soggy boots while Rami moved silently. Hero let his annoyance make him brave. He took another step across the arena. "Walter?"

The water before him churned into a hash of ripples as the dark shape shifted. Great curved ram horns sat above a misshapen head. Hero let out a breath. "See? I told you Claire couldn't kill him."

"Fairy tales," Rami muttered as Hero quickened his step forward.

"Walter? It's no time for a bath, old boy." The smell that assaulted Hero's nose as he drew closer said the minotaur could have used one. He drew to a stop. The creature was a bulbous mound of puckered skin and shaggy fur, and it had a mangy, rotted appearance in some places. Possibly from the damp, Hero surmised. A peculiar clump hung as if it had sloughed off his shoulder. Hero coughed delicately. "Though you do look in rough shape."

"Hero…" Rami warned, and the mound moved. The minotaur turned to face them. It wasn't wet, or mold; there was no denying the way the muscles of the creature's great jaw sagged with rot, revealing tea-stained bone beneath. One eye socket was a gaping wound, torn and ragged at the edges. As the creature shifted, a viscous liquid the color of ink dribbled past the flap of skin to dilute in the water below. It paired with the intact eye, which wandered before latching onto them with a dull, hungry gaze.

"That's not Walter. Death would have abandoned this place once Claire took his gate from him." The hiss of Rami's blade igniting into flame startled Hero into action. He stumbled back, and Rami put an arm out to step forward.

"Then what is it?"

"I suspect the only thing left here." The tension in Rami's voice turned Hero's head. The white webwork of a skull, nearly as tall as the walls themselves. It leaned against the wall near the entrance, initially hidden from their sight by the curve of the exterior. It was propped at an angle, long jaw studded with teeth the length of a blade. A terrible thought made Hero glance back and spy the dry pebble of scaled skin around the minotaur's working eye.

"The mad crocodile?"

"The god," Rami corrected grimly.

"But—" Hero glanced between the rotting minotaur that was

attempting to pull itself upright and the skull. "How?"

"You can't just remove a realm's gatekeeper without repercussions." Rami shook his head, nudging Hero to circle toward the middle of the arena in order to keep more space between them and the minotaur. It thrashed to its feet, churning the water as something darker and bilious streamed off its fur. It had a dragging gait, as if its limbs had been waterlogged for too long, but it turned its one eye in their direction and let out a wet howl.

Hero edged back and reached for his own sword. "What repercussions?"

"If I had to guess—"

"Guess fast."

"Claire defeated Walter the last time she was here, and escaped using his eye. Walter, as Death, is the gatekeeper. A gatekeeper that's been defeated serves no purpose. Walter left, and without a gatekeeper this forgotten realm was marooned even more than it once was. No accidental souls stumbling through to feed its hungry god. A hungry god can get desperate."

"It was already eating people! How much more desperate are we talking about?"

"Desperate enough to possess the corpse of their gatekeeper in order to eat itself."

"Delightful! No wonder this asshole lost believers."

"Yes, well, perhaps we should reconsider our intent for negotiation."

"If we wait for a landlord who will not eat us for his own benefit we'll be realmless forever, Rami. Leto told me about this once; it's called capitalism." Hero started forward. "You there! Remember me?"

The minotaur swung its single black eye in their direction. A grinding noise, like bone on bone greased with despair, howled from its chest. It lurched in their direction, sending fetid circles of waves across the water's surface.

"Disgusting." Hero leaned forward. "Come now, you talked enough last time. Remember? *BE JUDGED...?*" He tried to reproduce the horrible skull rumble the crocodile god spoke in the first time he'd entered this realm, but fell short.

As if offended, the minotaur used a giant claw to bat the boulder between them across the arena. Hero leapt back and nearly fell over his soggy boots.

Rami caught him by the shoulder before he could end up ass-first in the water. "He doesn't seem open to this 'capitalism.'"

"You caught that, did you? No matter." Hero regained his footing, starting to pant for breath. "We have swords! Finally! For once!"

"I don't doubt your skill," Rami said carefully. "But what, exactly, do you imagine happens to a realm when a god falls without another to replace it?"

"... Oh." Hero flinched as something crunched under the minotaur's thick hooves. "You may have a point. Run like hell?"

Rami yanked him back as the last of their precarious rubble barrier fell under a blow. "Go."

Trying to run through calf-deep water was not an elegant task, less so when the wall they'd been hiding behind collapsed in their wake. His boots were waterlogged, and too tall to kick off, so Hero could only pretend he wasn't flailing like a wet blanket as he ran. Rami stayed behind him, guarding their retreat. The swamp-water smell turned from methane to acrid oil as Rami ignited the flame along the edge of his sword.

They retreated down a long hallway and had just cleared the next intersection when a new section of wall crashed into the water. The minotaur wasn't going to give up pursuit that easily. Hero skidded to a stop at the center of three branching paths, and

Rami barely avoided colliding with him. "Do you remember the way out?" Rami asked.

"Do I—" Hero wheezed. "It's a labyrinth!"

A bilious wave soaked Hero up to the hip, causing them to both turn toward the way they'd come. The minotaur swayed at the end of the corridor, a shaggy blot against the waning forever twilight of the sky. It swayed, musculature having desiccated enough that it needed to support itself on one arm, but that still left one fist the size of a carriage to punch the wall as it began to lurch their way. It picked up speed quickly for a creature that was half hate and rot.

"This way." Hero tore down the right hallway at random. The flooding continued as they rushed down one maze path and then another. They passed several shadowed stairwells, but Hero knew better than to trust them. The last time he'd been here, stairs had only led to illusion and trickery. The maze continued, unabated, but the waters had made the rough paving stones treacherous. Rami's next step met empty water, and he stumbled face-first into a small sinkhole. Hero managed to avoid it, but they lost precious seconds of their lead as Rami righted himself, oily water cascading down his trench coat of soggy feathers.

"I do not like this place," Rami muttered. He wiped silt from his face as they ran.

"Don't be a wet blanket. Aside from the cannibalism and certain death, it's not so—" Hero twisted around the next corner and stopped as the path in front of them ended at a solid wall. Well, that wasn't fair. A frustrated whine rose up in his throat. "I do not like this place."

The churn of the water grew more violent and frenzied, and a grating sound grew as the minotaur attempted to shove itself between the narrowing hallway walls behind them. Hero drew his sword, and his shoulder brushed Rami's as they backed up against the unforgiving wall.

"Strike for the eye. It's our best chance," Rami said quietly. The line of his jaw was underlit with the eerie blue flame of his sword, tense but somehow beautiful. Hero should say something. Something snappy, something flippant or tender, but above all something with wit. But the icy water had seeped into his bones and drowned his humor. They squared off.

The lumpy shadow of the minotaur lurched and grew as a gnarled hand gripped the corner of the wall. Stone broke beneath the claws, shuddering down in a hail of rubble and dust that momentarily threw a smoke screen between them and their pursuer. Rami took a sharp intake of air, and abruptly Hero was yanked into a run.

Toward the monster.

He must have made a strangled sound because Rami shouted, "This way," into his ear before shoving Hero through the crumbling wall. The space on the other side angled upward, and it took Hero a beat to recognize the staircase. He recoiled, running into Rami's shoulder in the small space. "No, terrible idea—"

"Worse idea is right behind us," Rami said with a granite streak in his voice that wasn't going to be argued with or refused. The revealed stairwell that had been hidden behind the wall was tiny and forced them both onto the steps to dodge the claws as the minotaur revenant tried to widen the hole. Hero felt like a mouse cornered by a giant moldering cat. Rami nudged him. "Up we go."

"This is a *terrible* idea," Hero repeated. He allowed Rami to herd him up the steps at a plodding pace since they were safe for a brief moment. The alcove was too tiny to admit the monster that chased them, tiny—and far too convenient. Hero had learned not to trust anything convenient in this place. Convenient merely meant the hungry realm had thought up a new and delightfully innovative method to torture you.

Still, he climbed the steps with a cautious preparedness. The last time he had been here, the labyrinth had taunted him with doorways that appeared to lead back into the world of his story. Places where he'd grown up, people he had loved, and all of it had never existed. Only Claire, with her bloody-minded will, had kept him on this side of the threshold. Still, it wasn't as if he was going to fall for the same tricks twice. He knew the tricks now. Easy enough to resist. *And*, a pathetic voice added in his head, *your book is gone anyway.*

Maudlin brooding would have to come later, when he had more dramatically appropriate lighting and less soggy pants. They emerged from the curving stairwell into a second floor of hallways that shouldn't exist. The walls terminated a few feet above their heads in crumbled ruin. The sky was sour gray and choked with mounds of stagnant ash-colored clouds. It seemed lower and oppressive, pressing in on them from overhead, as if the entire realm was a trap closing shut around them.

"I am not one to easily admit defeat, but I can gracefully chalk this pit up to a loss," Hero said. "Why are we not going home now?"

"I want to make sure we're far enough away from that beast that we don't take anything back with us." Rami had sheathed his sword for the flight up the stairs but had the blade out and ignited again. It served only to give every crack and crevice in the lonely hallway a sickly flicker.

"At least our feet aren't wet." Hero stopped at the landing and scuffed the atrociously nondescript stone pavers. Time had worn away all color and detail from this place. It was almost like a realm forgetting itself.

"I'll scout ahead." Rami strode down the hall with a confidence he had only when there was a weapon hilt in his hand. The movement threw faint, tilting shadows as he stopped to cautiously check every crack larger than a finger's width, as if the minotaur was just waiting to pop out.

Hero followed at a wary pace. The farther they drew away from the stairs, the quieter the percussive thuds became—too quickly and too quietly for normal acoustics; the air turned silent and it suddenly felt as if they'd been transported to a new and forgotten section of the labyrinth.

The hallway had been endless when they'd entered it, but abruptly Rami was framed by a pool of pristine light spilling around the corner—no, not a corner. A *doorway*. It was a doorway that had not been there a moment before. Rami half passed it before twitching with a double take. He began to lower his sword.

Hero jolted into a sprint to close the distance. "Don't look!" But it was already too late for such asinine advice. Rami fully faced the door, and his craggy face smoothed into something softer and, strangely, younger than Hero had ever seen. "Ramiel!"

Rami had been told about the illusions that Claire and Hero had faced; he wasn't a stupid man. Hero would not fall in love with a *stupid* man. But that was the way illusions worked—by being attractive enough that reason didn't matter.

"Oh, Creator..." Rami whispered in a gutted, home-hollow voice, and Hero immediately knew what he must see.

Rami took a step just as Hero lunged for his shoulder. Hero caught the hem of his sleeve, which yanked him sideways as Rami stepped through the doorway and the world went sideways. The other side was a fractal of light. Hero squeezed his eyes shut as he was pulled across the threshold. He threw his hand out and said a silent prayer of thanks when his hand found stone strong enough to grip. Gravity tossed them about until Hero was wedged in the doorway, one hand holding on to the threshold by his fingertips while the other clutched Rami's coat.

"Let go." Rami's voice was rough and desperate. His big hands began fighting at Hero's closed fist, trying to extract himself. "We're almost there—"

"No, we are not! Wherever you *think* we're going, we are not. It's an illusion, Ramiel!" The doorway was no longer a doorway but a portal, perched above... *something*. Hero didn't dare open his eyes. Rainbow fractals blinded him even through his closed eyelids, and he knew—he *knew*—that if he lost hold of the doorway they'd fall into some greater illusion forever.

"Heaven is not an illusion. Hero—Hero, please." Rami's struggling changed to begging as his hand found Hero's wrist. "It's... I can't describe what it's like in the place of the Creator. I don't know why we've been given a second chance, but please, let me just *show* it to you."

The desire in Rami's voice shattered Hero's certainty. It wasn't desire in the normal, carnal sense as Hero was familiar with it. No, Rami's voice wrung with the desire for *salvation*. The painful desire to be whole, the belief that the answer to everything was at hand. "It's not real, Ramiel. Rami—" Hero kept saying his name, as if he could keep a hold on him through identity alone. "It's not."

"How can you say that? Of course the Creator is real. She's been missing, but now she's *here*, Hero. I found her. If we go back with her, they'll have to let us in. The Creator, she can *fix* you, Hero!"

"I..." Hero said through a strained breath. He found his voice impossibly small. "I... am not broken."

"Oh." Rami's voice was rough and hollow, as if he'd been punched. He stopped his struggling momentarily. "No..." He drifted at the end of Hero's reach. "No, of course you're not."

"And you're not either." Hero could feel his fingers slipping. If Rami started to fight him again, there was no way he would retain his grip. He felt his heart slipping from his ribs. "You're whole as you are, Rami. You're not broken, you're not waiting to be forgiven. You are you... you are *loved*, just as you are." Feathers slid between the knuckles of his fist. Hero's stomach lurched. "Please."

He didn't dare open his eyes. Hero knew instinctively that this doorway was entirely for Rami alone. If he looked, maybe his mind would shatter like a mortal's against something divine, or maybe he'd be lost in the same illusion entirely. Either way, that would mean losing Ramiel, so Hero didn't open his eyes, and he held, with the barest of fingertips, to Rami's sleeve. He didn't know what Rami saw in those moments, or what expression he wore when Rami's rough hands clasped around his wrist again. The angel's voice was hoarse but real, alive. "Pull me up."

His hands were rough with calluses and hot as life on Hero's arm. He pulled. In gratitude, he pulled with every fiber of his being and dragged Ramiel away from the wonders of paradise and back to Hell.

17

CLAIRE

Failure. No, stop. There is always another way, another path.
Think, Julia, *think*.

Librarian Poppaea Julia, 48 BCE

CLAIRE WAS NOT HOVERING. Of course not. Claire did not hover. However, with one of—no, now two of her people off to try to cajole the god that had tried to eat her, Claire decided to maintain vigilance at Walter's desk. Vigilance, yes. That was it.

"Ma'am, you're makin' the jars jiggle something fierce." Walter's howling baritone succeeded in sounding both apologetic and plaintive at the same time. He had one of his massive hands steadying a shelf, and Claire flicked her gaze down to where she was rapping her knuckles on the desk distractedly—and with force, and had been for some time, judging by the pain in her hands.

She clasped her hands together to still them. "Very sorry, Walter. I was somewhere else."

"This is a place for somewhere elses," Walter said, shoulders relaxing. He paused to straighten each jar just so on the nearest shelf before dusting his hands off. "I... I take it you 'n' Miss Brevity got yourselves an idea, then."

"A bad idea, but then most of ours are." Claire grimaced. "Your... judicious inattention was helpful, Walter."

"Glad to hear it and also don't have any idea what you're gabbing about." Walter put a finger to the side of his nose.

"Of course." Claire smiled ruefully. "In any case, Hero and Rami are off procuring... well, you could say a room of one's own."

"Aw, good for them!" Walter slapped the counter, which sent boisterous vibrations rattling the jars again. "I was rootin' for them... and you, of course. Those relate-in-ships you humans get up to was always kinda fuzzy to me, but—"

"Not—not like that." Claire bit down on her laughter. A shame Rami wasn't here—she would have paid good money to see the Watcher blush. "I mean a realm. They're scouting for the Library."

"Oh." Walter's face fell into craggy consideration. "So yer following in Mrs. Poppaea's path?"

"Of a sort." Claire smiled ruefully. "Hopefully with more success."

"You thinkin' Mister Ramiel and Hero will find a realm?"

"With any luck. Hero could talk his way into London Tower."

"An' you... figured out the god thing?"

Claire hesitated at the waver in Walter's deep voice. "The god—"

The jars in the office rumbled with a deafening chime as Rami and Hero returned. Claire felt the nerves that had been squeezing her chest ease and she schooled her face before turning around.

"I presume since you dallied that means you were success—"

Claire stopped short. Hero and Rami were sodden from the waist down and smelled distinctly of algae and bile. They both had the waxen survivor look that places like the dead labyrinth realm tended to impart. But that wasn't the part that caught Claire's voice in her throat and pierced her heart.

Ramiel's feathers were white.

One imagined an angel's feathers as white: this wasn't that. Angel feathers were supposed to be soft, immutable white, the pristine, untouched shade of hopeful, holy things. The bits of feather and fluff remaining to poke out ragged between the folds of Ramiel's trench coat were the white of nothing. Each pinion was a hollow cell, and the barbs of each feather stood out like lace ghosts. His comfortable gray feathers had turned translucent.

"Rami—" Claire started, then stopped again. She looked to Hero, half expecting him to be holding the angel up. Rami was standing on his own strength, much like a body rigors into death. Hero kept a hand and an inscrutably soft gaze on him.

Claire reached out tentatively. Her hand hovered above a clutch of ghost feathers on his chest but was afraid to land. "What happened?" she asked Hero without removing her gaze from those feathers.

"We slipped through one of the labyrinth's cracks." Hero's answer was serious and subdued. It was worse when Hero was serious.

"Ah." Claire dropped her hand by fractions.

"Heaven." Rami's voice was a husk of its former self as he answered the unasked question. "I saw the Creator. She was home. Whole. She looked at me and I—" He stopped short, craggy features appearing to crumble into the shifting sands of grief. He closed his eyes briefly. "I turned away."

"It was an illusion, love," Hero repeated softly.

She had sent them on this errand. Beneath Claire's palm, Rami's chest was still solid and warm, still as real as his feathers weren't. She felt him shift awareness. His eyes focused on her, still silver-gray and angelic and perhaps even more heaven-lost than usual. Now was the time he would need her to say something philosophical, something restorative and true. Both of them looked at her like they were waiting for a lifeline of wisdom, a deeper truth to make what they'd seen make sense. But that would just be placing her understanding above their own, giving Rami another god to look to. And Claire felt nothing like a god. Her back hurt too much, for one.

So instead she said, "To hell with them, then. Bugger realms and bugger the gods that made them." Rami startled beneath her fingertips, and Claire's smile felt brutal on her lips. "Let's burn them all behind us."

18

HERO

I tried reasoning with them. The other librarians, the others on the Sisyphean hill. It was all for nothing. Oh, they listened. The librarian of Xian was sympathetic; Indralok maintained polite disinterest throughout my entire passionate appeal. Even the thrice-cursed Summerlands librarian was kind enough to serve me tea. (Do not drink the tea.) But that is where the professional courtesy ended. Not one of them was willing to risk angering their host realm by supporting my cause. I wasn't even asking them to rebel with me! All I needed was some symbolic gesture—some crumb of unity to threaten Lucifer with. But no, they were timid as sheep, and twice as stupid. All sympathetic noises and courtesies, right before leaving me in the dust of their doorstep. Even Elysium, a realm I'd dreamed of all my mortal life, was nothing but an echo and empty promise. Not yet, my ass. Big puddle of cowardice.

I get nowhere talking to the librarians, and there's nowhere else to take my appeals. I am fated to do this alone. Alone in the Library and alone standing before Hell.

No, that's not right. There's Revka; I have Revka. I must not forget that.

Librarian Poppaea Julia, 48 BCE

"WELL."

"Don't start."

"Start what? Can't a man feel sentimental? You and me, the open road—"

"Hardly open. I should have been suspicious when Bird agreed to ferry us," Claire pointed out as she wrung the water out of one pant leg. It was still an odd sight to see Claire in pants. Hero pressed on.

"The open road, which happens to lead through a muddy lake, dragging me along on a ridiculous quest—"

"Technically, if anyone is being dragged, it is me. Brevity asked you to go as the apprentice librarian."

"Does that make you my assistant? Do you have to do whatever ridiculous impulses fly through *my* brain for once?" Hero clapped his hands. "Delicious, first—"

"Hero." If it was possible to sigh his name, Claire did it. He relented, extending a hand to help her up onto the grassy bank. His high boots had kept out the worst of the lake water, but the heels were caked in mud and made the most undignified squelching sound when he moved. Claire's damned pet raven had indeed ferried them safely through the raven roads to Valhalla but had been less than considerate depositing them in the mud-and-gravel shallows of a mountain lake.

Valhalla had been a logical first choice. A friendly first choice, at the very least. It was the only realm with a former librarian still in active residence, as far as Hero knew. And they'd already allied with Bjorn the Bard once before. If any wing of the Library would be amenable to joining their little rebellion, then the sagas of Valhalla would be it.

Rebellion. A secret burst of energy thrilled through Hero's bones at the word. Finally, finally, here was something Hero was an absolute expert at. Rebellion was something he knew, down to his bones, down to his book—

No. No book now. The world where Hero had been a rebel hero, then a reviled antagonistic king, was gone. That world lay in ashes on a lonely cliff in the Dust Wing. But Hero was still here. His memory and experience of fighting a rebellion, raising forces, making alliances... those still lived within him. This was something real that he could give—to the Library, to Claire, to Rami, to all of them. Hero was determined not to leave until he'd secured their alliance.

Even if he and Bjorn had not... exactly hit it off the first time around.

"Are you well?" The sudden, uncharacteristic concern in Claire's voice brought Hero around to the task at hand. She had finished shaking the mud and bog water from her shoes and had a scrutinizing look on her face. "The raven roads—"

"Are nothing to me, after the Dust Wing." Hero winced at how quickly his voice went from braggadocio to honesty. He straightened and tried again. "I lost my book, after all. What possible terrors could the raven road conjure to top that?"

"The road is an expert at torturing souls," Claire said skeptically.

"Still not used to having one of those," Hero muttered. It was a peculiar watercolor of emotions, having a soul. It felt like the ground dropping out from under you, the stable anchor of knowing your story gone. It felt warm like a kind of love, meeting Claire's eyes and knowing the undefinable something that made her brilliant also resided in him. He felt seen. He felt exposed. And all the emotional color of it muddled up to leave him confused. He'd thought it would be different somehow. Losing his book. Becoming something else. Having a soul.

But all he'd seen on the raven road were the things he now had left to lose. Rami and Claire, foremost, and the different ways that loss would kill him. Brevity, and her unflagging belief in the goodness of everyone around her. The damsels, the Library...

Home. That was it. That was the loss the raven road taunted him with, in the abyss. The loss of home. Belonging to no story at all.

"Shall we?" Hero extended his elbow, not bothering to find a more elegant change of topic. One of the true graces of time was no longer feeling the need to outquip Claire all the time.

Most of the time, yes. But that was just for the pleasure of it.

Claire looped her arm through his, and they began the long descent through the mountain meadow together.

VALHALLA WAS AN ALIEN world to Hero. He was a fighter and therefore could recognize the trappings of warrior culture that Valhalla was decked in. But whether by influence of pop culture or belief, it was like a war game in technicolor. All the blades too clean, bearded men too loud, ale too fizzy. It was the kind of place that may have started as an afterlife reward for the devout but warped, over time, to something that might have been found in one of the comic books of the Unwritten Wing.

Yes, he'd started reading the comics section. He'd been reading a *lot* lately. It was weird living alone in your own head for the first time. Reading helped.

The doors of Valhalla's main hall were banded with gold and

ribboned with carvings of every kind of creature adorning a great central tree. A serpent twined around the roots. Hero hadn't noticed that last time. It appeared as malevolent as the dim wind chime of bones hung above the arch.

Claire pulled them to a stop at the bottom of the steps leading up to the doors. She crossed her arms and squinted up at the rafters of bones and birds. "Arlid," she called.

The black birds chattered into a sullen silence.

"Arlid, I lack the patience to play this silly game with you right now. Don't play silly buggers, you brute."

"Perhaps 'amp up the imperialist voice' is not the way to go, considering the British history with the Norse," Hero murmured under his breath as a raven dropped its soil directly onto the step in front of them. Filthy creatures.

"I can't help the way I speak. It is called proper English. And I suppose you have a better idea?" Claire made a sour face. "Technically, they did most of the invading."

"Most! How novel for you." Hero cleared his throat, removed his jacket, folded it, and placed it in a disbelieving Claire's arms. Unencumbered, he pursed his lips into a whistle as he jogged up the steps.

He made it one step farther than he had expected before a whistle of air through feathers stopped him. He had just enough warning to plant his toes, drop the hilt of his sword into his hand, and pivot.

A steel weight met his, and the burn in his shoulders felt glorious. Hero dug in his toes and shoved the raven woman off. Arlid, sleek as a stiletto in leathers and feathers, grinned at him wickedly. She spun, nimbly sliding down a step to rise again on his flank.

Movement was a joy. It felt like a treat to have the weight of a hilt in his hands again. Hero had the misfortune of being perpetually caught up in situations without his weapon, and though Rami sparred with him often enough, there was nothing to compare with the feeling of catching guard against guard with someone who would gleefully spill his guts. Arlid wielded daggers, shorter but wicked and long enough to catch the basket of his hilt and throw him off. They pivoted and danced up and down the steps for what seemed like only seconds before they were interrupted.

Claire's bag hit the dirt with a thud. "This is nonsense, and while I expected it of Hero, Arlid, you should know better."

"The paper man wanted to play," Arlid said. It took her a long moment before she regretfully sheathed her daggers. Hero, even more regretfully, did the same with his sword. "Why did you bring the featherless scholar?" she asked plaintively of Hero.

"Claire is my assistant," Hero said with relish.

"We are here to see Bjorn," Claire corrected. She hesitantly placed a foot on the steps, as if still expecting an ambush. When none came, she joined them at the landing with a brusqueness meant to hide her nerves. "Library business."

One black brow on Arlid's narrow face arched hopefully. "A duel?"

"No, thank you," Claire responded before Hero could weigh in. Just as well. Trading blows with Arlid was a refreshing break, but Hero had no desire to spill his blood to Uther, the Valhalla gatekeeper, again. Claire crossed her arms. "I believe we've already proven ourselves to the realm's standards."

Arlid responded with a sullen look that could only mean agreement. She shrugged, turning her back as the shaggy mane of her Mohawk began to shift into a mess of feathers again. "Tricksy, you are, paper boy and book girl. I'll be watching you."

There was an imprecise moment, when the space that consisted of Arlid seemed to be some horrifying conglomeration of leather, claws, feather, and bone. Then the air made a popping noise and a large black raven spiraled up to the rafters again, leaving Hero and Claire at the door.

Hero shook imaginary dust off his shoulders and retrieved his folded coat from Claire. "Well, I feel welcome. Don't you?"

"Ask me after we've run the gauntlet of Vikings." Claire heaved on the handle of one of the great doors, succeeding in squeaking it open by inches. With Hero's help, she slipped inside, and they left the cackle of raven laughter behind them.

THERE WAS A MATCH going on in the long hall when they entered. The immediate crash of steel and roar of spectators made Claire flinch, which cooled any interest Hero might have had in gawking at the competitors. He made use of his height to scan over the shaggy heads of the crowd. A circle of drummers was gathered around one of the many fires banked throughout the hall, but Bjorn was not among them. Hero nudged Claire. "His office, maybe?" Claire nodded her assent and didn't appear to notice when Hero slid up on her right side, casually positioning himself between Claire and the trio of hirsute old men eyeing them. He recognized the look of a man trying to drink up the confidence to be obnoxious.

"Claire!" Bjorn industriously picked his way around the clutter. He was surprisingly agile for an old man who appeared to be mostly beard and sinew, Hero would give him that. The old Norseman swept Claire up in a mead-wild hug, which Claire allowed with a surprising level of tolerance. She only subtly straightened her blouse when he put her down again.

"Bjorn, you look well," Claire said. Which was accurate if "well" was a pickled liver and a grin that missed two teeth.

"Takes more than a fussed-up Valkyrie to get rid of me." Bjorn gave a gap-toothed grin. He leaned back expansively in his chair. "What brings Hell's Library to my doorstep? No angry angels at your heels this time, I hope?"

"No, we left him home to mind the shop," Hero said brightly, just to watch Bjorn do a double take.

"What—"

"It is a very long story. Suffice it to say that your assistance last time was fruitful," Claire cut in, reserving a scolding frown for Hero. "Why we are here is a slightly more pressing matter. Perhaps we could speak in your wing?"

Bjorn shifted his surprise from Hero to Claire, then his eyes narrowed. He ran a finger down his beard skeptically. "You want to see Valhalla's wing? Whatever for?"

"Library business," Hero said in a tone that ended the argument.

Bjorn's eyes were a faded blue, and crow's-feet multiplied around the edges as he considered. "You're up to something, lad. Hell is always up to something."

"We're not here on behalf of Hell," Claire said quietly. "I can promise you that much."

Bjorn's chair creaked on old joints. Finally, he heaved to his feet again. "Fine, but only because I trust Claire here. Not every wing takes to visitors like your Unwritten one."

If the Unwritten Wing, with its wards and its locks, was considered the hospitable wing of the Library, Hero thought they were in for a bigger challenge than he'd originally estimated.

"We'll be discreet as possible." Claire lied attractively, Hero would give her that.

Bjorn made a grunt that expressed his opinion on that likelihood. "Fine, but if we're going to the Unwon Wing, I'm gonna need me another drink."

BJORN TOOK HIS SWEET time securing an ale from the main hall. When he finally extracted himself from the crowd, at least he was carrying two smaller mugs as well. He handed Hero a simple cup, and Claire something that looked like a rough-thrown tea mug.

Bjorn drained his pint in one enormous pull, deftly managing to allow only a dribble to escape into his beard. Hero and Claire took more polite sips as they followed the Norseman around the edge of the hall and through a door down an unfamiliar corridor. Hero couldn't hide his surprise when Bjorn opened another door and ushered them out into the valley behind the longhouse.

Night had fallen in Valhalla, according to whatever internal clock a realm held to—Hell didn't so much have a night as a point in each day when Claire and Hero groused that their humanlike brains needed a break. The air was sharp with pine and frost. Grass crunched under Hero's boots and torchlight reflected in Claire's dark eyes and turned her skin to bronze.

"No tricks, Bjorn," Claire said warily, but he shook his head.

"No, not a trick, lass. The Unwon Wing prefers a bit of... distance, you might say. Better for everyone, really." Bjorn guided them through a field that had no visible path. As Hero's eyes adjusted to the dark, he could see they were skirting the lake they'd encountered their first time through... gods, a romp that already seemed ages ago. When Hero had mostly been preoccupied with the many ways he could lift his book and give Claire the slip.

Now he kept track of her in the dark as they approached a line of trees. The torch made shadows jump and stutter in ways that reminded Hero too much of the raven roads. He had the irrational fear that if he didn't keep close track of Claire, the dark would snare and steal her away.

Yes, very different from before.

Claire frowned. "I thought Valhalla's wing was unwritten sagas. Great war heroics or something like that."

"Something like that." Bjorn's voice had a somber quality that would have raised a red flag in anyone. Hero exchanged a cautious look with Claire, but she waved him on.

"Understood. Not my place to question a librarian's curation. Besides"—Claire forced a tight smile that was more of an accusation—"we trust each other, don't we, Bjorn?"

"Easy, lass. You'll see what I mean in a moment." Bjorn led them through a forested thicket in silence, following no discernible path. Finally, Hero strained his ears and heard running water a second before they broke through the bush. Water cascaded from a small rise, down a jagged frame of stones, into a small basin that wicked away to a stream.

"The Unwon Wing is just behind the waterfall," Bjorn said, pausing to kick off his boots by the side of the stream.

"There's nothing there but stone." Hero stated the obvious. There was the hint of an alcove beyond, but the moving water reflected the moonlight well enough to show it was nothing but a depression worn down by water.

"He don't learn too fast, does he?" Bjorn asked Claire philosophically. He gestured to the riverbank, and Claire made a face before crouching down to start unlacing her sneakers. "Must get by on his looks."

"Looks can be deceiving. Hero might surprise you," Claire said as she straightened. Hero absolutely did not acknowledge the small pool of warmth inside at the idea of Claire defending his intelligence. It was a very British kind of emotional defense, but Hero would take it.

They were waiting on him, Hero realized. He unbuckled his

boots, snatching Claire's sneakers from the dirt to stack next to his boots higher up on the bank. Really, good leather should not be risked. "Are we just... wading?"

"Through the waterfall," Bjorn said with a nod.

"I'd think you'd want to avoid bringing the damp into the wing," Claire said, scandalized.

"The wing doesn't mind," Bjorn said, lips pressed into a fine line again. "Now, are you two going to stand around bellyaching or are we going in?"

"We're going in." Claire squared her shoulders but flinched as her foot splashed into the river. The wide fabric of her trousers began to darken and wick up water. "Really, the one time when skirts would be efficient and..."

The rest of her complaint was lost under the roar of the waterfall. One moment, Hero could make out the water pelting over her shoulders, soddening her shirt to cling to her curves—Hero was not too much of a gentleman to notice, thank you very much—but in the next breath the waterfall held nothing but rock and freezing water.

Hero turned to look at Bjorn, who simply grinned that demented-old-man grin at him. Bjorn twirled his hand in invitation. "Oh hell," Hero muttered, bracing himself as he waded in. The water was just this side of ice, freezing even as Hero's bare feet appeared to find every sharp stone in the basin. He gritted his teeth and, knowing how the insane logic of the afterlife worked, charged through the waterfall into what appeared to be a stone cliff face.

It was reflex to close his eyes as the icy water closed over him. Hero half expected the sudden crunch of his face against granite, but abruptly the roar of the waterfall—if not the cold—was gone. Hero opened his eyes.

Then blinked to make sure they were open.

The darkness of the space they were in was absolute. He jumped when a cold hand slipped into his. "Hero?" Claire said, somewhat allaying the adrenaline that had dumped into his system. He could recognize her hand in his now, smooth but calloused at the fingertips from constant busywork, first with books, then with artifacts that sometimes bit back. Her hand was freezing, though. He gripped it by reflex, though his weren't much warmer.

"Where in the realms—"

A sudden roar, then a popping sound interrupted him with a cold draft at his back. Bjorn bit back a hoot as he shook the water from his beard—icy droplets hit Hero in the face. "Whooo! That gets yer blood a-goin' all right." His voice was pitched low but still rang loud in the darkness.

"I don't suppose you brought a torch through that," Hero said ruefully.

"Or a towel," Claire added.

"There will be a fire up ahead," Bjorn answered vaguely. Almost as he said it, Hero could detect a shift in the blackness; a glimmer of a shadow outlined a bend in the walls ahead of them, limned by the reflection of what could be firelight.

"Fire. In a library." Claire sounded as if she was starting to get a headache. "First the Unsaid Wing has a bloody pool, and you keep a fire. I can't—"

"Lower your voices, if'n you don't mind," Bjorn cut her off, despite being the loudest of the three of them. Hero felt him brush by and pat Claire's shoulder. "The wing is a bit fragile, you might say. Better to maintain quiet."

Rarely was Claire the one to be told to keep quiet. Hero studied her as she pressed her lips into a thin line, as if to keep the rest of that sentence from spilling out. Bjorn nodded approval before raising his hand to guide them down the hallway. Hero trailed his fingers along the cold stone in the dark, as a means to orient himself. If there was one thing he had learned about libraries, it was that it was very easy to get lost and end up somewhere you hadn't quite intended to go. The presence of dark and leaping firelight made this one seem particularly untrustworthy.

19

BREVITY

Don't underestimate Hell.
The quiet path is one where the predator already treads.
Librarian Ibukun of Ise, 808 CE

IT WASN'T THAT BREVITY minded taking care of the Library—far from it, since being librarian was all she'd ever wanted since she'd come to the Unwritten Wing. It wasn't even that she minded, really, the addition of the Unsaid Wing's inhabitants in all their chaotic, leafy green glory. No, what made her fist clench at her side wasn't the work or the change; it was the staying behind.

It made perfect logical sense when Claire had explained it. Brevity was the librarian and the Library was under imminent attack; it made sense that she would remain here while Claire and Hero traveled to the other Library wings as the emissary for the Unwritten. A librarian's first responsibility was to her wing, though that had never seemed to stop Claire when she had the inclination to travel. Someone needed to be here to welcome new wings, as the others (hopefully) recruited them, and get them settled. Taking care of the books and maintaining their defenses—holding the line—was a vital part of the plan.

But it felt ever so unheroic.

There was no heroism in breaking up a fight between the Unsaid's vines and a couple of the older, surlier books for the sixth time that morning. Little excitement in resolving a wandering tale that had been pushed out of its shelf by a pile of scrolls. If things were this contentious with just two wings sharing the same spot, she wondered, how in the world would the Unwritten Wing manage to hold all twelve wings together?

Ice water turned her socks soggy. Brevity looked down to see another puddle had sprung up beneath her toes. She hopped back and groaned. "Echo!"

There was, of course, no response. Brevity rubbed her hands over her face. The Unsaid Wing's discorporate librarian and her children had done little to rein in their charges. After Claire and Hero had left for Valhalla, Echo had slipped back into her reflection and Pallas had been cosseted off with the damsels. Iambe hadn't even waited that long—gods knew what she was getting up to.

But water in the Library was almost worse than fire. Humidity played all sorts of havoc with old documents. Bindings broke down, paper disintegrated, leather gave way to mildew. Those properties might not apply to magical water and magical books, but then again, fire had still burned, even in Hell. She wasn't willing to risk it.

"Echo! Iambe!" Brevity raised her voice again, but the only shape that stirred from farther down the stacks was a feathered one. Rami emerged from the direction of the lobby carrying an armload of books. He'd taken his reassignment from the Arcane Wing to the Unwritten Wing in stride and had already cleared two carts of repaired books back to the stacks. Brevity could barely get Hero to do one cart a *week* and idly wondered if that was precisely why Rami was doing them. Besides, the haunted look he'd had since he'd returned from the labyrinth's realm told Brevity he was looking for something to occupy himself.

"Can I assist?" Rami asked as Brevity passed him.

"No—yes—have you seen Echo?"

Rami shook his head. "Should I…?"

"No, it's all right. I'll find her and have a… a word." Brevity disliked the idea of conflict. The idea was to pull all the librarians *together* into a united front, after all. But perhaps if she worked out some ground rules with the Unsaid Wing, it would all go smoother when Hero coaxed the others to join them here. "Can you keep an eye on… things?"

Both of them gave an involuntary glance in the direction of the closed and barred doors of the lobby. Brevity had even managed to coax the gargoyle in from the hallway, and he was dozing in a storm of static and broken physics against the doors. The wards were up and, after the first barrage, reported only light incursions testing the perimeter. Malphas hadn't pressed her advantage after burning the Arcane Wing. Not even when Claire and Hero had left for Valhalla. The general of Hell might be patient, but it was unlike her to not press an advantage when she saw it.

Rami nodded, and Brevity appreciated the subtle military shift to his shoulders. "I'll keep watch."

She patted him wordlessly and took off down the Romance—Rivalries—Enemies to Lovers aisle, which she knew was a shortcut to the wider canyon-like intersection of shelves that ran like a main artery through the modern collections of the wing. When she didn't find signs of Echo there, she made a cursory check of the older collections, where a majority of the vines and heavy tablets of writing from the Unsaid Wing had migrated, then checked the damsel suite—Pallas was sleeping and, Rosia informed her firmly, was not to be wakened—before poking her head into some of the rooms of closed-off collections. The air was stagnant and chill as a tomb back here, lights kept purposefully dim. The books that lived here hadn't woken up during Brevity's tenure in the Library, possibly not even Claire's. The dust was still thick on the copper doorknobs, which left her reasonably confident that Echo hadn't gone this way.

"Right." Brevity had winnowed through her remaining patience. Sometimes the Unwritten Wing was just too big to find someone the old-fashioned way, like a human. Brevity didn't know how Claire put up with it. Thank gods she was still muse enough to shadowstep. It was the one perk she'd retained in Hell. It didn't extend beyond the bounds of the Library itself, but if she kept a firm vision of Echo in her mind's eye…

She lifted her foot off the hardwood, closed her eyes, and set her foot back down into shadow. The familiar rich smell of old books got wiped away by a cold rush that always brought a tingly pink feeling to Brevity's pale blue cheeks. She kept her eyes closed, focusing on the idea of Echo's location, and broke into a confident run. It should be only a handful of steps at most—

Her foot came down on nothing—a nothing even *more* nothing than shadows. Brevity lost her concentration as her stomach flipped and she opened her eyes. Soft shadows pooled around her, but the familiar chill of in-between places didn't sear her eyes.

She stood on a marble floor that was an ashy black. A circle of light lit up the floor around her but cast the rest of the room in impenetrable gloom.

This wasn't the Library. Brevity's flicker-quick shadowsteps around the wing had never been interrupted before. She hesitated and stepped forward. "Hello?"

The silence drew out. It was another several seconds before it broke with the crisp click of footsteps. Boots the color of dull brick stepped into the light. Malphas tilted her head. "Hello, Librarian."

Brevity didn't wait for her to say anything else. She took two steps back to reach for the easy escape of the shadows. They weren't there. The absence made her stumble, and her back slammed into an invisible barrier at the edge of the light.

"Settle down, child, or I'll have to get disciplinary," Malphas said mildly.

"I'm not a child, not to you," Brevity said as she felt unsteadily along the barrier of the light. It didn't feel like any ward that she'd encountered. It didn't even feel like magic; no porous surface for her to wiggle her will into. It was as smooth and cold as the stone beneath her feet. Brevity's pulse juddered into her throat, but she straightened up anyway. She'd had practice at being terrified, at least. "Maybe I'm older."

"Older than me?" That seemed to amuse Malphas. "You are an established spirit, I'll grant you that. Not a childish simulacrum of sentience like a human. That's why I'm affording you the respect of this."

"Respect?" Brevity's laugh was shaky and weak. She hated it; she wanted to be brave. Brave like Claire, strong like Rami, clever like Hero. But she was only Brevity. Only ever Brevity. "It doesn't feel like it," she ended softly.

"You were foolish enough to do your little muse trick in my realm. The Library may be sovereign, but the shadows have always belonged to Hell. I watched you do it before without caring enough to intervene. But now... Easy enough to divert you here. If you were Claire or that little pest of a book she keeps around and I

caught you in such a slipup, you'd be burning in a pit of flame."
Malphas shrugged. She leaned on an ebony cane, and though
Brevity knew it was simply for show, it gave her a wistful air, like a
parent about to hand down a punishment she regretted.
Grandmother of ghosts.

The mention of Claire spurred Brevity to ask the question that
she would have asked from the start. "What do you want, Malphas?"

"Interesting question, isn't it? First I wanted Andras, then the
Library, but I must be getting weary in my old age. What I want
right now, more than anything, my dear, is answers."

"You already interrogated us." The swoop in Brevity's belly was
something more than anxiety, more than fear. It was the first
inkling that this was not like the other encounters. This was not a
short visit, brief words exchanged full of vague threats and violent
promises. It occurred to Brevity that she didn't know where,
exactly, she was.

And that no one else knew where she was either.

"What is Claire after? You know this realm business is a fool's
errand." Malphas began to pace, stabbing the ground with her cane
more for emphasis than support. "Something has changed within
the Library. Even a demon can feel it. You're going to tell me."

"I don't know what you're talking about."

"You're the librarian. Librarians with access to books don't get
to beg ignorance." Malphas circled like a particularly slow predator.
"The books, is that it? The Library's grown in power, not
diminished since Andras's little stunt with the fire. Why is that?"

Brevity fell quiet.

"And then the way the Unwritten and Arcane closed ranks so
softly recently. The inventories tell us nothing, but something has
changed. It's sus—"

"You'd have to ask Claire," Brevity demurred, heart shuddering between her ribs.

"No... I don't think I do. The answer's not in the Arcane Wing, not anymore." Malphas slowed in her stalking as if a thought had caught her attention. "So protective of the one called Hero, a simple book. But that's—an interesting prospect. Requires skepticism, though; it will require confirmation. The books?" Malphas finished mulling to herself and narrowed her yellow hawk eyes on Brevity. "The books are the power."

"Books are always powerful," Brevity said faintly.

"No. The books *are* a power, and power that survives destruction is..." Malphas stopped, pivoting slowly on her heel. "What are books made of, little muse?"

Brevity swallowed and held still.

"Not cooperative?" Malphas straightened. "That's fine. We can continue this as long as it's necessary."

"I'm the librarian," Brevity said quickly. "You're not allowed to touch me."

"And I won't." Malphas took a predatory step and stopped just short of the light. "In fact, I plan to forget all about you."

"What...?" The stone beneath Brevity's feet grew hot. She had just enough time to lunge for the barrier, fingers scrambling against nothing, before the ground beneath her dissolved completely. Then she was falling.

"An oubliette." She could hear Malphas's voice grow faint above her as the world tunneled to an endless fall. "Hell is for forgetting, after all."

2 0

HERO

There's something that ties together the collections of the Library. Unwritten, Unsaid, Unwon, and so many more. Myrrh, they are all products of human soul, yes, of course there is that. But something more: regret. Regret lingers on. Regret fractures our souls into many. Maybe, just maybe, the counterpower to creation isn't destruction—that's just entropy, just natural. No, the opposite of creation isn't destruction; it's regret.

It's the stories we never tell that carry the most weight.

Librarian Yoon Ji-Han, 1801 CE

THE OPPRESSION OF THE stone hallway opened up as they turned the corner. Hero could tell that by feel rather than sight. It was still dark, smothering dark. But the air took up that decompressed quality of a wide space, spawning currents and eddies of warmth and cold. A breeze skimmed the droplets of water still clinging to Hero's cheeks, chilling him further. He hunched into his (also sodden) coat and followed Bjorn.

A flare bloomed into the darkness, forcing Hero to shield his eyes. A small campfire crackled to life, the likes of which one might make in the wood, at the end of the day when you're tired and bone cold and unable to go any farther. It lit up nothing but the bare ground around it, abandoned but crackling with a merry heat.

They moved toward it by instinct, letting some of the moisture wick from their clothes. Claire tried to discreetly shake out the long locks of her hair. "How much farther to this wing of yours, Bjorn?"

"Not far at all." He crouched by the fire, looking half-ghost himself as he poked at the embers.

"Not far. You said that a waterfall, one woods, and too much damned meadow back. How—"

"Listen." Bjorn held up a hand. "I warned you, be quiet. Listen."

The old man was being unnecessarily cryptic, but instead of arguing, Claire took a step toward the fire. He saw her eyes narrow as she studied it. Ember light lit her from below, softening the flickering light into something less than hellish, more sad. Hero took a knee beside her, then froze.

The voice was so soft, so well entwined with the crackle of the fire, he nearly missed it. But straining to hear, Hero could pick out a soft hum. It rose, querulous and unsteady, until it finally started to form words.

"Just wanted coffee. Get so damned few other pleasures in this pisshole. All the nurses and busybodies. A man deserves a little dignity." The voice was rocky with age. Hero raised his head, alert, but couldn't tell from which direction it was coming. He squinted, but his mind supplied half-formed faces in the dark that he couldn't be sure were there. *"Angina acting up again. This heartburn is a bitch. Where is that—just a little farther—feels warmer now."*

Another voice bled into the first, seamless and also without direction. This one was younger. *"He says if I'm quiet and good I get to go home. He brings me fries, lets me dip 'em into the milkshake like Mama doesn't. The salt's still on my tongue when he reaches for his belt."* The voice is distant—it could be on the other side of the campfire, or miles away. Safe, wherever it is, from the story it's telling. *"The carpet smells like my dog, Max. I want to go home."*

"What is this place?" Claire's voice was hoarse and hollow with horror.

"The Unwon Wing, as promised." Bjorn sat cross-legged at the fire now, and Hero realized he could see him better. Other fires had sprung up around them. Not close enough to see any other figures in the dark, but the fires bloomed in scattered patches for what felt like miles. They were at the edge of some huge camp, an army of ghosts.

"Everyone has one story, one story no one ever gets to tell," Bjorn continued, low and somber.

"The story of how they died," Claire whispered. Bjorn nodded.

"Those stories are worth preserving too."

"Valhalla was supposed to house the wing of war epics," Claire said.

Bjorn's smile was a husk of a thing. "Valhalla is the realm for fallen heroes. We listen to stories of battle, even battles you lost."

"The nurses try to mask the taste with yogurt," a young voice was saying, somewhere in the dark. It whistled around a missing tooth. *"But medicine doesn't taste like strawberries, or vanilla. They're not fooling anyone. Mom fell asleep in the chair again."*

"Even the battles you lost are worthy," Bjorn said. "Winning doesn't make a warrior; trying to live does that."

"This is ghastly." Claire had her hands clenched to her stomach.

"This is human," Hero muttered, to his own surprise. Claire turned to look at him and he shrugged. "My story contained plenty of death. We all want our stories to mean something, or to at least be heard."

"Some last stories never are," Bjorn said.

"Lost. Town has to be over that hill. Has to be," a voice like hoarfrost muttered. *"Was cold but now getting warm, so warm…"*

"At least in a book, you know your last story will be told. It will be written down and lived, moment by moment, by every reader that comes along."

"To die over and over again," Claire sounded horrified.

"To live over and over again," Hero reminded her.

"They take the village. We run, and run, but they come again." An old woman's voice rang out. *"This time, I do not run."*

"Is everyone's last story here, in your wing? Is mine? Is—" Claire's breath caught so sharply that Hero had to glance her way. But she wasn't injured, not physically at least. "Is Leto here?"

"The wing holds stories, not the people themselves." Bjorn gestured to the miles of campfires around them. "Do you see any dead here?"

"We know where Leto's soul is. We saw him off," Hero murmured softly. "It's not here, Claire."

"But the tale and the teller are the same," Claire said with a feverish tone. "If Leto's story is here, then it's a sliver of his soul—"

"What did you say?" Bjorn interrupted sharply.

"The road is icy," grumbles one voice, as another whispers, *"Oh god, the turbulence."*

Hero was abruptly reminded of this mission, the point in coming here. He glanced at Claire, but she appeared still caught in the suffering idea of Leto. He shook his head and stole the stick from Bjorn to poke at the fire. "Right, didn't we mention? Stories have souls. Bit of a surprise to even me, really, being told all this time I was a bit of imagination and paper—"

"Myrrh," Bjorn muttered to himself.

"Myrrh," Hero affirmed. It was the code word previous librarians had used to index specific entries in the Librarian's Log. Specific entries that cataloged their joint efforts to unravel the secret that the Library was hiding, the reason for the Library itself. The Library didn't simply exist because the unwritten stories of humanity were important. The Library existed because stories were a part of humanity.

Souls.

"If that's true…" Bjorn's brows beetled together, and then he shook himself. "I spent six hundred years tryin' to puzzle that one out."

"Well, some of us are slower than others," Hero said generously. He knew what Bjorn was really asking. "There was a fire, when Andras made his move."

"Never liked him."

"You never liked me either. Even a broken clock is right twice a day." Hero grimaced and continued. "Books were destroyed in the fire. Or we thought they were, until a cistern of ink turned up. Unwritten ink."

"The books?" Bjorn's voice took on a gruff kind of wonder.

"The stories," Claire said weakly, though she appeared to be gathering herself. She wrapped her arms around her chest, as if trying to hold on to the heat from the campfire. "The souls of the stories. Souls are immortal things. They can't be destroyed by mere fire."

"Immortal and powerful, which makes them valuable to every creature of every realm without a soul." Hero tightened his grip on the bit of wood in his hand. "And the secret is out."

"Hell knows?" Bjorn ventured.

"I suspect at least Malphas does." Claire drew her shoulders up, but Hero knew the signs. Her eyes searched the dark, a constant roving. And the fingers of her left hand rubbed at the wrist of her right. That had been the tell of her nerves ever since the injury of the ink. "I think she knows, and she's trying to back the Library into a corner. So we gave her a feasible excuse to move against us. She's burned the Arcane Wing."

"You and your friends would have sanctuary here," Bjorn said softly, jamming his thumb in Hero's direction. "Even this idiot."

"Bjorn, I'm touched," Hero cooed.

Claire's laugh was so sudden and sour that it stopped them both. "You think she'll stop at the Unwritten Wing?" Her face was a twisted echo of misery. "Her ambition is greater than that, Bjorn. She's a demon, the ranking demon in Hell. She's not coming for the Unwritten Wing, old man. She's coming for the Library."

Bjorn straightened up from the fire at that. "What? No, the realms keep their own."

"Mind isn't what it used to be, by the end," a frustrated voice muttered to their right. *"The children wear each other's faces. It's not fair..."*

"It's not as if Hell doesn't have a history of meddling," Hero said dryly.

"She can't." Bjorn looked ready to dig his feet in. His beard jutted mulishly. "Lass can try, but 'tain't no one who can invade Valhalla."

"But the wings of the Library are not of Valhalla," Claire said gently.

"And are but merely hosted here," Hero finished.

"Valhalla protects its own," Bjorn insisted. He threw his hands up and took a step back from the fire.

"Yes, that must be why the wing is annexed here, out in the woods, behind a waterfall, in the dark." Hero stood as well, stretching his back as he made a dramatic turn toward the ocean of disembodied voices and fires in the dark.

"*I was a soldier once,*" a young man's voice said.

"We only survive if the Library works together, Bjorn. The Unwritten Wing needs its allies," Claire said. She hadn't risen, and to Hero's eyes she suddenly seemed to wear every single one of her years—lived and unlived—there by the fire. She stretched out her legs to allow the volume of her pants fabric to dry. She looked tired, and even knowing their goal, their plan, Hero faltered and wanted to go to her again.

"*Everyone's here, even little Jane...*" a voice like brittle paper whispered.

Bjorn shook his head as his shoulders hunched and crept toward his ears. He began to pace around their small circle of light. "No, lass, no. I'm sorry, it can't be done. The Library only exists in parts; it's for the best. We can't risk the safety of every wing for one. I want to help you, you know I do. I was in your place once—well, your past place. I'll put in the good word for you here, vouch for you with the longhouse. But to put all the Unwon at risk and join a resistance? Against Hell? My answer is no."

Claire turned wordlessly to Hero, and the absolute confidence in her gaze made his stomach flip, just for a moment. He made a show of straightening his courage and his jacket.

"You're certain, Bjorn?" Claire said, without removing her gaze from Hero.

To his credit, Bjorn at least did have the grace to sound regretful, perhaps even a bit ashamed. "Final answer, lass."

"I see. It seems we have just one small problem, however," Hero said, studying his toes, then purposefully raising his gaze beyond Claire, beyond Bjorn, far beyond to the blurry forest of shadows past his shoulder. "It was never you we were here to petition for aid."

An absence descended on the cavern with absolute quiet. It was an absence of thousands of voices, the ceaseless cirrostratus veil of whispers that had been crashing over them like a tide since they entered the wing. Each point of campfire burned steady, but it was as if the entire wing had taken a thoughtful breath.

Bjorn spun, uneasily trying to follow Hero's gaze into nothing. "What trickery are you up—"

"Souls of the Unwon Wing!" Hero clenched his hands in his pockets, where hopefully no one could see them shake. He wasn't sure what would happen next, but he only hoped his voice would not be remembered for wavering. He stepped fully away from the fire and felt the dark wrap around him with cold fingers. "I am not just a librarian; I am your brother—a story. You have heard our argument. The Unwritten Wing calls for aid; it's time for the Library to rise together. What do you say? Will you join us? Or will you allow Valhalla to protect you as you cling to your last story, here, in the dark?"

The air grew thick, thick enough that even the flames appeared to slow, churning through the dark to cast shadows thick as molasses. It sank into his lungs, making it hard to breathe. Bjorn was sputtering; Claire was saying something. Hero didn't dare glance over his shoulder, dare to check on Claire, or challenge Bjorn to interrupt. They were peripheral to this moment, spectators to the question mark that hung over the fate of the Library.

It hung, and it hung. A sword of Damocles would have been kinder. Hero trembled with the effort of holding still. This—it all started or ended with this. Either the wings would join together, starting with this one, or they would all fall alone. The Arcane Wing already had. The Unwritten would be next, and once the demons confirmed the souls in the books, their armies would turn ravenous. Every wing would fall. And the story would end, for good. All stories would end.

Would Hero end too? Caught as he was now, somewhere between the read and the reader? If so, was there a point to going on without a new story?

The fingertips that brushed at his wrist nearly sent Hero through his skin. And when his hands spasmed out of his pockets, an unseen set of fingers laced with his. It was not Claire's, for it was too cold. It wasn't Bjorn's—too soft. The gentle pressure of its grip grew more solid, and another unseen presence took Hero's other hand. He shifted, unable to really feel the forms of what gathered around him in the dark, but the warmth was that of a thousand fires. The strength of a thousand fires that had held back the night for eternity, and would do so again. Soft, solid hands rested, one by one, on his back, his shoulders. A whisper, one he'd heard before but softer now, repeated itself in the dark. *I was a soldier once…*

"Thank you." Hero's cheeks felt wet in the dark, though his skin had dried off long ago. He blinked furiously, unable to wipe his face. He took a ragged breath, staggered both by relief and by the enormity of what this meant he had to do next. "Thank you."

RAMI

I wish I were human, sometimes. Is it okay to admit that here?
Boss said the logs are private. But Boss also says the librarians
of the Unwritten Wing have to be human. There's never been
a nonhuman librarian of the Unwritten, not once. So what am
I doing here? I know the corps exiled me, but I thought at
least I could be useful.

Humans are weird in the best ways. They're brave and
contradictory and terrible and lovely. It would make sense
that something special like a human would be needed to
contain all the unwritten stories. I'm not *any* of those things.
Boss acts like I'm an inconvenience. I think she wishes I'd
leave. Says I don't know anything. But there's one thing I do
know: she's lonely.

I think I'll stay.

Assistant Librarian Brevity, 2007 CE

THE LAST THREE BOOKS on the cart were stymieing Rami. There
was no discernible reason why they should. They were not

particularly unruly books to classify. Two were literary works, the kind of unfinished navel-gazers with titles stolen from Shakespeare—it was always Shakespeare, Brevity confided to him once—and the third was a perfectly average urban fantasy featuring two brothers and a muscle car. But every time he picked up that volume it would take him into the depths of the fantasy collection and past the shelves where Hero's book should have resided.

It had been logical for Claire to accompany Hero to Valhalla. Hero represented the Unwritten Wing and could speak to the books; Claire had a previous friendship with Bjorn. Rami had only ever visited Valhalla as an interloper. He'd let them go with little objection. Still, it left him with an uneasy feeling. They were careful as they'd left, gentle even, a behavior even Rami had to admit was suspect in Claire and Hero. They were worried about him.

It was no secret that the others thought of Rami as the anchor of their group, the stabilizing influence of the Library. It was normally a role that Rami enjoyed. But it was an illusion. The Library was populated with *runners*. There was Hero, who took his running away literally, greasing the way with false bravado. There was Claire, who ran to the safety of books and processes when threatened. And Brevity's flight was the width of a smile, quick as a shadow behind her eyes.

Everyone forgot the fact that before Rami ran, he fell. Falling from a perfect Heaven was not something one forgets. And as Hero clutched the sleeve of Rami's coat, as Rami dangled above a great divine, the illusion of possibility that was there—that felt so *immediate* and there—he'd nearly fallen again. He'd been willing, for just a guilty moment, to abandon all he had for the possibility of something else. The yearning for home that ate in his chest. That feeling had steadily decreased since joining the Library, but the labyrinth had ripped the scab away. Heaven was nothing but an illusion to torture him now. Even the color of his feathers had fled out of reach. It had been his *choice*, a choice he would make again, every time, but that didn't mean it didn't still hit him like a slug in the gut.

Please. He heard Hero's voice in his head again. His hand stuttered over the book he was shelving. And there it was, a fact that was important and had been rolling around in his mind. Rami held on to it like a drowning man.

This time, when he fell, someone caught him.

The accompanying swoop in Rami's gut was disorienting enough to propel him away from the book cart. He started down an aisle picked at random. The formerly tidy stacks were clogged with new residents. Scrolls spilled from the upper shelves, catching randomly on vines that trailed and pooled into verdant tripping hazards on the floor.

He was forced to slow and pick his way—destination nowhere in particular—deeper into the stacks until he found himself at the mouth of a dim corridor.

It was one of the many crooked alcoves, doglegs of shelving that the Unwritten Wing seemed to sprout and move around at random. Gloom had settled over this particular stretch, as if the Library had neglected to take the lights in the last reshuffle.

Shadows danced at the far end of the aisle, thrown by something erratic flickering just around the corner. Rami approached slowly, not drawing his sword but giving the corner a wide arc as an old caution rose in his mind.

The sight of a campfire stopped him short. It could be nothing else: a little circle of rocks and a hut of tinder crackling quietly in the middle of the otherwise abandoned aisle. Fire didn't quite raise the instinctive terror in him that it did in other Library inhabitants, which allowed Rami to approach with caution. The hallway seemed abandoned, nothing else casting shadows on the rows of books besides himself.

"Hello?" His voice was clipped short by the shadows, seeming to be muffled the moment the words left his lips. It was different from the Library's usual silence. Rami cleared his throat and tried again, without response. He shook himself and approached to kick out the flames.

"*I told them,*" a small voice leaked out of the air. Rami spun, but his eyes told him he was still alone.

"Hello? Rosia, is that you?"

"*I told them, but I fucked it up. I fucked up everything.*" It was the thin voice of a teenager, sapling green timbre threatening to break under distress. "*Mom called it a sin. Said I was too young to know what I want, that they could fix me. Dad... Dad... he was silent. That was so much worse.*"

Rami fell to sudden silence. All angels could recognize the shattered edges of a confession.

"*Mom, she was talking about some church program, and Dad wouldn't look at me. He wouldn't look at me and I just... I ran. I don't know what I was thinking. Em lives three states away and I'm broke. It's snowing, and I'm cold. I can't go back. There are people passing on the street but no one will make eye contact. No one looks at me. Maybe I want to disappear. I... I'm sorry, Em.*"

The voice broke into soft, wet sounds, and faded. In the following silence, Rami could hear other whispers, other dead stories, hidden between the crackling of the campfire. Souls. Stories. This was another wing of the Library. Claire and Hero must be finding success in Valhalla. He put it together silently and took a slow breath before whispering into the fire, "Welcome home."

The whispers paused, and maybe a trick of the eyes made the fire appear to flame brighter, if only for a second. Rami retreated slowly, but he found himself reluctant to draw entirely away from the fire.

A watercolor memory came over him, fragile and muddled, of another teenager, in a cluttered bedroom. Perhaps it was the desperation in the ghost's voice that reminded Rami of Leto, the lost soul—and the Library's teenager turned demon—that he'd last seen departing for Heaven in the aftermath of the coup attempt on the Unwritten Wing. Leto had been haunted, and lost. He'd called himself broken. He'd been condemned to dark places but had still found his way to the Library and found the resources to draw his own path. Humans were like that. Building new connections. Stronger than any angel or demon or spirit, in that way. Put a human in darkness, and they'd start building a fire. If Rami was lost in the dark again, lost in the way he was before he came to the Library, he'd want a human to find him.

It had been a human that'd found him, now that he thought about it.

"Sir?" Rami started out of his thoughts and he realized with surprise that the fire had disappeared and the glow of the Library was at his back again. One of the damsels stood at the end of the aisle, hesitant to intrude. She cut a strong silhouette against the faerie lights—strong jaw and a warrior braid, wearing a rough weave like armor. Rami fumbled for a name.

"Katharina." Rami straightened, realized he was still holding a book in a death grip, and relaxed his hands enough to set it back down on the cart. He cleared his throat. "Can I help you?"

"Well…" The woman appeared to hesitate, then held up the square clutched in her hand. "It's my book."

As she approached, Rami could see the thread frayed from the top of the binding. Books were miraculously well-preserved in the Unwritten Wing, but the damsels had a tendency to carry theirs around, subject to the little daily wear and tear. No character liked having their book repaired, but they were generally responsible about reporting damage to the librarians. Which Rami was not. "Miss Brevity will be glad to take a look at it, I'm sure," he demurred.

"That's just it," Katharina said, fidgeting with her book. "I went looking for the librarian and I can't find her."

"Can't find…" A cold lump began to form in Rami's stomach. He shook his head. "Surely she's just in the back sections—"

"Brevity is not within the stacks of the Unwritten Wing." Rosia materialized at his elbow, and had Rami's hands not already been empty, he'd have dropped more books. She clasped her hands in front of her and had a grave look, which with her ghostly eyes felt quite literal. "The librarian has abandoned the Unwritten Wing."

2 2

BREVITY

Hell operates on forgetting, on fear. Fear can make mortals do the most terrible things; forgetting is what lets them live with it, and do it again.

But fear is present during the best things too. Ask any hero, and they'll tell you they were afraid. Fear is not antithetical to heroism.

It is the prerequisite.

Librarian Ibukun of Ise, 820 CE

BREVITY FELL LIKE A star.

Not bright or shooting like a star, no. She fell so long that the air rushing past her face chapped and turned her skin red. Until the air itself became an abrasive weapon she was being driven through. It numbed her body and her mind, so much that when she landed she barely felt the impact. Brevity pushed her cheek off cold stone and assessed. She wasn't injured—Hell would never make its tortures that easy. The crevice in which she'd landed was no more than a meter wide, barely enough room to kneel, let alone recline. The stone was smooth and bone white underneath her fingertips. She was at the bottom of an incalculably long shaft, the opening not even visible overhead, but instead of darkness, the stone was its own light.

Not a shadow to be found—or stepped through—anywhere.

The air was the nothing flavor of Hell. Anise and absence made it hard to breathe. Brevity tried to extend her arms but found the wall before she even got them halfway up. She was at the bottom of a long, long shaft dug into the foundations of Hell itself.

Hell is for forgetting, Malphas had said. And suddenly Brevity knew what this was, and she collapsed to the ground.

Malphas had left her in this oubliette with the expectation that Brevity's mind would torture her better than any demon ever could. Her thoughts could be a weapon used against her—Brevity already knew that. She'd spent hundreds of years understanding the dragon-like thoughts that surfaced from seemingly nowhere to gnaw on her mind relentlessly. Trapped and unmoored, Brevity's muse imagination would spin out her worst fears, and in an oubliette, where the skin of reality, unobserved and unremembered, rubbed thin, her fears would become reality.

Malphas might not even bother to return to pick up the pieces.

Brevity pressed her fingers against the stone until the tips went white. *Think.* No one knew she was here. Even if Rami suspected Malphas's hand, it wasn't as if they could find her here. Hell was vast and wide, and Brevity had no idea where forgotten things were consigned. No one was coming to rescue her. Brevity would never leave this hole in the earth.

Not unless she saved herself.

Her thoughts could be a weapon, it was the truth. But Brevity refused, desperately and completely refused, to accept that there wasn't a way to wield them. Her fears could become real here in the oubliette. Could her hope? Brevity squeezed her eyes closed.

For a while she tried to imagine her way out. She thought about a secret door in the stone in front of her, easily missed. She conjured up how the hidden seam would feel, smooth and dust crusted under her fingers. She imagined the grinding growl and hollow thunk as she slid the door back and light spilled out to a corridor that went... well, anywhere at all. She wanted to go back to the Library but didn't fancy the notion of imagining a shortcut from Malphas's torture chamber to the Library lobby. She'd settle for anywhere with shadows that she could use to shadowstep home, far, far away from here.

She envisioned and she thought, she imagined and yearned. She pushed every wish, every dream, every hope beyond hope, into the idea of a door. Then, eyes still closed, she reached forward until her fingertips found the wall and could run over the surface.

Nothing.

She opened her eyes to verify what she already knew. There was no door. Nothing but stone and the piercing light that splintered into her head like a migraine. She felt like an idiot. Hell didn't respond to positive emotions. Hope, dreams, survival— these worked in the Library, but they were alien matter to Hell.

The hope drained out of Brevity. She shoved her fist in her mouth to keep from whimpering. She would not cry, would not. Would not give Malphas the privilege of her fear.

Even Malphas isn't watching. This is an oubliette; you'll never be seen by anyone again. The soft dragon-thought slithered into her head and took up residence. It paused before it added, in a voice that was much like her own, *Maybe that's for the better.*

It wasn't that Brevity thought she was worthless—she knew by now what she contributed to the Library. But there was a tension in her that never left, the idea that failure was on a knife-edge. That it would be Brevity who slipped up and cost the Library everything. Being here, being forgotten, could almost be a *relief.* Maybe Malphas had done her a favor when she threw her in a hole, falling through the air so long that she fell beyond reach, beyond memory. She felt like she was still falling; she—

The stone beneath her knees trembled. It was so brief, so faint, that Brevity could have imagined it. But she'd already been preoccupied imagining falling and...

Oh.

Imagining the fall hadn't been a hope. It'd been fear, despair, guilt. Those weren't Library emotions. Those were Hell emotions, which had power here. Imagination had power both in the Library and in Hell; it was simply a matter of how you felt it. Brevity knew imagination. It was what she was made of—made for. The what-could-be was a tool, a weapon, specifically Brevity's own.

It was nearly impossible to force yourself to be *afraid* of something once you wanted it. How fortunate that Brevity was half-anxious all the time. She closed her eyes and considered the *possibility* that the stone beneath her knees was paper thin. Hell was old, and reveled in decay. It was feasible that the stone at the bottom of an oubliette cracked, weathered, crumbled away. Perhaps it sat, a spiderweb of cracks that held undisturbed for centuries, only for a muse to fall—at high velocity, oh so fast—all pointed elbows and the weight of guilt, and snap. And where would she fall through to? Who knew, but it was not here, and surely terrible—

The ground beneath her gave one last shiver that sent Brevity's pulse rabbiting up into her throat—and that was the fear that tipped it. A deafening crack rippled through the stone, and Brevity fell. She fell, once again. This time into the underside of Hell.

23

HERO

You can be done with a story, but that doesn't mean the story is done with you.

Librarian Bjorn the Bard, 1401 CE

THE WALK BACK—THROUGH THE dark, another soaking under the waterfall, and a miserable, soggy march through the woods and across the meadow back to the longhouse—was completed in terse silence. Bjorn was able to hold his peace until the final click of the door to his study closing behind them, at which point he calmly walked over to his desk, picked up his clay tankard, and hurled it at the fireplace.

It was mostly empty, so it only succeeded in making a terrible crash and scattering pottery shards over the front of the hearth. Bjorn was rightfully upset, and his accent got thicker and thicker with emotion until his words became simply a wall of heavily glottal fist shaking. He appeared not to be slowing down anytime soon. Hero found it easy enough to tune out the theatrics. His attention was on the fine furrow of thought lining Claire's forehead.

Something in the dark had flustered her back there. The Unwon Wing had unnerved her in ways that Hero hadn't thought the unflappable woman could be disquieted. Hero couldn't suss it out. Granted, going in, he had expected more of the masculine nonsense along the lines that Valhalla excelled in. He'd expected epics and ballads and war drums, bloodthirsty victory. But instead there'd been only the hollow echo of ends. Claire was dead; death shouldn't bother her. But she'd been different since the unwritten ink had stained her hand and haunted her mind. *Haunted*, yes… Hero was no writer, but that was the word for it. The unwritten stories had haunted Claire and left her not quite the same after the revelation that they were, indeed, souls. Claire had resisted that, though eventually Hero had learned to not take it personally. She'd said souls should be singular things, embedded in a body as is proper, then ascending (or descending, in Claire's case) to their eternal reward. She'd said she'd always envisioned them as generally filling up the same space and shape as a human body, just… ghostlike. Souls should not be splintered, many-faced things. Should not be sharded and scattered in many places at once. Souls should not be ghosts and songs and letters and stories.

But they were.

Considering that Hero was the one being redefined, he'd accepted it almost immediately. He'd never understood the fuss, souls and no souls. He'd always felt *human* enough, and if humans had souls, then why shouldn't he? But Claire had survived for three decades in Hell by clinging to a very rigid and precise categorization of the world. Every time that categorization defied her (Hero) or betrayed her (Andras), she struggled to change with it. Sometimes he caught a look in her eye as if *she* were the one with the fragmented soul. And the shards were sharp enough to draw blood.

"No right," Bjorn was saying. His face was red, scrawny muscles clenched. "You had no right to come in here and do that."

"It was my understanding that we were welcome in Valhalla—" Claire started to say, but Bjorn moved fast for an old coot.

"You lot had no right to stir up my wing." He had a finger in Claire's face before Hero could stop him. It took considerable restraint to not remove said finger from Bjorn's purview, but Hero supposed it would be counterproductive. Claire could stand on her own.

"Your wing?" Claire arched her brow. "Bjorn, I understood you were in Valhalla enjoying your rightful retirement."

"Librarians have a hard time retiring." Bjorn crossed his hairy arms with a pointed look. "You would know that as well as anyone, girl."

"Don't call me 'girl.'" Claire met his eyes for a long, cold moment before turning and beginning to busy herself with heating some water. Bjorn hadn't offered them tea, which was equal to a declaration of war to Claire. Hero made himself useful by poking around Bjorn's desk for tea leaves. "We weren't here to stir anything up, as you put it. We simply wished to speak to the…" Claire paused. "What do you call them—ghosts? Deaths?"

"Stories," Bjorn said grumpily. "Same as yours. Ends are stories too. Perhaps the most important kind."

Claire sniffed, frowning into a battered pot before filling it from a pitcher of water and setting it over the fire. "Not more of that soldierly rot about good ends and honorable deaths."

"I didn't hear many good ends in there," Hero added.

"It's not the winning that makes an end good." Bjorn had a pained look as he watched Claire take over his hearth, but he reserved the venom of his glare for Hero. Ah yes, there was the tea. Hero fished a small packet of paper out of the back and shoved the drawer closed with his hip. Bjorn slouched into a chair by the fire. "An end that feels right, that's all a story wants."

"No." Claire shook her head. "You tell a story, you promise a reader something. A story should deliver on that."

"Speaking as a..." Hero paused. "Speaking as a *me*, I think you're both full of rotten shit. Have we forgotten that we're talking about people's deaths here?"

The water in the pot began to boil and captured Claire's attention. Bjorn grumbled as he reluctantly heaved to his feet to begin rifling his office for a clean pair of cups. "It ain't right. You can't just walk in here and—"

"I believe," Hero said, as he moved out from behind Bjorn's desk, "I have every right. From the denizens of one wing to another."

There was a pronounced silence as Hero handed Claire the packet of tea. Her fingers lingered against his as she took it, and her mouth crooked up at one side. It was an apology for losing herself in the argument earlier. Or perhaps a thanks for calling her out on it. That appeared to be Hero and Claire's language of love, reminding each other not to be monsters. Or villains.

It was a wonder that Rami could put up with either of them. Claire busied herself with making tea, then obliquely inspecting the pile of scrolls left out on the end table. It was an odd reversal, having played Claire's backup often enough. But Hero was here as the librarian. The consultations of Valhalla's stories had shaken him, but this—this he could do. He returned his attention to Bjorn.

The Norseman still had an expression to curdle milk, but he appeared to be picking up the shards of clay with a singular intensity. Buying time. Hero cleared his throat. "Well?"

"I reckoned that I had a theory," Bjorn said slowly. He rested on his haunches and weighed a large shard of cup in the palm of his hand. "It's not like a clay pot, a soul. You realize that, right?"

"Well, I'd hope not," Hero said, as if he had any clue what the old man meant.

"A sliver of soul, a shard of soul, made of the same stuff... that's just awkward mortal words we clumsily try to slap on fancy immortal things we don't understand." Bjorn slipped the jagged curve of clay between his fingers like a claw and held it up. "You ain't this."

"Broken?" Hero supplied mildly.

"No!" Bjorn made a motion as if he intended to chuck the piece at him but changed his mind. He scowled and shook his head as he finished sweeping up the crockery. "A part, a missing piece. Not whole. Reuniting with your kin, even joining with your author, ain't going to put it back together again."

Air hitched in Hero's lungs. He'd met his author once. It felt like so long ago, the start of a very sad fairy tale. Isn't that how it went? Once upon a time, long ago and far away, a story had run away to find his author, the one person who could make him real and whole. Only she hadn't recognized him—she'd been attracted to him, of course, many were—but even after he'd awkwardly bared his soul to her, his creator, his maker, she hadn't seen him. Not as he'd wanted to be seen. It'd put him in an awful, vicious mood by the time Claire had hunted him down, and gotten them off on the wrong foot entirely.

And then, of course, his author, his maker, his other part of his soul, burned him out of his book.

"No, I suppose it won't," Hero said quietly.

Bjorn read his face and nodded. "Souls aren't fragments. She might have made you, you are made of the same stuff, but you're not her. Suppose it's more like a reflection. Or parents and children."

"Oh, bugger to that," Claire swore reverently from the hearth.

"Daddy issues?" Hero singsonged, though his voice felt like sandpaper. Yes, damn it, he would latch onto the first distraction that would allow him to flee from that memory.

"I wouldn't know—I've forgotten, I suppose because they're long dead. But judging from the depth of my displeasure at the concept, I'd say so." Claire shrugged. "But to the matter at hand, we've secured the support of the Unwon Wing, at least."

The tension in Bjorn's shoulders reasserted itself. He turned away and chucked the broken cup in a basket that must have operated as a trash bin. "Yeh had no right," he muttered again.

"The souls in your care have every right to choose." Hero was unsympathetic at whatever little bruised ego the Norseman was nursing.

"You can go with us," Claire said quietly, and obviously more sympathetic. "We're not trying to steal anything out from under you, Bjorn. You can go with us back to the Unwritten—"

Abruptly the bin basket slammed against the wall, showering bits of clay and discarded parchment at Bjorn's feet. His fists were white knuckled at his sides. He didn't turn, but Hero noted how his hunched shoulders heaved with deep, forced breaths. When he finally spoke, his voice was rough and deep as a rocky seabed. "What, in all of bloody brutal Midgard, makes you think I would want to go back?"

Claire had risen with the pot of water in hand but held very still. The only movement was the steam rising off the pot, curling and snaking around her like a halo. It was evident they'd stepped into unexpected territory by the caution in her voice. "You don't?"

"You're an idjit to ask that question." Bjorn twisted around. His eyes were rheumy and wet. He bunched his fists in his beard, as if to give them something nonviolent to do. "I spent over six centuries in that damned place. You've spent, what, thirty years? How sick are you of those same walls, girl? I learned every creak in every floorboard, every goddamn dusty corner—"

"The Library doesn't get dusty—" Hero said, and it really was a testament to Bjorn's restraint that the wreck of a man didn't slug him. The glare Bjorn sent him was violence enough.

"A mind ain't made for it!" Bjorn's voice was raised, shaking with a barely contained slurry of emotions Hero couldn't identify. "You die, think you'll get some sky-blasted rest, and they plop you in a dark, windowless tomb of a place in a damnation yeh didn't even believe in." Slow breathing had failed. Bjorn crossed his arms over his chest like a ward and tucked his chin. "You don't starve; you don't even need to piss—them powers that be think of everything except one. You can sure as hell go mad."

"You seem perfectly within your faculties to me," Claire objected.

"Mad ain't a destination, girl. Sanity is a journey that just goes on." Some of the anger drained out of Bjorn's wet eyes. He shook his head. "Maybe you're too early in yer tenure to understand that. You fall in a dark, deep place, you claw yourself out, hand over bleeding hand, but that don't mean you won't fall again."

"I… I understand a little of it." It was Claire's turn to look away. She set down the steaming pot of water, all thoughts of tea apparently forgotten. Hero could guess what thoughts crowded it out. Loneliness, temptation, and betrayal, and a handsome woman left behind in a faraway city. Claire's darkness had come early, and though she'd come so far, opened up so much, it never left. Standing in the light now just meant you cast long, deep shadows.

"I didn't stay in the Unwritten Wing; I survived it. Six hundred bloody years, and not even a good battle scar to show for it." Bjorn appeared to roughly draw himself together. His shoulders dropped, if only by force of will. He sniffed and lifted his head. "Forget how I died. That's my unwon battle right there. That place."

"I'm sorry," Claire said softly. She glanced at Hero, and he knew what she was asking. He nodded. "You don't have to come. I didn't want to do this without you, but I understand. We need the wing, but you—"

"—go where the story leads me," Bjorn said ruefully. "I'm a storyteller, Claire. Same as you. Don't matter what fancy titles they give or take away. You think I could stand not knowing how this plays out?"

"Are all humans this suicidally curious or just you two?" Hero asked.

Bjorn pivoted and jutted a finger in Hero's direction. "You! Don't think I've forgotten about you, you sapling. You are a librarian now. The cheek of you going over my head and talkin' to my charges. Talking to the stories! It ain't done! If Claire here ain't going to teach you right—"

"Brevity's his mentor, not me," Claire said.

"—then I'm gonna hammer some wits into you myself." Bjorn continued as if he hadn't heard her. He let out a long breath and glared at Hero another moment before turning back to his desk. He dug a ragged gunnysack out of a drawer and dropped it on the surface.

"You'll come with us, then?" Hero guessed.

"Seems like it," Bjorn answered as he grimly began to sort through the chaos of his shelves. "If you lot are dead set on starting a fight, you're going to need at least one good Norseman on your side."

Hero opened his mouth to argue that, but Claire stepped up and knocked his shoulder with hers. She shook her head, then smiled softly as the old man made quick work of his preparations. "Couldn't ask for better."

2 4

BREVITY

Humans love to make things complicated. Look at belief. They build whole morality and judgment systems on it—who believes what, believes in the right way, believes strongly enough. It's so unnecessary. Belief, when you get right down to it, is just a powerful story. Tell a story well, and the reader doesn't just want it to be true—they *know* it is. Get enough souls to believe in a story, and you can change the world.

Or make one.

Librarian Fleur Michael, 1763 CE

BREVITY FELL THROUGH SOLID stone.

She didn't break through. There was no crunch and snap of rock around her as she fell, simply a curious lack of wind. The stone didn't give way beneath her so much as it became less *real*. She fell through a phantasm of solid rock. Strata of countless eons blurred in front of her eyes, so dizzying that Brevity could only distantly wonder what Hell's geologic record could even be based on. Couldn't wonder about that, not now, because she had to focus on the terror of the fall.

Easy to do, as it wasn't ending anytime soon. Brevity's arms swam through the not-stone, trying to find some purchase to slow her descent, but there was nothing there. She was falling through the nothing underside of a realm. At least the oubliette had been a *place*. She had made a horrible mistake.

If anything, that thought increased her fall speed. It took a surprising moment to realize when the stone faded away entirely. A shot of wind, so cold it seared her skin, startled her to her senses. She fell through a cavernous space, but it felt solidly real. Brevity was suddenly not in the liminal underside of Hell but *somewhere*. Somewhere hidden deep in the foundations. And, to her shock, she wasn't alone.

Tiny black flecks roiled and frothed over the walls of the cavern in an infestation. It took another two minutes of falling to recognize those flecks were not insects but *demons*. Ranks of figures seethed along the walls of the cavern. Brevity had always known, technically, that Hell had armies. Malphas was a general after all. But to *see* it was something different. All of Hell's legions littered the staging ground of the giant space. Along one edge, coils of what Brevity first had mistaken for borders resolved into scales as things came into view. Wyrms, like the snakelike monster that Andras had rampaged into the Library with, writhed in frenzied nests. Dozens—hundreds?—of them.

Brevity let out a gasp. She was still falling, rushing through the air so impossibly high above the cavern floor that none of the demons should have heard her. But there was a single figure at a dais in the center of the space that jerked her head up.

Malphas.

"What are you doing out of your cage, little mouse?"

The voice was sinuous and purring inside Brevity's head. Below,

Malphas barked an order and a trio of winged lieutenants shoved off the ground. Brevity's heart leapt into her throat, but she was still falling toward the dark cavern floor below.

... *Dark* cavern floor.

There was no time to think it through. The space was huge, but that made the shadows cast by the lights below long and deep. They jumped up to meet her as Brevity reached out and threw herself into a step through the shadows.

BREVITY SKIDDED THROUGH THE shadows and into the light. She had just enough time to register a whirl of wood shelves and bright colors before she collided with something large and meaty. Said large, meaty thing said, "Ooof."

At some point during the panic, Brevity had screwed her eyes shut, and now it took a concerted effort to open them. The world resolved into the whirling red eyes and hideous face of Death itself, and she'd never been so relieved to see it. "Walter? It's..."

She wanted to ask if it was really him, if the jumbled clutter around them—it appeared Walter had caught her a second before she would have careened into a shelf of glass jars—was really the transport office. If she was really safe. But she wasn't sure she wanted to hear the answer.

"Miss Brev! What're you doin' blinking all willy-nill— Oh hey, shh there." Walter juggled her around in his arms until he could set her on the edge of a stool that was near the office counter. As the counter was made for Walter, Brevity's head barely came level with the wood top. "There, now. Easy does it. Yer shaking like a wee pup."

Was she? Brevity looked down with blank confusion at the tremors shivering through her hands. She was still staring at them when a giant-sized jacket dropped around her shoulders and Walter pressed a sloshing mug half-filled with hot liquid in her hands. "You look a fright, Miss Brevity, if you don't mind me saying."

The liquid in the mug wasn't dark enough to be tea. Brevity took a numb sip. Walter looked embarrassed. "I don't got anything proper like Miss Claire's tea, so I just heated some water quick. I heard hot things are comforting to mortals. Not that you're a mortal! I don't mean to—oh!"

To her own surprise, Brevity fell forward, mug and all, and began to sob. Walter caught her against his chest and patted her back awkwardly with a hand the size of a dinner plate. "I'm sorry, I always go an' say the wrong thing—"

"Walter, you..." Brevity sniffed against the rough fabric of his cobbled-together suit jacket. The mug was trapped between them and sloshed a wet spot on Walter's delightfully ugly tie. "You are the only right thing that happened today."

"There, there..." Walter eased her back to scrutinize her. Walter's face was not made for concern, and his bulbous features took on a constipated look. "What got you in such a state?"

The question welled tears in Brevity's eyes again. But before she could speak, an army of footsteps thundered down the steps to the transport office. Walter flailed as much as Brevity did, and somehow she ended up clutched to his chest like a shield as the gentle giant peered over her shoulder.

The first thing that emerged from the gloom of the stairwell was the glint of a blade. It was joined by a gun barrel, and then a thornbush of other weapons. The figures that crowded into the transport office's cramped space were bristling with weapons and fury. Walter was being invaded, and the force was *incredibly* hostile.

"You will take us to Hell's court, or else."

Brevity had been busy preparing to reach for a shadow again, but she stopped at the familiar ghostly lilt of that voice. "Rosia?"

"Librarian?" Rosia's impish face rose over the sights of a positively *monstrous* blunderbuss gun. The other damsels were equally armed. Brevity hadn't even been aware that the damsel suite contained such an arsenal, but here they were, fitted for war. And there, at the back, lighting the curls of the tops of the damsels' heads with holy fire, was a very familiar sword.

"Rami!" Brevity was too exhausted to be embarrassed that her face grew hot with tears again; to be embarrassed that Walter held her or that she half jumped, half crawled her way out of his arms and across the counter and landed on the other side with a *thud*, all while making quite pathetic sobbing sounds. She had been scared and had to pretend to be brave for so *long* and *she had been so, so scared*. She didn't care how she looked; she had made it home.

Rami, to his credit, immediately had his sword sheathed and stepped forward. He barely managed to catch Brevity as she plowed between the damsels and caught her in a hug. This one wasn't awkward, not like hugging Walter; this one was large and all-encompassing and *safe*, and oh, how very good it was to have an angel as a hugging friend. Brevity buried her face in his feathers.

"We couldn't find you," Rosia was saying calmly. The damsels appeared to be less bloodthirsty now that they'd found Brevity. They'd stopped pointing their weapons at Walter—Death! They'd been willing to fight Death? Brevity squelched a hysterical giggle—and they'd gathered around Brevity and Rami like a protective swarm. "We looked everywhere. We cannot lose our librarian. It is against the rules."

"I knew Hell had to be involved," Rami explained softly. His voice was a rumble through his chest under Brevity's chin. "I was going to come alone, but the ladies would not hear of it."

"She is our librarian," Rosia said simply.

Theirs. Brevity had people. People who would notice when she was gone, who would go looking for her, even to the point of challenging Hell itself, to make sure she was okay. The tears choked her again and Brevity covered her face with both hands.

"Hey. You're safe. You went ahead and saved yourself and you're safe now, shhh." Rami was right there, pulling her arms gently down. He wrapped her up in a hug again, safe and undemanding. "We were coming for you. We'll always come for you. You're home now."

And Brevity believed him.

2 5

CLAIRE

I would have thought that death would rid us of this classist buggery that humans are obsessed with.

I thought wrong.

Librarian Fleur Michael, 1733 CE

NOT BEING A CONDEMNED soul had its benefits. Freeing Bjorn to travel to Hell appeared to be a simple matter of him throwing open the door to the hall, settling up his tab at the bar—which appeared to consist entirely of favors and gossip—and, finally, giving up his place in the drum circle. They sent him off with a new fur cloak and a small keg of something potent. Valhalla seemed earnestly sad to see Bjorn go, and Claire managed to feel only a mild stab of envy at that observation.

A feathered riot greeted them as they exited the longhouse. The air was thick with ravens, wheeling and cursing in a frenzy. Claire clamped her hands over her ears and quickly located the focus of their ire. At the apex of the roof, one black bird, fatter and scruffier than the rest by far, roosted with a smug kind of calm.

"Bird," Claire grumbled.

"I confess I half expected your pet to abandon us here, myself." Hero's cheer diminished slightly when a questionable fluff of feathers and detritus caught on his hair. He had to duck to avoid the flight path of a particularly upset raven.

"That…" Bjorn said, flapping his hands irritably. He had to raise his voice over the screeching. "That is your transportation?"

"Our transportation," Claire corrected. Bird had begun industriously ripping at the bone-and-gristle wind chimes the ravens preferred. A knucklebone plinked at her feet and down the flight of steps. "Assuming Arlid's folk don't kill her first. What is the issue?"

Bird managed to rain down a whole section of trophies. Claire ducked back under the arches to avoid a particularly large string of jawbones, but a blur of feathers and teeth intercepted it. There was a jarring crunch as something hit the stairs.

"Traitors! Deviant!" A raven woman, indigo-black hair feathered into a Mohawk nearly as impressive as her eyeliner, rose from where she landed. She had the string of jawbones in one fist, which she shook like evidence at a trial. "Honorless scabs!"

"Hello to you as well, Arlid," Claire replied placidly.

"You." Arlid pointed her finger with an extraordinary amount of accusation. Arlid was prickly in the best of circumstances, but they appeared to have done something that genuinely aggrieved the raven guard. "I knew Valhalla should have fed you to the flock from the first."

"Then you'll be pleased to hear that we are now leaving and I doubt we'll have much cause to return to this realm again," Claire said evenly. "Now, if you'll just return us our bird and let us be on our way—"

"*You* brought the traitor here?" That appeared to be all the spark

Arlid needed to start up again. "Cowards! Milk drinker! Foul cheats!"

"Don't you mean 'fowl'?" Hero muttered under his breath.

Claire was usually immune to Hero's remarks, but it took some effort to suppress that one. She pursed her lips rather than smile. She exchanged looks with Bjorn, who just shrugged. The old man appeared entirely content to let Arlid verbally abuse Claire to her heart's content. Claire sighed. "I had wondered if Bird was one of yours."

"No." Arlid's kohled eyes narrowed and she clattered the jawbones against Claire's chest to emphasize the point. "That traitor is not one of ours. We exiled her, cast her out from the flock for her crimes." Her voice rose to a screech again. "Honorless!"

Even Arlid's human voice took on a cawing tenor when she was worked up. Claire winced and held up a hand. Bird appeared to take this as the signal to descend from her perch and land on Claire's shoulder with enough weight to make her stumble. It was, of course, the worst possible time for Claire to say, "I have no place nor allegiance in flock politics, as you continually remind me."

"If that were true," Arlid said, kohled eyes suddenly narrowing as she stepped back, "then you would have no problem handing over the traitor."

"I thought you said Bird was outcast."

"Yes, and the price for returning from an exile unforgiven is unpleasant." Arlid's smile was composed of sharp points and grudges. "Very unpleasant. Give her over to us, book people, and we will ferry you back to your realm."

If Bird was aware her future was being bartered, she didn't act like it. Her claws stabbed through Claire's thin shirt and her beak idly plucked and yanked through her hair as if looking for crumbs.

Hero tilted his head. "Tempting."

Claire couldn't deny it was. It wasn't as if Bird had ever shown any fondness for or fidelity to the rest of the Library. Claire had merely inherited one loud, messy, ill-tempered raven along with the rest of the Arcane Wing. It shrieked and bit and clawed and only halfway minded Claire when she had a biscuit in her hand. The idea of being able to return to a crumbless desk, to leave papers out without fear of torn and pecked edges, had definite appeal.

But then again, there was no returning to her desk. Her desk, her papers, any remaining place she'd had at all, had burned up with the rest of the Arcane Wing. Claire took responsibility for every artifact they'd lost, every way she'd let Malphas prove just how unsuitable Claire was for the job. All that remained of the Arcane Wing was Claire, Rami, and a dagger containing a demon.

And one very unlikable raven.

"Why hasn't she changed, like you do?" Claire gestured vaguely at Arlid's wicked human form.

"Because she can't. Not without the flock's forgiveness," Arlid said. "We do not forgive traitors, cowards, weak things. Will you hand her over?"

"I wish I could," Claire said ruefully. "You haven't even started in on the number of names I call this creature." Bird made a stab at her hair again, and Claire shrugged her off hard enough to unsettle the claws digging into her collarbone as Bird fluttered into the air. "I have no doubt she's just as terrible as you say and deserving of every unpleasant fate."

Arlid nodded. "Her crimes—"

"Are unimportant to me," Claire interrupted shortly. She raised her chin. "You say this dratted creature is an outcast. You say she's worthy of punishment and done the unthinkable. You say she's without home or honor. Is that correct?"

Arlid could smell a trap when one was nearby. Her expression turned sour even as she nodded slowly in agreement.

"Then I say that sounds like just one thing: mine." It was nonsense, it was stupid, it was absolutely picking a fight for no goddamned reason, but all that just sent a vicious thrill up her spine as Claire smiled. All teeth. She clicked her tongue, and for once Bird was biddable enough to sweep down and return to her shoulder. Her weight really was monstrous. "Hell—no, the Library—claims this horrible oversized and terrible goose as its own. Bird belongs to the Arcane Wing, what's left of it. We'll be taking her back with us, as is our right."

The ravens overhead had fallen strangely silent, and behind Arlid two more women dropped into being with a quiet rush of feathers. Arlid didn't look at her backup; she looked at Claire, long and hard. "We came to your aid when you needed it, ink girl. You would throw that away for a beast?"

"No," Claire said. "I have few allies in the world. I cherish the ones I have."

The point of Arlid's chin inched up, a pleased kind of justice. But Claire wasn't done.

"But an alliance that is based on rage and hate will eventually fail. It took me losing what I loved, twice, to understand that. We do not trade lives. Not anymore. I can't be your ally on this, Arlid. But I would like to still consider myself your friend. Hero?" Claire was relieved to hear the quick ring of a blade sliding free from its scabbard behind her. She smiled. "We're leaving now."

It was difficult to turn on your heel with the weight of a very large bird digging into your shoulder, but Claire managed to not stumble. She picked a random direction away from the longhouse and started walking, trusting Hero and Bjorn to follow. It was a long, tense moment when all she could hear was the grass crunching beneath her feet and the disgruntled click of Bird's beak in her ear. She half expected a counterattack, a raven or dagger in her back to take her down. But eventually only the sound of two sets of feet fell in behind her.

The lighter step lingered until they were clear of the rise, then sped up. Hero pulled up next to her with his sword resting jauntily against his shoulder. "Well, that was bracing."

"Don't start."

"I had no idea you were such a sentimental animal lover, Claire."

"I didn't—" Claire stopped in the middle of a denial and released a long sigh. Because she was never going to hear the end of it now. She shrugged Bird off her shoulder, and the raven gave only a mild cuss before launching itself in the air. "She is simply our ride home. I was being practical."

"Yes, practical." The corner of Hero's mouth quirked up in that irritating and irresistible way he had. "Any humanity is merely a coincidence. Funny how that always works out for you."

Claire refused to deign to respond. She cleared her throat. "Home, Bird. If you please."

"YOU SHOULD HAVE TOLD me it was your first time traveling the raven roads," Claire chided as she guided Bjorn's head between his knees. "I would have thought you had used them hundreds of times."

"Not all of us go gadding about like a mayfly," Bjorn mumbled, still wiping viscous bits from his beard. They'd arrived near the gargoyle, which Bjorn had promptly emptied the contents of his stomach onto. Claire still wasn't sure whether to blame the raven road or the gargoyle's disconcerting multidimensional nature. Bird had taken it as a personal offense and fled with a grackle of cussing.

Hero, ever fastidious, made the quick excuse to go acquire a towel. It was a pleasant surprise when he actually bothered to return, bringing towels and Brevity with him. "Bjorn! Oh hey, wow… I didn't know we could do that." Brevity took the towels from Hero and distributed one to the Viking and the gargoyle.

"The persistent glories of the human experience never cease to amaze," Hero said with distaste.

"The first trip is always the worst," Claire reminded him. "You should know that."

"A fair point." Hero tilted his head. "What did you see on the road, old man? You don't strike me as the angsty haunted type."

"Hero," Brevity whispered with a stricken look. "It's rude to ask."

"Is it? I had no idea."

"Get yer—hng." Bjorn coughed into his hand, still half-crouched. "Get your jollies in now, sure. See how funny it is when I—"

"Water?" Brevity produced a flask from one of her pockets. Bjorn looked at it dubiously before taking a swig. He smacked his lips with a grimace. "Water in a flask. Aye, this is Hell."

"I'm new here and even I know that joke gets old," Hero said. "So what did you see?"

Bjorn straightened with effort. He appeared to chew on his water a moment before deciding to answer. "Live on long enough after you die, and it isn't who you see, it's who you don't see."

"True enough, that." Claire made a shooing motion toward the Library doors. The hallway, with the way the lacquered floor dropped off into sudden nothingness, was deeply disquieting. "Perhaps Brevity…?"

"Let's get you settled." Brevity's eyes lingered warily on the empty hallway. There was a wounded air about her, though it was not the time to ask. Something had happened while they had been away. Claire took careful inventory as they walked into the Unwritten Wing, but it seemed as it always was.

"It's my job to welcome you, right," Brevity mumbled, appearing to shake off the lingering unease as they approached her desk. She always stood an inch straighter when reminded of her duties. It used to be a nervous habit, but her shoulders held a quiet line now. A steadiness. She was settling into her role as librarian.

Claire examined the way that observation dropped into the surface of her thoughts, alert for any ugly ripples. Not too long ago, the comparison would have stung, drawn up a poisonous muddle of regret and resentment. But like poison, those feelings had already done their damage and burned themselves out in the aftermath. Instead, she was pleasantly surprised to find her first thought was: *Attagirl.* A distant, not quite proprietary pride warmed her chest. Brevity was librarian, and she was a bloody good one.

Claire couldn't take the credit for that, but hell if she wasn't going to be proud anyway.

"If you need a bunk, there's a couch in the Gothic Retellings section." Brevity didn't notice the way Bjorn recoiled in horror. They headed through the doors, with Claire and Hero following behind. "Echo seems happy in her pond, but you'll want to meet her eventually. And your wing...?"

"They keep to their own. I doubt you'll even notice they're here." Bjorn tilted his head. "Unless the lights go out, of course."

Brevity managed to keep her reaction buttoned behind a perky smile. "Double the lights, then. Got it."

They reached the librarian's desk, and Brevity pulled out the log to record the events of Bjorn and the Unwon Wing, with minor murmurs of correction from Bjorn himself. Claire stood to the side and allowed her eyes to drop politely. Her gaze wandered across the expanse of the desk. The inkwell had changed, from brass embellishments to silver. There was a book with a persimmon cover stacked on the corner that Claire didn't recognize, and she ached to crane her neck to take in the title.

"I'll just... go start some tea." She turned without waiting for an answer and headed toward where she knew she'd find the tea cart near the door to the restorations room. It was a transparent excuse by now, but no one said anything to call her back.

Acid burned in her throat. But it wasn't jealousy; it wasn't, to Claire's surprise, even regret. No. Claire forced her hands to steady on top of the already warm teapot. It was a sense of place, or the lack of it. Claire had relinquished her hold on the Unwritten Wing and begun to make a home amid the creepy and bizarre residents of the Arcane. But now that, too, was gone. Her supposed place now existed as nothing more than a smear of ash on Hell's heel, and Claire wasn't certain what, exactly, was next.

Claire had to dig to find her favorite Ceylon, but Brevity had been too thoughtful to throw it out. She measured out the spoonfuls meditatively. It wasn't that she wasn't a librarian; it was that she was still *here*. She didn't have the Unwritten Wing, she didn't have the Arcane Wing, but Hell still had its hold on her. She was here. There had to be a reason.

But did there?

Claire's hands flinched and she took a moment to steady them before picking up the kettle. A reason. A plan. A fate. Claire didn't know if she really believed in those anymore. She'd barely believed when she was alive, and in her contrary way, her tenure in Hell had only released her from her remaining illusions about it all. Yet here she was fomenting a rebellion against the natural order itself. What use was an atheist in Hell, when you got right down to it?

Either she was useless, or she was free. Claire breathed in the
clay-metal smell as the tea steeped and contemplated that.
Useless or free. Claire felt as if she was neither. The tea turned
both dark and clear.

26

HERO

The hero's journey is a real sonovabitch, on that much we can agree.

Librarian Gregor Henry, 1974 CE

Oh, *fuck* Joseph Campbell!

Apprentice Librarian Brevity, 2013 CE

Brevity, please refrain from swearing in the log.
    … But yes, bugger the monomyth and all that tired nonsense.

Librarian Claire Hadley, 2013 CE

CLAIRE STAGED HER RETREAT to the tea cart, and Hero let her. He waited until she was at the far end of the giant lobby before turning and pinning his look on the others. "All right, what happened?"

"Something *else* went wrong?" Bjorn asked with weary resignation.

Brevity and Rami found spots on the floor in urgent need of examination.

Gods, this Library was full of terrible liars. Hero rubbed his temple a moment before snapping his fingers impatiently. "Rami scuffs his shoes like a schoolboy, and our dear librarian looks like someone kicked a puppy. Details, please. I'd rather stab whoever needs stabbing before Claire gets back."

"No one is stabbing anyone... already tried that," Rami said with censure. Hero just smiled.

"So there *was* a problem."

"Malphas," Brevity said in a mouse-small voice. She looked up with haunted eyes. "She caught me in a shadowstep."

"We got her out," Rami said hurriedly. "Well, she got herself out, but the damsels and I found her with Walter and brought her home."

"The damsels are a formidable lot," Hero agreed, reaching over to squeeze Rami's arm. One part reassurance for the angel, one part reassurance for Hero himself, that Rami was still in one piece. It had been a harrowing tale, when Brevity proceeded to tell it. They'd been lucky. One day their luck would surely run out. The thought settled like ice in Hero's stomach.

"Don't tell Claire," Brevity said, suddenly urgent. She leaned forward in her seat. "It was my own fault. She couldn't have stopped it. And it won't happen again."

"We'll see about that." Hero exchanged a glance with Rami. Hero was making a concerted effort at getting out of the business of secrets. Out of the villain business. But old habits were hard to shed. He saw how Brevity's brow crinkled. "But you're not telling me everything either."

"I... In the oubliette, I think I... saw something," Brevity said slowly. When Hero nodded, the story emerged in halted bursts from the two of them. Brevity's prison, Rami's rally, and a brief, vast glimpse of Hell on the move. The ice in Hero's stomach spread to his heart.

"Well…" He broke the ensuing silence with a sigh. "Nothing we didn't already know, I suppose."

"Shoulda stayed in Valhalla," Bjorn grumbled.

"There were so *many*," Brevity said in a small voice.

"And Malphas won't wait forever," Rami added. He had that old look on his face, the look Hero saw when he was remembering hundreds, even thousands of years in the past. Remembering the memories of Ramiel, Thunder of God, not Rami, the shabby Watcher of the Library. His arms were folded and his gaze was somewhere far away.

"How will it go?" Hero asked softly.

"She'll gather her resources—maybe even other allies—and then proceed. First to weaken, try to drive us out of the place we're most secure. Then she'll strike." His silver eyes were dark when they shifted attention back to Hero. "Decisively."

"Then…" Hero tapped his knuckles with one hand as he thought, rasping a thumb along the calluses. Calluses! Really, he would need to charm the damsels into sharing the alchemy of hand cream at this rate. "Then we shall just have to move faster. We have a plan after all." He stood, clapping his hands against his pant legs. They were, at least, dry now.

"You only just got back," Brevity said.

"So no one will notice if I am gone again. Tell Claire I'm working hard—No, Rami, I can do this on my own." Hero paused, looking between the doubtful faces before drawing a deep breath. "I think I… I have to."

"But—"

"Stick to the plan, remember?" Hero grabbed his jacket off the back of the chair and slid around the cluster of chairs. "I'll be back with friends. It will be a party!"

HERO'S JOB DIDN'T START and stop with just the Unwon Wing. Not until the Library was safe. He knew it as he walked through the doors of strange realms, whether under hospitality or under suspicious guard. He cursed it as he greeted the last remaining librarians and each one looked away from his steady gaze. He greeted them not as a book to a reader but as equals. The librarians had heard of him by now—"the broken book," they called him. But the books themselves, the souls of the Library, had a different name for him: the reader. The soul that let the stories of a million lost works flow through him, to be a conduit with the wisdom to release his own and become something more.

He greeted the librarians, but he was welcomed by the stories. He was embraced by them, recognized for what he was: free. And while the librarians fretted over requests and plans and risks and obligations, he made his true appeal to the souls of each wing. Because here's a secret only fractured souls know: we decide our stories. What happens to you is not the story. The plot is not the story, the conflict is not the story, the world is not the story.

The story is *you*. You, the character; you, the reader; and the liminal watercolor of magic that happens between those two. Love a story, hate a story, tire of a story, all the possible magic a story has is contained between those two immovable, unknowable forces.

Everything else—well, it matters. But this is another story.

His steps slowed in the paths between those final wings. The libraries that joined him should unite in the Unwritten Wing, but souls have never been that biddable. They clung to him, limned his hair with possibilities, dragged at the tilt of his shoulders. They stayed with him because he listened. He was the reader and he was the story and he was free. And stories walked with him.

Stories walked the breadth of the afterlife, they circled the empty places left by gods, and all the realms trembled in their wake.

The Unwritten Wing was quiet when he returned from his last—dear gods, let it be the last—trip. The souls of the Unsung Wing made a whistling sound as they swept past him to roost, like invisible birds, among the rafters. Brevity had already intercepted the highly irate librarian, and Hero all but stumbled to the nearest couch.

He'd just closed his eyes when he heard a floorboard creak and recognized the weighty footstep behind it.

He cracked open his eyes. "Here to punish me, warden?"

"I'm not in the habit of punishing people for efficiency." Claire stood with her hands clasped in front of her, as if she wasn't quite sure what to do with them as she gazed at the overstuffed shelves. "You've been… efficient."

The Library hummed with stories—no, it *vibrated* with souls. The air tasted of anise and cardamom and *possibility*, ionized with all the wide wondrous space of what-ifs in between. It was glorious and mildly terrifying, and if Hero had been less exhausted he would have been smug.

Instead, he settled for dragging his feet off the couch with no small amount of effort. He fluttered a hand. "Sit, Claire. I feel like I'm being scolded when you stand like that."

"I'm sure you did something worth scolding." Claire took a seat nonetheless. She smoothed her trousers. "All of them?" she asked.

"All of them." Hero closed his eyes again. "Every damned last one."

"Not—" Claire stopped with pressed lips, as if dismissing whatever she had been about to say. She let out a breath. "It's never been done before. The Library has never been under the same roof, sharing the same fate. Not in any histories I've found, at least. One wonders if there wasn't maybe a reason for that."

"Second thoughts? Too late. I've already given you a rebellion for a present. I shan't go shopping again," Hero said with a dismissive air. He slitted open his eyes to watch her. She was a shadow against the lamplight, shivering and not quite distinct. She was... softer like this. He had thought he preferred Claire bold, but perhaps he simply preferred whatever parcel of Claire she let him have. "We can hold it, warden," he said softly. "We can hold the Library and keep it. Poppaea may have never managed it, but we *have*. You've made me believe that."

"Poppaea may not have gathered the Library, but she alludes to having worked out the issue of a god and realm somehow." Claire shook her head. "We haven't."

"Just give me a nap and I'll take a crack at that shambling minotaur again. Last time he just caught me off guard."

"No." Claire chuckled. "That realm has never been good for any of us."

"Then I'll find another. Valhalla! I'll duel the bloody Vikings one by one till they hand it over."

Hero's eyes had been drifting closed with each word, but they pulled open again at the soft, oddly charming giggle that escaped Claire. She covered her mouth as if it surprised her. "You would, wouldn't you?" she said wonderingly. She hesitantly touched his hand. "You really would."

Hero held her gaze in the low light. "I would."

The moment hung, soft as a hush, there over the couch. The Library might have been full to bursting with souls, but for one moment, this story, this, was world enough for him. Claire's mouth opened on a thought, then closed again. Her tongue flicked out and she looked away as she licked her lips nervously. Oh yes, Hero was lost. He'd always been lost with all these fools.

"I'm afraid." Claire's voice was low, as if she regretted breaking the silence. "Afraid that I've brought all the Library here just to destroy it entirely. We have no idea where to find a god, let alone a guide or a realm."

Hero didn't want a god, or a guide, or even a realm. He wanted more. He *wanted*. He was written that way and it was the one thing that *hadn't* changed. He was full of wants. Wanted to shrug off the exhaustion of a dozen realms and leap off the couch. Wanted to finally cradle her face between his hands, to look at her and kiss her until she believed. Or else drag her off with Rami so he could show her that she was the only god—goddess? oh, how Claire would *hate* to be called a goddess—the world needed. That they needed. He wanted. And because he was a villain, he could have so much and *still* want all he'd been told he couldn't have.

Instead, Hero squeezed her hand, just once. "We'll find one. If I know you, you'll dig up some dusty book of some forgotten god that gives his home address." Hero shrugged. "Or a recipe to make one."

That was finally an absurdity that broke the caul of despair off Claire's face. She snorted, which turned into a laugh, and Hero watched the way light played like a hymn across her skin.

27

CLAIRE

There are twelve wings of the Library, in twelve afterlife realms. You'll find a list in the appendix of this log—it is our responsibility to make sure it is updated when we hear of changes to our colleagues' ranks. There are twelve wings of the Library, but as you'll soon find out, each wing is as unique as the collections it carries. Do not expect logic from Duat, for example, nor empathy from Xiabala's curator. You should know your colleagues, but don't become overly familiar.

Ultimately, every wing of the Library will have to tell its own tale.

Librarian Ibukun of Ise, 821 CE

HERO HAD BEEN THOROUGH at his job of bringing the other wings of the Library into the fold, and each librarian had, of course, come with the infinite wing in their care. The result had become a maelstrom of creation. The Unwritten Wing was overflowing with strange new stories, and the librarians gathered, uneasy as storm clouds. The Library had always been the Library, single but separate. Each librarian had their wing and their charge; that was all. Other wings were heard of merely as theoretical entities, as even the interworld loan did not require librarian intervention. Still, all of them had heard the tales of the Unwritten Wing. Some regarded it with suspicion, others pity or respect.

And now they were here. Claire absorbed the tableau from her seat near Brevity's desk. Librarians were of every shape and shade. The gathered group—twelve in all, counting Brevity—represented the spectrum. The majority were humans, like Claire, but there were other spirits besides Brevity and Echo. A man with an ibis head came with Duat's wing, and one librarian appeared to be some kind of shape-shifter that was currently a bespectacled orangutan. Claire couldn't fathom a guess of what wing that one was attached to. At least he made a proper cup of tea.

The Unwritten Wing, already invaded by vines and letters of the Unsaid, now had to make room for the whole of humanity. The contents of a dozen wings crowded a single space, and the entire wing had begun to shiver with an unreal quality. Books and art, poems and poets, fans and phantoms, crowded the space. The air was thick with dust and webs of dreams. Words and whispers and weaves warred for territory. Between the nearest stacks of books a wandering song seeped down, thick like golden honey.

The librarians had sequestered themselves in a far corner of the wing's lobby, somehow beating out vines and craftwork and sentient poetry by force of will alone. Brevity had procured a mismatched set of chairs and arranged it around a study table that was not quite large enough for the task. The work surface was scarred with centuries of inkblots, repair nicks, and phantom rings from countless careless teacups. The librarians were, inevitably, a fractious bunch. The wisp-like librarian from the Tantarus refused to keep her feet off the table, even when Sheol's librarian, a dour golem named Anik, threatened to pull her off by her hair. Jannah's librarian was an academic swathed in brightly colored robes that positively could not keep the peace with Xi, the inkblot from Xian's Unlearned Wing. Nour, the librarian from Duat's Poetry Wing, carried a smoking pipe, and occasional wreaths of heather fogged around their stork head, painting the entire scene in a dreamlike haze that left the taste of dates on the tongue. Xibala's librarian appeared to be drinking a chalice of mist. It felt more like a mad tea party than a conference.

"So the way I see it, the best chance of survival we've got is to stick together." Brevity was outlining, for the tenth time, the events that had brought them to this unprecedented, crowded place. Claire studiously tuned it out, not needing to hear a retelling of the destruction of the Arcane Wing. Or her many failures before that: the ink, Andras, the list went on.

It was easier, instead, to study the librarians' reactions to the news. Bjorn had heard it before, and instead intently sipped from his mug—tea? coffee? mead? the contents were uncertain at this distance—with a focus he usually reserved only for ale. The trio of spirits looked bored, but then, nonhuman librarians were always an unreadable bunch. The curators who had once been flesh and blood varied. Jannah's young man, with skin several shades richer than Claire's, took notes intensely in a small notebook. The scholar next to him—Indralok, maybe?—was folded in so many layers of ink-blotted fabric that the only distinguishing feature was the deep, growing furrow of their thin eyebrows.

"We all appreciate the efforts of the Unwritten Wing and understand the threat. However, I would like to discuss alternatives to your plan." A woman older than Claire, with laugh lines highlighting her plump cheeks and a pencil stuck in the twists of her curly silver hair, cleared her throat as she spoke up. Claire tried to place her, using what she knew of the other Library wings. Summerlands, maybe. She could recall some wing there relating to verse. She'd never bothered herself with much thought for the other wings, as librarian. Perhaps if she had, none of them would be in the room now.

Brevity hesitated. "There's so much to do—"

"The Unwritten Wing can't expect to be made de facto leader," Nour objected. They puffed at a reed pipe. "There are procedures for this form of congress."

"Procedures?" Brevity echoed with a crestfallen expression.

It was inevitable; it was exhausting. Claire knew the arguments were a reflexive demonstration of rhetoric. The wings of the Library would ally with one another, if only because they had no other choice. But Claire also saw the hard truth under the skin and sinew of philosophical debate; the other librarians were not Hell's librarians. The majority tended to wings in paradises, or realms of neutral enough morality to be benign. Few had curatorship over artifacts that resisted them; none had ever learned how to fight, every moment, in a realm covetous of their existence. They would ally, but it would be Hell's librarians doing the heavy lifting.

Well, Hell's librarian, and Claire. If Claire was no longer an official librarian, then she wasn't obliged to form a consensus with the table of scholars. She withdrew by inches, waiting until Brevity was involved in a passionate debate with the Duat librarian before slipping away. It was an easy thing to drift to the wall of card catalog drawers. She'd hidden it under "TIGERS; origin stories." She emptied the drawer of its hidden contents and turned for the open arms of the stacks.

She felt eyes on her as she passed the table. Let them think she was a disgraced librarian; let them think she was a traitor or, worse, an idiot. There was more to libraries than keeping books; there was community outreach. Libraries needed allies, and Claire knew just the devil they needed.

2 8

RAMI

SCRAWLED AND UNDERLINED WITH A HEAVY HAND, A
STAND-ALONE ENTRY:

Demons!!

Librarian Ibukun of Ise, 983 CE

I agree with this sentiment entirely.

Librarian Yoon Ji-Han, 1809 CE

IN RAMI'S EXPERIENCE—HIS VERY lengthy experience—any building develops a personality over time. The Library in Hell was no different. Not a soul, not precisely; that was too loaded a term for any era. But anything was capable of a little sentience if shown enough time and love and hate. Rami had observed how the Unwritten Wing glimmered when Brevity was delighted, or how the Arcane Wing struggled to polish up its gothic edges to meet Claire's standards. How even when it had been burning to ashes around them, the Arcane Wing had delivered its curator to safety.

Libraries and their stewards existed in a confounding equilibrium that was strange even for the vast wonders of the afterlife. Which was why, when the shelves appeared to sigh dust motes into the air without moving, when a book fell off its stack of its own volition, when the Unwritten Wing appeared to stir, just slightly, around him, Rami's gaze went first to Brevity, then to Claire.

Brevity remained pinned behind the librarian's desk, deep in what appeared to be a lengthy explanation of interactive narratives to a rather disapproving pile of robes.

Claire was skulking away from the card catalog. That would be Rami's cue.

He caught sight of her near the Gothics section. (A brass plate helpfully indicated: SUBGENRE: GOTHIC ANTIHEROES. Someone had crossed it out on the plate and scribbled in "assholes" below it.) He followed her for a long way, farther into the stacks than he'd had cause to go in a while. When he realized where she was going, he sped up.

She barely slowed down when he fell in line. Rami had no difficulty keeping up, and asked with the mildest interest, "What is your plan, then?"

They approached a shuttered section. Claire barely slowed to throw open the barrier and step through. The smell of smoke and tarred remains of books remained in this aisle. The section where Claire's books had been housed, and where Andras had burned them. Even the Library carried scars.

Her chin inched up and he could practically see the denial brewing, so he added, "It's me, Claire."

He stopped. It was a considered gesture. Once Claire would have barreled on, glad to be rid of any pesky help, but once was not now. Claire's momentum carried her a couple of steps to the end of the aisle before she stuttered to a stop. She appeared to debate something to herself before turning.

"I'm going to release Andras," she said with a steeled kind of calm.

He could see the item she carried in her hand now. Recognized the wicked curve of blade beneath a heavy wrap of linen and leather. Andras's dagger, the weapon made a prison when the Library had bound him into it. He regretted, again, not chucking it into the void between realms when he had the chance.

"Why, in all Heaven and Hell, would you do that?" he asked, begging for an answer. That was the maddening thing about Claire; she always had one.

"The Arcane Wing is lost; the librarians will talk themselves to death before deciding on a course of action—believe me, I know. Our best hope for a vacant realm is gone. And all the while, Malphas simply cinches the noose tighter and waits for us to strangle ourselves with it."

"You think inviting a demon who tried to kill us all into that mix will somehow make that better?"

"I think it may be the only thing that can," Claire said quietly, too quietly. "Even if we succeed, even if we unite the libraries and find a realm and find a spare god wandering around and figure out what the hell a gatekeeper is…" She caught her hand trembling and gripped a fist over top of it. "Even if we do all that, we are still left with a war with Hell, a realm that will not let us go without a fight. I'm tired of fighting, so tired of fighting, aren't you?"

"Despair is no option," Rami said quietly. "Not for us."

"No." Claire's fragile calm shattered with a sudden laugh. "Would that it were. No, despair is not our business here. But fighting dirty and calling in a ringer is."

"Andras would destroy us all."

"Not," Claire said calmly, "if I promise to give him exactly what he wants."

Andras had wanted the Unwritten Wing, all the restless, malleable souls of stories he could devour and trade to fuel his own vendetta against Hell. He'd been willing to sell out the Library for it, to sell out Claire for it. Rami knew, because he'd been the angel Andras had tried to sell them to.

He hadn't taken the deal; Uriel had.

But Claire wouldn't give Andras the Library. Rami had come too far to believe that. She'd been willing to risk total obliteration rather than give up the Unwritten Wing.

Claire held herself taut, as if preparing for a blow. She expected Rami to think the worst of her, because she had been honed to accept the worst of everyone else. She was a cynic, their Claire.

But despite that cynicism, she'd told him anyway. She would see this story through, damn the expectations, damn the cost. That—that was why Rami had followed the strange dead woman literally into Hell. She flinched when he let out a long breath. "I don't like this. Surely we can find some other way."

Claire nodded, and for a moment Rami clutched at relief. Yes, she understood. Yes, she had not lost her senses. Yes, there was an alternate solution to the problem at hand.

But then he remembered that agreement had never meant compliance in Claire's worldview.

Her wrist twitched into a wide arc. She let go of the dagger and sent it hurtling to the burnt floor with all her strength. Rami supposed such abuse wouldn't have dented a sturdy dagger in the mortal world; physics and metal alloy would have prevailed. But in the afterlife, intention was more powerful than gravity. The blade hit the floorboard hilt first, and the stone eye set into the grip shattered. Fragments of the tiger-stripe jewel turned to brown and amber stardust in midair, clearly rising from the ash that littered the floor. The floorboards beneath their feet groaned in something like a scream.

The ghost of soot and kerosene that had hung in the air sweetened into a sharp, invasive bouquet of anise and iron. What little light remained in the burnt annex seemed to dip, then swell, painting shadows on Claire's resigned face. She was no longer looking at Rami, all her attention focused on the gemstone dust that swirled at their feet. If he'd wanted, she'd left him a wide-open avenue to strike, to at least disable her and drag her away from the maelstrom building in front of them. She might have even thanked him for it.

But Rami had watched Claire grow from a woman who ruthlessly smothered and hid from her demons to a woman willing to walk through fire to save one for a cause she found worthy.

The whirlwind had picked up; metallic fragments started to coalesce into the outline of something human. Or something that pretended to be. Starbursts shuddered where fragments collided and stuck, gradually building mass. The ambient light swelled. Each piece of glittering dust appeared to cast a shadow, and it was from that shadow that something new stepped into the wing.

Rami kept his sword drawn and directed it at the demon in his view.

A well-heeled dress shoe, polished to a void black sheen, stepped out of the shadows, followed by impeccably tailored trousers and an expensive vest and coat just slightly too extravagant to look old-fashioned. The demon that stepped into the annex was not much taller than Claire, and gray and narrow with a scholarly air. But he pulsed with a vitalness that was at odds with the soot and decay surrounding him. A gaze the color of spoiled gold took in his new surroundings, and Andras tilted his chin as if amused.

"Hello, pup," he said.

"Andras." Claire drew still and tall. A chill whispered over Rami's spine. Like this, cold and resolved and ready, she reminded Rami of something eternal. It was, in Rami's most private thoughts, something sacred. The comparison was so apt that it was a sin he couldn't feel sorry for. Claire's ice cracked. "You are intelligent enough to not do anything foolish, yes?"

"I wouldn't say that. I did move against you. That didn't prove to be a wise investment." Andras inclined his head with a paternal look that sent Rami's skin crawling. "But I have wits enough about me to not confront a Watcher unarmed. How long has it been?"

"A little over a year, by the mortal clock," Claire said. "Not nearly long enough."

"A year?" Andras removed imaginary dust from his cuff as he surveyed the ruinous aisle of ash. "I thought you would have tidied up more in that time."

Some things are not so easily fixed, Rami thought. But Claire was wise enough not to grant Andras that indication of power. She inclined her head. "I prefer to preserve it. You never know when rubbish will be useful in the future."

"Did you just call me trash, pup?" A delighted laugh sounded wrong as a rusted hinge coming from Andras. "Oh, Claire, I have missed you."

"How curious that I have not," Claire deadpanned. She made an impatient gesture. "If your curiosity is satisfied, I am here to make you an offer."

"My curiosity is never satisfied—where would the entertainment be in that? But do go on."

"I have trapped your soul in a device of your own making, Andras. I need not explain to you how it works. This is not a negotiation.

Should you turn down my offer—or even consider the thought of betraying me again—I can blink and lock you right back in."

"Is that any way to treat an old friend?"

"I really couldn't care less."

"Now, that's not true."

"Perhaps not," Claire said. "In fact I care a great deal. If I had my care, you'd have been handed over to suffer the eternal suffering of Malphas's idea of justice long ago. I'd want to watch you suffer, but I know suffering is what demons enjoy most, so instead I would want to watch you flail. Helplessness, Andras, is what I would wish upon you. A complete and utter helplessness and a failing of power that strikes what you cherish the most. A scenario where you gain ambitions only to watch them be ripped away from you, piece by piece, with the thorough knowledge that nothing you can ever do will ever change the outcome. That is the hell I would wish on you, Andras."

Andras was quiet for a long moment. "Oh, pup." He finally drew in an emotional breath. "You make me so proud."

The muscle in Claire's jaw twitched, and Rami thought he might have to intercede. But as ever, Claire marshaled her will. She smoothed her hand over her hips, as if straightening the skirts she no longer wore. "But I will go on unsatisfied in that desire, provided you and I come to an agreement faithfully."

"Why in the world would we do that?" Andras was entirely amused now. He sauntered forward a step and had to be reminded of Rami's presence when he raised his sword to stop him short. "And whyever would you trust me again?"

"I won't. But I'll settle for a reasonable confidence in your behavior," Claire said, unmoving. She met Andras's eyes. "Because only I am able to give you exactly what you want."

"Claire." The warning escaped Rami before he could stop it. No. This was too much. Claire was clever, but Claire was mortal. Rami, above all, knew there was absolutely no dealing with a devil. "You can't do this."

"Would you stop me?" Claire carelessly turned her attention from Andras to Rami. When she did so, she flinched, then stowed it away swiftly. Rami realized he'd tilted the tip of his sword toward her. Aghast, he pointed it at Andras again.

"That's not what I mean. You can't strike a deal with one of his kind."

"Mark that we are made of the same material, Watcher. If mine is a little more honest about it." Andras watched the exchange, amused. "Any perfidious capacity is in you as well."

"Demon," Rami growled. Claire stayed him with a touch at his elbow.

"I know what we are all capable of, sinner and saint. And, more important, I know what you want."

This last statement caught Andras's attention. "Do you, now?"

"I do, and it is in my power to grant, if we can reach an accord."

"And how do you propose we do that? I, after all, am not the one threatening imprisonment despite claims of good faith."

"A simple trade. You help me secure court approval for the Library's independence, and I help you secure your heart's desire."

"Which is? I regret to inform you my aspirations are no longer set on the Unwritten Wing, dear."

"Regaining your rightful place in Hell's court." Claire paused, as if to savor the surprised silence, before smiling thinly at her former mentor. "You were a count of some kind, if I recall?"

"Duke," Andras corrected coldly.

"Oh, duke, that's right." Claire's thin smile waxed into something confident. "But you were cast out in a bout of normal demonic politics. You thought you could buy your way back into favor if you deposed me and could offer the books of the Unwritten Wing in return."

"But he failed," Rami said, just to see Andras's frown deepen.

"But you failed," Claire agreed. She lifted her shoulders in a dismissive shrug. "Not the first to try to burn a library in pursuit of power or politics. It's practically human of you, old man."

"Don't insult me, pup." Barely contained disdain twitched at Andras's nose.

"I wouldn't dream of it. But the fact remains that instead of returning to court you have been imprisoned in a knife of your own making. Malphas knows, by the way."

Again, Andras's nostrils twitched at that.

Claire smiled. "She was dearly interested in getting her hands on you. I am the only reason she didn't."

"You expect me to be grateful?"

"No, I expect you to be curious." Claire crossed her arms. "If I can protect a miserable traitor from the all-powerful general of Hell, what else can I do to affect the demonic court?"

Andras opened his mouth, then reared back with the impact of a thought. "If you expect me to believe you can reinstate me in court, you must be desperate. You can't."

"I am confident that I can," Claire said levelly. "In fact, I have a plan that would do precisely that. If, and only if, you help me preserve the Library from Malphas's machinations."

"And what is the other option, Claire? Else you'll bottle me up in the dagger?" He cast a disdainful look at the shattered gem at his feet and stepped over the detritus. He stalked, leisurely, toward Claire. "The books don't rise to your beck and call anymore. You may not find it so easy a second time around."

"I agree. So much easier to just let Rami strike down a threat."

"How pedestrian," Andras murmured. He turned on his heel, sharp and fearless, and fast enough to make Rami brace his grip on his sword. "Is that what you're here for, then? Decide to trade one loveless object of worship for another?"

"You wouldn't know anything of love," Rami growled between clenched teeth.

"I have the capacity to know just as much as you." Andras paid no mind as a blue flame formed on the sword and began to dance along the killing edge. "We're the same, you and I. Our differences are merely a matter of context."

"Choice. I remained true; you didn't."

"Did you? Is that how you find yourself in Hell's service?"

"I serve the Library, not Hell."

"What fine distinctions you cut." Andras lazily dropped his gaze to the sword tip. "It must be a relief, to exercise your darkest rage and call it justice."

Rami gathered himself, the blade in his hand steady. "You will not bait me."

"Won't I?" Andras said mildly. "A shame." He appeared to dismiss Rami in a glance and turn his attention to Claire. Escaping his regard was like the relief of a cold edge of metal leaving your skin.

If Claire felt it, she showed no sign. But Rami could detect the tension in her eyes, the coil of plans and desperate contingencies she didn't want to spring. She affected a bored sigh. "If you are done picking fights, Andras, I really do have other business to attend to."

"More important than me? I am intrigued." Andras could change his demeanor with a whiplash precision. His snarl faded into a scholarly interest swiftly. "I don't doubt your intelligence, my dear. But if you have summoned me because you need my expertise with the courts, I fail to see how you can promise anything I haven't been able to gain for myself."

"Malphas knows we are trapped. She intends for me to barter dearly for the Library. You are just a bargaining chip I can slide into the pile when she's not expecting it. Besides, I've surprised you once already." Claire lifted her shoulders with a casual dismissal. "Are you certain I couldn't do it again?"

The silence answered her question. Andras's gaze sharpened as he ran inward calculations, infernal odds. After a drawn moment, he nodded. "I may be willing to play your game out. But I want a security."

Claire's eyes narrowed. "You have no position to make demands, Andras."

"Yet I have nothing to lose. If I refuse your deal, you're still going to have to deal with me and the hassle of containing me again." His fingertips flicked at Rami without looking at him. "I promise I can make that quite a task. You don't need another distraction right now, hmm?"

Claire's lips thinned. "What do you want?"

"I help you, you regain my standing in Hell's courts. I lack your confidence in your ability to deliver. So." Andras drew out his words, lining them up like dominos. "If you fail, I want something else I know you can deliver."

"For gods' sakes, Andras, just spit it out."

"If you fail to deliver my return to court," Andras said, "you forfeit your soul instead. To me."

"My soul is already tied here, to the Library. I have never had a say in my fate."

Andras smiled. "Let me worry about the paperwork."

"You're no match for Lucifer."

A horrific scraping sound escaped Andras. Rami realized with a dawning terror that it was a giggle. Demons were not made to giggle. "Lucifer? That's a name I haven't heard in ages. Oh, Claire, how I've missed you. There's so little you understand about the realms you inhabit."

Claire was too proud to ask it, so Rami asked for her. "What does that mean, demon?"

"It means you're right: you do need my help more than you know." Andras tugged at his tailored sleeve and removed an imagined speck of lint. His cool gaze slid to Claire.

The charred floorboards creaked as she shifted, and it sounded like a warning. "I agree to your terms."

It felt as if the Library itself flickered. Rami felt as if he'd been punched. "Claire!"

"It's not as if it matters." She crossed her arms as if suddenly chilled. "My plan will work, and Andras will have his infernal playmates back. And if it should not…" She faltered, and Rami read the way she clenched her jaw to keep the ghosts at bay. "If not, we'll be lost anyway. So, fine, if I fail you can damn me, or lead me around by the nose for all eternity. If I fail at this, my soul is forfeit anyway. You're welcome to the ragged ends of it. God knows I've never had much use of it."

A smile, cold and bilious, crept up Andras's face. Claire held up one finger. "You will honor the intent of the terms—"

"No need to wrap me in a djinn's promise, Claire. The spirit of the game as you propose it is far too enticing as it is. I will not need loopholes." Andras clicked his tongue as Claire opened her mouth again. "And yes, yes, I will behave as your ally on all things as far as this arrangement goes. I will not hurt a precious hair on your assistant's head, or so much as dog-ear a page of a book."

Claire pursed her lips into a fine line. It gave Rami a chance to step up and touch her arm. "Don't do this. You cannot possibly believe you can trust or control a demon—"

"We have an accord?" Andras prompted.

"It is done, Rami." She finally looked at him, and the dark of her eyes was wet and unreadable. She gave him the slightest shake of her head: *Don't, leave off, follow my lead.* She turned her attention back to Andras. "Brevity is librarian now, you should remember that. Hero is her assistant."

"A book minding the books? What an absurdity."

Hero was many things, but Rami wasn't certain a mere book could be counted among them anymore. Just as well. The more secrets they held over Andras, the safer they would be. Rami would not be the one to correct him.

"And what does that make you?" Andras always knew the question to strike the most emotional damage. Claire was braced for it, and only Rami saw the thin flinch of the papery wrinkles at the corners of her eyes.

"A patron of the Library. As are you. Come. We should get back to the others." Claire turned on her heel, as if Andras was a pesky book to be ordered around. "This will require some explaining."

"Oh, you do spoil me with such entertainment." Andras brushed past Rami's shoulder and fell in step with Claire, side by side, out of the ashes and into the Library.

A sigh of air ruffled Rami's feathers, and he craned his head to the shadows of the ceiling. The Library settled uneasily into the silence. Rami agreed with the sentiment.

2 9

CLAIRE

Hold tight to those who have earned your trust, kiddo. Hold
tight to those who have earned your trust, your softness, your
fury, and your fire. Hold tight to those whose stories resonate
with your own.

A heart is a kind of library.

Librarian Fleur Michel, 1720 CE

ANDRAS GOT HIS ENTERTAINMENT. Claire had thought she'd
steeled herself when she emerged out of the depths of the Library
with her former enemy at her side, but the way Brevity flinched,
then looked hurt, undid all Claire's certainty. Brevity faded back a
step like a wounded animal and didn't say a word during Claire's
brusque, thorough explanation.

It was still better than Hero's reaction. Claire forced herself to
look at him. He'd flinched as much as Brevity when Andras had
made his entrance, but it was a flinch forward. He hadn't removed
his scabbard since the Valhalla interview, and his hand was on the
hilt and the blade free before Claire could speak a word. When she

finally did begin talking, instead of staring at Andras he turned his gaze to Claire with a stark, unreadable look.

Claire barely spared a moment to consider the other librarians' reactions. Bjorn was the only one who had known Andras, and Claire didn't need to look to feel the aggrieved insult radiating off the Norseman. Their opinions didn't matter anyway—not as much as her people's did. Once, the Library had been her world. Strange how a heart could grow but narrow to a pinpoint of focus.

The thought slowed Claire's defense. Brevity appeared to have been waiting for the opportunity of the pause. "Why?" Her voice cracked at barely a whisper. "Why him?"

Regret was oily in her stomach. Claire swallowed hard. "The Unwritten Wing has rebelled once before. While our case is more formidable with all the Library united behind it, I don't trust Lucifer to play fair."

"You think Andras will help us? Out of the goodness of his heart?" Hero was acid and hurt.

"Bold of you to insinuate I have a heart, book," Andras said.

"No." Claire bit down on the explanation of the deal she had made. She didn't dare look at Rami to see if he would keep her secret. "We don't need him to help; we simply needed leverage."

"Boss—" Brevity said in that low tone that threatened to morph her hurt into pity. No, Claire didn't want that. She turned sharply and faced the skeptical faces of the librarians.

"We've already explained the import of the situation. The Library does not choose the unintelligent. None of you are stupid enough to fail to grasp how dire the need is. This is not a discussion. You can speculate and debate all you like, but we have no other choice. The Library rebels, or the Library dies."

"Stories don't die," the young man with the notebook mumbled.

"Souls do. Or will wish they did. Go ahead and ask any demon." Brevity leveled her gaze around the room. "Most of you come from paradise realms, so maybe you think you can come to an agreement with your hosts. But ownership isn't safety, no matter how benevolent."

"A leash is a leash," Hero said quietly.

Hero had won the right to talk about leashes. Claire nodded but hesitated to open her mouth. There was a granite line to the turn of Brevity's chin that said she wasn't done, and didn't need Claire to justify herself.

"Pup." A voice in her ear made her flinch. It wasn't the menacing purr she heard in her dreams, but Andras's voice always contained a threat where there'd once been reassurance. He had drifted to a stop just behind her chair, arms crossed, a kind of calm curiosity on his aquiline features as he watched the librarians continue to debate plans. His eyes didn't drift, but he knew Claire was listening. "Have you given any thought to after?"

"After?" Claire found herself murmuring out of the side of her mouth too. She told herself it was because she didn't want to disrupt Brevity's progress with the librarians. Not because she didn't want to be seen speaking with her supposed prisoner. "I wouldn't think that'd be your concern."

The edge of Andras's frown twitched. "You've always been my concern, pup."

"Don't—don't call me *pup*." Claire breathed calm through her nose. "Your concern only ever existed to the extent it served your machinations. I'll grant you played a long game."

"I'm a patient creature." Andras tapped a finger on his crossed arms, as if contemplating how much to say. "You are underutilized."

No. Absolutely not. She was not bringing this divisive nonsense to the discussion. Claire slipped out of her chair and drifted to the kettle in the corner. Andras, predictably, followed. "Some people don't seek to control and use everyone around them."

"No. You've acquired… *friends*." He made the term sound like *lice*. Andras sighed as she sedately set about the ritual of brewing a new pot. How many pots of tea could put off the inevitable? "And that's why you'll fail."

"I believe I can convince Hell to release its hold. One way or another." They were sufficiently far away that their voices wouldn't carry to the table. Claire portioned a scoop of stout black tea leaves into the pot and checked to make sure her strainer was at hand as she waited for the water to boil. "I believe Hero could persuade the sun out of the sky, if need be. I believe that if anyone can draw a room full of librarians together, Brevity can."

Andras appeared to grant that with a roll of his hand. "And then what?"

"And then…" Claire bought time for her thoughts by fishing for a spoon in the drawer. "We build something new."

"Simple as that." Andras's sarcasm was acidic. "You know what you need, then?"

"A realm, a guide, a library, and a god," Claire said to herself. She'd repeated it, like a perverse kind of prayer, since she'd picked it apart in Poppaea's memories. The afterlife wasn't all whimsy. To exist as a realm—not a hosted barnacle as they were now—they would need four things.

"I'll grant you that you'll have a people." Andras tilted his head at the discussion taking place at the table. "I'll even give you the unearned belief that you'll find a way around a place and guide. But gods, Claire? Those are in rare supply these days."

Hell and harpies. Claire had hoped that he wouldn't have

bothered himself with her strategy beyond what he wanted. The water came to a quick boil—thank Hell—and she poured it into the teapot with unnecessary caution. "We shall manage."

"No. You won't." Andras may have been a patient demon, and a vicious enemy, but when he decided to press a point, it was quick. "There are no gods left, Claire. Not anymore."

Claire jostled the teapot and nearly sent the kettle flying. She cursed under her breath and finished the pour before twisting her attention to Andras. "You're lying."

"Oh, the schemes I could make if I were." Andras's smile was bitter. "Really, my girl, hadn't you noticed? There hasn't been a real god ruling a realm since before you were born."

"That can't possibly be true. When I first arrived, Malphas—"

"Malphas gave you a peek of a minor illusion that you were still new and freshly dead enough to fall for." Andras scoffed. "Lucifer is hardly the only one to have wandered off. Didn't your pet angel ever tell you what sent Uriel spiraling, desperate enough to hunt you?"

"He said—" Claire paused, gaze flying involuntarily to where Rami stood, a good sentinel behind Brevity. He'd likely tracked that Claire had stepped away, but he kept an intimidating countenance reserved for the librarians at the table. Ever the good soldier, Rami was. Strange how Heaven let him go so easily. "He said Uriel was manic. The angelic host had been left to rule on their own, and she was frantic to—" Claire stopped and took a sharp breath. She stared at Andras. "She was frantic to draw back the attention of their Creator. But that doesn't mean—!"

"Lucifer, the Almighty, Odin—even the quieter notables like that bloody Monkey King. No one's seen hide nor hair of them in centuries." Andras sighed, as if it was a family embarrassment he was admitting. "I suppose I can't blame them. All those eons, epochs, generation after generation of the same old whining and needy creation? Anyone would need a vacation."

Claire refused to believe what she was hearing. She reached for her tea but found her hand shaking, to her distaste. She glared at her palm. "But for the afterlife to exist, there must be gods somewhere."

"Perhaps. But the only ones left in the realms are us. Demons, spirits, monsters, and mortals." Andras was quiet for a breath, just long enough for her to look up. "There will be no almighty to save you."

"I do not expect to be saved." Claire couldn't help but cast a glance over her shoulder. The only ones who had taken notice of her absence, outwardly at least, were Hero and Brevity. Hero's alarm was watchful while Brevity's was... sad. Undefinably sad. Claire looked away again. "You said something about being underutilized." She drew herself up to meet Andras's stare again.

"Me? I'm just a spectator. How could I know anything?" Andras demurred, chuckling at whatever surely murderous expression appeared on Claire's face. "I only wanted to counsel you to think about the Library's future, and yours. I am deliriously curious to see a new realm born. What kind of god could become a library, after all?" Claire frowned. Andras was circling something he apparently felt was incredibly clever—and important—but she didn't see how. When she didn't say anything, Andras merely smiled. "It will be spectacular. I'm sure. Your tea is getting cold, dear."

"Andras, you—" Claire paused. Rami approached, having lost the inner struggle to his deep distrust of demons. Timely enough, as Claire wasn't sure what she'd been about to say. There was nothing to say—to the disappearance of gods, to realms and a doomed future. To all of it. Why would Andras see fit to warn her? She narrowed her gaze with blatant suspicion, but Andras merely smiled. "You are not my friend." It was a weak finish, a reminder more to herself than to Andras, but she hurried away to rejoin Rami and the others before Andras could get in a response.

What makes a god of the Library? Like a burr, it tunneled its way into her mind.

"We're doing this. The Library can't survive fractured and under attack across multiple realms. And we can't survive if the stories don't. Humanity can't survive without stories, not in the ways that make it worth living," Brevity was saying as Claire rejoined them. She exchanged a glance with Claire and Rami and evidently found confirmation in what she sought there. She took a deep breath. "You can say what you want, but you weren't the ones that decided to come here—your stories did."

"My wing deals in a higher form of craft than stories—"

"Songs, poems, letters, memes, whatever!" Brevity threw her hands up. "Souls! That's the point, right? When people create things, they create a little spark of soul. People recognize that. That's what gives them their magic. The Library is nothing more or less than humanity making meaning of the universe. Whatever you want to call it, *that's* why we're here. The souls of the Library chose to fight, with or without you. You can whine and sulk all you want, but I..." Brevity faltered and took a steadying breath. "I'm afraid too. But I've wasted too much time waiting to not be afraid. I'm going to fight. I can be afraid *and fight.*"

The Library did not choose the unintelligent, but it certainly chose the unwise and the stubborn. The silence around the table only held until Duat's librarian clicked his beak. "Fear is not the issue. Our primary duty is to our individual wings. The Library has always valued independence."

"How grand, you'll each independently be enslaved." Andras's tone was low and light with amusement.

"The Library is something a demon couldn't understand," Bjorn grumbled. The debate picked up again, rising from a low murmur to raised voices that Claire couldn't focus on. There was a thought, a realization, burning through her chest like an ember. Her gaze fished around the table, drifting past everyone before she came to a stop at Andras. Narrowed gold eyes met her gaze. Andras was watching, waiting for something. Patience, that's what made a good demon. They could wait it out, present a united front until it was the precise moment to stab an ally in the back. Andras was a very good demon, because he was calculatingly patient.

"The Library..." Something about her voice must have been odd, the way Brevity cut off in mid-argument to turn to her. The quiet eddied around the table, but Claire didn't care. The thought took shape, and then the thought grew teeth, and her voice was a frosted edge. "This was never a *library*. What do you think makes a library? A room full of books? A coincidental accumulation of shelves and paper? We were never a library. A library is an integral part of the community it serves. A library is for the needs of people, not librarians. A library changes to meet the needs of those who depend on it. We were *never* a library! Where were our predecessors when Poppaea fought and lost? Where were you when the Unsaid Wing sought sanctuary? Where were *any of you* when the books of the Unwritten Wing burned?"

Bjorn was the only librarian who had the grace and guilt to flinch. The others eyed her as if she were a new threat, a feral animal. Perhaps she was. She wasn't a librarian anymore. So she could say this without doubt. "A library is a place made for sanctuary. A library helps, and serves, all who need it. None of us have run a real library for hundreds of years. At best, we've been shadows. Archives, collectors, clutching our treasures in the dark. That's not a librarian's job. You talk about preserving a library that *never was*."

"*Never was.*" Echo looked thoughtful. Andras's smug lips were pulling into a slow smile, as if he was proud of her. The rage Claire felt got funneled into her words.

"Brevity was right. We've forgotten why we are here." Claire glanced at Brev, who's eyes were wide but who gave a fierce nod of assent. "We can't go back to how it was, because how it was, was broken. The way we did things was what allowed creatures like Andras to hurt us in the first place. We forgot our own souls. The tradition of our Library is the reason books burned and the Dust Wing exists. That farce of a library is gone, and good riddance." Her fist hit the table, and even Rami startled. "What we're here to decide is what we replace it with. Are any of you strong enough to stand up and become real librarians? Any of you?"

The accusation echoed against the silence, against the table, fluttered past the blank-faced librarians to ripple like a wave and crash against the tall library stacks. Every book, vine, letter, poem, song, and soul felt it and listened.

But Claire couldn't. She couldn't stand to listen to the answers, not with the shame burning hot in her chest. Her teacup wobbled as she abandoned it and shoved away from the table. Someone raised their voice, calling out her name, but Claire didn't slow down. There was only one place to retreat. There was only ever one place to retreat. She didn't know where she was going, but her feet did. Aisles passed in a blur until she was running. Running—so much easier to do in slacks, but she missed the protective perimeter of her skirts. She could hear the books whisper as she passed. Whispers, always whispers.

"Claire." It wasn't the voice she'd expected to hear behind her, but today was not a day for expectations. She had stopped. She didn't know how long she'd stopped, staring at the same shelf. It couldn't have been long; her breath was still heaving, burning and thin in her lungs. Her hand gripped the shelf in front of her for support. She closed her eyes and rested her forehead against the row of books. They pulsed softly under her skin and echoed against her skull. Souls and stories reaching out to her. Claire shivered.

"Claire."

She drew a breath and turned. "You should be back with the others, not chasing after me."

The sconce above haloed Brevity in a soft, flattering glow. The Unwritten Wing loved to embrace her like that, far more kind and accommodating than it had ever been to Claire. That thought would have hurt once; now it was a kindness. Brevity deserved all the hugs.

"I'm a librarian," Brevity said, quiet but firm as steel. There was a note in her voice that made Claire take a closer look at her. Brevity's chin was up, teal eyes sparking with intensity. "What you said back there, everyone was listening. I want to be *that* kind of librarian. I think you do too."

"I am not a librarian anymore."

"You are to me." Brevity hesitated, a question on the tip of her tongue. But instead she said something altogether different. "I've found you back here before."

"Habit, I suppose." Claire shrugged. "It was the only privacy I had." The books here were simply bound, the titles stamped in simple boxy lettering. The oldest ones looked like the kind of manuscripts one would tap out on a word processor in Claire's day, but new additions, ones added since Claire had left this place, were modern creatures, sans serif lettering and mimicking some digital page in white and red. Her fingers sought out a small paperbound story emblazoned with an illustration. Two long-haired figures, frequently wielding swords or embracing.

That had been a good memory—the wonder of it. In Claire's lifetime, it had been exceedingly difficult to find a story representing love as she felt it, especially if one was a proper middle-class woman from Surrey. They existed—they had always existed—but always between the lines. Subtext. Hinted at but never seen. It had been a revelation to come to the Unwritten Wing and see books—generation upon generation of books—telling the story of people like her that had never been written. Or never had been permitted to be written. Stories that had always been, of people that had always been, but never seen. That was the power of stories, the ability to find a mirror when you felt invisible.

Claire wiped at her eyes and returned the book to the shelf. "I suppose I ran here without thinking about it." She shifted her gaze to Brevity pointedly. "To be alone."

"You're never alone in the Library," Brevity said.

Claire flinched. "To be left alone, then."

"Why him?" Brevity immediately clutched a hand to her mouth, as if the question had escaped. Her eyes widened but she didn't look away.

There it was. She'd asked the question before, and this time she deserved an answer. Claire couldn't deny that. "Andras?" she supplied softly. Brevity nodded and closed the distance between them with caution.

"Why'd you let him out, boss? What he did—what he is—why?"

There was a pleading note in Brevity's voice that was a barb straight into Claire's chest. She looked away but didn't find any easy answers on the shelves. "We needed an ally. Andras knows the demon court—"

"Andras *is* the demon court." The breath came out of Brevity like a hiss. Her face was pale and taut. "After what he did to us—what he *tried* to do."

"We can use Andras." Claire tried to reach out with a placating hand. "We don't have to trust him—"

The outburst came with a fist slammed into the bookcase next to them. "I saw them! When I was falling, I saw them. Hell, full of demons just like *him* that are going to—" Brevity stumbled over a wet breath.

"You knew what Hell was," Claire said, not unkindly.

"It's so much *worse*." Brevity's eyes wobbled and moistened. The anger drained from her and she slouched against the bookshelves next to Claire. "It's so… I didn't realize it before today. It's awful, what they do. Torture would have been one thing—I read all your human books about that—but… there was a dark place I was just prior to that…" Her eyes went distant. "The anticipation, the what-ifs, I can see how that's worse."

"People create their own Hell," Claire said, remembering some distant quote from a time when it had all seemed more metaphorical.

"No one deserves that. No one." A vehement edge cut through Brevity's voice. "I mean, I can see bad guys getting their comeuppance. And I know you mortals have a thing about serving your time, but … forever? Forever is such an awful long time. Even longer alone in the dark." Brevity's hands clenched and found Claire's. "No one deserves that. No one."

"You should run against Lucifer. You'd have my vote." Claire shared a smile. She'd never seen the sharp edges of Brevity, not like this. Hard, and strong. She asked it before she could think it through. "How'd you get out?"

"I… fell." Brevity's brows furrowed. She shook her head sharply before starting again. "No, I... I imagined it, Claire. I got scared, so scared, and... and I realized that was okay. I got scared, and imagined, and then I fell."

I realized that was okay. Claire didn't struggle with the same anxious circles that Brevity did, but she felt a distant step off the spiral that she hadn't known she was on. She understood the relief. Not to deny the fear but to take it with you. "I see. You got out. You saved yourself."

"I—" Brevity hesitated. "I was still so scared. I still am."

"But you acted anyway. That's a very human sort of bravery, I hear," Claire said. "I'm so proud—no, I'm so *impressed* with what you've done, Brev."

Brevity's cornflower cheeks turned lavender. She appeared to wrestle her emotions under control before redirecting her thoughts to less pleasant things: Andras. This fierce, terrified and fierce, new version of Brevity would not be turned away from terrible things. "He shouldn't be here."

"None of us should be here," Claire said helplessly. "You should be in Muses Corps leadership, bringing dreams to people. Hero should be written and in the world, being read and loved. Rami should be in Heaven. I..." The sentence failed her. Claire sank back against the bookshelves. "I lived my life. Heaven is not anything I'm interested in. Perhaps I am the only one meant to be here, and I have brought the rest of you down with me."

She squawked when Brevity stepped on her toes. "Stop," she said softly. "Or I'll tell Hero and Rami."

Claire didn't give her the satisfaction of pretending not to know what she meant. She, Hero, and Rami spun around their own complicated, nuanced orbit, and Brevity had always been perceptive. It was no wonder that she sussed it out so quickly.

Besides, Claire was tired of denying that she had a heart. It broke far too often for that. "Oh, that's hardly the case—"

"Why not? I mean, I've been meaning to ask that. You're all half in love with each other. And I am all in love with all of you." Brevity stopped, reflecting on that. "Muse love, I guess. I never had much interest in the sex stuff, even if there's an *astounding* amount of human dreams devoted to it. Why is that? Sex is so basic, so why do humans put so much thinking into it?"

"I..." Claire chuckled. "Religious guilt, jealousy, and no doubt an innate propensity to overcomplicate things as a species."

"Yeah, humans do that," Brevity said with the same depth of fondness one might have for an especially stupid puppy. "It's great." She straightened. "But you don't *have* to do any of that stuff now. You are dead. Enjoy it."

Enjoying death was such an absurdity that Claire could only blink for a moment. "I don't think... It wouldn't be a good idea."

"*I* think..." Brevity said, looking at her with a level assessment. "I think it's the best idea." She paused. "Is it me? Am I in the way?"

Claire's hand caught her by the shoulder. She felt herself smiling now. "Oh no you don't. You're part of this."

"Part of what?" Brevity threw up her hands. "That's what I've been *asking*! Humans are so complicated. What *are* we?"

It was a struggle to pin the laughter up. Claire took a moment to give the question the thought it deserved before answering. "We are... family," she said simply. "You, me, Rami, and Hero."

"Just family?"

"There is no 'just' about family. Not when I use the word."

Brevity's face was made for emotions—possibly a muse trait. The slow bloom of warmth and joy that came over her face was enough to break Claire. In the next moment, Brevity had thrown her arms around Claire's waist and buried her face in her shoulder. Claire staggered in surprise, and Brevity hugged her tighter. A wet hiccup escaped her, though all Claire could see was the mop of teal curls against her face. "Family," was all she said, repeating it at a nearly inaudible whisper.

The earnestness, by its very nature, made Claire deeply uncomfortable. A proper British woman didn't dwell on earnest feelings, let alone discuss them. It was vulgar. These kinds of things were just best left... assumed. And even years around Brevity and her font of feelings couldn't unlearn that discomfort. A knot of something hot and momentous had lodged in her throat. Claire made a noise to clear it. "Well, I think we can leave—"

The rest of the words were drowned out by a thundering, sonorous groan that shook the floorboards beneath their feet. "What—?" Brevity started, but Claire had already extracted herself to fling herself past Brevity at a run.

The hollow groan continued and deepened. The wood floor beneath her feet flexed and bucked, wood screaming against wood. Claire gripped the shelves and nearly lost her balance before Brevity caught up and offered a steadying arm. They ran back the way Claire had just fled, away from the shadows of love and fear, and toward the next emergency. As librarians. As family.

30

RAMI

There's another ward, fallen. The characters have all retreated back to their books—good. No use they experience dying when they haven't even lived.

That is what will happen. No use pretending at softness here and now. Malphas will break down our pitiful wards, crush our paltry resistance, and the rebellion will be over. Hell cannot touch the books themselves, but she won't need to once she's defeated me. She will pull the foundations from the Unwritten Wing, and all will fall into chaos. Order requires a mind, requires comprehension. Without a librarian to order it, the unwritten stories of future generations will be lost.

I can't win against Malphas, but I can't surrender to her either. Both paths lead to the destruction of the things I swore to protect.

But this is a fairy tale. When have we ever remained on the path?

Librarian Poppaea Julia, 48 BCE

THE WAKE OF SILENCE that Claire had left at the table lingered. Rami had a clear view of the hunched shoulders and ruffled feathers from his post away from the table. He felt like an outsider, which was nothing new. But worse, he felt like an intruder. The gathered librarians were not all as emotionally contained as Claire, and what she'd said had struck each of them with different wounds. Echo, wearing her son's form, peered introspectively into the middle distance. The gnarled knuckles of Bjorn's hands tightened around his untouched mug of tea while he bickered with the Duat librarian. Rami hadn't caught their names, and even if he had, they all seemed like distant concerns compared to the way Hero leaned back in his chair, relaxed as ever on the surface but meditatively cracking his knuckles, one by one.

A sound like thunder nearly startled Hero out of his chair. It had everyone on their feet, thankfully, because the next tremor that shook through the Library crashed a tower of books across the conference table.

"Stay with the librarians." Hero had already drawn his sword and loped toward the front doors, entirely negligent of the fact that he was a librarian. He disappeared for a moment, and it took all of Rami's reserve to stand guard in front of the gathered scholars rather than chase after him. He reappeared, sword lowered and face perplexed, a moment later. "The hallway is clear."

"No demons?" Rami asked cautiously.

"Not a one. Quiet as the grave out there. I interrupted the gargoyle's nap. What's going—" Hero's question was interrupted by a sonorous creak followed by a crack that felt like it rent the earth. A cascade of sound followed as the floor shuddered: stacks of books hitting the floor, wood scrolls cracking and chipping, sheaves of loose parchment fluttering into the air like a froth of moth wings. Rami immediately looked to the floor, expecting a chasm to have split the very ground, demons crawling up from the depths of Hell. But the wood floorboards seemed intact, only venting lines of dust into the lamplight, shook loose from the slats.

It took time, a disturbance that large, to settle into silence in a space as big as the Library. The books had been stirred by the noise, and Rami saw a couple of heads peering out at them curiously from the far end of the stacks. The damsels would be sending a representative in no time—probably Lucille, Rami thought with a wince. The damsel's elder matron was formidable enough to make even a Watcher quail.

Claire came skidding out of the stacks, Brevity behind her. "Status?" she yelled, but no one had an answer. Murmurs came from the librarians' table until Bjorn's voice cut them short.

"The fires are going out." His voice was low but streaked with alarm that spread around the table.

Hero rejoined Rami, holding his sword out warily for lack of a clear target. "What fires?"

Tension inched through Bjorn's old wiry shoulders, as if pulled by a wrench. His hand inched along his waistband looking for a weapon he'd long since discarded. Bjorn's keen gaze met Rami's. There was no humor in them now. "My fires. The dead fires."

Hero breathed in a curse, and Rami flowed into action. A few steps took him down the nearest aisle, though he was slowed down by the debris of fallen books and dust-shivered vines. The campfires of the Unwon Wing had accompanied Bjorn along with its spirits and made all the librarians nervous until Brevity had managed to coax them into the shielded containers and lamps that dotted the intersecting paths of the shelves. The fall of shadow warned Rami before he even reached the first intersection:

the sturdy copper brazier was out. Cold smoke still curled from the embers, casting a strange frosty anise scent on the air. Rami's brow furrowed as he stepped forward.

The floorboards flexed like a sponge beneath his boot. Rami recoiled on instinct, and by the time he stepped forward again, his boot made a small wet splash. Beads of water, dark and oily, rolled off his toe to rejoin the thin puddle forming on the hardwood under his feet. In the dark, he couldn't make out how far it spread, but he placed the cold smell now—water. Rami's chest thudded. "Echo?"

The Unsaid Wing's librarian and her mystical reflection pool were the only permissible source, and Rami dearly hoped this was the spirit playing jokes. If there was a worse enemy to libraries than fire, it was water. Fire burned, but water lingered, festering mold and rot with a reach farther than the flames'. If a fire raged a book to ashes, water inflicted the trauma of bloated corpses of stories long after the ground had dried.

The Library was a magical entity. Thankfully, the dead needed no water closets. It had no plumbing to speak of, except the niceties conjured by the damsels out of their own books. Even Claire's beloved tea was steeped from a kettle that never emptied. There should be no real water in Hell.

An icy feeling nipped at his toes as the water penetrated the lining of his boots. There was definitely water in Hell. His toes were soaked through by the time he returned to the front lobby.

"There's flooding." His warning was unnecessary. The water only puddled in the seams of the floorboards here, but already the librarians were in action. The Duat librarian was hurriedly rolling up the unmade rugs, slinging them across any higher surface at hand. Brevity had marshaled several others to relocate the books and scrolls that had stacked up on the floor for lack of space. Hero had enlisted the gargoyle, who was attempting to lever one of the tall standing shelves up without spilling its inhabitants—unsuccessfully. It was an operation both efficient and pointless. The Library was an endless sprawl of shelves and stacks. The water would outpace any efforts. Even if it never reached the lowest shelf of the stacks, it would snatch hundreds of books from their hands.

At the eye of the fruitless activity, Claire hunched over the desk, flipping through the Librarian's Log with a desperate fervor. "The wards," she explained, not looking up as Rami joined her. "The wards fell just before. This has to be Malphas's doing. If we can get the wards up again, the water may stop."

"Why would she want to flood the Library?"

"Invasion didn't work for Andras. Malphas is more clever." Claire raced her finger down one page, then another, searching. She was too occupied to see Andras frown in offense from where he idled in an armchair. "She doesn't care about preserving the stories. She intends to make us surrender to her."

"Flood you out." Andras had a petulant if thoughtful look on his face. "You would surrender before seeing the entire Library flooded and lost. And even if you didn't—a waterlogged book is unreadable but still useful."

"Only for a demon." Hero gave a full-body shudder before continuing to stack boxes of scrolls on top of a chair. "A story needs to know how it goes too. If the ink runs, we could forget who we are."

"Ink…" Rami jolted as a thought ran through him. He lunged, throwing Claire over his shoulder. She barely had time to squawk before she was deposited—gently, if urgently—on top of the desk.

"Explain yourself this instant!" Claire fumed as he stepped back.

"Ink. There could be unwritten ink in the water, or it could bleed from the books."

Just one drop of unwritten ink had been enough to corrupt Hero's book and nearly kill Brevity. It had stained Claire with a bleak possession of souls that she was still haunted by. The fury fell from Claire's face and, reassured that she wouldn't move, Rami turned to help Brevity up to perch on a side table. When he spun around again, Hero stopped him with a raised hand. "I get the idea. No need to manhandle me, you brute." He clambered on top of a chair and joined Claire on top of the desk with all the awkward dignity he could manage.

Bjorn was quick to catch on and took refuge on top of a carpet-cluttered table. Echo gathered her own pond around her and her children in a way that made it crest at the edges, like a wall. The other librarians had no idea of the threat of unwritten ink and what it could do to a mortal or a spirit, but they more or less followed suit. Soon the furniture of the front lobby was dotted with a particularly anxious and awkward flock of librarians. They all regarded the floor with new apprehension. The water seeped slowly, gathering in puddles no more than an inch deep but already murky with malice.

Only Rami had been able to touch the ink, however briefly, and remain unaffected. Even so, the chill seeping into his boots felt vicious and biting cold.

"But we can't just do nothing!" Brevity said plaintively.

"The collection is too big," Claire muttered desolately. Hero looped an arm around her shoulders with an ease that was still new between them. It appeared a comforting gesture, but Rami suspected Hero was also braced to hold Claire back from whatever ill-advised heroics typically followed despair in Claire's brain. "We can't save it by hand." The streak of certainty in her voice was bitter, and there from experience.

"But we're librarians. This isn't just one wing; this is the entire Library. We have to do something." Brevity's voice threatened to break.

The water had crept up to Rami's ankles. It was an uneven murky pool across the floor now, floorboards quickly disappearing. It hadn't reached the bottom row of the Library's shelves yet, but a quick calculation said they had minutes, not hours. The librarians had been efficient in sweeping up any stacks of books scattered around the front lobby, but Rami knew that somewhere deeper in the stacks, books and scrolls that had settled on the floor were taking on the first damage to their ancient pages. Bleeding ink, disintegrating paper, soggy vellum that would warp and stick to each other like decaying mulch. It would be a slow and agonizing death by water.

"We ain't just gonna give up, dangerous or no." It was Bjorn this time who looked ready to jump into the low tide. Rami tensed to stop him. "We're librarians, still?"

"Librarians will." Echo said in the warped mockingbird speech she had. The edges of her pond frothed, still a clear Mediterranean blue that held back the gray floodwater. Pallas slept on, unperturbed, at her feet, and Iambe stood protectively in front of him. Fractious as that Library wing's relationship was, it appeared they united against threats, like any family. Echo stared past Rami, gaze locked on Brevity expectantly. Rami couldn't do the same. Looking at Brevity was like watching a heart break in real time. She'd only just become comfortable with the mantle of librarian in time to lose it. The cherry floorboards spongy with water were her choice, and the dizzy little faerie lights overhead reflected on the water's surface. All of it, the Library of Brevity's making.

Librarians, and will. Echo's words chased the tail end of that thought. Rami sloshed his way over to where Brevity was perched. "Change it." Brevity blinked her watery eyes in confusion, first tears forming. Rami took her hand urgently. "Change it. The Library. This is your wing that we're sheltering in. A wing changes to reflect its librarian, does it not? Tell it to change; protect the books."

"I don't know how," Brevity protested. She dropped her voice, hoarse with creeping fear. "It just did it on its own after Claire left. I didn't really control it."

"You wished for spiderwebs," Rami reminded her. Brevity had confessed the idle fancy in the weeks after they'd escaped the Dust Wing. It had taken some looking, but Rami had begun to notice faint gossamer puffs hidden in the nooks of the very deepest parts of the Library. Maybe they'd always been there, but Rami chose to believe not. He gripped her fingers. "Wish for something else."

Brevity's eyes widened even as her small pointed features remained frozen in place. For a moment, Rami feared the common thing would happen. Anxiety and fear would overwhelm the muse's ability to create. It was a real battle, and Rami could see the ground lost and gained in the way Brevity's breath sped up to a gallop. But then, an uncommon thing happened instead. Brevity didn't become less anxious, not that Rami could see at least, but he could track the shift. Her eyes squeezed closed briefly, then opened. They were still bright with spinning fear, but also sharp with focus. "Will you help me?" Her voice was small but steady.

Rami was doubtful of how much help he could be, either as a Watcher or as a former assistant librarian to the Arcane Wing. But rather than voice that, he nodded firmly and loosened his grip on her fingers. Brevity pressed her palm against his and breathed deep.

Frosty flood still nettled its way up Rami's ankles. The hem of his trousers had turned heavy with water. It amplified the small shudder that spread across the water as something in the depths of the Library roused. The air stirred with the peppery smell of old paper and time. It drifted and mixed with the moss and oak swamp water to sharpen into a breeze that stirred the feathers in Rami's coat. Brevity's fingers tightened around his. The knuckles went from propane blue to white, then relaxed.

"Try—" Rami started, but the rest of the encouragement stuttered in his throat as the water crested up his legs like a tide. His heart stuttered. No, they were too late, the water was rising too fast—but then the water sloshed away again. He traced the origin of the wave back to the towering shelves of the Library. Wood flexed, books breathed, and... and grew.

The Library grew like a plant unfurling before the sunshine. Brevity's rose-stained shelves trembled, disturbing the floodwaters as they reached. Spindly legs, like tendrils of the vines that draped them, shot out from the bottom of the stacks. The rails along the shelves just barely managed to keep the books in place as the rows of the Library stacks grew taller, raised on legs that curved and coiled into complicated, vaguely eerie graceful arches. Farther into the shadows, a commotion echoed against the rafters. Wet thuds and the faint drip of water muddled into a frothy roar as the Library rescued its charges and realigned for a new purpose.

When silence reasserted itself, the lowest shelves of the stacks rose several feet above the water on decorative wood legs. What scrolls hadn't fit on the shelves had been rescued from the floor and were now twined in loops of the Unsaid Wing's vines like lush literary fruits. The Library's rugs billowed from the rafters like particularly heavy banners, the paintings reached farther up on the walls, and even the furniture itself, festooned with stranded librarians, stood on vaguely stilt-like legs.

"My god," Hero breathed. And it felt miracle enough to make even an atheist curse. Next to him, Claire ran her fingers over the desk they sat on—now several feet higher in the air—with disbelief.

"You did it, Brev," Claire said.

Brevity's hand twitched and she slowly blinked open her eyes—which weren't her eyes. The pupils had been swallowed up by a soft shadow, and the iris flickered wood tones, then the shade of old leather, then parchment white, cycling through a spectrum of stories. "The Library—" Brevity's voice sang with multiple chords, and she grimaced. The eerie light faded somewhat from her eyes and some of the natural blue returned to her pallor. She swallowed and her normal light tone returned. "I mean, the Library did it. I think."

"The librarian did it." Awe was a strange look on Bjorn's bearded face. His thick brows knit together and he shook his head. "I ain't never seen it happen like that, though, lass. You are a wonder."

"She's a librarian. When a librarian and a library work in tandem, anything can happen. She's a librarian." There was a chip, more like a mosaic, behind the tone in Claire's voice. A chip of wistfulness, a chip of wonder, mortared together with a deep pride. She hugged her knees to her chest from her perch on the desk with Hero. Her smile was wet and true. "Best one I've ever seen."

HERO

A Norseman's not made for land. The walls of this Library close in on me sometimes, and gods do I miss the smell of the sea. Telling a story or singing a song isn't the same unless there's the scrape of salt in your throat. Not all my kin were seafarers, but we were all born with the tidal pull in our veins. I was born on a boat—ha! I thought I'd forgotten that!

There's a magic to a boat. You can't stand still, no matter how uncertain you are. On a boat, you're always headed somewhere.

Librarian Bjorn the Bard, 1112 CE

HERO SWUNG HIS LEGS where they dangled over the edge of the desk. "As much as I do love a good waterfront property, do we have a plan for how to wish away this water next?"

The water was still flooding up between the floorboards at a slow pace, but the Library was keeping ahead of it. Not that Hero had any idea how, mind. They never caught the Library growing as dramatically as it did the first time. He'd just notice how close the sloshing water was getting to his toes, and then the next time he glanced down it would have retreated several feet. Nonetheless, Hero didn't fancy spending an eternity sharing the librarian's desk with Claire while Rami flopped about like a fish below them. The murky water reached up to his ribs by now, and the layers of his feathered trench coat bloomed about him like a bedraggled cloud. The water droplets that speckled his cheek and clung to his hard, rough features were particularly appealing, and he looked like nothing so much as a thunder god rising out of the depths. Not that Hero would say so.

"All of you are staying where you are," Rami said, daring him to argue, and really, he should have known better.

"Fancy words from a drowned pigeon who—" Hero paused as movement caught his eye. "Look."

The aisles of the Unwritten Wing had become tributaries when the water rushed in. The giant bookcases channeled the water with an impossible current all their own. Out of one of these glided a boat.

Hero didn't bother to rub his eyes. He'd seen weirder in the Unwritten Wing—though not by much. The craft was a fine thing and far above an emergency raft. The boat had a curved prow like a gondola, piloted expertly by a sturdy-looking damsel, and sitting in the center like the queen herself was Rosia.

Even Claire was too stunned to say anything. The boat drifted to a stop beside the desks where the rest of them had taken shelter. Rosia looked up, smiled, and stated the obvious. "There's too much water."

"We're working on that," Brevity said faintly. "Um, not to assume, but did you come to rescue us?"

"Okay," Rosia said, as if responding to a different question. Her gaze slid to meet Hero's. He didn't like the expectant glint in it.

"Well, it's not as if we had much of a choice." He was the first to abandon his perch and step lightly into the boat. Hero could see more boats now, floating out of the shadows after their leader. Enough for all the stranded librarians. How terrifying. "Mind the gap."

IT FELT LIKE A river, the water, as they navigated the boat between the legs of the Library shelves. Hero craned his head back. The stacks of the Library stretched like canyon walls above them.

"How long can this go?" He craned his head to find the boat behind him, which Brevity and Claire had claimed for their own. Claire made a face.

"Which 'this'? Malphas's flooding or Brevity's ability to adjust the Library ahead of it?"

Hero raised his brows and shrugged. "Both?"

"Forever, to the first," Brevity said, the corners of her eyes crinkled in concentration. "And... not forever... to the second."

"You're doing great, Brev," Claire said quietly. Her hand tightened on Brevity's, and the unspoken passed between them. "But Hero's right: we can't wait for Malphas to tire first."

"We're in no position to counterattack," Rami reminded them from the boat bringing up the rear. Water still dripped from his shoulders and flattened the feathers in his coat like a drowned bird.

"You think too small, Watcher." Andras tsked. To Hero's infinite displeasure, the demon had claimed the other seat in his boat and sat as if it were a pleasure cruise.

"We don't attack," Claire said with a thoughtful look. "We negotiate."

Hero scoffed. "When has diplomacy ever worked for us?"

"First time for everything. We need to send a message." Claire rose in the boat and cleared her throat. "Bird!"

Cursing, in every non-language one could imagine, pealed down from the rafters, quickly heralding a swoop of dusty black feathers. Bird landed on the tip of the boat, heavily enough to make it bobble precariously. Claire ignored the waves and discreetly used Brevity's shoulder for balance. "Bird, I would like you to carry a message to Malphas and the court."

For a terrible bird who spoke only in expletives, Bird could express fathoms with her silence and insulted ruffle of feathers. Claire sighed. "No, I don't have crackers."

Bird turned away and unfolded her wings lazily. A preflight stretch, and Hero was sorely tempted to see if Bjorn's ghost fires were strong enough to roast a raven. "Fine!" Claire stopped her with an irritated sigh. "Crackers. I'll… ask one of the damsels to bake us one or something."

"We already made you boats," Rosia said with a prim air from the next boat over.

"I'll ask very, very nicely," Claire grumbled.

Bird, apparently satisfied, refolded her wings after a leisurely stretch. She hopped up on Claire's arm and regarded her with beady, suspiciously intelligent eyes. She waited, expectantly, for the message.

"How do we even know they will be willing to talk?" Brevity asked hesitantly. She added, a little softer, "Last time didn't go so well."

"They're already flooding the wing; at least we'll be provisioned if they try fire," Hero noted with a dry curl of his lip.

"They'll want to talk. Even if Malphas doesn't want to negotiate a surrender, there's one thing we have that will get her attention," Claire said. Bird deigned to allow her to stroke a hand down her sleek back, clacking her beak quietly. Something unspoken passed between the two, and the raven gently launched into the air. "There's one thing you can rely on demons always wanting."

"Souls?" Rami said quietly.

"Power?" Brevity guessed.

"Pathetically on-the-nose aesthetic choices?" Hero chimed in.

Bird circled once overhead, disappearing into shadows, then out again. Then, curiously quiet, she dropped into a dive that caused everyone but Claire to duck and startle.

"Revenge," Claire said.

A low grunt of discomfort made Hero frown behind him reflexively. Andras, who had been suspiciously quiet up till then, held a hand to his hair, gingerly patting at a patch of the tiger stripe while Bird fluttered overhead. Andras studied a wetness on his fingers with a frown. "Your pet bit me, Claire. Poor sportsmanship."

"Just borrowing a tuft of hair, Andras. I thought you'd prefer that to a sample of flesh." Claire paused as Bird perched momentarily in front of her, a clutch of gray and gold hair in one claw. Claire nodded, and Bird launched into the air again, quickly gaining height until she was swallowed in the dusty shadows of the rafters overhead.

Hero watched her go. "Ah, a hostage exchange."

"Don't give me that much credit, book." Andras had recovered his dignity, though a cowlick of hair still stood at disarrayed angles above the widow's peak of his forehead. "Malphas hardly cares for one exiled demon."

"Precisely." Claire was still watching the dark overhead. Bird must have made her exit when Claire turned around to face him with a positively terrifying smile that sent a thrill through Hero. He loved it when she let herself play the villain. If it wasn't so much fun, he'd be worried she was too good at it. "She cares so little about you she's going to be very interested in your reappearance. You two had a bit of a history before your fall, didn't you?"

Andras's cool expression curdled. "Everyone has a history if you live long enough."

"I think Malphas will be very interested in our plans for your future, don't you?"

"You intend to hand me over." Andras's lips formed a disgusted moue. "We have a deal, pup. Don't think I won't delight in torturing your soul if you betray me."

"Torture?" Brevity's head came up in alarm, and Hero narrowed his eyes as Rami didn't react. He suspected they'd made a deal with a literal devil, but he wouldn't have thought an angel—their angel—would have gone along with it. Rami's face settled into a craggy grimace, and Hero made a note to have a very strenuous conversation. Later.

"I thought you'd be proud, old man." Claire let the threat hang, acidic and brilliant, in the air before dismissing it with a wave of her hand. "I have a plan that satisfies both our goals."

"A plan? Some ruse to fool Hell? My, you have grown up bold, my girl." Andras appeared to weigh his options for a moment before shrugging. "And what's my role in this plan?"

"Trusting me." Claire's smile was viciously bright. She regained her seat in the boat and smoothed out her trousers with meticulous care. "For now, we wait."

"For what?" Rosia asked from her perch. The damsel at the prow was incredibly competent and had navigated their little line of boats down the twists and turns of the aisles of the Library, made all the more treacherous by the continually rising water. Ahead, Hero could see a square of light and what looked like a ramshackle dock composed entirely of emptied bookcases and one soggy divan. The occupants of the damsel suite had been much more industrious and quick to respond in the face of an emergency than their gaggle of librarians had been.

"For Malphas to get greedy." Claire's voice was quiet, her head tilted down over the side of the boat. Her reflection held a frown and wavered as the bleak, dingy water continued to slosh and gather.

THEIR RIVER PATH EMPTIED out, as Hero had suspected, at the damsel suite. The damsels descended upon the arriving boats like a team trained for the purpose. Several brawny women dressed in homespun helped secure the boats to the dock, while a charming boy offered blankets and tea as the librarians reached solid land. With Brevity's librarian pull for preservation, the damsel suite had responded along with the rest of the Library. The threshold, once barely a bit of wood trim marking the door to the damsel suite, was now a block of hewn timber that jutted out like a plinth. It extended down into the depths of the water and had evidently raised the entire damsel suite above the tide line. Hero lingered as the poor hospitality lad made an entire fuss over the state of Rami's soggy coat. It was quite a delightfully awkward show when the boy, intent on his duties, tried to take the coat from him and Rami demurred. The big man finally extracted himself—coat intact—only after accepting enough blankets to swaddle an elephant. He joined Hero at the door with a grimace. "Not a word."

"That's the delightful thing—I don't have to." Hero gloated only a little as he accepted one of the blankets and tossed it about his shoulders like a gallant cloak. Rami narrowed his eyes—whether in fondness or annoyance, it was impossible to tell—and tossed a second blanket at his face. Playfulness was also a new development that was Hero's fault, and he was so delighted he almost forgot to dodge out of the way.

The interior of the damsel suite had not escaped unchanged. The floor felt sturdier, lined with thick mortared slate rather than the more porous wood panels of the Library. And it was a hive of activity. A carpentry staging area occupied the corner nearest the door, with several book characters covered in sawdust and satisfaction as they crafted boat parts that Hero couldn't identify. Deeper into the parlor, he could only make out various tables of potions, wires, and weave. The characters of the damsel suite might have started out their existence as poorly written mascots of little expertise, but none of them had remained that way. Characters could grow, change, even with their books still attached. Maybe that was what it meant to have a soul.

"Oh, that looks heavy. I can—" It had taken all of ten seconds for Rami to be recruited into the wood preparations. He fell in easily, soggy feathered coat and all. The lead carpenter, a dour-looking woman with shaved hair, eyed him prospectively before shoving a tool in Rami's hand. A creature that had lived on Earth for most of its history would have to have learned a thing or two about boating, Hero supposed.

Brevity was elbow-deep in some arcane book repair, with several of the refugee librarians watching over her shoulder. Echo and her daughter appeared to be calling up more vines from their wing to wind and shore up the dock outside. It occurred to Hero that the only skill he really could contribute was making people bleed, literally or figuratively. A poor offering in any real emergency.

Perhaps one of the damsels would teach him… something. The idea of self-improvement was a radical thought, and Hero lost himself considering the options for a moment. Medicine, perhaps, if he could no longer rely on the superior healing of a book character. He told himself that was a satisfactorily self-serving skill to master, but the second thought, which came quick on its toes, was that the important people around him had the pesky habit of perishing, and he refused to allow more of that.

Claire had Andras cornered in an armchair far across the

room, probably committing more delightful villainy. That brightened Hero's mood and he started to make his way toward that entertainment until something snatched at his coat sleeve.

"Reader. You will come." Rosia was still a wraith child, half Victorian gothic and half nightmare elf, dainty and ethereal. But she felt as if she took up more space since she'd lost her book. The Rosia that had emerged out of the pool was less flighty, more solid and thoughtful. She held on to Hero's sleeve without a hint of reproach as he frowned at her.

"I really don't know what you could possibly have to do with me," Hero said. He should feel a kinship with Rosia, the only other character who had seen her book destroyed—dissolved into the unwritten ink—and remained material and whole. Instead, he felt uneasy around her.

"The realm, the guide, the librarians. You are the Reader. Your job isn't done." Rosia may have become less of a ghost, but it hadn't diminished her proclivity for eerie pronouncements. She gestured vaguely at the room and looked at him expectantly. Hero glanced away uneasily, but the others of his strange people were deep in new tasks.

He was the sole idle person in a hive of rather irritating competence and productivity. Might as well. Hero sighed and gestured to Rosia. "Lead the way, spirit."

Rosia beamed up at him—less innocent, but more satisfied than she used to be—and the wall behind her, which had been a solid set of shelves, now sported a narrow hallway. The damsels working near it didn't even appear to notice the change and merely moved as their tables and settees were abruptly a meter shifted. Rosia didn't release her grip on his sleeve as she turned and tugged Hero away from the hum of a Library in the act of rebellion.

HERO

A realm. I knew I was never going to find a realm. I'm not sure what I was thinking. I had probably hoped that, banded together, the Library could claim some kind of public commons. In my wildest fantasies, I imagined a benefactor. Perhaps Elysium's heroes would welcome us into their green fields and I could feel the sun again.

But I knew we were never going to find a realm. The only home we had was the one we carried with us.

Librarian Poppaea Julia, 48 BCE

THE DAMSEL SUITE HAD started as an underutilized reading room. A handy place for detaining the most stubborn of characters who escaped their books, which soon evolved into a kind of refugee center for misused characters—damsels, sidekicks, love interests—to live more of a life than their stories allowed. Under Claire's and Brevity's tenure, it had grown into a suite of rooms, then a complex that sprawled and grew to match the inhabitants' needs. The Unwritten Wing appeared to approve of their continued presence, however much Claire had objected to the risk of unwritten books changing.

The result was a cozy amalgam of architecture. Rosia led Hero down a narrow passage with wood panel that matched the main lounge but quickly turned down a set of iron spiral stairs, through an industrial workshop, and apace down a round hallway apparently built for hobbits. Hero emerged at the other end with a backache and was still stretching the kink out of his shoulders when Rosia stopped at a door and motioned. "In here, if you will."

Hero stepped into a concrete room. It took a moment of muffled silence and discrete warning signs on the wall to identify it as some kind of soundproof bunker softened with a rug and parlor chairs.

"Expecting the worst, are we?" he said lightly, despite his growing nerves.

"Not precisely." Rosia shook her head. "Some of us come out of our stories with our own needs. Some need space. Even the Unwritten Wing can be overstimulating from time to time."

"Oh." Hero considered the thick walls with new ideas. Cooling and calm instead of cold, serene rather than stark. "Should Brevity have a room like this?"

Rosia's smile was soft. "She's always welcome, but external stimulation isn't where the librarian's shadows hide."

Hero couldn't argue with that. Rosia gestured but he opted to lean against the back of the armchair rather than sit. Strange: when Rosia was an eerie ghost child she hadn't bothered Hero in the least, but there was something about this new, self-composed version that constantly made him feel as if he was walking into a trap. "Are we here to talk about Brevity? I see how you look at her."

It was a jab designed to level the playing field, and Hero did feel a vicious bit better as heat flooded to Rosia's cheeks. She sat herself on the couch opposite and took a moment before giving Hero a level look. "The librarian needs you. The Library needs you, Reader."

She kept calling him that. And it raised a thrill up Hero's neck each time, a muddle of emotions he refused to unpack. "Of course they need me. Have you seen how much trotting over hither and yon I've done for them?" Hero shrugged, comfortable in his verbal armor. "I should get a knighthood. Or at least a pocket watch and some frequent-flier miles."

Hero had never owned a pocket watch, not in his story, not here, but a thousand alien concepts had flooded into him since he'd read the stories of the Library. For a former denizen of a high-fantasy novel, "frequent-flier miles" was just as nonsense a concept as light-speed spaceships, and not nearly as grounded in the material world. But that's what stories did. Let enough impossible things pass through you and they gain a kind of reality. Stories grant the impossible emotional gravity, create new orbits—and your mental universe expands.

Hero found it entirely irritating, in point of fact.

If the words were gibberish to Rosia, she was too composed to show it. Her wide full-moon eyes blinked at him slowly. "But your work is incomplete."

Hero reeled back with the offended air of a cat before water. "I beg your pardon? I have gathered every wing of the Library in one place! Even Poppaea didn't accomplish that!" If there was one thing Hero excelled at, it was taking offense. He was still building up a good self-righteous steam when Rosia's next words gutted him.

"Every wing except one."

The air in Hero's lungs was biting. He knew, but he didn't. "What do you mean?"

"You have gathered every wing of the Library, except one. And the stories missing dwarf all of us here."

Hero's spine turned to ice, then to iron. "I am never going back there. I died there."

But I got better, was the way he preferred to finish that joke to others, which served the dual purpose of being entertaining and entirely avoiding the truth.

"That's why only you can go back. Only you can speak to them, the stories of that wing." Rosia looked sad, near apologetic. "Reader, you have one more journey ahead of you."

The silence, the filtered air, the dim lights, it all turned on a coin flip, from soothing to suffocating. Hero looked away with the taste of dust gathering on his tongue. "Claire would never ask me to go back."

"But you will go nonetheless."

"Why?" Hero was shouting though he didn't intend it. "Why will I go? Why me? Why not you? You keep calling me 'Reader,' like it means something. But you're just the same as me, story without a book." His voice was thick. He swallowed and tasted ash. "You go to the Dust Wing."

"I am not the Reader," Rosia said.

"What does that mean?" Hero exploded into a yell and realized, distantly, *Ah yes, this is why Rosia led me all the way down here. Comforting, my ass.* He began to pace. "Tell me. If you know what I am now, tell me."

Part of him felt light with hope. Part of him hoped she would, right there. That Rosia would use her eerie wisdom and explain, give a name and understanding to the book-shaped hole he was now. Tell him his place in the story again.

Fate had never been that kind to Hero. Rosia tilted her head. "You are Hero."

A frustrated groan rose in his strangled throat, and Hero

collapsed on the armchair to dig his hands through his hair. "I'm not what you think I am."

Rosia was unperturbed. She advanced on him. "Anyone can be a reader; everyone is a reader from the start. We are what stories we tell ourselves, the ones we choose to believe in. Being the Reader isn't about reading stories. It's about sharing them."

"I didn't—"

"You listened to the Dust Wing. The stories sang to you, lingered, passed through, and left a haunt in their wake. You carry every story with you now. You lost your own story, but you gained millions of others." Rosia took a breath and paused, as if crossing an important boundary line. "Will you help others find their own?"

"I have no idea what you're talking about," Hero said, faint with resignation because he knew the shape of the plot he was in. His story sense was excellent, and he knew when a weird woman started talking about fate it was already too late.

"You will. You just haven't read that far yet." Rosia nodded to herself with some satisfaction.

"The Library won't be complete unless the Dust Wing joins. Our attempts to rebel will fail without it. Is that what you're saying?"

Rosia was maddeningly silent. Hero dropped his head back against the armchair, stirring up a specter of dust that almost made him vomit. He squeezed his eyes tight against the memory. "I thought I was done."

"Your story is not over." Rosia's voice was soft and certain.

"I'll go. Just—" Hero felt the tide of messy emotions in his chest. It was harder to swallow this time. He kept his eyes closed. "Just go. I can find my way back myself."

Rosia was silent. Hero barely heard the click of the door closing again before a jagged sob escaped his hold.

33

CLAIRE

I suppose you could consider fiction a kind of lie. But you'd be wrong to assume all storytellers are good liars. We're terrible at it—we admit the truth up front.

But sometimes the appeal of a lie is stronger than the one who's telling it.

Librarian Ibukun of Ise, 787 CE

IT WAS A THIN pastiche at best, but it would have to hold. Claire assessed Rami and Andras one last time before nodding brusquely. "That will do. At least for our purposes." Her gaze skimmed wearily over the damsel lounge again and came to land on a figure emerging from between two bookcases. "Ah, Hero." She cast a quick appraising glance behind her before crossing her arms in front of her chest. "Where did you hare off to this time?"

Hero was blurry around the eyes. Odd, but Claire could assign that to strain—who could blame him?—and perhaps a lack of rest. Still, the edges of his smile were more false than usual as he wheedled his way into the group. "Rosia caught me."

"What did she have to say?" Andras asked.

"Cryptic nonsense. What else?" Hero chucked his chin up, challenging the interest in the demon's voice.

"Well enough." Claire really didn't think it wise to foster small talk but was at a loss for where to direct the conversation that would inhabit less dangerous waters. So when the door swept open and a middle-aged damsel made a bid for attention, Claire was relieved.

"The water's stopped," the damsel said.

Across the way, Brevity made a gasp that was half relief and followed the damsel out the door. Claire glanced between Andras and Rami, but their faces were equally unreadable and unfamiliar. She followed Brevity out the door.

The dock had grown since they'd left it. Whether it was the sweat of the damsels or the imagination of Brevity's power as librarian, the jetty extended nearly across the aisle now. The more agile among them could have made the leap from the dock to the nearest bookcase of the Library stacks. (Claire, it should be noted, was not in that category.) Claire couldn't guess how much higher the waters had risen—with the stacks growing to stay ahead of the waterline and the ceiling lost in the dark overhead, there was no point of reference. But the churn that lapped at the edge of the dock looked ominously deep, fortified by depths of floodwater as Malphas's attack wedged its way in between the cracks.

There was no visual point of reference, no way to tell how many meters of water the Library floated upon now, but the ripple of relief as tension drained from Brevity's shoulders said it was no longer growing, no longer forcing her to keep the books one step ahead of destruction. "It stopped," Brevity confirmed, quiet voice almost dizzy with relief. Her gaze sharpened as she glanced up at Claire. "What's that mean?"

The silence on the dock lengthened, settling heavily until all she could hear was the gentle slosh of corrupted water against lacquered wood. Claire scanned the shadows of the stacks, but nothing emerged. No raven, cursing on the wing. Her nerves fluttered and she tried not to think about where Bird was. "It means our message was accepted. We are invited to court."

"Trap," Hero said blandly.

"What else did you expect?" Rami muttered.

"They expect us to just walk on out of here?" Brevity eyed the water suspiciously.

"Not us." Claire met Brevity's questioning look with a sigh. "You should stay here in case the... waters rise again."

"In case the negotiations fail and the court takes its vengeance anyway." Rosia had no qualms about stating the unstated. She looked rather calm about the whole matter, unlike Brevity, whose pixie face folded into a frown. Claire had braced herself for protest, or at least the recrimination of hurt in the muse's eyes, but Brevity surprised her with a fragment of a nod.

"I have to stay with the books." There was no regret in Brevity's voice, no hint of bitterness at missing out on the excitement of risk. The yearning Brevity had harbored once—which had burned, which had hungered—had grown into a steady self-confidence. "I am the librarian."

"You are the librarian," Claire said, and tried, with all her heart, to impart the muddle of gratitude and pride that welled up inside her. Brevity was the librarian of the Unwritten Wing, and Hell should tremble at her door. Claire put her hand on her shoulder. "I'll go. I can negotiate on behalf of the Library, and I'll take Andras with me." Moreover, she was expendable.

"You shouldn't go alone," Brevity said, as if she'd heard that thought.

"I'll escort her." Rami spoke up, no doubt in his voice.

"Rami, no…" Hero breathed.

"I'll go." Rami repeated. He turned, a smile playing at his lips as he brought a hand up to Hero's face, cupped a little too dramatically. "I have to do this, my love."

A little thick, don't you think? Claire drew a deep breath that struggled not to turn into a sigh. "Fine, Rami can escort, if he feels prepared to face Hell now. He'll know their tricks, anyway."

"Indeed I do." The angel's smile was sharp.

Andras cleared his throat with a disgruntled look. He reached over and removed Rami's hand from Hero's cheek stiffly. "If we are going, let us go."

"Cheer up, Andras," Claire said pointedly. "This will be a family reunion for you. You're a demon, are you not?"

The look Claire got was withering, but Andras straightened his shoulders. "I know my role."

"Remember it," Claire admonished, frowning as Rami winked at Hero once before boarding their little boat. This plan was holding together by the seams, but she had no choice but to make it work. She nudged Andras in next and graced Brevity with one more reassuring look before leaving the dock last. "If anything happens, don't wait for us. Protect the Library."

"Protect the Library," Brevity repeated softly. Claire scrutinized that but was stopped from asking a question when the boat tipped downward again.

"What do you think you're doing?" Claire hissed.

"Pushing off. Bon voyage!" Hero kicked the boat away from the dock with his foot and waved to the gathered damsels with a dramatic flourish before settling in on the edge of the prow. "You didn't really think I was going to let you two go off with that creature without me?"

"No, it is your duty to stay with Brev—"

"Claire." An intense quiet in Hero's voice stopped her short. He drew a calm look, first to Rami, then back to Claire. His lips pressed into a fine line. "It is not a matter of debate, not anymore. Where you go, I go."

34

HERO

I've seen enough revolutions in my time to say it with some authority: rebellions are built on love and hope. You can't reject the status quo unless you are hopeful enough to imagine something better. Of course, that doesn't make a lot of difference once the killing starts. My homeland was always good at that.

It's not such a ridiculous thing, to be willing to die for an idea. Sometimes, that's the only thing worth a good death.

Librarian Fleur Michel, 1734 CE

CLAIRE AND RAMI WERE curiously quiet the entire way. The boat floated in silence between canyon walls of bookshelves, bobbing gently against the sides when Rami allowed the boat to drift. Andras muttered quiet corrections in his navigation, but Hero tried to filter out most of what the demon said as a matter of principle. Hero had expected Rami would move aside so Hero could take up a place in the stern next to him, but Rami appeared to barely notice him. Fine, if that was the way it was to be, the ungrateful oaf could sleep on the damsels' couch alone tonight.

Assuming any of them made it back to the Unwritten Wing. According to Rosia, they were doomed to failure if he didn't return to the Dust Wing. A jaunt to Hell was preferable to visiting the place where his book—his story, perhaps just he himself—had died. Hero would take damnation over graves any day. He felt a tinge of guilt at the thought—and guilt itself was a novelty Hero had begun to experience with more frequency lately. He reached for a comfortable distraction. Claire's sour face was a perfect target. "Don't tell me my company is that repulsive, warden. I've been told I have my charm."

"It's not your charm that concerns me." Claire turned her attention to him with a surprisingly concerned knit of her brows. "Couldn't you have, just once, stayed behind?"

The alarm in her voice caught Hero off guard. "What, you still don't trust me?"

"The true question is if you trust me." Claire's gaze strayed to the other end of the boat, where Rami and Andras minded the oars. "Can you follow my lead in there, Hero, no matter what happens?"

A glib answer would have been easy—Hero kept a dozen on hand at any time. But there was a soft fear in Claire's dark eyes that forced him to reach for the truth. "I've trusted you with my life before, and I will do so as many times as you need me." His voice sounded more fragile than he liked; Claire had that effect on him.

"I'm—" Claire glanced away briefly. "I have a plan, but out here, anyone could be listening. It'd be too much to say aloud, anyway. You're going to have to trust me, Hero." She met his eyes, earnest and bleak. "More than ever."

"I—" Hero closed his mouth and glanced at Rami's back. Surely he heard them, but he hadn't turned around, hadn't said a word. Rami was notoriously close-lipped, but he could communicate a thousand opinions with the twist of his stoic face. They knew the plan; Hero did not. He was used to being an interloper, but not among those he cared about the most.

This was his cue. It was practically bright in lights above Claire's head, a villain's cue. To extract what he could, to above all protect himself from whatever struck the worry into Claire's eyes. But one couldn't be a villain without a book. The tragedy granted a moment of freedom that was disorienting. Hero took a sharp breath before shaking his head. He discovered the words as he said them. "I am here to support you. I'll follow your lead. You have my loyalty and my word, Claire."

The last time he'd given his word, it had been to Claire. Sour and smarting from his return to the Unwritten Wing, freshly bound to the Library, he'd sullenly promised to look out for its inhabitants. The memory seemed sepia distant, worlds away from the words he said now. He repeated it, only partially to himself. "I swear it."

Claire's lips parted, but Hero couldn't guess what she was going to say. He never could. She closed her mouth with whatever it was unsaid. Nodded once. "All right, then." The boat jostled under them abruptly. The hallway around them had changed, from wood and stone to something glossy and sinister white. The floor rose, or the water tapered off—it was impossible to tell which—and their little boat beached itself against a tile floor.

"We're here," Rami said with a strange tilt to his voice.

Claire nodded to herself and rose. Rami and Andras were already on dry land, securing the boat with reluctant cooperation. Andras offered a hand, and Claire frowned at it for a conflicted second before accepting. She stepped up to the prow, then hesitated as she looked over her shoulder. She met Hero's gaze for a fleeting moment. "For what it's worth, I trust you, Hero. My life, the

Library, the books. With everything."

She looked away again just as quickly, hurrying on to the shore. It was as near a love confession as they got, librarian and book, author and character. Nobody and nobody, as their roles currently stood, Hero amended silently. Hero swallowed the stone of feeling down as he followed the others down the hall to Hell's court.

35

HERO

None of this makes sense. Hell, Heaven, the afterlife. Not if you think about it logically. What are afterlife realms? Which came first, the human idea of Hell, or the realm that claims that title? The mere fact that the realms exist in tandem means it can't be totally a creation of man's imagination. One true god—unless you hire a carriage and swing by the next neighborhood over? The prophets and holy books would have surely mentioned a small detail like that.

No, the realms have to be something else, something truer than imagination, belief, or even gods. They're primordial. These spaces we take up, but not merely to occupy. They adapt, absorb, adjust in response to their inhabitants. The realms become.

It begs the question, If the realms become the occupant, could an occupant become the realm?

That is a question that shall require coffee.

Librarian Gregor Henry, 1971 CE

THE VESTIBULE WAS CLEAN; the vestibule was terrible. White lines rose in simple patterns up the walls. Hero almost preferred the grime and human suffering of their previous court appearance to this. At least then there was some trace of life, however miserable. Here the marble under their feet was soulless and eternal. No mark of anyone who had passed this way, no chance of leaving their own traces behind. It had no past and held no future. Nothing would remain here; nothing could remain. If there was a philosophical opposite to a story, it was this white page of a hallway. It made Hero's skin crawl. No one met them at the shore, and no guards or sentries intercepted them as they proceeded along the wide corridor to a single inconspicuous door at the other end. The oppressive noncolor surrounded them, pressed down on them. It drummed against the ink—blood? whatever—that ran in his veins. Hero had the wild impulse to look at his hands, as if the white could erase his existence, bit by bit.

But some things were immovable, uneditable, and true. Hero held on to the sight of Rami's square shoulders, feathers fluffed at precise angles under the collar of his trench coat, a sturdy block of gray and brown against the absence. And Claire, warm brown skin and hair inky black, blots of rebellion in this place. Small fragments of beads still clasped the ends of her locks, flashes of color and spite. They carried their own stories with them, even here. They could forge their own words and worlds. Hero could not exist in a blank page, but he could hold on to them, mortal and immortal and both all too human, and follow them across the gap. He could, though each step against the white stone felt like falling into nothing.

He would do it, for them.

Out of the corner of his eye, he caught a flash of color. Andras had fallen back to walk in step with Hero, and his features were collapsed into a strange and alien expression that Hero couldn't interpret.

FORGET ALLIANCES, FORGET NECESSARY evils. Hero understood all that, but the memory of seeing Andras's satisfied face as the pages of his book tore still clung to Hero and soured his stomach. He didn't slow his pace. "What are you looking at, demon?"

Andras had the nerve to actually flinch as if he was surprised. The cruel line of his lips thinned momentarily before he looked away. "You seemed... uneasy."

"Uneasy? On our way to gently lay our necks on Hell's chopping block for the good of the cause? Uneasy in a void-like prison made by our enemy? What a stunning deduction." Hero's stomach roiled behind his protective wall of snark. His loathing for the demon beside him was the only thing that kept his mask in place. "Are all demons so astute? No, of course not; otherwise you wouldn't have lived the last year inside a tchotchke." It was a word Hero had just learned from a Slavic book, and delightful to enunciate with a sneer.

To Hero's horror, Andras actually smiled at that, before getting his expression under control. He lifted his chin and looked away. "I didn't mean—"

"Oh, you mean," Hero growled. "You mean everything. You are planning something, don't deny it." The pent-up feelings—of rage, of fear, of everything that had started when this one frivolous little snake had decided to meddle and play at king—they all bubbled up and drew Hero to a halt. He stabbed a finger in Andras's face. "You—I see you. Don't think you're fooling all of us. There's no redemption story for you here, demon. You are fallen and irredeemable and I don't know what you are planning, but I will stop you. And if you so much as inconvenience them"—Hero pointed his finger ahead, where Claire and Rami had begun to approach an end to the endless corridor—"Heaven's wrath will seem like a mere slap compared to what I'll do to you."

Honestly, this was when Hero had expected a smile. Andras loved nothing more than to rile people up and roll in their darkest emotions like a pig in mud. But the demon looked strangely taken aback, then solemn.

"Andras. Hero." Claire's voice shook Hero out of his thoughts. She'd stopped with Rami before a white expanse of wall. Something still constricted Hero's chest every time he looked straight on, but upon inspection he could just make out the fine break that signaled a door. Not the grand double doors of the Unwritten or Arcane Wing, but simple, utilitarian. The kind of door that would lead to a doctor's office or a conference room or an accountant's office. It was disappointing, but also fitting. In Hero's experience, the worst evils were done in innocuous nothing rooms like this one.

It was easy to ignore Andras as he drew up beside the others. Rami shot him a questioning look, but Hero shook his head to dismiss it.

"Ready, gentlemen?" Claire asked.

"Ready," Andras said.

Hero nodded his agreement but caught the heat of Claire's concern anyway. "Hero," she said slowly. "I wish you would wait outside. We might need an escape—"

"I'm not letting you—either of you—walk into Hell alone."

"The Unwritten Wing and the Arcane Wing, representatives of the Library," Claire said primly. She nodded to Andras and added, "And company."

THE ROOM WAS NOT any of Hero's definitions of a court. Neither was it the farcical horror that they'd navigated last time. There were no pens, no cages in sight, when Claire opened the door.

Instead, there was a masquerade.

Brevity would have called it a party. Rami and Claire would have called it a bother. But Hero knew the only proper term for it was "masquerade." Any other word would have been an insult to the swirl of satin and gilded claws that swirled around them. The hall boasted an elaborate painted ceiling, every surface decorated like an ivory wedding cake. Traces of lily and amber hung in the air, first enticing, then suffocating as it drew them into the dizzying whirl of the crowd.

It was beautiful and dazzling and exactly the kind of event that had made Hero break into a cold sweat when he was... well, when he was his story. A country rebel turned king was unaccustomed to the dangerous waters of royal social functions. He'd had tutors and advisers, after his rise to power, and Hero was accomplished at feigning confidence, but he'd always dreaded these things. Later in his reign, he usually just drank himself into oblivion to get through them. He was fickle and impulsive when in his cups. Performative cruelty was expected of royalty. It made for a better party.

Perhaps he hadn't been a good king, in retrospect.

The idea of facing this milieu dead sober proved they were still in Hell. Hero turned, but as expected, the door behind them had disappeared.

Claire made an irritated click of her tongue. "Ugh, wide lapels. Those were ugly even when I was alive."

Hero squinted, but every courtier in his gaze was decked in trim velvets and sateen. Rami and Andras wore similarly bemused expressions. Hero's mind ground through the possibilities to turn the corner. "I am guessing you are not in the middle of a vaguely French gala, warden."

Claire shot him a dubious look and grimaced. "No, worse. One of those endless holiday functions for the office where I clerked. All tedious old white men who—" She stopped, blinking as if trying to clear the memory from her eyes. "Oh."

"I just see demons," Rami volunteered.

"Heaven," Andras chimed in with an unhappy note.

"Hell is a tailored experience," Hero mused. "It would make sense we all see whatever situation makes us most uncomfortable."

Claire regarded the crowd with a new eye. Hero didn't know what she saw, but he saw free drinks. He intercepted a waiter that passed through their orbit and snagged several slender champagne flutes off the gilded tray. He took a sizable sip of one before passing the rest out to the others. Andras regarded the glass as if it were a trap, Claire declined to taste, but to his delight Rami sniffed once, then downed the whole thing.

"Easy, old man." Hero touched the curve of Rami's forearm. Hero wasn't exactly sure if angels could get intoxicated, but he assumed if there was anywhere it was possible, it was Hell.

"CLAIRE, CHILD, HOW GOOD of you to make it." Malphas did not match the courtiers in silks and shadow. In any milieu, she was the war mother, grandmother of ghosts. She'd traded in her bloody leathers for a suit, impeccably tailored to her trim frame, in the style of the false-courtly conceit of the room. It was done in a fine weave the precise shade of rust and shadow, the oblivion color of blood just before it disappears into the dark. There was a carnation, bright and pink, adorning the right lapel.

"I had expected you to choose something more martial," Claire said, sweeping a hand to indicate both Malphas's dress and the aesthetics of the room.

Malphas smiled that fond, grandmotherly smile she had that chilled Hero straight to the bone. No grandmother looked so about to eat you. "So naive, child. Fine suits and satin gloves have more blood on them than brute armor and brass ever will. We're beyond such base intimidation measures, wouldn't you say? Come, you are the guests of honor after all."

Malphas led them a circuitous route around the ballroom, allowing every minor demon and hopped-up imp in a corset to take a gander. Hero strode on the outside, providing what protection he could from the prying eyes. He risked a measured glance at Rami. The stoic Watcher had paled before at the merest hint of facing the demons he had fallen from Heaven with. Hero was prepared to shore him up, to provide what comfort their burgeoning relationship could offer. But when he glanced at Rami, the angel had a calm, almost half smile on his face. As if this were an afternoon walk. The emotional stability was really quite unfairly galling. Hero wasn't sure whether to take offense or pride in the fact that Hell couldn't ruffle Rami's calm, but Hero could.

Over Rami's shoulder, Andras had a dour expression on his face. Hero relished a new target. "Not the welcome you hoped for, demon?" Hero delighted in the discomfort on his face. "I thought you'd be overjoyed to be coming home."

"You would think," Andras said, voice tight with something that felt familiar but Hero couldn't place.

"Go easy on him, dear." Rami captured Hero's hand and gave it a forward squeeze. Hero had tried forever—days, even—to get Rami to start using affectionate names, but he'd always refused. "He's only a demon."

Andras's expression was schooled into a distant look that

almost hid the anger that flashed in his cold gold eyes. "Aren't you supposed to be escorting Claire, Ramiel?"

"I would never leave this one's side," Rami said, squeezing Hero's arm again, and Hero resisted the urge to stare at him in surprise.

"I appreciate the invitation, General," Claire was saying ahead of them. "But as I said in my letter, I am here to negotiate for—"

The slap came out of nowhere. Even Rami, who was ostensibly on guard at all times, must have missed it. Hero had been lulled by the press of coifed hair and powdered hands, lulled by the civilized cruelty of it all. Physical violence felt too pedestrian for this lot, but one of the nameless courtiers had slithered from the crowd and struck fast. It was only Andras who reacted when Claire's chin turned with the force of the slap. He caught the aggressor's wrist with a stony strength Hero hadn't thought the old demon capable of.

"Return them." It was impossible that Hero had ever mistaken the warrior in Andras's grasp as a courtier. The knight was tall, with a cascade of pale hair skimming past the sword at their waist. Hero blinked and their clothing appeared to melt from the European bustles and lace into a brilliantly colored sash that rested on top of a strange armor of brass. Their face had a long aquiline quality that was wonderful for sneering.

"Return what?" Claire sounded tentative, as if spinning through a mental Rolodex. She didn't rub her cheek or give any indication that she'd just been struck out of nowhere. "I don't believe we've met—"

"You steal something you can't even recall. That makes you ignorant and a thief."

Hero had a rule; he was the only one allowed to call Claire names. This nonsense was going too far. He took the opening to step in smoothly. "Hero, knight gallant, at your service, sir."

The curl of the knight's lip got more severe, as he knew it would. They turned their focus on Hero. Andras released their wrist slowly. "Knight errant, perhaps. Our guards had reports of a strange pretty creation stealing our Library away with false promises. That was you, wasn't it?"

"Hear that, Rami? I'm pretty."

"You're beautiful, darling," Rami said.

"You're a diplomatic representative from another realm." Claire paused, tilting her head with obvious calculation as she looked the woman up and down. "Tír na nóg? The Summerlands?"

"I am Aithne, Duke of the Far Halls, and you have committed the worst treason against my people."

"It's only treason if one is a citizen," Rami murmured politely.

"Charmed." Claire crossed her arms across her chest. Hero couldn't help but notice the pause that had pooled into quiet around them. Courtiers had turned their masked gazes to the exchange. Hunger was in the air. "But I have no business with the Fair Folk, so if you'll pardon—"

"I will not."

"But faerie aren't an afterlife belief," Hero objected.

Claire shook her head. "They are if enough belief lingers. How many generations mourned their loved ones, stolen away by the faerie?"

"We do not need to steal, unlike you," Aithne interjected.

Claire didn't rise to the bait. "Take a trip to Ireland. No one may worship the faerie anymore, but see how many are willing to bulldoze a hawthorn tree in an empty field. I'd warrant the Fair Folk are given more circumspect *respect* than many modern religions."

"They know better than to make an enemy of our people," Aithne said. Their hand rested on the pommel of their sword.

Hero hadn't seen it move, and alarm spiked through his nerves.

"We have not stolen anything from you," Claire snapped, and Hero thrilled at the way she straightened, chin rising with the anger he loved so much. "The Library belongs to no one."

"You invade our land without invitation, you raid our treasure house—"

"The Library is not gold to be hoarded." Claire took a step forward, heedless of the fact that the elf knight had a longsword, a head of height, and a couple of stone of muscle on her. "That was your mistake from the start. The tenants of the Library are..."

Andras cleared his throat and Claire hesitated. To her credit, she didn't let herself glance at Malphas, who had been silently reveling in every word. "The Library is sovereign from its host realm. Faerie has not been singled out with this inconvenient fact."

"No, we have not... How bracing it was to arrive and realize I didn't come alone," Aithne said, voice taking on an edge. At the edge of his vision, Hero thought he saw cloth and courtiers shift. "Though I would not presume to speak for them."

The blind bustle of the crowd melted away from some distinctly undemonic figures. There was a rotund bearded man in a fur-lined cape, and there, an elder woman swathed in a turquoise sari. Another wore weave covered with what might have been depictions of Mayan gods and a gold snake around their wrist. There were half a dozen emissaries from other (former) Library realms there. None of them had a sympathetic look for Claire, or the Library. All of them looked aggrieved and prepared for violence.

This was why Hero had come, of course. Claire had that effect on people.

Aithne took a decisive step forward, but then Malphas was in the gap, one hand raised. "Now, now, ambassadors. I appreciate your spirit, but what kind of host would I be if I let you disembowel a guest before refreshments?" Malphas tilted her hand out in a *what can you do?* gesture. "At least have a glass of wine first. Ours won't trap you."

Aithne's cheek twitched. Their glare didn't leave Claire when they reached for a glass and took a long, disdainful sip. The threat of violence in the air receded somewhat, from imminent to merely portentous.

Malphas clapped her hands and turned away with a cluck of her tongue. "Such manners in the youth these days." She ordered them to follow her with an imperious twitch of her battle-scarred fingers. Claire allowed them to be herded, but Aithne watched them over the rim of their wineglass as the Library contingent passed.

"I can see whose idea this was, and you're not that clever. The next step you take outside the Library, little human, I guarantee you will see me."

Hero was used to threats. Frankly, he enjoyed a good, colorful oath to end one's life; it added zest to the day. But there was a dark grain to the statement that turned it from threat to prophecy, an oily certainty that hung in the air and clung after them as they walked away. Hero made the decision then and there that Claire was never, ever stepping so much as into the hallway without a full guard.

Malphas spoke into the silence as they put distance between them and the emissaries. The demon courtiers pressing in around them felt downright safe, in retrospect. "Now is when you would express gratitude if you were wise, girl."

Claire sniffed. "It's not as if you could have done otherwise. You'd have looked weak if you allowed another realm to take your prey; isn't that the way of Hell?" They were being guided toward the long table at the end of the room. In a normal setting it would have been a place for honored guests. Instead, the dais looked like a scaffold. Claire showed no reluctance as they reached the steps. "Besides, we are here to broker an understanding, are we not?"

"You are in a poor position to negotiate, child. You set yourself in rebellion to Hell and then walk willingly into my court? You are foolish if you think you'll walk out again."

"Your court, General? I thought it was Lucifer's."

The remaining air died out of the room. The air chilled, though not a breeze stirred the lights of the candelabras. The animosity between Claire's and Malphas's locked gazes grew and thickened until it shattered on the sharp edge of Malphas's laughter. "You are an imaginative human, I'll give you that. Come sit in a place of honor, mortal."

Hero watched Claire bristle, but then take a moment to cagily measure the width of the audience. The farce of a fete had been suspended; every demonic creature in the court had their covetous attention centered on their backs. It was enough to make Hero's sword hand itch. Claire weighed their options, then appeared to come to a decision erring on the side of caution. She inclined her head and accepted a helping hand from Rami to ascend the dais. She took the indicated seat next to Malphas at the center of the table, and it didn't take long for other seats to clear for Hero, Rami, and Andras as the rest of Malphas's underlings took the hint. Hero beat out Andras for a seat next to Claire—no way he was being pushed to the peanut gallery for this entertainment.

"Where is our vile benefactor anyway?" Claire feigned ease as she settled into her seat. She reached out for the glittering glass of wine that had been set in front of her, then thought better of it. "This is quite the gathering, Malphas. I'd think Lucifer would be present."

"Your childish snit is hardly important enough to rise to the attention of a god," Malphas drawled with a strained edge. "Mind yourself, Claire."

"Oh, I am. Minding, that is. And what's come to mind is a peculiar pattern. I and my people have been to an awful lot of afterlife realms by now, and I have yet to speak to a single actual god in their domain. Isn't that curious?"

Technically accurate, Hero supposed. The monstrous crocodile of the labyrinth realm was more of a demigod squatter than a divine creator.

Malphas didn't seem amused. "I have more than enough authority to destroy you and every person, book, or"—she curled her lip at Rami—"thing that you hold dear."

"Careful, General Malphas," Claire said, cool as an exposed blade. "Someone will think you're setting yourself up as a god." Frost raced across the back of Hero's neck in gooseflesh, but Claire continued before Malphas could make good on the murderous look she had. "But then, I suppose absence is as good as permission, isn't it?"

The feints were subtle in this dance Claire was having, but if Hero read the acid in Malphas's eyes right, it was Hell that came out of it bleeding. She inclined her head as if acknowledging a point. "How I'll miss our little talks when you're gone, Claire."

"Is that why you're drawing this out, Malphas? Sentimentality?"

Malphas's smile fell into a grim line. "I could blot you all out. Right now."

"Your ledger isn't the one our names are in." Claire smoothed her lap and crossed her ankles. "Try again."

"You offered me the clever brat." Malphas flicked a dismissive finger toward Andras. If he took offense at being called a child, he had a good enough poker face to not show it. "For that, we can forget your indiscretion with the books. Step aside and let Hell do what we do best, punish souls."

Claire's laughter was sharp as a razor. "Try again, Grandmother of Ghosts."

It was obvious Malphas hated that moniker. She sucked on her cheek a moment, looking for all the world like one of those aunties at the village market in Hero's distant memories that would call you sweetie before fleecing you. "Give us Andras, and the Library can expand."

"No," Claire said simply. "You relinquish all hold of the Library—and all souls within it."

Malphas made a snorting noise. "Retribution on one bastard duke—even one as annoying as Andras—is not worth that. Nothing is."

"Nothing?" Claire said with a mild smile.

The negotiations were interminable. Hero stopped paying attention after he sipped his way through the first glass of wine. By the second, he was out of demons to study and bored, and by the third, he found he didn't mind anymore. He was idly curious to see what would run dry first—Malphas's threats or Claire's scheming.

She really was devastatingly attractive when she was like this—not in a sexual way, because in this mode she was also incredibly terrifying in that all-powerful way authors were to books. But attractive, like a natural disaster.

"The angel, then." Malphas's cool tone ripped Hero back to attention. The demon general slouched back in her divan with a syrup-slow smile. "Forget the duke. Let's talk your pet Watcher."

"Ramiel is not here for negotiation," Claire said stiffly. She still hadn't touched her wine, and if anything she rose straighter in her chair, hands folded in her lap. Beneath the table, Hero could see they were clenched.

"You've rejected every other reasonable concession, child. Let's just explore one more," Malphas said mildly. "Or are you the one now wasting time?"

"We don't barter people."

"But Ramiel is not a people, is he? He's a fallen angel, same as all of us here. Same as Andras, and you were certainly quick to trade him away." Malphas's tone took on the eminently reasonable, inoffensive watercolor of logic that all the worst people used to do wrongs to others. "If you've grown fond, remember he's immortal. I doubt we could hurt him if we tried."

"You would," Andras said in a granite voice. "Try."

Malphas shrugged. She repositioned the silk wrap around her shoulders. The illusion of some beneficent old dowager just settling in. Granting boons instead of curses. "Even demons have to find something to pass the time."

"You ask for a member of my family but offer nothing. It's not worth a crumb of freedom."

"What about the whole cake?" The entire table fell silent and Malphas took a prolonged pause to sip from her glass. "Andras might buy you a crumb, but leave Ramiel here and the Library can leave the realm with Hell's blessing."

"You're not serious," Claire said softly.

"I'm a demon. What do you want, a pinkie swear?" Malphas's chuckle was ghoulish. "If you don't trust my word, perhaps you'll take Hell's." She struck the side of her glass with a spoon, and the crystal ring was sharp enough to make everyone else at the table wince. She cleared her throat, though her voice carried well through the immediate silence. "Attention, you lovely beasties."

"What's your game, Malphas?" Hero muttered. He gave a reassuring shake of the head to Rami. Claire would rather chew off her own hand than abandon any of them in a place like this. She would not take the bait. Hero was more concerned about what Malphas's next play would be when she refused.

Malphas stood, rising from her seat every bit the queen she said she wasn't. "The Library wants to abandon the generous protection of our realm." The crowd began to rumble with the appropriate disapproval, but Malphas held up a staying hand. "Aye, but Lucifer knows mortals are shortsighted. However, the Library is a... significant resource to Hell's community." The wrinkles around her eyes multiplied as she squinted cannily at Claire. It was all but admitting Malphas knew how many souls were hidden in the Unwritten Wing alone. The confirmation sent a chill down Hero's spine.

"It is a great loss, but we are nothing if not reasonable, aren't we, boys?" She was in military-commander mode now, psyching up the troops, making everything look like her idea. Perhaps it was. Hero smelled a trap. "Now, I've made the former librarian here a completely reasonable offer that includes the return of our long-lost brother, Ramiel, who I know you've all missed so dearly..."

Malphas trailed off for their benefit. So Hero could precisely taste the malevolent interest as all demon gazes in the room slid to take in Rami. The oily underside of the pause made Hero's jaw clench. He may not have understood the finer animosity between Watchers and the fallen angels who had embraced the demonic place in Hell, but Hero did understand revenge, objectification, possession.

It was ridiculous that Claire was allowing this farce to go on this long.

"I'll go," someone whispered to Hero's right. Claire's expression fell as she processed who'd said it a second before Hero did. He jolted out of his chair, causing a terrible racket as he stood. Rami had his hands folded in his lap, shoulders tense and turned in but resolved. "I'll do it."

"The hell you will," Hero growled. He swung around to get support from Claire—she was very good at reining in Rami's handsome idiot tendencies—but she was looking at her hands as if she was contemplating a great evil.

Well, there was no contemplating that.

"The hell you will," Hero repeated firmly.

"So much spirit in the young ones. This will be bloody," Malphas muttered into her wineglass with relish.

"Hero—" Claire raised a placating hand, but he didn't like the pity in her eyes. No, pity meant he was wrong. Hero was wrong about many glorious and impressive things, but not this. Not Rami. If there were two truths in his life, the first one was that Rami belonged with them. The second one was that Claire, in different ways, did too. They were the cardinal points on his compass, and the hesitancy that hung in the air right now sent the arrow spinning.

"Tell him he's not. Tell him." The thread of fear in Hero's voice was agonizing, but he didn't break eye contact with Claire. He didn't like the way she blinked, hated the way the fine muscles along her stubborn jaw tightened. It broke his remaining certainty, and he added, more softly, "Please."

"Why shouldn't I?" Rami interrupted the thick silence. A strange, sharp edge to his voice brought Hero's head around. He had a challenging look in his eyes, the soothing gray darkened to coal. "I'm of no other use to you."

"You are of use to me," Hero snarled viciously. The barbs winding around his chest were so tight he nearly jumped out of his skin when Claire laid a soft hand on his arm.

"Hero," she said quietly. "You swore to follow my lead here."

"Your lead can go hang—"

"What use am I to you?" Rami asked, contemplatively.

The calm—the resignation—in Rami's voice incited Hero. It altered the usual flippant answer he might have given. Without it, his need was exposed and raw when he answered.

"Because I love you, you ignorant bastard."

A grunt came from Andras's direction, but Hero kept his eyes locked with Rami's. Hero expected any number of reactions. He had grown to relish the velvet-tender way Rami's eyes could soften when looking at him. He might have even accepted seeing pain and pity, with Rami set on his self-destructive course. But the crook of his lips was a gut punch, followed swiftly with a mortal wound as Rami simply tilted his head in calm, curious interest.

Hero felt as if he were bleeding from an unseen wound.

"You said you trusted me." Claire's hand tightened on him, and a shuttered look came over her face. It was a look Hero was infinitely familiar with by now, and it caught and fizzled the anger in his throat. She didn't look away, but emotionally she hunkered down, braced for a terrible answer. "Do you trust me?"

The air was stale with avarice. The demons that crowded the room had ceased their farce of partying to watch the argument unfold. The crumbling of Hero's world was nothing but a melodrama for Hell. He couldn't breathe. It'd been so long since he'd been betrayed that he'd forgotten, like old scars, how much it hurt.

"I trusted you," he finally answered, and he felt his tone crack. He forced himself to look at Rami, face the calm and ease with which the angel could walk away from him. "I trusted you," he said in a broken whisper.

"Let's make this distasteful business official, ____ n. I will hand over this one, and he will return to your realm—as a member, not a prisoner. And will not be punished for whatever slight you have perceived in the past. All obligations of the Library to its host realm will be terminated, furthermore—" Claire was saying, wrestling through the possible loopholes with the sturdy finesse of a barrister. Hero couldn't find it in him to care. He abruptly shifted his attention to the table and snatched the wineglass. He drained it in one snarling gulp. He'd lost the chance to disseminate or pretend indifference, but he would not fall apart in front of his enemies. He clenched his jaw until he tasted his own blood. The Library had softened him, made him able to bleed like this now. But the demons would not taste his tears; he would give no one that pleasure.

"We have an accord," Malphas said.

He must have a masochistic streak, because he found himself looking at Rami again. The angel seemed unruffled by Claire's betrayal and the horrors of his future in Hell. Hero had the distant thought that it already seemed unreal. The creases of Rami's trench coat seemed too clean, his rumpled feathers too straight. His craggy olive features cool as stone, and the silver in his eyes yellowed. Had Rami changed or had Hero just never seen him clearly? Had he been so easy to walk away from?

The infernal wine roiled in his stomach and threatened to rise.

"It's done. Let's get out of this disgusting place." Claire tugged on Hero's sleeve. Hero nodded, reaching gladly for the numbness that threatened to set in. He stumbled away from the table. He saw his feet manage a series of successful steps across the court as something dark and desperate welled up in his chest.

He never reached the door.

He twisted and surged back. He only made it a single step before he felt Claire catch his arm. "You can't mean to stay here. You're not one of them!" His voice was raw. Hero twisted it over the line to anger rather than heartbreak. "Giving yourself over to Hell won't absolve you of whatever damned sins you think you've committed."

And Ramiel's stony face never moved.

His heart wasn't in his chest. His heart was there, at the table, with Malphas's cruel hand gripping hard. Hero's stomach gave a lurch, and he was only mildly aware when Claire hauled him back and shook him, hard. "Hero, look at me."

"Rami—" Hero lurched, and was stunned at Claire's strength as she used his momentum to spin him around instead. Her chin was set and tense, eyes shining with pain. Good. If she would betray them, if she would just sell off those who loved her like chips on a table, if…

Claire wouldn't do any of those things. The dissonance was what finally split Hero's heart in two. "How could… Why, Claire? Why?"

He saw the question hit her like a slap. Her eyes were wet and furious. "Fine. Make me the monster. Hate me if you want, Hero. But listen to me. Remember what you swore before we came."

Hero's chest felt strung tight as a bowstring. But he'd run out of ammunition. He cast one glance back at Rami, but he had already diverted his gaze to Malphas and the court. His hope deflated. "I'll listen, warden." He felt the dull anger stinging his eyes as he glared at her. "One last time, I'll be your leashed dog. But after we walk out those doors, we are done."

36

CLAIRE

Hell is not the place for matters of the heart, and the Library is no place for frivolity. Don't let passing whims ruin a good index.

Apprentice Librarian Yoon Ji-Han, 1818 CE

Forgive my language, Librarian, but what the hell? The Library is made up of nothing *but* passion. What books have *you* been reading?

Librarian Gregor Henry, 1819 CE

IT WAS A MARVEL that the boat did not sink under the simmering accusation Hero brought in with him. Claire hated herself when he would not meet her eyes, but when he finally did, the betrayal was a stab in the gut. It wasn't that it wasn't well deserved, Claire knew that. But it was that she'd gotten out of practice. Once, she'd deserved those looks. Once, the extent of Claire and Hero's relationship was a perverse argument in the language of betrayal.

Warden and book, human and idea. He must think that was what she had defaulted to now, for this. After all this.

Claire silently cursed herself again for allowing Hero to tag along. She should have seen that coming. She should have ensured he was occupied with work for the damsels when she, Rami, and Andras had departed. Sloppy. She used to be better at this.

The thought didn't bring her any comfort.

The doors closed behind them; the dam broke. "We can't leave him—" Hero started pleadingly.

Claire made a silencing motion that brooked no argument. Miraculously, it worked. She perched at the end of the hull and remained still and composed as Hero slunk in after Andras and silently took up one of the oars. She could still feel eyes on them as they pushed away from the flooded hallway. Malphas had spies all up and down this route, of course. She'd kept her silence on the way in, but the way out seemed to stretch interminably as Hero hunched his shoulders and rowed. Only a fictional character could successfully turn rowing into a study in angst. He attacked the task with mechanical ferocity, a mortally wounded beast ready to strike out at the nearest obstacle—in this case, the murky water.

The silence held for a time before Hero's voice broke. "You abandoned him."

Claire squeezed her eyes closed. "Hero—"

"You just traded him like he was nothing. He served you faithfully. We... He loved you—" Hero's voice wobbled. He didn't look up, didn't stop rowing, but his hunched shoulders hitched higher. "We all knew how hard it was for Rami to face Hell again. It tore him up inside but he did it—for us, for you. And then you sold him to those jackals like a piece of meat."

"That's not what—"

"Don't defend yourself!" The oar paused out of the water and Hero clenched it in his fists as he stood, throwing the boat into a precarious wobble even as they continued to drift. "Rami wasn't—isn't—like you and me, Claire. Rami is *good*. He could have destroyed us whenever he wanted—every other immortal creature we meet in this goddamn place is a bastard, you will recall. But not Rami. From the start Rami has been good. He is patient and kind and against all gods-damn odds he fell in love with you—with me, I…" Hero's voice was beyond a crack. It threatened to dissolve, but he wasn't ready to let Claire off without verbalizing her crimes. "Ramiel is the best of both of us. He would have died for us and you just… used him. You used all of us like we were nothing and—" Hero stopped short, flinching back with a shake of his head.

Only the slosh of thick water against the hull punctuated the silence. Hero sat frozen in the center of the boat as he stared at Claire as if he couldn't recognize her. Neither spared a glance for Andras, sitting still as stone between them. It took Claire time to speak around the knot of self-loathing in her voice. "You are right. All of it. I am not good, never was."

Hero's expression crumbled into pain. "Claire, it's Rami. Turn the boat around, we have to go back and—"

"Three more meters, Hero. Trust me for three more meters. That's all I ask of you." Claire studied her hands, then looked up to hold his gaze. It was a request—Claire had no illusion about her ability to steer the boat on her own. "Then I'll be whatever monster you deem me."

It was a cruel thing to ask. Hero's lip curled as an interior war raged. His sword hand trembled before he twitched a nod. "Three. Damned. Meters."

There was no more to be said. Hero's eyes challenged her to

look away, so Claire didn't dare. The air had turned less briny as Hell waters gave over to the flooded stacks of the Library. Still, Claire didn't move until the shadow of the Library's great doors fell over the boat. "All right. Go ahead. That should be far enough."

Hero tilted his head, confused, until a blur of shadow and feathers spun between them. The shadow moving across the boat passed over Andras and left behind Ramiel, whole and sitting in the boat between them, in his place as the illusion swept away. He looked nearly as pained as Hero had, but the stricken look was colored with an air of wonder as he looked between Hero and Claire.

A strangled sound clawed its way out of Hero's throat. Claire hadn't thought it possible to strike Hero speechless. But amusement quickly passed as she caught the expression on his face. His misery melted into shock, which then melted in the furnace of something much darker and harder. Claire backpedaled as he rose to his feet. She was too familiar with Hero to be scared of him, but the intensity of his gaze made her... well, nervous. "Hero, I'm sorry, but it was a tactical decision—"

Claire didn't quite believe it when Hero reached out and, with a graceful push, tilted her over the side of the boat.

The water wasn't cold, precisely, but Claire still got out a yelp as it folded over her head. Her feet hit the bottom after a short dive and she pushed off, bobbing to the surface and coughing up most of a wave's worth of water. The water must have been clear of any harmful ink or residue, because she felt fine if sputtering furious.

"Hero!" The boat had drifted down the flooded hallway with the momentum. Hero stood at the side staring inscrutably at her. Behind him, Rami had risen, but before he could reach out, Hero dove into the water without a sound. He broke the surface again a second later, water coursing off his hair and high cheekbones like some gods-damn Byronic antihero. Claire gulped another mouthful of water in surprise.

The water wasn't deep, but it was deep enough that Claire had to tread to keep her head comfortably above water. Hero, with his height, had no such encumbrance. He began to forge through the water with a dark glint in his eye.

"Now, you have every right to be upset—" Claire tried to backpedal but it turned into a flailing splash.

"You lied to me." Hero's shirt was soaked through and plastered to his pale skin. A bit of froth clung to his absolutely ruined velvet jacket but he didn't appear to care. "You let me think you would hurt us."

Claire heard a muted splash that she assumed was Rami abandoning the boat to save her. She grimaced and lost her footing again. "It's unforgivable, I admit it. We couldn't risk—"

"You…" Hero reached her, clutching her upper arm too tight, which at least kept Claire from drowning. But he didn't stop there. He took another step and water drenched her neck again as Claire's shoulders hit the hallway wall. She could feel the heat radiating off him. "You were never going to leave Rami behind."

"… No," Claire admitted in a bewildered voice. She was no longer flailing in the water, but Hero still had his grip on her arm, bracketing her in against the wall. She couldn't read Hero's intense expression at all, but at least she felt he was no longer at risk of drowning her. The chill of the water pricked goose bumps up her spine. "What do you think you're doing?"

"A tactical decision," Hero muttered. He paused, water sloshing between their chests where she was caged in against the wall. "Go ahead. Call yourself a monster again."

"I'm—" Claire hesitated, regret sinking like a stone in her

stomach again. "It was necessary. I am a monster. I understand if you don't—"

The air between them grew smaller as Hero leaned down, nose almost brushing hers. His eyes were furiously dark and green, but this close Claire could see tiny streaks of violet, which was distracting. "I. Don't. Care." He bit out the words. And *Oh, he's so mad that he's going to bite me.* Claire just had the time for the utterly ridiculous thought to flit through her head before Hero caught her lips.

The force of the kiss pressed Claire against the cold stone of the wall. The chill sank into her skin and muddled with the heat flooding up her face, coals at her lips, arms, collarbone, anywhere Hero touched. She anchored herself by the velvet lapels of Hero's coat, and when Hero finally eased back she was horrified to hear herself gasp for air a dumb moment.

"I don't care," Hero repeated at a fair growl. "I don't care if you're a monster or not. If you're a monster, then you are *our* monster. We can be monsters together."

Claire opened her mouth again, but this time, Hero drowned her. He kissed her again, and his foot slipped and they slid underwater. This would have normally been much more alarming to Claire if Hero were not currently doing the most *distracting* cleverness with his tongue.

A new set of hands gripped her waist and dragged them back to the surface just as she was running out of air. Hero surfaced with an indignant kick, but Rami didn't let go of either of them. "God, I thought you were drowning!"

"No, you glorious idiot. We were kissing." Hero's laugh was a little drunken and he grinned at him through the wet hair that hung in his face. Hero turned just enough—without letting go of Claire—to place a very waterlogged kiss on the corner of Rami's startled frown. "I thought I'd taught you the difference."

The heady rush of heat was slowly draining from Claire's cheeks, just enough for reason to get a foothold. She gaped at Hero, "Why—why would you—"

Hero sighed and allowed his weight to rest on Rami's arm, dragging Claire back with him. "Why would I kiss you?"

"We agreed, I… not that I didn't enjoy it, mind." Claire did a mental stumble to find that positively true. She hadn't thought she could feel that kind of heat again as a dead woman. "But we agreed it wasn't what we should do—what we should be, you and me. There's too much history. There's too much—I'm an author, and you're—"

"I am a former character from a story," Hero corrected archly. "Yet I appear to have lost my book along the way. As you have lost yours. Well—" Hero made a face. "Long-lost Beatrice doesn't count. Exes never do."

"But—"

"So you are not a book," Rami said with a somber tone. He glanced shyly at Claire. "And you are not an author, or an acting librarian. It would seem the question is, What do you want to be?"

"No, not you. Us," Hero said almost to himself. "What do you want us to be?"

"I…" Claire swallowed her impulse for a quick response and considered. Things usually went the way Claire planned, but then, things never did when it involved Ramiel and Hero. It was a strange alchemy, the family she had found. It was nothing so straightforward as a sexual attraction, and nothing as well trod as a romantic entanglement. No, the lines between them had always been more thorny than that. Hero was a book, she had been an author, and both of them had unfortunate pasts with that power dynamic. That had been enough reason to maintain her distance.

And then the magnetic pull between Ramiel and Hero had convinced her it was for the best. She hadn't counted on being pulled into their orbit, but it felt natural, like all gravity did. And Claire was so tired of struggling against gravity.

They will not thank you, a pitying voice said in her head.

No, Claire thought, *but they will love me.*

"I..." Claire tried again. It was a struggle for every syllable, but not because of the water or the cold. She felt... she felt warm. "I want this," she admitted. "Even if I'm... I'm not sure I'm meant to have it."

Hero chucked her chin. "That's what makes it fun to take. Steal it. Take it, Claire. Whatever your terms, whatever you want, take a little bit of happiness."

Claire was already shaking her head. "Now is not the time—"

"Of course it is. You beat Hell itself! Who does that?"

"You deserve happiness, Claire." It was a simple comment, nothing more. Said as simply as everything Rami did. He was the only one of them moderately dry above the shoulders, and he kept them afloat, their anchor when Claire and Hero, in their bladed natures, might lose sight of shore. A small furrow appeared in his brow as he studied her and saw—no, Claire amended, he couldn't suspect. "You deserve happiness. Even for just right now."

Claire didn't have an answer for that.

"What we deserve," Hero announced, breaking the pause, "is to get out of this freezing water."

"You're one to complain," Claire grumbled, even while accepting Hero's hand to drift toward the boat. Rami had thankfully made sure they didn't lose it down current. At least one of them had been thinking. "You pushed me in."

37

RAMI

Never trust a demon with the details. Hell is full of lawyers, accountants, and other lesser thieves.

Librarian Gregor Henry, 1988 CE

SCRAWLED LATER, IN THE MARGINS:

Really, Gregor? A lawyer joke? I expected better from you.

Librarian Claire Hadley, 1991 CE

THE HULL OF THE boat scraped against the floorboards before they reached the stacks. The water was receding, if slowly. Claire trudged on ahead of them, the ankle-deep water dragging at the fabric of her trousers. Rami thought of offering to carry her, but if the waters had not harmed her with a full plunge, he supposed a few more puddles wouldn't hurt.

It was a relief to be back in his own skin. Rami had recoiled when Claire explained her plan to fool Hell, but the experience had been so much worse than he could imagine. It wasn't being in the demon's skin. It wasn't even the way Hell had welcomed him as one of their own—a cruel kind of twist, considering how many countless years he'd spent looking for just such a realm to call him. No, the worst of all of it, the knife that twisted in his stomach through all of it, was a single glance. The wild disgust in Hero's first glance almost broke Rami's will over the illusion right there. Every subsequent barb and cruel interaction that followed… well, Rami would have almost preferred to be left to the mercies of Hell.

Almost.

He slowed enough to risk a sideways glance again. The iron tic of displeasure in Hero's jaw was still there. It underlined his fine features, reminding Rami that the man was far stronger and unyielding than anyone—including himself—thought. Normally, he admired that. Now, it promised he was going to have to earn every inch of conversation. "I'm sorry."

"You said that already." Hero managed to barely move his lips as he stared straight ahead.

"I…" Rami resisted the urge to squirm under the silence. "I wanted to say it again."

"The definition of madness is repeating an action and expecting a different result." Hero's chin did that careless chuck to the side that Rami knew well. The more angry—truly hurt—Hero was, the more full of smiles and ease he became.

"I'm sorry," Rami said again, like a dunce.

"For what?" Hero said sharply, catching him by surprise. He stopped walking but didn't turn to meet Rami's eyes. His gaze was pinned forward, but not on the point where Claire was rapidly disappearing down the aisle. Perhaps he looked at the books, or simply tallied Rami's crimes in his head.

"For… causing you distress." He studied the high color in Hero's cheeks and considered everything he knew about the man before taking an awkward guess. "It's no embarrassment, what you—"

"You think I am embarrassed of my feelings?" Rami took an unintended step back when Hero reeled on him, eyes blazing. He was disheveled, still soggy and wild from the dunk in the water. His velvets were soaked and wrinkled. Normally coifed bronze curls splayed every which way on his head. His lips were still bruised pink, and Rami felt a small thrill of distinctly unangelic pleasure wondering whether it had been he or Claire who had done that. Hero looked terrifying, he looked eternal, and he looked glorious, and all Rami could think was, *Be not afraid.*

It was difficult to focus on words. "Y… Yes?" Hero was a proud, proud creature, and it grieved Rami that he'd been driven to that point.

"You are a terrible and beautiful idiot." Hero's lip curled and he took another step until it was Rami's turn to back into the sharp edge of a stack of books. "I am a creature of fiction. Feelings are what make me feel alive. It'd take a coward to be ashamed of them. I love you. I love Claire. And the idea that either of those statements could be a shame is, frankly, a bitter insult."

Every time Ramiel thought he understood humanity and… well, the human-adjacent, he found a new way to be confused. "But—yes, Claire is Claire—but I'm fallen—"

"You beautiful idiot man," Hero said the way others might have cursed someone's parentage. His hand sank into the front of Rami's coat and clenched until Rami could feel the heat of his fist against his heart. "I told you this in the labyrinth realm. You heard what I said about your qualities earlier. I've read a Dust Wing full of stories, and nowhere have I found a story once where a man can't be redeemed by his choices. You are not broken, or found wanting. I am not angry because I am ashamed. So." Hero abruptly let go of him and stepped back. "So try again."

Rami was somewhat of an expert at falling, being a Watcher. "I am sorry for deceiving you. I should have tried to tell you Claire's plan, but you joined the boat and there wasn't time—" He stopped as Hero's face darkened and thought carefully about his next words. They felt impossible when he found them. "The idea caused you pain. I'm sorry... for scaring you. I will never do it again, on my oath."

"Oh, you terrify me regularly. You and Claire. So determined to throw away your lives for a ridiculous cause." Hero's frown softened by degrees. "But that's what I get for loving hero types, I suppose. Even Brevity is exhaustingly altruistic and she should know better."

"You're a hero too," Rami said, because he wanted Hero to admit it.

"Shut your pretty mouth." Hero drew closer. He was smiling now, and it had a fizzy effect on Rami's stomach that he hadn't thought he could feel. "Unless that's an invitation to show you just how wicked I can be in priv—"

Hero was abruptly on the other side of the aisle. He looked surprised and frowned. "I'm sorry, I didn't mean to—"

"I didn't move." Rami frowned at the expanse of wood floor that hadn't been there between them a moment before. He opened his mouth to say something else but was drowned out by a groaning sound that had both of them looking up to the shadows of the ceiling. The Library shuddered.

"There you are!" Claire wheeled around the corner, out of breath. She flashed a vexed look between the two men. "Are we finished here?"

"Claire, what—" Hero sputtered as she grabbed both of their hands and yanked them into motion.

"Andras didn't buy us as much time as he promised he would." The floor lurched and a small flock of books tumbled over their rails and onto the floor. Hero bent to gather them but Claire dragged him into a run. "Our trick is up."

"Malphas has defaulted on her word?" Rami asked.

Hero let out a yelp as the wood floor beneath his feet appeared to turn to putty and caught his heel. Rami struggled to pull him out until Claire bent down and undid the buckles around his ankle. The leather boot remained half-submerged in a birch-colored puddle as Hero yanked his foot free.

"Oh no, Malphas is honoring her side of the agreement, with the precise amount of technicality as we did," Claire corrected grimly. "Hell's releasing its claim on the Library, all right. But they're not waiting for us to pack our bags—the realm is ejecting us."

Rami felt his heart stop.

"What does that mean, for us mere books?" Hero snapped.

"Nothing survives adrift outside a realm. There's nothing— Existence doesn't, well—" Rami managed, and was deeply grateful when Claire found a metaphor that summarized the disaster unfurling before them.

"It means the Library is unmoored." Claire winced as a bookcase to their right appeared to shatter, then reverse in midair to put itself back together again. "And trying to hold together will tear this place apart."

3 8

CLAIRE

Maybe what makes a library isn't what it has, but what it does.
Librarian Bjorn the Bard, 1433 CE

I won't surrender to Malphas, but I will surrender to the Library. Walter says this will work—technically, he doesn't say it will *not* work, which is all I have to go on. I'm sorry, Revka, there's no time to tell you why I have to do this. But if it works—if there's the narrowest chance it works—I'll never have really left you. The Library will belong to itself.

A demon can't conquer what isn't there. When Malphas breaks that door, she will find the librarian's desk empty.
Librarian Poppaea Julia, 48 BCE

"OH." HERO SOMEHOW MANAGED to hobble next to her, shoeless on one foot, and make it look like a casual stroll in the midst of chaos. "Is that all? I thought it was something bad."

"It is bad! Stop being cheeky." The beams in the ceiling of the

Unwritten Wing abruptly decided to sweep down, and Claire had to duck to miss getting beaned as they lurched their way through the stacks. It was urgent that they get back to the others in the damsel suite. The Library was tearing itself apart trying to contort to fit the space where Hell had once been. "If we don't anchor the Library to a new realm or something solid in short order, we'll…" Claire stopped as she realized she wasn't sure what happened to spirits and souls that fell into the void of pathways between afterlife realms. Judging from what she'd seen on the raven roads and elsewhere in the afterlife, it couldn't be anything good. "How long do we have?" She directed the question to Rami.

He startled, as if just realizing that he was likely the closest thing to an expert they would have. The effect was to turn his craggy features even more troubled. "It would be difficult to say. The Library—anything in the afterlife—is a construct fueled by divine—"

"Guess faster, dear," Hero murmured as he stepped around an armchair that had sprouted something that appeared to be cosmic tentacles. Books had scattered everywhere across the floor and it was hard not to cringe. Claire knew they were presented with bigger problems, but books were lying with pressed spines, for gods' sakes.

"An hour, maybe," Rami admitted grimly.

"We need more time than that." Claire was relieved when the front pier of the damsel suite came into view. With the water gone, the wing had regained some of its proportions, which made the path to the door scalable. Figures were clustered at the edge, and Claire recognized Brevity's blue and tattoo-scarred arm as she pulled her up.

"Inside, quick!" Brevity dragged Claire into the damsel suite and Claire did not waste time arguing. The suite was packed, and it appeared every awake book and guest librarian had crowded into the sitting room to avoid the chaos outside.

Claire's mind raced, trying to tally who was here and who wasn't, but the sense that a final countdown had inevitably begun to tick drove other logical thoughts out of her head. She looked to Brevity. "When did it start?"

"Not long before we spotted you. Is it Malphas... ?"

"She's not attacking, just the opposite."

"We're being set adrift." Bjorn came to the correct assessment swiftly. His beard jumped in a furious expression. "Left ta shipwreck by ourselves."

"We did ask for our freedom," Hero said dryly.

"Free to destroy ourselves," Claire said. "And with all the wings gathered here, if the Unwritten Wing is destroyed, so is the entire Library."

"The souls." The teal blush drained from Brevity's cheeks.

"Ours included." Claire accepted a cup of tea from Echo. The spirit laid a hand on her, and abruptly her sodden clothes and locks were dry again. She nodded a silent thanks before focusing on the doom at hand.

They had been spinning their wheels up until now. Hero and Rami had tried to secure them a realm and only returned by the skin of their teeth. Claire had tried to recruit Walter but only returned with a riddle. The one thing they had managed—securing a deal with Hell—now threatened to destroy them in short order. She thought she had tricked Malphas, but it was Claire who had been outwitted. If the Library tore itself apart in the void, anyone, including the grand general of Hell, could swoop in and sweep up what was left like vultures.

Malphas would probably enjoy gnawing on the remains of Claire's soul. The same way she likely enjoyed Poppaea's.

"Did she know?" Claire wondered.

Rami ignored the question entirely. "We need to move quickly. We have to find something that will shore up the Library's…" He faltered. "The Library's sense of self."

Hero finished toweling off his hair—Echo had not helped him dry off. He gave Rami a rueful look between the limp curls of copper hair in his face. "What do you want us to do, whisper affirmations and sweet nothings to it?"

Hero might have been remarking on the weather for all Rami noticed his snark. Rami turned to Claire and Brevity. "There's always a logic to it. No matter how mercurial a realm seems, it's got a logic that holds it together. Values, metaphors." When neither of them proposed a solution, Rami sighed in frustration. "What is a library made of?"

"Books?" Brevity offered uncertainly.

"Pah!" Bjorn sat on the back of a sofa and crossed his arms. "Not always."

Bjorn's library housed ghosts and memories. Duat had brought songs. Echo's pools had guarded letters and missives. No, a library wasn't just a pile of books.

"Stories," Iambe suggested.

"Yes and no," Rosia murmured. She was at the forefront of the collection of damsels that had the constitution and desire to stay awake while the chaos storm wreaked havoc on the books. She'd lost some of her dreamy quality since her encounter with the unwritten ink, but she still had the maddening habit of speaking in riddles.

Claire chewed on her thumb and tried an answer that felt wrong even as she said it: "Souls."

"We've never had to steal souls before; ain't gonna start now," Bjorn said to the stout agreement of the other librarians in the room. She felt a distinct chill from the damsels listening in.

Claire rolled her eyes. "It wasn't as if I suggested to go snatching children off the street," she grumbled. She understood that she'd garnered a reputation for being harsh and unorthodox, but, really, was she that bad?

Perhaps she didn't want to hear the answer to that.

A handful of other suggestions came from the gathered group, but Claire was distracted by the intense way Rosia stared at her. The damsel had been a character from a gothic ghost story until she'd sunk into a pool of ink—the last remains of the destroyed books lost to Andras's coup—and it had somehow disentangled her from her book. It had done much the same to Hero, only under much more traumatic circumstances. Claire still wasn't sure how that had worked, or what, precisely, that made Rosia and Hero. No longer characters, certainly. They lived fates and stories independent of a book that no longer existed. They still retained all their fictional qualities—could still "read" any book in the Library simply by touching it. The Unwritten Wing had still accepted them both as part of the Library, though the damsels seemed to treat both Hero and Rosia with a kind of respect. Rosia, because she had become one of their internal leaders. Hero, because he had read—listened, lived, remembered—the stories of the Dust Wing while he was there. They called him...

"Oh." All eyes swiveled to focus on Claire. She weighed the answer again, but it felt too true to disregard. "Readers. A Library's purpose is to exist for future readers, people."

"How do we get more readers?" Iambe asked with a skeptical air. "It's not as if we have a list of patrons with borrowing privileges."

That had always been the isolationist nature of the Library. Just librarians, no readers. Occasionally denizens of their host realms wandered in, but no one ever borrowed a book or story of any kind, at least not long enough to learn it. They hardly even had a right to call themselves a library. An archive, perhaps, or a tomb. The only difference between the Unwritten Wing and the Dust Wing was better lighting. Claire's confidence flagged until a thud on the table behind her made her nearly startle out of her skin.

"We got plenty of readers. Right here." Brevity leaned on the tall stack of books she'd just dropped on the table. Rosia perched beside her with a look at the librarian that was half adoration. "When's the last time any of us have had a story hour?"

At the bashful murmurs around the room, Brevity straightened up, alarmed. "When's the last time anyone has read any of their wing's own materials?"

"You can't just go reading feral like that!" Bjorn sounded scandalized. "It ain't allowed!"

"Reading books runs the risk of waking them up, we're warned," Claire said with a dry half smile and glance at Hero. Not that all librarians listened. It was cruel to condemn a booklover to a trove full of new books and tell them not to touch them.

"Good!" Brevity pounded the top book and clambered up on the table. "Don't we want them to wake up and fight for themselves? We can't do this on our own. The wing needs to save itself."

"You want us to read?" Iambe sounded amused.

"No, I want y'all to tell the stories. Read 'em out loud if you have to. I..." Brevity's confidence stumbled a little. She looked to Claire for support. "It could work, right?"

Reading always did something. Especially in their Library. Even in the living world, reading did things. That was the magic and that was the danger. Some stories entertained you; some intrigued you; some saved your life. If Claire hadn't sought out her own books—or if Claire had just written them in the first place—would any of them be here? It was always a gamble, beginning a story. You could never be certain of the end.

But that had never deterred any reader.

"It's worth a try," Claire said.

Brevity grabbed a book at random. It was navy and dappled with specks of silver that spun into a nebula of stars. She threatened the crowd with it. "Who'll read first?"

"Oh, give it," Bjorn grumbled. He grabbed it out of her hand and lowered himself into the armchair nearest the fire with a groan. "Gods, this place needs some good furs and ale. Okay, librarians and letterfolk, listen close."

He began to read, jumping into what sounded like a fantastical description of a salvage mission in space. He started out slow, his rough Scandinavian burr stumbling over the technical and make-believe. But Bjorn, a born storyteller, quickly found his cadence and the room changed.

Quiet gathered, spreading out of the empty spaces of the damsel suite to pool and transform into something focused, something alive. The damsels drew up blankets and settees. Librarians gradually loosened their shoulders. Echo settled to a mere reflection in her pool to listen, quietly repeating words now and then for dramatic effect.

The alchemy of word and will was a subtle one. The story was engaging enough that even Claire almost missed the slow pulse of air against her cheek. She turned and saw the sturdy frame of the suite door reassert itself, unwinding its wobbling ribbons to become solid wood and iron again. It felt as if a thin bubble had formed, pushed outward with each breath Bjorn drew to speak, and the Library found a fulcrum of new resolve.

The glass pane in the door wobbled, undecided on whether it

was made of glass or chaos-laced Jell-O. "Bubble" was the right term—fragile and temporary.

"This only buys time," Iambe almost echoed her thoughts in a low voice at her elbow. "We still need a realm."

"If you have any ideas, I am accepting suggestions." Claire drew her attention back. Bjorn was in the warp and weft of a tale now, gesturing with his free arm as he occasionally glanced at the book and read a particular passage. The stars in the book's leather cover appeared to almost twinkle. The book had readers, readers for the first time in centuries, and it was glowing under the attention.

They had no shortage of books, but Claire wondered how long the attending librarians and damsels could hold up. It took no small amount of effort to tell a story. And a good story asked something of its reader as well. Iambe was right; this would only buy them time.

"I have one." Hero sat with his elbows on his knees on the couch, inspecting his hands. He looked up reluctantly. "There's one more wing we haven't tried."

Claire frowned. "Nonsense. All twelve librarians are accounted for—"

"There's thirteen wings of the Library," Rami said softly. He was standing behind the couch at Hero's back.

"Thirteen—" Brevity gasped, then forced her voice low in order to not disturb the story that was in progress. "You mean the Dust Wing."

"You can't be serious." But the way Rami and Hero exchanged a glance told Claire that they were. She took a breath. "But the Dust Wing has no librarian."

"This was never about gathering librarians," Hero reminded her, and there was a muddle of gentleness in his voice that Claire immediately hated. "It was about gathering wings, gathering stories. And the Dust Wing counts."

Claire felt the fear in her gut harden. "No. I won't send you back there. Not if there's any other way."

"You don't need to," Hero said with a stunning smile. "Ramiel can take me. Angel express."

Rami was already wincing as Claire pivoted. She resisted the urge to point. "*You* are condoning this?"

"Hero knows the books. Even better than you, and definitely better than me." Rami spoke slowly, as if trying to telegraph the most understanding with each word. "If he says we need the Dust Wing, then we need them."

"They don't deserve to be forgotten. Again," Hero said to his hands.

Claire was shaking her head. "That place nearly killed you, Hero."

"Actually, it did kill me," Hero corrected brightly. "It just didn't take. Listen—Claire, I can do this. I know I can do this. I have to do this."

The anger drained out of Claire. "The last time you convinced me you had to do something, it also ended in the Dust Wing. No."

The tilt of Hero's smile fell. They both remembered their desperate bid to understand the unwritten ink, how Hero had convinced Claire to try it on his book. Claire could still see the elation on his face when he'd started to remember the missing pages of his story. She could still taste the ash and bile of terror as it had instead eaten through his book from the inside out and he'd fallen apart.

"This is different," he said softly, after too long a pause. "You said yourself that this is all for nothing unless we gather them all."

Claire was already shaking her head, hardening and frosting over. "Not like this. No, I won't do it, Hero. We'll find a different way."

"Claire—"

"You'll do it," Brevity said.

It was said with such utter confidence that Claire only managed to blink at the muse for a moment. "I certainly will not."

"You will. Because Hero's right, and you know he's right. Either we do this all together—all the libraries, all the stories—or we don't do this at all. If anyone can speak to the Dust Wing, it's Hero. He's the only one who the books there have ever spoken to. We're running out of time and I can't name an alternative." Brevity's voice grew stronger as she rattled off her reasoning, steel growing in her stance as she raised her chin to defy Claire. "Can you?"

"I—we don't—I won't sacrifice anyone else! Not... not anymore." The only reason Claire was able to keep her voice down was because it trembled and broke. And then it wasn't so much that the icy veneer of Claire's composure cracked, but the whole glacial reserve of her walls came down. A shudder ran through her, her breath caught, and the words came out in a stumbling, halting whisper. "The last time broke me."

Hero's hands came up and cupped Claire's downturned face in a soft way he'd never dared before. They were not made for soft things, Claire and Hero. Their history was a prickly beast of antagonism and tension and then reserve, love spoken in the way they were unwilling to hurt each other in the ways they knew they could. But to hell with reserve, with history.

Hero's expression was open, tentative, when he gently turned her gaze up. He dragged his thumbs through the tears. And Hero, written to be glorious and dramatic and endlessly witty and reviled, said nothing. And for once, Claire had no words for him either, not here at the end of all their stories. Hero put his lips to a different use instead, placing a feather-soft kiss on one cheek, then the other.

Claire gave one tremble, just one, then fell into his chest, holding him tight. If Rami was the anchor, the stone, then Claire was the water. Ice turned water turned air. He wrapped his arms around her. But then, like water, like air, she knew they couldn't stay this way. Water and air were meant to let go.

"Not a book," Hero muttered softly into her hair, and Claire hoped he could feel when she smiled.

"Not an author," Claire said into his chest.

"Um..." Claire opened her eyes to see Brevity standing a hesitant distance away. She hadn't even noticed she'd slipped off—presumably to give them this time—and had returned with a Library loan slip in hand. "Are you sure? Really sure?"

"Really, really sure." Hero's voice was subdued and rough. "I'll come back. I promise."

Claire's eyes were still wet, but she drew back with a long breath. "I'll be here. I'll come find you if you don't."

"I know you will." Hero smiled. "Warden."

"Book," Claire returned fondly.

Brevity put a hand on Hero's arm. "Do what we got to do." Hero was already off the couch and headed for the door, Rami a step behind. Brevity raised her voice. "And be careful, yeah?"

Hero raised his hand in acknowledgment without turning around. Claire thought they would depart without a word, but Hero slowed as they passed the couch again, just long enough to press an uncharacteristically soft kiss to her temple. Rami, ever mindful of propriety, kissed her hand. The door closed, and she found herself clasping the hand to her chest, holding on to the lingering ghost of warmth they'd left behind. Heart and head.

It felt like a long time after the door closed before Claire lowered her hand from her chest and straightened. She gathered up her teacup and focused on the storytelling session in progress. Bjorn's story would wrap up soon; they would need another reader to keep going. They had to keep going. Without a realm, a god, or a guide, they still had one another. That was enough for any story, wasn't it? Claire picked up the nearest book from the stack on the table. "Let's get to work."

39

RAMI

Maybe I was doomed to fail. There are some wings of the Library, after all, that are beyond my reach. Beyond the reach of anyone but a forgotten book. I was never certain if the Dust Wing counted, when tallying the resident souls of the Library. It had been arrogant of me to think that it didn't. I was too afraid to try. No librarian I know of has entered the Dust Wing and returned. Forgotten books have a right to be hostile to humanity; we're the ones that failed them.

Librarian Poppaea Julia, 48 BCE

THE QUALITY OF THE Dust Wing was its own particular flavor of darkness. It wasn't simply the absence of light; it was the oily feel of shadow upon shadow. Even Rami, who had excellent dark vision, thank you very much, could feel the change as they arrived.

The Unwritten Wing murmured of ruffling pages and dreaming books, but that was a whisper compared to the staccato chorus, over and over again, of ripping pages. Hundreds of them. The shallow flat area where Hero and Rami landed was as close to an approximation of a front lobby as the Dust Wing got. Hero had called it the killing fields, last time they were here. Garlands of papery entrails drifted in midair, books caught in the act of self-mutilation. Beneath his feet, the pages were so old they crumbled into a slick slurry as he took a step. The shadows were almost absolute, only stabbed by twists of bone white parchment catching the light.

And everywhere, everywhere, was the muted sound of ripping pages. Forgotten worlds destroying themselves.

"Gods..." Hero stumbled, his weight sliding against Rami until he could get an arm around him. "It's so loud—why is it so loud?"

The tearing-paper sound was unpleasant, but Rami wouldn't have described it as exceptionally loud. He supported Hero and drew his sword with the other. Even ignited with blue flames, it did little to push back the shadows. Nothing moved. "What are you hearing?" he asked Hero quietly.

"It's..." Hero grimaced, closing his eyes to swallow laboredly before answering. "Loss. Despair. Last time I was here, it was stories, millions of books telling their stories. But now..." His fine brow furrowed. Rami disliked how pale it looked in the firelight. "Something's changed."

Rami's sense of alarm was fine-tuned. He scanned the shredded paper forest around them. "Do you want to go back?"

"No!" Hero's eyes shot open and he shook his head. "There's nowhere else we can go. It's our best shot at a home. I have to do this."

The haunted look in Hero's eyes did not convince him, but Rami resolved to hold his peace. "Then we'll do this together."

Hero flashed him a smile—a mere ghost of his usual spirit—and straightened, composing himself until his hand slipped back into Rami's. It felt smooth and fragile. "Tag along, then. We ought to head... there." His eyes unfocused for a moment before pointing at a wide break between the cliffs of crumbling books that dominated the "lobby."

Neither of them moved.

Rami cleared his throat. "As I said, there's no shame in going back—"

"This way," Hero bit off, and took off at a grim march. Rami followed. After what had happened last time they were in this place, he certainly had no intention of letting Hero out of his sight.

The chorus of ripping pages gradually faded behind them the deeper they hiked into the crumbling canyons of the Dust Wing. There were no tidy bookshelves and discretely indexed stacks here. Books piled upon codices piled upon slates piled upon stone tablets piled upon even more obscure and rudimentary modes of storytelling. The whole place was a layer cake of history, stratum after stratum of stories written, then forgotten to humanity by neglect or by malice. Somewhere in here were the lost works of Sappho. Unrecorded plays by Shakespeare. And millions of other lesser-known voices, either forgotten or silenced by the march of time. These were books that had been written, once. Had made it to humanity and been read by someone. Seen sunlight, touched a reader's heart. Instead of lending the memory of life, that somehow made the wing all the more eerie and sepulchral. Which was a worse fate, Rami wondered, the failure of death or the wasted potential of never living at all?

Hero was muttering. Rami wasn't sure when he'd started. Hero came to a sudden stop at the base of a cliff, a stricken look on his face as he stared into the dark. "Why? You need a reason?"

"Hero?" Rami kept his voice gentle. His hand hovered over Hero's shoulder, suddenly afraid to land. "Talk to me."

"Talk, talk, talk..." Hero clutched his head as if he'd been struck. "They're talking, all right. Vile nonsense—What about me? I will tell you about me, you—" He started, twisting around to Rami in horror. Wet tracks streamed down his waxy cheeks. "They don't want to help."

"The wing?" Rami inched the tip of his sword up again, eyeing the crumbling artifacts warily. Nothing moved, nothing breathed, for Rami at least. Hero twisted as if he were in the midst of an arguing crowd.

"The bloody entitled—" Hero was breathing shallow and labored now. His fist struck the nearest pile of books, sending a cascade of dust down on their heads. "What's it to you? To you? You want the whole Library to fall because you got forgotten?" Disgust added to the tears muddying his voice. "And they dare to call me a villain."

"Can you explain—"

"What makes you better than any of us? I've read you, *all* of you," Hero seethed at nothing Rami could see. He began to dig through the rubble of disintegrating pages. He pulled out one leather-bound square that was almost holding together. "This? Trite."

"What are you doing?" Rami asked.

"I'm reading." Hero shrugged and tossed the "trite" book over his shoulder. "I read all the books last time I was in here. Though I suppose maybe 'read' is not the technical word…"

"You said there were ghosts."

Hero sniffed. "I was being generous. Look at these. Boring. Drivel. This one's got every 'ist' and 'phobia' covered…" Hero crouched down and began to scramble deeper into the debris. Flakes of dried paper and leather began to billow and settle on him in a fine layer of filth. "Dull. Predictable. Hack. And this one? A love triangle? Really?"

There was a moment, when Rami blinked, when he thought it

was a trick of the shadows and the dust. A shift in Hero's pallor, which had been painted gray by the swirl of filth in the air. But it felt like the world shivered, and as Hero's fingers touched the next book, he... changed.

The dust rippled over him in a shiver, leaving a luminescent skin of not-quite-light. Hero was still muttering invectives and commentary, the losing side of a debate that Rami couldn't follow. But Rami wasn't truly alarmed until he watched Hero pick up another book, carelessly flick it up with a twist of the wrist, and... disappear.

It was only for half a second. Hero didn't seem to notice, caught in mid-mutter as he stuttered out of existence and then back in. He tossed the book over his shoulder, picked up another, and it happened again. A flicker. This time, Rami was watching closely enough to see that Hero didn't merely reappear; he filled in. Roiling text scrolled over his skin and then disappeared into his hairline as he returned to reality.

The warning in Rami's gut hitched up to an alarm. "Hero, stop a minute."

Another book was discarded and a crumbling scroll picked up. This time Hero phased in and out in some Latin script. He reached out again: a decree in cuneiform, followed by what looked like Phoenician. He'd stopped muttering at some point. Hero had become a dust-covered automaton digging through the rubble, as flickering and insubstantial and gray as the ghosts that surely inhabited this place.

"Hero! Stop!" Rami lunged forward as he saw him reach for a precariously wedged slate that would surely bring the entire cliff sliding down on top of them. He wrapped his arms around him, but hauling him away, he lost his footing. They skidded farther down the rubble.

Hero was still blindly reaching. In the dim light, old languages that Rami recognized—and a couple he didn't—slid over Hero's skin like fast-moving shadows. His skin had turned the shade of parchment, his eyes gray as charcoal and fixed straight ahead. Wherever he was, he was not here with Rami. Not for much longer.

Rami was acquainted with loss, but not this. Not this. Not here, and not again. Angels were not supposed to be arrogant. All their action, power, and authority came from the god they served. But it was only Rami who decided, here and now, this would not happen.

"Hold on a little longer," Rami croaked as Hero shuddered beneath his grip. There was no time for a graceful exit; the edge of the cliff crumbled beneath them and Rami breathed one final lungful of dust and malice as he charted a path home.

40

HERO

My apprentice calls me heartless. He is incorrect. I had a heart, once. I don't remember why I chose to lose it. Perhaps my heart was better off without me.

Librarian Yoon Ji-Han, 1803 CE

HERO CAME TO HIS senses amid a hurricane. The nothing-void of the pathways between realms roared with not-quite-wind, and the static cyclone drowned out the ghosts in his head long enough to realize his surroundings. To realize his rescue.

Arms vised around his chest impossibly tight and trembling, as if Rami wasn't certain that Hero's body was still there. The force of the angel's will kept the worst of the howling darkness at bay, and Hero made a precise decision not to look too closely at the dark beyond Rami's flickering translucence. Instead, he looked up.

Realmfire wreathed the curve of Rami's close-cropped hair, creating a jagged, broken halo that spilled wispy light across his cheekbones and down the broad curve of his shoulders. His eyes were two points of light, focused on navigating them safely in the void between stars.

The voices of the Dust Wing rolled back in on him like a tide. The pull was too strong. The stories had swamped him, rushing in all at once and trying to make a home of the new, human place where his story used to be. He'd been pulled under, and Rami had pulled him out.

Resolve settled in Hero's bones. Maybe it was the effect of the stories. Maybe it was the changes he'd undergone. The loss of his book, the acceptance of the Library, the love of Rami and, in her own way, Claire. Or maybe, just maybe, it was the ridiculous idea that this was only the end if he told the story that way. This couldn't be the way the story went.

"... go," Hero croaked, unable to hear his own voice in the airless space.

Rami's starlight eyes dimmed, focusing abruptly on Hero's face. His voice was low and clear over the static haunting of the between places. "Hold on, love, we're almost home, don't—"

"Let go," he repeated.

"What?"

Hero licked his lips. His head was ringing. And the ghosts were singing. And the words he didn't want to say slipped through his cracked lips anyway. "I have to go. The Dust Wing. I have to go back."

There was no perceptible change, no velocity to slacken, but Hero felt like their progress slowed as Rami blinked at him. "The Dust Wing isn't safe. It tried to—"

"Nothing in this world is safe, not for us." Hero squeezed a clutch of Rami's feathered coat in his fist. "I have to go back. Right now."

"You're... injured," Rami said with a gentleness that made Hero's heart ache.

"I'm not. Or if I am, it doesn't matter. Rami—" He put all the forbidden, nameless things he was feeling into his voice, and it cracked. "I have to do this. I think I am the only one who can." He glanced down at the dizzying dark. "You have to let me go."

"Here? Hero, you can't—" Rami's arm around his waist gripped tighter. "I will *never* let you go. I promised that." His voice turned choppy with fear. "We promised that."

Hero tried to pry Rami's fingers from his ribs; he might as well have been plucking at granite. He felt the Dust Wing getting farther away, the ghosts quieter, the pull of the story less true. He knew if he lost it, he wouldn't find his way back. A different story would play out for the Library, for all of them. He would not let that happen. "I'm the only one who can do this. I have to go back there, right now."

Rami's frown deepened. "If that's the case, I'll go with you."

"No—no, that's not..." Hero struggled to find a way to explain it, the undeniable certainty the ghosts had left behind. "That's not how the story goes. I can do this; I have to do this. You believe I'm more than a villain, right? I need you to believe in me—I know I don't deserve it, but please." The air in the nowhere place was thinning. Hero found it hard to breathe. "I need you to have faith in me."

"Faith..." Rami repeated like a wound. His frown broke into something so much more raw, desperate. "You held on to me when I was falling. Please let me hold on to you. *Please* don't ask me to do this."

"You don't have to do anything." He gave up fighting Rami's grip and reached out fingers to touch the plane of his cheek. Soft; Hero was always so surprised by how soft it was, when Rami looked like something eternal carved out of craggy stone. He cupped his jaw and memorized the zephyr light in Rami's eyes. "You just have to believe. And let me go."

Rami took a stabbing breath. "Hero..."

"Believe in me. You gave me something to believe in. Let me return the favor." Hero's vision blurred as he felt Rami's arms slowly begin to relax. "Thank you."

Rami's throat worked. One of his arms shifted from holding on to him to wind in the loose curls of his hair. "Hero, you should know, I—"

"I love you," Hero said quickly—and, gods below, he'd expected the words would bring a new swoop of terror, but it was as if he'd found an anchor. A gentle certainty bloomed in him, so he pressed his palm to Rami's mouth and said it again. "I said it in court, but I didn't get a chance to actually say it to *you*. I love you. You save anything else for when I get back."

Rami's eyes widened, and god, the desire to kiss him rose fierce in Hero's chest. But there was no time and, besides, his hand was already covering Rami's mouth. Instead, Hero smiled, took a breath, and leaned back out of his arms.

And Hero fell away.

RAMI

Meh. Ji Han, Odin bless him, was so obsessed with the idea of gods and power that he didn't notice the wyrm in the room. Why wonder about the gods? Ain't no one seen one of them around here for as long as I've been here—and that's saying something. No, the only immortal god I've met around here is Death.

"Walter," ha! What kind of name is that? In our tales, Death was many things. An absence of ravens. A fearsome woman offering you rest. A old man with one eye. All the gods carried a little bit of death with them, way my people told it. Same as life.

No, only all-powerful being I know of is Death, and he calls what he does a gate. Does that speak to the power of the afterlife? Or simply the power of gates? What is it about a doorway?

A doorway only exists for you to pass through. Then you're on your own.

Librarian Bjorn the Bard, 1313 CE

RAMI LANDED ON THE floorboards of the Unwritten Wing, alone and hollow. He closed his eyes, clenching his fists tight until the urge to dive back into the nowhere of the Dust Wing abated. Faith. *Hero* had asked him for faith. The absurdity of a villain asking an angel for faith was bad enough, but what was worse was that Rami had not wanted to give it. He believed in Hero, but he feared losing him more. When fear lost out to faith, that was when the worst evils of the world happened.

He'd seen Hero's eyes—Hero's, not the thousands of stories that fluttered and licked at his soul as the Dust Wing had tried to claim him—*Hero's* eyes. He'd had faith in Rami, a belief that Rami was strong enough to let him go, and a new fear had won out. The fear of disappointing the ones he loved.

Rami had let him go.

Something alarming and wet touched his cheeks, startling Rami's eyes open. He touched his face hesitantly, but the liquid on his fingers was clear. *Another miracle*, Rami thought grimly, and took a shuddering breath. He started to navigate his way through the stacks. It required him to double back several times and perform a minor acrobatic maneuver when the floor gave way to what appeared to be a vortex of jellyfish, but he entered a sudden bubble of calm as he reached the damsel suite.

The air warmed and stilled. The dock had melted away to leave the simple frosted-glass door that sheltered the remaining hopes of the Library. Shelves went in their prescribed directions. Rugs lay in accordance with gravity. At the threshold, the soft crackle of a fireplace was audible above the soft hush of a voice speaking in a cadence Rami recognized in his bones.

He'd loved enough humans to know when he'd stepped inside the bubble of a story.

The air held its breath, and Rami softened his footfalls without realizing it as he slowed at the edge of the circle that had formed near the fireplace. Bjorn sat in the center chair for the moment, flapping his leathery arms like a bird as he wove his story. Around him the librarians and remaining damsels were arrayed, some sitting pin straight in chairs, others wrapped in blankets on the floor with what appeared to be hot cocoa. All of them hung on his words.

"... an' them dragons blinked themselves all the way to the sun and back, burned the invader from the sky. But that's a tale for another time."

The sphere of quiet wobbled in the pause, but soon the stork-headed librarian—Duat? Rami could not keep them straight—stretched his long neck and cleared his throat. "I know what happens next."

Bjorn appeared to sag with relief. Rami belatedly noticed the dark hollows under his keen eyes. He was slow to rise from the chair, as if he'd been talking for a while. "Tell me, Master Librarian. How does it start?"

The stork-headed librarian rose, smoothly picking up a book and taking the seat vacated by Bjorn even as he already began speaking. "The dragons traveled the great dark, but not alone. This is the tale of the generation ship that marked their passage..."

In the circle, the low hum of the storyteller's voice kept up its cadence, thrumming with the attention it held. The damsels listening seemed to glow in the dim light. Fresh blush to the cheeks, sleek muscles picked out by candlelight, fire burning in their eyes. From this angle, they looked healthier, stronger.

More real than real, that's how Claire had described characters once. The librarians weren't just buying time for the Library by telling stories. They were strengthening it. Stories were not just words; stories were action.

The stillness spun up again, wards strengthened, vigil maintained. The world outside the story continued to make no sense. Disasters and danger did not cease to loom. Simply reading and telling stories would not save them from bodily destruction. It should have made the act of storytelling pointless; instead, it made it something... holy. Rami... Rami knew holy. He'd be twice damned for using that word, but he wouldn't deny it when he felt it. There was something to this moment that he hadn't understood before. There was a power in a gathering of humans, huddled together against the coming dark to tell stories of light, of hope. There was a kind of power in the bleakest times, of telling stories of another way to be. Another world they could be. Telling stories of perseverance and survival in the face of a world that wanted you gone.

"I understand now," Rami murmured.

Stories were weaponized hope. And if that was true, and Rami was at least still some part of this story, then he could be weaponized too.

Rami slipped back out the door and into the chaos. His feathers ruffled when he crossed the invisible boundary constructed by the librarians, as if he were ducking out into a storm.

RAMI HAD FAITH.

He hadn't wanted to leave Hero. Not in the nowhere spaces of realms, not with Hero threatening to shatter in his arms. He hadn't wanted to leave Claire, or Brevity, or the Library on the precipice of destruction. If he could have, he would have encompassed them all. In his arms, in the wings he no longer had, in his immortality, to preserve them forever.

But Rami did have faith, and it was only by faith that he was moving now. Not faith as it once was. Not faith in a divine being setting all things right. Not faith in a plan that explained away the suffering he saw. Not faith even in good winning out over evil.

The faith Rami had was in humanity. Not in the messy parts—and humans were gloriously messy—but in their souls, their stories, their potential for endless re-creation. Humans could be bad. They could be cruel and vicious and selfish and self-destructing. But there was a quality above all that, and Rami had been reminded of it standing there in that bubble of stories told against a storm. Change.

Rami had faith that humans could *change*. Uriel hadn't had that faith. Perhaps none of the remaining angels, Watchers, assorted Heavenly host, did. They were made to serve absolutes, after all. Good and evil, Heaven and Hell. But the one thing stories proved, to anyone willing to see it, was that humanity held the endless power to change.

Maybe that was why each story was made up of soul, just a little bit of that potential that humanity carried. The realms were a static place without mortals. It took a human soul to shake things up. Stories. Claire had said librarians were there to keep stories from waking up and changing; they should have known that stories were souls even then.

Maybe that's why Rami was drawn to the Library in the first place. And maybe, just *maybe*, that's why Death took such an interest.

There was only one way to find out. Rami hurried through the stacks and to the big double doors. The Unwritten Wing had devolved further in the short time since he had returned. The wooden planks beneath his feet seemed half-replaced with nonsense and dreams. Here a sliver of the black void of space, there a threshold made of candy canes. The Library was doing its best to create patches to span across the long dark of oblivion, but entropy always won. He had to move fast.

Hell, as chance had it, provided a slight problem. Rami passed the gargoyle (who had been morphed into a violet octopus that Rami was reluctant to admit was adorable) and turned into the hallway to run straight into... nothing.

The hallway he was familiar with was there, stone pavers, mishmash of wood panels and appropriately long shadows and all. But three steps ahead of him the pavers stuttered out, the wood splintered, and the shadows swelled into complete absence.

Hell had granted the Library its freedom, as agreed, and in the process had sent it spiraling adrift in the nowhere seas of the afterlife. There would be no timely miraculous escape via ravens, angels, or candlelight for the Library's residents. Even Rami, a divine exception to many of Hell's rules, could not walk freely into the miasma of eternity.

That wasn't to say he couldn't walk there at all, however. He would need some costly stepping-stones. He stopped and reached up to grab a fistful of the white feathers that stuck out from his coat. Plucking them hurt, in the same way losing a friend hurt humans. Each feather was what remained of his power, and the grace he'd been granted. He stared at the fistful of broken pinions and, with grim regret, added another handful of feathers from his other shoulder.

It would have to be enough. He knew where he was going. He held the memory of glass jars and Walter's booming voice in his mind. He only hoped they had not drifted too far from Hell already.

He set his jaw, steeled his reserve, and cast a fistful of hope into the broken shadows. White fluff fluttered then stuttered in place, like static catching a signal. Before the feathers could disappear, he stepped into the dark after them.

THERE WERE SMALL PERKS to being a Watcher. He didn't want to remember the mad things that made the nowhere their home, so he simply didn't. When the familiar jingle of close-packed glass jars reached Rami's ears, he opened his eyes to Walter's office with only the faint aftertaste of sour salt and cold on his lips. A thin layer of rime, frosted and faintly green, evaporated from his coat lapel in anise wisps.

Walter's office was a blessed touchstone of normalcy after the chaos of the Library adrift. Wooden shelves lined the walls, reaching up to the far rafters and burdened with countless glass jars of varying sizes and colors. The labels were all in the same childlike hand and applied haphazardly. Death himself was standing on tiptoe to slide a deep blue-and-gold jar labeled *Capri* back on its high shelf.

Rami waited until the fragile jar was out of Walter's hands before clearing his throat. The boulder of a man turned with all the grace of a small rockslide. "Oh! Messir Ramiel," Walter drew Rami's name out to a full three syllables. He tapped his knuckles together sheepishly. "I was just... ah. What can I do you for?"

It was difficult to keep in mind that he was speaking to the avatar of Death when Death was currently looking like a guilty three-year-old child. Rami schooled his face to its most polite neutrality. "I would like a moment of your time, if you can spare it."

"Sure! 'Tain't been much activity in here since Hell went and..." Walter trailed off, looking altogether stricken. "Oh no, Messir Ramiel! They didn't leave you behind, did they? I know

Miss Claire can be hasty but I'm—"

"I came here on my own, Walter." Rami had to halt him before his flailing hands knocked over the counter. "Actually, the Library's endangerment is why I am here. I would make a formal petition to you."

Walter paused. It was unlikely that, beneath his pebbled hide, he had anything so mundane as a circulatory system, but it appeared as if all blood drained from his face anyway. "Me? Aw, I hate for you to waste your trip, but I already told Miss Claire I can't take sides. No way, nohow."

"Why? Why must you remain neutral in the face of suffering? It's obvious that Hell and the other realms aren't doing the same."

"It's different for 'em little folk," Walter said hesitantly.

It was certainly the first time Rami had heard anyone refer to Malphas, the armies of Hell, or the greater afterlife realms as "little." Rami's expression didn't change and he did his best to keep his voice careful and light. "How is it different?"

"It just—" Walter looked pained and quickly diverted himself by beginning to draw doodles in the polish of the countertop. "Them rules are different for gods and all."

"But you're—" Rami paused as he considered it. Walter was not simply the gatekeeper for Hell. He was, as best as Ramiel understood, the avatar of Death—all death. Death held a binding position across the realms because, after all, it was the one power on earth all the afterlife realms held in common respect. Without death, there was nothing. If that didn't place Walter in the echelon of gods, then Rami didn't know what would.

As a divine being, Rami felt a muddle of conflict at the idea of acknowledging multiple beings as gods in the first place, let alone petitioning one for help. "Uriel said the Creator was gone." The words were soft and slipped out from him before Rami had a chance to consider them.

"Ah." Walter grimaced and sat down heavily on his stool. "She shouldn'ta told you that."

"But you know what happened," Rami persisted. He told himself he was here to help the Library, but now the idea of getting answers took on an urgent need all its own. "Is it true?"

If it was possible for an ogre in menswear to look queasy, Walter did. He studied the top of the countertop intently and doodled a little harder. Rami thought he heard the countertop veneer creak. "There's a bit of a, whatcha call it, natural order to these things. Gods 'n' such."

"What do you mean, 'a natural order'?" Rami struggled not to feel defensive. He had been one of the Creator's original divine creations. He'd been there since the beginning. There was no beginning to god, not in Rami's book. Because if there was a beginning, that meant there would be an end, and that was unfathomable. But was it more or less unfathomable than hundreds of realms of hundreds of other gods, with creations like him? Was it any more sacrilegious than aiding a Library in Hell? Rami reflected on the number of impossible things he'd done in recent memory and suddenly felt queasy himself.

He'd traveled the realms for the Library, with Hero at his side. They'd visited Elysium, a realm of one of the most active pantheons in human history. But they'd only dealt with inhabitants and demigod spirits. At Chinvat, they'd met Sroasha, but the all-powerful judges of the place had been misty figures in clouds and the bridge itself. When, come to think of it, was the last time Rami had actually dealt with a god directly?

A long time ago, the answer came. Perhaps not even since the

Fall. Rami had been eager to avoid gods for a while, with good reason.

"It's not just the Creator, is it?" He didn't dare say it at full volume, so it came out as a whisper.

Walter's gaze flicked up, and the whirl of his bottomless eye sockets flickered from its customary red to something darker. "Happens to 'em all, eventually."

"What happens?" Rami struggled not to lose his patience, but even angels had their limits.

"Gods. Humans got it all wrong, y'see. Everyone thinks a god is a thing someone is, but..." Walter fidgeted and looked down again. "All gods I seen started out as a thing someone does."

Rami furrowed his brows. He was a Watcher, a spirit as old as humanity itself. He was used to dizzying points of view, but what Walter said made no sense. "Gods start... You mean gods are made?"

"Starts as a choice, always does. Then action, will... throw in the right set of circumstances, enough magic in the air, a willing reality, and a good story to believe in and—" Walter made a mixing motion with his hand. "Bam, you get yourself a god. Kinda like a whatchercallit, soufflé."

Rami wasn't certain he had the emotional space to deal with the idea that gods were made like... like soufflés. "Right... I came here to—"

Walter seemed to be warming up to the topic now that he'd broken his silence. "Course that's just the start. Be a lot more gods around if it weren't for them becoming realms."

"What?"

"What? You think a place like Hell runs on its own steam? Ain't enough classic believers for that now. Eventually a god's gotta choose between being a *them* or being a *there*. They start takin' up the slack and..." Walter shrugged. "Poof."

"Poof..." Rami was rarely surprised. His face didn't quite know what to do with the contortions his brain was doing. "The gods become their realms? That's where she... where they've all gone?"

"Or the other thing," Walter said with a drop in his mood. "That un's always a sad one."

"The other..." Rami stopped, suddenly remembering the labyrinth realm. The way the crocodile god had cannibalized the corpse of his own monster. The way the stone pavers and walls crumbled. The whole place had appeared to be sinking under its own weight. A forgotten god's last-ditch attempt to retain their immortality.

"Worst is when even that ain't enough," Walter said with a gravelly sigh.

Rami realized he was holding his head with one hand. He shook it, but it did nothing to clear the confusion. "We need a god, Poppaea said. Does Claire know what you just told me?"

"I..." Walter's eyeless gaze settled on a distant contemplation, and a look, a muddle between sadness and pride, settled on the knobs of his cheeks. "I think she does."

Thank gods. Rami wasn't sure he could relate and explain all these revelations to the others without having an existential crisis. He drew a deep breath instead. Later. He could figure out the fate of his Creator later. "But that doesn't explain why you can't help us."

"I'm not a god. I can't claim a realm. People need it too much for that. What would happen if death faded?" Walter shook his head sadly. "People need death; stories need an end. So death doesn't discriminate."

Rami felt his hopes fading, but he had to try anyway. "Poppaea said we needed a gatekeeper—a guide. That could be you."

"Me?" Walter's eyes widened, and his bulbous face was blank for a moment before it cracked into a swelling laugh. It went on loud and long enough that when he stopped, the room was filled with the faint hum of glass jars vibrating in his wake. "I'm no guide."

"But you're Death."

"Death is the gate. That's the tricky thing about power, Messir Ramiel. Surely you've noticed it. Hold on to too much of it and it holds on to you too. I got a whole lot of wiggle room here, at the gates. But between the realms? That's none of my business." Walter shook his head a little sadly. "Gates never travel themselves, and a guide is one who knows the ways. Mortals have to walk the pathways between realms themselves. Some realms, if they feel like it, try to send out help in a way their chosen believers will understand. That's them guides. If you're looking for a guide, you need yourself someone who's died and walked those paths, someone who has a natural affinity for the Library."

"Who's died." Rami frowned, deep and protective. "You can't be suggesting Claire."

"No, no, sir. Miss Claire has different work in mind, I imagine." Again, that conflicted look appeared that made Rami's stomach clench in warning.

"We don't have time to find someone who fits the role. The Library is falling apart now." Rami's stoic patience was fraying. Even now, things could be getting worse. Hero, Claire, Brevity. He could lose the only family he had, just as he found them. He wiped a hand over his forehead as if that would help him think.

"Strikes me you won' have to look too far," Walter said slowly. He was again muttering to the table, which was Rami's only clue that he was saying something quite important that skirted the edge of the rules. "Though it's gonna be a path you're not gonna like."

"I've already made one trip to Hell's court. I'll go anywhere to get what we need." Rami's mind paced over the possibilities.

Walter knew the answer but couldn't say it. He seemed confident enough that Rami could know it too. That meant it had to be someone in their shared acquaintance, but that was a limited crowd. The Library, Hell, who else? Since Walter was Death, he supposed he could know the lost souls Rami had once—

"Oh."

"There ya go," Walter said softly.

HERO

Listen. That's the part of the librarian's job that everyone forgets. *Listen.* Listen to your books, listen to your patrons. Listen to your enemies, even; when they're maddest is when you know you're doing something right. A librarian's job is to listen. A library's job is to be a place where the hopeless can feel seen and heard too.

Librarian Gregor Henry, 1977 CE

BY NOW, HERO HAD become familiar with the many ways a soul can be disassembled and reassembled somewhere else. He had traveled by trick, by bird, by boat and bridge, by painful corrosive destruction, by Watcher and will.

By far, his least favorite method was the IWL, at least up until now.

Falling back into the Dust Wing, as if pulled by an overwhelming gravity, was becoming a contender. He felt as if a small black hole had opened up inside his heart and he was being pulled apart from the inside out. He'd kept his eyes on Rami at first. He willed his face composed and unafraid. Unafraid as the ghosts chorused in his head, unafraid as the darkness swam in on the edges until a bone-shaking pop felt like it shattered every nerve in his body and there was darkness. Not the darkness of nowhere roads, where only Rami's certainty stood out like a beacon. No, this was a darkness he recognized.

He didn't land in the grisly killing fields of the Dust Wing's lobby. He didn't even land on solid ground. He fell, as all the books arriving in the Dust Wing must fall, through infinite darkness. Hero only had a moment to pinwheel inelegantly before he felt, more than saw, the crumbled ruins of the wing rushing toward him.

Hero tucked and protected his head, taking the brunt of the impact with the roll of his shoulder. It helped, if only because Hero felt a tiny crack and blinding pain rather than landing poorly and not feeling anything at all. The momentum carried him down a hard incline, and Hero lost his form entirely, tumbling like a die tossed into the dark. He came to a stop not because he'd run out of momentum but because he encountered something harder than him. A thick chunk of stone caught him in the middle. Hero held on and ran a damage inventory as he tried to remember how to breathe.

At least one broken rib, that was for certain. His ankle throbbed, and there was something distinctly Not Right going on with his shoulder and sword arm. That thought sent him pawing for his scabbard with his one good arm, but that had been ripped away in the landing. Injured, disoriented, and unarmed. That was how he was to face the haunting of a wing that had already defeated him twice. The pain at least quieted the whispers clotting up his thoughts. He gingerly slid off the outcropping and rolled onto one knee with effort. Something hot and wet dribbled into his eye. It was too dark to see whether it was black ink or red blood now.

That was a shame. He suspected a number of damsels had good money placed on the answer.

A small valley between the mountains of abandoned books created a path before him that Hero could barely pick out in the dark. He should have asked Rami for a light before he let go. He should have... asked Rami many things before he let go. This was the trouble with being a written creature; Hero was realizing how much he relied on subtext.

That sour fact amused him enough to lighten the stabbing pain in his side as he got to his feet.

"Well?" His voice sounded frail in the darkness. He grimaced and tried to correct that. "Speak up!"

The expanse of dust had no answer for him.

"I gathered the stories of every other wing. I read them, each and every one, as they passed through me. Don't you want to remember what it is like to be read?"

Hero frowned as only his own voice rebounded back at him. The Dust Wing had never been silent, not for him. That was why he'd been certain that he had to do this. Could do this. Doubt began to trickle in. "Answer me!"

It was more silence, but he could feel eyes on him now. The eyes of the Dust Wing souls, of course, but it felt intensely more. He felt the attention like a sentence strung out along a page. Could feel the muted press of paper against his skin. Somewhere, the gods watched him to see what he would do. Somewhere, the gods sipped tea, or idly checked in on his story in snippets of their bigger god lives. He felt it, all the avatars of readers that were here with him now, in this moment. The critic, the curious, the skeptical, the wondrous, the tearstained, and the weary. They were here, and Hero's heart silently whispered, *I see you. You, you.*

They said Hero had escaped his story, burned his book, but it was a lie. The truth was they were all stories, human and character, sinners and saints. Every soul a story, and every moment fresh ink on the page.

He was being read, even now. He'd run so far to escape his story, to escape his fate as a character in a set plot. Only to run back here, to realize there was no escaping the page of the greater book. This chronicle of time, the index of souls, this library of lost things.

Freedom wasn't freedom from the story, after all.

Freedom was making the ink count for a damn.

His injuries were unimportant and drowned in that thought. His pace picked up and drew him deeper into the Dust Wing, past the modern tablets and lost hypertext, past books and paper, past parchment and vellum, slate and stone. Hero knew what he was looking for now.

"Fine," he said. "I'll come to you."

He followed the story to the heart of the ghost.

43

RAMI

I almost lost him to that vision. Don't think I don't see how he pauses, looks over his shoulder of feathers turned white, and gazes into the middle distance awhile. I kept the man I love from his version of paradise. I dragged him back to Hell, literally. I should feel guilty about that, but I don't.

Heaven doesn't deserve him. Heaven doesn't deserve any of them.

Assistant Librarian Hero, 2020 CE

IT MIGHT HAVE BEEN fair to imagine that it would be easy for an angel to return to Heaven. Rami could be faulted for the assumption, the way he had pined to return and enter past the Gates. But the fact was, for any Watcher, or angel who had been cast out, the way back to Heaven was a crawl over scorched earth. Not physically, of course, but it felt that way. Rami would have crawled over broken glass to help his friends, however.

The Gates never failed to dazzle, even to jaded old Watcher eyes. The light sang along the boulevard, reached in blinding columns and rows that funneled every approaching soul to the same elevated point just in front of the Gates. It was impossible to miss, and it was the way Rami allowed himself to be directed.

The desk seemed grander from this angle. When Rami had attended to it, it had felt like merely a shabby raft in the tossing sea of disgruntled souls. Now it rose above the crowd like an altar. Wide slabs of white riddled with filigree fretwork and gold details. Impressive and divine, just the kind of desk one would expect at the Gates of Heaven.

The only problem was, it was unattended. Rami frowned, but before he could find cause for alarm he heard a familiar voice.

"Well, it's not my place to tell you where to go, but I hear Duat's nice if you like poetry."

The shuffling crowds parted for a breath and Rami caught a glimpse of a pair of stooped shoulders, only half there, the way all souls were until they crossed the Heavenly Gates. It drifted in a small orbit around a familiar slight figure wearing an ill-fitting suit and topped with a head of messy curls.

Rami smiled in spite of himself. "Leto."

"One minute. I'm with some—" His head whipped around, and Leto, former lost soul, former junior demon, current caretaker of the Gates of Heaven, gasped. "Ramiel? Who—what—"

The teenage boy forgot the soul he was advising and began to forge gently through the crowd. Rami took the moment to take inventory. Most souls after they died reached a happy default in their preferred outward age and physical appearance. Leto had died as a teenager and remained much the same as the last time Rami had seen him. Still gangly, soft brown skin still freckled. He still wore a cheap suit, though somewhere along the way he'd ditched the tie and split the cuffs so they were easier to roll up to his elbows. An informal modification that reminded Rami of Claire with a pang of fondness.

But there was an assurance that had not been in the freshly dead teenager before. A quiet sense of self as Leto placed a gentle hand on shoulders in the crowd to slip through without disturbing a soul. The teenager Rami had known had been coltish and spun tight with doubts. All that tension, all that regret and fear, seemed to have drained away from the young man who stopped before him.

Leto barely hesitated a second before wrapping Rami in an effusive, if quick, hug. "I didn't think I'd see you here again!"

"Is that why you're directing Heaven-bound souls to Duat?" Rami asked, chuckling as Leto's eyes went wide. "I couldn't help but overhear."

"It's not like that!" Leto wrinkled his nose, and a brief flash of the awkward teenager trying to not get in trouble appeared. "I do my job and get to know everyone who comes in! Most of them go on. It's just… well, Heaven is not some people's idea of paradise, you know? Especially since …" He drifted a hand back toward the Gates, as if to indicate the complicated state of affairs Uriel had left things in. Left, after Claire had discorporated her.

"It started with just this one mortal—supercool lady. She did roller derby! Like for serious." Leto got animated with his hands. "She was telling me all these stories and I just couldn't help thinking how well she'd fit in with what I saw of Valhalla, so I mighta… kinda suggested that. And she liked the idea, so I sent her there."

Rami was too tired to be scandalized at this point. "You're diverting souls from Heaven to Valhalla?"

"Not just Valhalla. After that I started thinking about it and doing some research on world religions—do you know how hard it is to ask for books around here? Really made me miss…" Leto trailed off with a small grimace. "Anyway, now I interview everyone and help them figure out where they want to go next. No one's ever been sent back, so I figure the other guys are okay with it?"

"The other... guys," Rami repeated slowly.

"Sorry, right, my bad," Leto apologized, missing Rami's concern entirely. "Not just guys, obviously. I mean the other folks that do what I do. In other realms."

The young man before him was so joyfully calm and confident that Rami didn't have the heart to describe how he was flippantly upending, oh, several eons of religious doctrine and realm operation. And evidently drawing the affairs of several other active afterlife realms into the act. Did Walter know he had been doing this? Death had to know.

Walter's suggestion began to make a lot more sense. "That's great, kid," Rami said absently.

Leto's relieved smile was almost more blinding than the Heavenly lights. "Thanks. I kept on thinking about what you said about souls, you know?" Oh god, this was his fault. And then Leto's head tilted. "How's things back—you know. How's everyone?"

Rami took a deep breath and began to talk.

44

BREVITY

So here I am, Library, prison and sanctuary, torment and blessing in one. Here I am, unwritten dreams, untold ends, forgotten stories. Here I am.

My soul was consigned to the Library at the start of my tenure. I thought the only way out was to hold on to myself until I was free. Stoic nonsense. My freedom will be here, foiling Hell, to become something more than I am. Stories are made of us, and we are made of stories.

I'll do more good as a story, as a library, than I will as a woman in rebellion against time. I will walk softly among the stacks, one last time. And if the Library will have me, I will not walk out again.

Hell wants to remake the Library, but they will not remake me. *I* will remake me. The Library is more eternal than any realm.

Listen for me, Revka.

Librarian Poppaea Julia, final entry, 48 BCE

IT WAS OBVIOUS TO Brevity that the librarians were flagging. They could all feel it. Story after story went around, and every one of them had exhausted their memories several rounds ago. Now they were improvising stories on the spot. It wasn't that they were running out of stories—gods no. They were librarians, story keepers and storytellers to the last. They could have unwound stories like an eternal Scheherazade if that could have kept the Library intact.

The problem was the listening.

It took skill to really absorb a good story. It took skill to tell one, but a brilliant tale performed for an unwilling reader leads to the type of crimes high school literature essays are made of. Telling the story was only one half of the bubble they'd created. The other half, the sustaining half, was the rest of the audience, listening and losing themselves in worlds that never existed. That's what gave a story life beyond the breath in the storyteller's lungs—the reader. That's what asserted reality against the chaotic forces attempting to tear the Library apart.

But the librarians were, for the most part, mortal. Even the nonhuman spirits of their number needed some form of rest. Imaginations flagged, attention drifted, and slowly the preservation of their bubble shrank by inches. The door to the damsel suite warped, and then flames dribbled out of their fireplace and crystallized into yellow taffy that smelled like hot violets. Divans and ottomans melted into the ceiling. Paisley fractals spilled out of teacups. The assembled damsels gathered in a tighter and tighter cluster around the speaking librarian, but Brevity knew it was only a matter of time before the abyss started pulling at them too.

Bjorn was up now. Having exhausted his typical repertoire of heroes and battle, he was telling a soft, cozy romance of two ice dancers that had Brevity tearing up a few times. The tears helped, she'd noticed. The bubble had expanded then, if only for a moment. Tears helped prove a story real. But they'd already passed the third-act dark moment and were winding down into a happily ever after, and the rest of the librarians looked distracted with the same worry: of who would dig up another story next.

Brevity's gaze fished over the group and landed on Claire, standing, as if on guard, at the edge of the bubble near the door. Something was going on. Secrets didn't quite have colors, but Brevity still had an affinity for sniffing them out. Brevity knew secrets, and there was a big one brewing in the space between Claire's ears. Brewing and, she had the foreboding feeling, about to come to a boil.

The door to the damsel suite made a flatulent sound. Someone had likely knocked, but the door had ceased reliably identifying as wood half an hour ago. Claire, being the nearest, dragged it—the door oozed, oozed!—open. Beyond, Brevity could see the outline of Rami's feathered shoulders and head silhouetted against the chaos. There was a moment's murmur, then a pause that was broken by a startled gasp from Claire.

From Claire.

Brevity knew better than anyone that Claire was not as calm and composed as she appeared, but nevertheless, hearing a gasp from Claire immediately spiked her pulse into action. Brevity was at the door before she knew it and had somehow grabbed a fire poker on the way—always best to face surprises armed.

Hellhounds, demons, muses, ghosts, betrayal—she was a librarian, and a librarian was always prepared.

Except for this.

"Leto?!" The young man standing under Rami's protective arm looked like the confused mortal boy she had known. The same polyester suit, same bony wrists and ankles sticking out above the too-short cuffs. The same briar-patch hair of curls that he didn't seem to know how to care for. He looked the same, but it was as if it fit him better. Like his body had grown into his soul rather than vice versa, as he would have on earth. He didn't slouch anymore, or cringe his shoulders up to his ears—human ears! No longer demon-pointy. Brevity had never had a chance to get used to that. He stood there, shoulder to shoulder with an angel, and still as a pond amid the chaotic thrashing of the Unwritten Wing around him. His gaze was steady, and Brevity felt a deliriously unexpected flutter in her stomach.

"Hi," Leto said, with just enough of that old human trepidation for Brevity to know—to believe—it was him. She felt a laugh bubble up in her chest and she threw herself forward to wrap him in a hug. The Library was falling, she'd failed yet again, she'd be the librarian on watch to see everything lost, everything was awful, just as it had been a moment ago. But now everything was awful and Leto was *here*.

He made a surprised sound when she squeezed his ribs, but quickly hugged her back just as hard. He felt more solid, more real, than he'd ever felt as a supposed demon. He smelled weird, the residue of Heaven and sterile lines and graphite rules still clinging to him. But it was him. Brevity pulled back and couldn't stop grinning. "What happened? Did you actually get thrown out of Heaven? I was joking about that."

"Nope. I'm here to help out." Leto reflexively raked his hair back. "Rami told me... well."

He trailed off, glancing to the side with a look that was equal parts hope and caution. Oh, Claire. Brevity had gotten swept up in the surprise, but she wasn't the only one. Claire stood frozen in place, and Brevity worried that she was upset until she saw the slow-motion softening of the perpetual lines at the corners of Claire's eyes. Her lips parted, she drew in an unsteady breath, and when Claire smiled it was like a small piece of her heart had stitched back together.

If they were all family, of a kind, Leto was blood. He'd been a confused Hell-bound soul, swept up in their pursuit of the Codex Gigas. It wasn't until nearly too late that Claire had realized that Leto was a descendant of the mortal family she'd left behind, his death and subsequent appearance in the Library another play in Andras's elaborate plot.

She'd found him, and then she'd promptly lost him.

Brevity kept hold of his hand but stepped to one side, and one small step brought Claire the final way to Leto. She regarded him in silence, absently straightening his lapel, dusting his suit pocket with a motherly air. "You've grown," she said quietly, though Leto was still an inch shorter than she was.

He smiled shyly. "I learned how to make tea too."

"That'll do. Welcome…" Claire's low voice caught, snagging on something beneath the surface. "Welcome home, Leto."

"I'm here to help," Leto said again.

"That's great," Brevity said with a grimace. "But I don't think it's looking too good for the Library right now." Brevity was at a loss where to start. "We're falling apart. We need to find a god and a realm and—"

"And a gatekeeper," Rami finished softly. "Or to be more precise, a *guide*."

Claire's attention snapped to Ramiel. "A guide…" Her mouth dropped open and she glanced at Leto, then back. "But… a human? You're certain?"

"I spoke with Walter."

"He... I suppose he would know." Claire paused, staring at Rami with a question hesitant on her lips. "Hero...?"

"He had something he needed to do. He said—in the Dust Wing—" The softness of Rami's voice was tamped down by pain and worry. He met Claire's eyes again. "He needs to do it."

"He's..." Claire stopped. Her expression fell. "Trust him to indulge in... heroics. Just so."

She stared at her hands. A weird wind blew through the gaps in the shelves around them to thrum a wailing, whistling sound. Claire turned back to Leto and touched him on the cheek. "I've missed you so much. You have no idea. But are you sure you want to do this? You were in Heaven, Leto. Even if the Library survives, it will never be that. You shouldn't give paradise up."

The wind shrieked again, filling in the space as Leto gave that question the consideration it deserved. "Heaven was okay to visit. But..." Brevity could see his fists flex at his sides. "I'll take home over paradise every time."

Claire sniffed, but her lip trembled, just a hair, before she patted Leto's cheek and placed a swift kiss on the other. "Then it appears foolishness runs in the family."

Leto's grin brightened. He squeezed Brevity's hand as he looked around the tattered remains of the Library. The wind had picked up in pitch as the shelves nearest them iced over with peppermint and algae. "It does. So I have an idea, but what's fir—"

The howl and cracking of floorboards drowned him out. A patch of solid ground beneath them snapped and melted away, but instead of falling down into the void, Brevity suddenly felt her center of gravity shift and she fell up. The librarian's protective bubble had shrunk again. Brevity twisted in the air to snag the edge of the damsel suite doorframe. She quickly looped an arm around it, which was the only reason she didn't slide again when Claire grabbed her free hand to stop her own fall.

The ceiling of the Unwritten Wing lay "beneath" their dangling feet, while above them, the hole in what had been the floorboards howled like a storm door blown open during a hurricane. Brevity was relieved to see that Rami had secured himself to an upside-down endcap across the aisle. The shelves surrounding the damsel suite had turned into a cliff face, though it took a moment to process that all the books stayed tidily on their shelves.

The Library had reversed gravity just for them, to save them. "Thank you, Poppaea," Claire whispered as she switched her grip from Brevity's forearm to a shelf and wedged her feet in. "Hold on just a little bit longer."

"The wing is tearing itself apart. We need to get down," Rami called from across the way. He paused with a grimace and corrected. "Or up."

"No, climb away from the suite! The Library should let you back down when it's safe." Claire had to shout just to be heard above the mewling wind. "We're running out of time. Leto—do you know what to do? To become our guide?"

Leto paused, and his curly hair snaked in the wind as he considered. He looked at the books clinging to the bottom of the shelf before staring up, as if contemplating the vortex, before nodding slowly. "I think so!"

"Good. Rami, go with him."

The feathers in Rami's trench coat were depleted, but the few remaining fluttered in the wind like a wounded bird. The look on his face screamed his misgivings. "We still need to find a god—"

"Leave the god nonsense to me." Claire turned her back to him and began to painstakingly try to drag herself up the shelf to where

Brevity was at the doorframe. "Just get Leto to the front door."

It was too far away for Brevity to make out the complicated emotions that filled up the pause before Rami nodded, securing a hold on Leto's arm and pulling him along the shelf. "As you say, Librarians."

Brevity managed to swing a heel over the edge of the doorframe, and a hand caught her on the other side. At least someone else in the suite had noticed the doorway had gone wonky. Brevity smiled her thanks as Iambe helped haul her to what was supposed to be the damsel suite's ceiling. Brevity reached down to offer the same assistance to Claire. She took her arm.

"And, Leto!" Claire called, looking over her shoulder one final time. Brevity was close enough to feel the tremble in her biceps as her breath caught. "I'm so, so proud of you."

Brevity looked across the howling space in time to see Leto pause in surprise. He twisted precariously to meet and hold Claire's gaze. He opened his mouth to say something but nodded instead. It was enough. Claire drew a breath, turned away, and allowed Brevity to haul her across the doorframe. The wind dissipated until they could hear only their own labored breathing. By the time Brevity looked out into the stacks again, both Rami and Leto were gone.

She caught Claire staring. Her gaze locked somewhere just beyond, not in the direction where the others had gone, but deeper in the stacks. Her eyes looked like she was already mentally on a journey Brevity could not follow. Brevity shook her shoulder, Claire blinked, and they slowly made their way back to the group of librarians at the eye of the storm.

They found seats at the edge of the circle, near Echo's pond, though both of them took care to not sit so close as to cast their reflections in it. Xi, the ink-stained librarian from Xian, was finishing up their story, illustrated with some really fantastic sumi-e deftly drawn in midair with their inky fingers. Slowly, the final images drifted and the air inside the bubble wobbled precariously.

The pause drew out. Every face gathered, librarians and damsels alike, was heavy with fatigue. Stories could go on forever; storytellers couldn't. Bjorn was ashy with exhaustion, but he began to fumble for another book. Claire interrupted him.

"I have a story."

That injected a shot of curiosity through the suite. Claire had yet to participate in their end of the world story session. Though the Unwritten Wing had regained her, it was obvious the other librarians no longer considered her one of them. Bjorn's hand hovered over the books stacked beside him. "You sure, lass?"

"I am certain." Claire flicked a long look at Brevity. It was a look that said something, something important. Brevity couldn't read it, but she felt the weight of it settle on her shoulders like a mourner's shawl. All eyes were on Claire now, but she didn't reach for a book.

"This is a walking story," Claire announced and stood, flicking invisible dust away from her skirts—she'd found clean skirts again somewhere; when had that happened? When had Brevity lost track of Claire's story? She gave an imperious gesture to the gathering. "Up, up. Let's go."

"But the chaos—" Brevity tried to object.

"Let it come. This is the kind of story that welcomes chaos." Claire had a determined stomp to her stride. Gravity had reasserted itself, though there was still a large hole in the floorboards outside to skirt around. "Come along, everyone. And do listen closely. There will not be an encore performance for this one."

45

THE LIBRARY

A library does not have a name; a library has all of them.
A library is not a place; a library is a purpose.
A library does not have eyes; a library has *I*'s.
And this is what the library saw.

"ONCE UPON A TIME, there was a soul. And the soul was lonely,"
Claire said, stepping fearlessly out into the hallway. Her foot
dropped for a frightful second, before the floorboards solidified
under her feet. Claire didn't look down. "It was in the dreamtime,
when the world was as new as a tender bud, and the soul was
alone. To keep herself company, the soul whispered to the bud
what would happen when it bloomed. And the world listened.
That was the first story."

*

HE WAS IN THE dark, but Leto wasn't afraid. He'd been running,
Ramiel right behind him, toward the front doors of the Unwritten
Wing as reality broke around him. A wrong step, and the void had
dropped like a curtain. It made sense. Leto had died often enough

to understand that it was one final journey you took alone.

Two crimson lights swirled out of the dark. Eyes.

*

THE WAY FORWARD WAS the way back. Hero strode through the Dust Wing for what felt like hours. His eyes became used to the dark. His skin became as dry as paper. He walked the pathways through forgotten paperbacks. Stacks of fanzines, snippets of poetry no one could any longer recall. Small gems stumbled upon once, then lost forever. Where there was a path, he ran; where there wasn't, he stumbled, then he crawled.

*

THE AISLES OF THE wing were a maelstrom, jagged with the sharp edges of insanity. The Library felt the thread of a story—there, and the Library listened and held true. Bird darted overhead, in and out of shadow. Always appearing, another inkblot in the light. Claire kept walking. "Eventually, the world bloomed and grew, as worlds are wont to do. It remembered the story whispered to it while still in the bud, and loved the soul so much it worked very hard to make the story come true. And when it was done there was one more soul in the world, because the world could not bear to miss another story."

"This was the first reader," Brevity whispered with wonder. She'd caught up and slid her hand into Claire's to hold on tightly. She'd caught on to the rhythm of the story, as Claire had known she would. It felt good to not walk this final story alone.

*

"OH, WALTER!" LETO FELT dizzy with relief as he made out the white of the giant's shirtsleeves emerging through the gloom. "You scared me."

Walter's shoulders ducked sheepishly. "No need to be afraid,

Mister Leto." He paused and eased his weight down to the invisible floor of the nothing-space they were in. Leto could almost look him in his glowing red eyes now. "You know that now, eh?"

"I do," Leto said softly. Walter was big enough that it was hard to take him in all at once at this distance. His edges were beginning to shiver and shift into something new.

"You ready to get started, then?" Walter asked.

*

WHERE THERE WERE WALLS, he climbed. The hardcover cliffs slowed his progress. Centuries had built crumbling strata of clapboard and linen and leather and wood. His nails split, his hands bled. He climbed, spine over spine, until sweat and ink dripped in his eyes. He didn't dare look down to blink it away. The ghosts had followed him to the cliffs too. *Jump*, they said, pitying. It would be easier than questioning. Easier than answers.

Hero kept climbing.

*

"THE OLD SOUL AND the new soul reveled in their company. They told stories to each other, of what might be, what might have been, what might-have-never-was. The best were repeated, and even if it was just them and their little world in the dark, they felt true." Claire took a deep breath, finding Brevity's hand in hers and squeezing. She sensed the others following at a distance—close enough to hear, but huddled back for safety. They felt the hold of the story now, even if the Library was dying. Bird landed on her shoulder, heavy and real. She would stay with her until they found the end. Claire kept walking. "These stories passed back and forth between them like a river, wearing a presence in the world like water wears down stone, until one day the souls woke and then there were three. This was the first character."

*

LETO WAS READY. He took Walter's hand, which was a sliding sensation in his grip. First the familiar meaty mitt that he'd been expecting, then a hairy claw, then nothing but bones. Death was showing all of himself to him. Guide and Gate could see each other plainly.

Walter coughed, almost as if he was embarrassed. "I'll give you a tour, but you'll have to find your own way back," he warned.

Leto nodded, and they set off down the forgotten pathways of the afterlife.

*

THE SEAS OF PARCHMENT were the hardest. The cliffs dropped off to a beach of debris, whittled away by a strange kind of tide. Paper, linen, silk screen, parchment, and papyrus roiled and curled against one another. One drop of moisture made it a slurry. Pulp and progress pushed up onto the beach, then away. Hero had the ridiculous thought that this was the end. Somewhere, in those sea depths, were his lost pages. His story was there, like a driftwood siren, if he'd only stop to look for it. Wasn't it a beautiful place to rest? A sea of words, silence, and the dust-speck stars above?

Hero bent and scavenged the remains of codex covers to make a boat.

*

"THE WORLD GREW FAST after that, and spun far out of the first soul's reach, as worlds are wont to do. More souls were made and wandered far. The soul grew old, so old she could not travel far to tell her stories. This made the reader souls sad, for though they could tell their own memory of a story, each story is new with the teller. So the world birthed up language and writing and words, and the souls told their stories on the skin of the earth, for all to read." Claire walked across fractal swamplands, books and memories splintering into thorny brambles. She reached out and touched a thorn. It sprang into an English rose. "This was the first book."

*

HUMANITY TELLS A LOT of stories about Death, the one thing that will always remain unknown and fictive. Death is a tunnel, Death is a bridge, Death is a gray field, Death is an endless sleep. Leto followed Walter through laudanum-cloaked mists and across narrow catwalks of smoke. Across fields of poppies and chrysanthemums. Through stone cairns and toward bright blue-and-white lights. He followed, and each step he took gained a place in his memory. It was suddenly effortless; he could trace every step.

That's when he began to see the fireflies.

*

ALL SEAS HAVE A strange relationship with time. Hours flowed into days, which pooled into months and seeped into the foundations of Hero's mind like years. It made sense; the forgotten time of the Dust Wing had to go somewhere. Hero sailed, paced, shat, and slept amid the sea spray of stories. The friction of fiction chapped his pale cheeks. His injuries healed, then his injuries ached. He grew a beard. He was capable of growing a beard! Hero had never been written needing a shave. It itched.

At night, he lay on his back, stared at the constellations of dust motes hanging in the air like fireflies, and wondered if those he'd left behind were lost too.

*

BOOKS RIGHTED IN THE CHAOS. The Library was burning itself up to give Claire a clear path to walk. It would sacrifice them last. Bird's feathers bristled and ruffled Claire's cheek when the unreality got too close for comfort. *Almost there, Poppaea*, Claire thought. "Now the first soul was very old indeed. Their story had grown and meandered for such a long, interesting journey, through hardships and wonders the soul could not have even imagined. The soul's story had told so much, but it still felt incomplete. 'What is missing?' the old soul wondered to the sky. 'An ending,' the sky wondered back. And the soul was gone, though the stories were not. This was the first death."

*

WALTER LED HIM INTO darker places, and that's when he could see it. Lights flickering, lingering when they should have been passing through. Leto drew near and reached out to touch one. Oh.

"They're souls. Dead, like me," Leto said with wonder. "Why aren't they moving on?"

"They still got stories in 'em," Walter said kindly.

Leto thought. He cupped the soul-light in his hand. "I think I know a place they'd like, then."

Walter smiled. "Lead the way."

*

THERE WERE NO STORMS on timeless seas. It was still a small miracle when the tide drew Hero to a rocky shore. His boat broke up almost immediately, shredded on the small white shards of stone that turned the sea of paper to pulp. He stepped onto slate shores. Countless slabs, clay pottery dotted with cuneiform, sticks burned with tally marks telling the story of trade, some of the earliest writing. A broken stylus stabbed at him through the disintegrating parts of his boots. He took them off and walked barefoot toward the only landmark on the horizon: a wide hole set into the crest of salt-white stones, a cave.

"THE WORLD HAD A secret it kept from Death. It had loved the first soul so much that it had bloomed for its story; no other soul had done that. It had cherished the first soul so much it could not let it go." Claire couldn't hear the footsteps of the other librarians behind her anymore. Her world had narrowed to the pulse of her story, the ground precisely one step ahead. One word after the next. Her voice echoed oddly in her own head. "'Would you like to go on?' the world asked. And the soul was wise enough to say, 'I cannot go on as I am, for it is important for my story to have an ending.'"

*

LETO WALKED THE PATHS of the afterlife, and this time he was not afraid. It was a little like the work he'd done at the Gates, picking up souls, redirecting them where they needed to go. But oh, this was so much better. It wasn't furtive; it wasn't hard. It wasn't guessing where a soul belonged—he was finding those with library souls, story souls, and sending them home. Home was easy, once you recognized it.

He smiled.

*

THE ENTRANCE TO THE cave was a wide mouth, toothed with stalactites dripping stale water on his head. He took a closer look at one that reached farthest down, and he could see other artifacts caught in the stone. Knotted-rope languages, pierced wood, stories told in weaves of colorful thread, feathers, red clay, and twisting lines. Stories caught like creatures in amber. Echoes died away in the frost. It was eerie, but Hero was forgetting what comfort was. He stepped off the broken slates and onto the smooth floor of the cave.

And then he heard the voices.

*

SHE FELT, MORE THAN heard, Brevity's gasp beside her. Of course Brevity would find the truth first. She knew Claire's heart better than Claire did herself, at times. Claire squeezed her hand, just once, and kept on. "The world thought about this. 'Then, would you like to go on with me?' it asked. The old soul thought about this a very long time. 'I think,' she said, 'that would be a very good story.'

" 'Because it feels true,' the world said.

" 'Because it is true,' said the soul. And so it was.

"This," Claire whispered. "This was the first god."

*

LETO'S PATH LED HIM through a dimly lit bedroom. Teenage posters on the wall—video-game art, mostly; Leto had never been sporty when he was alive. He stepped over a bed of rumpled blankets. Tiny blue pills speckled it like teardrops. He looked down and felt a weight drop off his shoulders.

"Let's go home," he said to the small quavering light cupped in his hand.

*

BEFORE WRITING, BEFORE INK and charcoal and chalk, humanity told stories. The first library was a song, Hero remembered Bjorn saying. Being a creature of the written word, he'd never paid much attention to the Norseman's affinity for spoken storytelling. But now Hero sank through a gauzy forest of lost voices. Stories, passed down from elder to child in a continuous chain, until war, pestilence, or colonialism had broken the links. Stories of people who no longer existed, or a multitude who were merely *told* they no longer existed. Stories of people who filled the world with a song that was a stamped-out echo.

It was too much. Hero tried to cover his ears, but the voices were impossible to block out. The pressure built in his head, ghost upon lonely ghost. It only eased when he let go. When he listened.

His feet were slow now, one step in front of the other, silent so as not to disrupt the stories. He walked in the dark, and heard and remembered everything humanity had forgot. The dust followed him, spectral and alive. It was just enough light to see, when he came to the very back of the cave.

*

"THIS WAS THE FIRST god," Claire repeated and slowed as they reached the front lobby of the Unwritten Wing. The seams of the chaos were showing here. The floorboards splintered and the edges of colorful rugs flapped into the absolute void of the gaps, colors bleeding out of them like water. Librarians and damsels alike slowed at the edge of the stacks. But each step that Claire took, the wing was there to meet her with steady ground. Each step, the surface rippled but held. The effect was unsettling. Claire glided across the lobby as if walking on water, not wood. "There was a librarian named Poppaea Julia," Claire said. Her hands rested momentarily on the battle-scarred surface of the librarian's desk as she neared it. Her cadence faltered as she stared down at the desk at the eye of the unraveling.

Stared, as if she wasn't going to see it again.

A small rabbit tremble sounded a warning somewhere in Brevity's gut. "Claire…"

"It's okay, Brev." Claire raised her gaze. She was smiling. "I'm not going anywhere."

Her attention shifted over Brevity's shoulder. The librarians had followed, all eleven of them, but so had the damsels that had stayed. Rosia peeked out from behind Bjorn, eyes solemn and wide. She broke away from the crowd to skitter over to Brevity. It was a small gathering, but enough. Enough to build a future of stories on. Bird launched off her shoulder and looped over her head, almost appearing to caw a blessing over the gathering, and then the raven melted into the dark.

Something was happening. Everything was happening. Brevity fought against the headwind of the vortex that divided the lobby. "Boss, you don't have to do this."

"No, I don't," Claire agreed. She'd found the page she was looking for, and her fingertips rested on the Librarian's Log.

"Then don't sacrifice—"

"This isn't a sacrifice. Brev, remember that. There are no martyrs here." The wind had caught the tips of her locks and they writhed like ribbons around Claire's head. "I don't have to do this. I choose to, though. I choose to be here. I choose to stay. I choose all of you. I choose this. *This* is what a library is." Claire reached out with her free hand and touched the scarred gilt tattoo on Brevity's arm. "The story you stole. You wanted something to call your own, didn't you? This is yours now, Brev. All of it. You are the librarian. Take care of them."

Brevity couldn't speak. The whisper of wind rose to a howl. She was distantly aware of the huddle of librarians clutching the shelves behind her. Echo fluttered in the reflection of every drop of water that flew through the air. Many of the remaining damsels had returned to their books for reinforcements, but a few remained. Rosia clutched Brevity's hand like an anchor.

Somehow, above the wail of wind, Brevity heard Claire's voice.

"There once was a mortal named Poppaea Julia. She was a soul who became a librarian who became a god who became a story. She gave us a hidden story. She gave us an unfinished story. She wanted to give us a home, but she failed and found she could only give us hope; that's what a god does. She has been the god of the Library for generations now, but it is time for her to rest. My name is Claire Juniper Hadley..." Claire drew air into her lungs. Tasted anise and old paper on her tongue. "I'm ready," she whispered.

Bird let out a grackling cry in the dark. The books to either side of them whipped color in a frenzy, whether from panic or ecstasy. And then, just then, the streaming colors, the reaching, yearning souls of every book in the Library, stretched in one direction.

Toward Claire.

"There was once a soul named Claire Juniper Hadley, and…" Claire said, meeting Brevity's eyes across the divide. Her eyes were bright. She smiled. "There once was a Library."

The spectrum of souls, every spirit of the libraries they'd gathered, streamed like falling stars into the place where Claire stood. The lobby was bright as the sun. The world righted. Brevity blinked.

And Claire was gone.

*

THERE WAS NO LIGHT, but there was no dark either. The dust permeated the air, his skin, his lungs, and by dust-light Hero could see the lines, done in ash and clay, on the flat wall of the cave. Bison and other large creatures, strangely graceful on their spindle-stick legs, fled from hunters. An antlered beast twisted in midflight. Whether it was a recounting of a hunt past, or a hope for bounty future, it was a story. And at the center, done in brick-red clay, was a single handprint.

Hero understood time now. Could ride the crest of it and not drown as the history of moments came sweeping down on him. At some point, when the universe was already old but man still so very young, a single human had stood here, telling stories in the night. Stories were how humanity made sense of the dark, of the chaos and the time. Hero could have stood there for another eternity, losing himself in the arc and whorl of the picture tale. He could have stayed there, choosing sane fiction over the challenges of reality. But that was not what stories were made to do.

Hero reached out. His velvet coat was torn and disintegrating at the cuff. His hands were no longer smooth but calloused with memories. He took a long, ragged breath and placed his hand over the palm print. It fit perfectly.

"Hero," a voice said behind him.

And Hero turned away from the back of the cave.

*

THE DOORS OF THE Unwritten Wing stood before him again. Walter had his hand on Leto's shoulder. "Now you know," he said with a soft rumble. He was suit-shaped and kindly again. "Are you ready?"

*

THE DUST WAS ALIVE, whirling and gathering. Wind rippled through the cave like a soft sigh. Thin bits of material—papers, no, it couldn't be—blew in from the sea and danced in the updraft. They danced around Hero. Text squiggled across them, like the text of the Unwritten Wing. Hero tried to grab at one, but they slid out of his grasp. Lines and images began to form on the pages as they fluttered away.

Images overlaid one another, like a thumb, an ankle, a tattered ruffle of skirt, the corner of a frown, a critical eye. The pages aligned, just for a moment, and Hero gasped.

"Claire." His voice was weak and rusty as a ruin. It felt like years since he'd spoken, but maybe it was only hours. The cave shivered around them and he stumbled. He'd come so far, he'd lost so much, but change was coming. Hero had no idea whether it meant he'd failed or succeeded. "Are you really…?"

The pages fluttered, reshuffling into chaos one moment, then the animated sketch of Claire the next. A short, perfunctory ripping sound rang in the air and suddenly the storm of paper burst. Claire stepped out of it.

The ground shifted again, but that wasn't why Hero stumbled. His chest went tight as a hand reached out to keep him upright. "I tried, Claire. I couldn't do it but I tried—"

"You did it, Hero." Her voice was blurred, soft like rain. "We both did."

He pulled back. The dust-light flared, and Hero got a good look. Claire's long braids were black and watery at the edges, like brushes loaded with paint. Her eyes held a kind of sepia light. Her brow and lashes looked soft and liquid, as if inked on, and they crinkled as she studied him. Hero wondered if she was shocked at how much he had changed too. "What did you do, Claire?"

"The Library needed a guardian," Claire said simply. A constellation of inkblots circled lazily around her head. She touched his hands and the years-abused skin healed.

He swallowed his wonder. "You mean a god."

"Poppaea did it, years ago, to keep the Library whole when Hell remade it. She failed to free us, but she protected the story. She told the story, to make sure it went on. That's what makes a library what it is. The people."

"You're the Library now?"

"I am part of the Library. Always was."

"You promised you'd be there when I got back." Hero's voice hurt; everything hurt when exposed to light after so much darkness.

"I'm still there. Here. I'm not going anywhere, Hero. This is the way I can stay." Claire's hand touched his cheek. It felt like lambskin. Like buttery-soft vellum. "Come home."

"I've been gone so long." Hero unconsciously brought his hand up to his beard, his chapped skin.

"Only in story time. Not so long for the rest of us. All those thousands of lives, you listened to them, Hero. You promised not to forget." Claire smiled. "You know better than anyone, that's what any story wants. The Dust Wing is willing to be our realm. Come home, Hero. Rami's waiting."

"But you won't be there." He realized it as soon as he said it. Gods didn't sit behind desks and allow their tea to go cold. Gods didn't fall asleep on the arm of the chaise while reading and drool in endearing ways. Gods didn't grumble about the crumbs he left in reading chairs. Gods didn't squawk when he kissed them on the nose. A wound opened in Hero's chest that he knew, in an instant, would never completely heal.

"I will. I'll be there. It's the best way I could protect all of you," Claire said. The crown of ink circling her head slowed. And then, a little quieter: "The best way I could stay."

"But we know what happens to gods now."

"Yes, in a millennium or two I'll fade away into the Library rather than let it fall, just as Poppaea did." Claire smiled, not at all apologetic. "That's why I had to do it. I know what I'll choose. Besides, that's so much more time than most souls get."

"Will you be there, like this?" He gripped her hand a little tighter, worried she was already fading away.

"That depends."

"Depends on what?" Hero resisted the urge to whine. "Warden, enough with the mysticism. Don't taunt me now."

"It depends on what story you decide to tell." Claire's laughter was tinkling as Hero grimaced in confusion. "Don't look so surprised. You are brimming over with stories now. Who else would I have tell ours?"

"I'm a book, not a writer."

"Not a book," Claire said fondly, throwing his words back at him. "First rule of stories, Hero: they change. I never could stop you from changing, remember?"

"I ran away," Hero said faintly.

"And I went after you." The inkblots haloing Claire's head disappeared briefly into her braids. "Go home. Help rebuild with Rami. Take the Librarian's Log, tell our story."

"I won't know the right words," Hero said helplessly.

"No writer ever does. The words will be right eventually," Claire said, soft as a promise. "I'll be there every time you try."

The cave was changing, melting around him, though he sensed Claire's presence kept him safe. The outcroppings were eroding into shelves, stalactites into reading lamps. "No one will read it."

"Wait and see." Claire squeezed his hand, and ahead of them the sea crested into stacks, familiar and deep and infinitely wider than the Unwritten Wing had been. Horizon to horizon, stories swept like a flood into the Dust Wing, vibrant and alive. "It's time we became a real library, don't you think?"

EPILOGUE

It is important to end well, I think. We have so little control over how we start, and barely know ourselves when we're in the business of going on. But the end? I like to think I owned it. I remember less about my own mortal life every day. I was a linen woman. I lived in France. I was called mad, a witch, among other things. I don't remember how I died, but this I believe: people tried to take up bits of my life the entire time I was living. No one gets to take my end from me.

Listen up. Here is what I know about endings: they don't exist.

Librarian Fleur Michael, 1782 CE

YOU. LISTEN TO ME, you. You reader, you interloper, you glorious wandering god. Listen now, little soul.

Can you hear it?

There's a new myth in the world, and it is told in whispers. It's caught in the dissolving memory of a dream on waking. The dead sing of it. Children know it intuitively, as with all truer-than-true things. The clever steal pinches of it, here and there, when they can.

It's an afterlife that requires no prayers. No offerings or vows. After the disorientation and non-euclidean maze of death, seekers might stumble upon a young man waiting in a bit of light. His suit doesn't quite fit, but it's soft and rumpled around the edges, just like his smile. He greets you by name, and soon enough lost souls find themselves on the threshold of great doors opened wide. The first breath tastes like peppermint and sunshine. The librarian is a cheerful one, with blue skin and bright clothing and a smile that is so familiar it reminds you of something. A man sits at a table nearby, content and remote in his own thoughts, tousled copper hair hiding his face as he scribbles across an empty page and mutters to himself. Another man brings him tea, a pot clutched carefully in big hands, silver eyes gentle.

There are warm fires and deep chairs. There are green things growing between the cracks. There are spots of sunshine and rainy windows. There are hot drinks and little pastries and color, so much color it breaks your heart.

And there are stories. So many stories.

You recognize it, little soul. Of course you do; it is known to all who arrive here. It is a myth of an endless library, a place for souls to pause, rest, and regather themselves after death. It is a place of sanctuary; it is a place of homecoming. And, like any good library, it is open to all.

There is a question you are asked when you die, and it is Ramiel's abiding honor to ask it.

"Would you like to tell me your story?"

ACKNOWLEDGMENTS

I wrote this, the final book of the Hell's Library trilogy, during the COVID-19 pandemic of 2020. I wrote this while quarantining with vulnerable loved ones in a claustrophobic city apartment, writing an end to the series during a time when it felt the world—a version of the world as I knew it, at least—was threatening to end. If this caused me to favor good ends for the Hell's Library family, to indulge in more "I love yous" and "I cares" than a cynical reader cares for, I apologize for nothing.

If you're lucky enough to find yourself a family at the end of things, you damn well better tell them you love them.

These books were possible, especially during this time, only because of the family I've found. This book is dedicated to one of my oldest and dearest friends, Becky Littlefield. She who read my terrible first drafts when we were sixteen-year-olds on the internet doing NaNoWriMo for the first time, who was my rubber duck for a weird idea about a library in Hell, who was one of the first to read the first halting words of what would become this trilogy. Becky's a hell of a first reader, and an even more formidable friend, and I'm lucky to have her in my corner.

Thank you, as ever, to my publishing family. To my agent, Caitlin McDonald, who was the first to take a chance on Claire and me. To Miranda Hill, my patient and supportive editor, who trusted me to get there even when I doubted myself. To the entire Ace team: Alexis Nixon, Jessica Plummer, Stephanie Felty, cover artist Jeff Miller, and everyone at Ace who believed in the books enough to get them in front of readers. To the UK publishing team at Titan Books, including Cat Camancho and Julia Bradley—thank you from the bottom of my heart. I also want to thank Rebecca Brewer, a brilliant editor and accomplice in smuggling these books out of the Unwritten Wing.

I'm lucky enough to have a writing family in the people of the Isle and the folks at the pub. Special thanks to Tyler Hayes, C. L. Polk, Karen Osborne, Valerie Valdes, Jo Miles, Amber Bird, and Chris Wolfgang for propping me up at various points during the drafting and revision process.

My Patreon patrons held me up during this hard year, and they are some of my favorite people. Special thanks to Haviva, Caleb, Kristi, Katharina, Becky, Bruce, Karen, Alastair, and Savannah—classy muses, all of you.

Thank you to my sister, Kate, for always being the best sister—every anxious writer should have a sister who's a psychologist, y'all. Even when she's not telling me "Your brain is bad, buddy," she's the most supportive friend I could ask for. And I owe every word to my partner, Levi, who was locked in this madhouse with me throughout quarantine and somehow can still stand me and my books.

I also want to thank my mom and dad. When I started out writing, my mom was my biggest cheerleader and wanted to read everything—everything, even the sexy romances—that I wrote. She painstakingly hand-punched an early draft of *The Library of the Unwritten* to keep in a binder—she nicked herself, and so I have a copy literally bound in blood. Sadly, by the time I finished this book, my mom had lost most of her ability to read and enjoy books due to declining health and age. I'll forever be sad that she likely won't read how this story ends, but I know she's there on every page. I love you, Mom, and... I'll see you in the Library.

What else do you say upon finishing the trilogy that's stewed in you for years? What do you say when it's your *first* trilogy and you're still marveling it made it out of the Unwritten Wing at all?

You say thank you. Thank you for it all.

Next story, Claire. Next story.

A. J. Hackwith is almost certainly not an ink witch in a hoodie. She's a queer writer of fantasy and science fiction living in Seattle with her partner, her dog, and her ghosts. A Novel From Hell's Library is her first fantasy series, beginning with *The Library of the Unwritten*, followed by *The Archive of the Forgotten* and *The God of Lost Words*. She is a graduate of the Viable Paradise writers' workshop and her work appears in *Unncanny* magazine and assorted anthologies. She has also written sci-fi romance as Ada Harper. You can find her on Twitter @ajhackwith and in other dark corners of the internet.

For more fantastic fiction, author events,
exclusive excerpts, competitions, limited editions and more

VISIT OUR WEBSITE
titanbooks.com

LIKE US ON FACEBOOK
facebook.com/titanbooks

FOLLOW US ON TWITTER AND INSTAGRAM
@TitanBooks

EMAIL US
readerfeedback@titanemail.com